IN THE WRONG SIGHTS

A BAD KARMA SPECIAL OPS NOVEL

TRACY BRODY

Copyright Page

This novel is entirely a work of fiction. The incidents portrayed in it are the work of the author's imagination. Any resemblance to actual persons, living or dead, events or localities is entirely coincidental, unless you're my friend as I do occasionally, with their permission, name a character after friends as a thank you for their support. So be nice to this author and you can show up in a book.

In the Wrong Sights

Copyright © 2020 by Tracy Brody Books 2020

All rights reserved. No part of this publication may be reproduced, stored or transmitted in any form or by any means, electronic, mechanical, photocopying, recording, scanning, or otherwise without written permission from the publisher. It is illegal to copy this book, post it to a website, or distribute it by any other means without permission.

Designations used by companies to distinguish their products are often claimed as trademarks. All brand names and product names used in this book and on its cover are trade names, service marks, trademarks and registered trademarks of their respective owners. The publishers and the book are not associated with any product or vendor mentioned in this book. None of the companies referenced within the book have endorsed the book.

ISBN: 978-1-952187-07-0

First Edition

Also available as an ebook

ISBN: 978-1-952187-06-3

❧ Created with Vellum

PRAISE FOR TRACY BRODY

"The Bad Karma series just gets better and better. Do yourself a favor and start reading. You won't be able to put them down." ~ Liliana Hart, New York Times Bestselling Author

"Toe curling romance, heart-stopping suspense." ~ Sandra Owens, author of the bestselling K2 Team and Aces & Eights series.

"Seat of the pants action with true military insight!" ~ Robin Perini, Publisher's Weekly Bestseller.

"Tracy weaves action and heart together with crisp writing that kept me turning pages." ~ Colette Dixon, author of Love at Lincolnfield series.

"Tracy Brody has quickly become one of my very few one-click authors." ~ Heather, Amazon Review

*To my awesome and supportive husband and family.
To our military members and their families. Thank you for all you sacrifice.
With thanks to God for my overactive imagination and persistence.*

ONE

THE WEIGHT of the casket and lifeless body of Master Sergeant Hal Boswell matched the heaviness in AJ's soul. If he hadn't been the one to discover Hal, to press two shaky fingers to the cold flesh of his throat, he might not have accepted the death of his mentor.

A heart attack. AJ's jaw locked recalling what the coroner had speculated. No way. It had to be something else. Hal was as fit as when he'd served on Special Forces teams. He'd endured multiple tours of duty. Survived too many dangerous missions to count. For him to die of a heart attack was like surviving a gunfight, then dying from the flu shot.

AJ wanted this to be a bad dream. Instead, he joined five other elite warriors—men Hal had molded into the best of the best—and moved toward the open grave. Even at eleven hundred hours, the heat and humidity of a cloudless North Carolina morning made sweat trickle from the rim of his dress uniform hat, down his neck, and under the crisp collar of his shirt. His white-gloved hand gripped the casket's handle as he and the other pallbearers took short, precise steps. Steps closer to the void in AJ's life left by Hal's passing.

Had he done enough to show his appreciation while Hal was alive? There'd be no more weekend trips to Hal's fishing cabin. No more wrangling over who caught the biggest trout. God, he hoped Hal had no doubt of his respect and the father-and-son type of bond that went beyond Hal's mentoring.

The forty or so mourners seated were other lives Hal had touched: members of the Army's Special Forces community; former teammates; members of the Selection cadre; men he mentored. All of them turned out in uniform to pay their respects.

However, there were no grieving widows at this funeral. Chief Lundgren contacted at least two of Hal's ex-wives, but the few women among the group were wives attending with their husbands. No true family to hand the flag to.

A flash of movement to his left drew AJ's gaze to the lone woman in running shorts and a T-shirt. Her long, lithe limbs churned, and her dark-red ponytail swung as she ran along the asphalt drive bordered by tall pines. Right toward them.

Protesters at military funerals usually had signs and typically didn't come solo. Was she curious? Her questionable choice of locations aside, with its acres of white tombstones standing like rows of dominoes, why intrude on the one ceremony taking place?

Jeez, lady. Have some respect. His teeth clenched. This wasn't a show. Hal served his country and deserved better than gawkers.

The runner disappeared behind a small mausoleum. AJ focused on his duties as the honor detail set the flag-covered casket onto the lowering stand beside the grave.

"Order arms!"

The honor guards moved to stand in formation for the service.

IN THE SHADE of the mausoleum, Cassidy labored to draw a breath. She slipped the ropes of the gym bag down her arms and pulled it off her back. The stitch in her side kept her bent over while she dumped the bag's contents on the ground. She shook out the dress before grabbing the bottle of water. After she downed half of it, she pulled herself upright and drew in another gulp of the humid air.

She'd made it. Despite her mother's lack of urgency in relaying the news. Despite having to drive all night. Despite the blown tire two miles from the cemetery. She had made it.

A scan of the cemetery turned up no one but the mourners gathered for the service. She yanked off her sweaty shirt, used the remaining water to rinse off as much of the perspiration as she could, and hastily dried herself with the workout towel. She'd stink, but there was nothing she could do about it.

She was drenched in sweat from trying to loosen the lug nuts. Swearing like Hal hadn't worked any magic for her and waiting for AAA would have taken too long. She hadn't driven the whole damn night to miss Hal's funeral. She had the rest of the day to worry about the car and getting back home.

Okay, not exactly *home,* but the only home she had until Flores went to trial.

She took another scan of her surroundings, then stripped off her shorts and tugged the black knit dress over her head and sticky limbs. After she shoved her dirty clothes in the bag, she traded her running shoes for black pumps, undid her ponytail, and secured her hair with a clip.

Ready.

Almost.

She inhaled, closed her eyes, and slowly exhaled. Her racing heart calmed but still beat—despite the hammering of grief it'd taken.

She stepped out from behind the shelter of the mausoleum. Not as many as people had turned out as she'd hoped for her to go unnoticed in the crowd. Most of Hal's old teammates had retired, probably moved on. Just as well. It lessened the chance she'd be recognized. Though if someone did recognize her, Hal hadn't told anyone her story. Being recognized here wouldn't put her in jeopardy.

As she crossed the grassy expanse, her insides quivered. She took the vacant seat at the end of the last row of chairs. *It'll be okay.*

Except her gaze settled on the flag-draped coffin holding Hal Boswell's spiritless body.

Cassidy's heart revved again from how close she'd come to missing this. Her mother had passed along the news almost as an afterthought at the tail end of their bi-weekly call. *Oh, I got a call that Hal died.*

Dead?

He seemed invincible. The shock of his death had slammed her like a tsunami. *Did I make enough time for him?* College. Moving to Chicago for work. Two years ago, he'd insisted she come visit. When he balked at her mention of bringing her boyfriend, Parks, she'd postponed the trip. Then an EMT wheeled Reynaldo Flores into her Emergency Department and screwed up her life six ways to Sunday and Monday and Tuesday.

She'd lost two years of her life she'd never get back, and now she'd lost Hal.

While her mother hadn't bothered to note the details of the service, Cassidy found the online obituary with a simple internet search. It'd taken her less than ten minutes to pack a bag and hit the road because she *had* to be here.

This wasn't how I wanted to say goodbye. But I'm here. Would it give her closure?

Tears welled once again. Her hands shook, not from the caffeine flowing through her veins, but from the loss of the one man, the only man, who'd invested his time in her. He'd made her feel she mattered.

Even after her mother and Hal divorced, he'd been there, continuing to help with her college tuition, which enabled her to get her nursing degree. He called on her birthday. Had been there when she had important decisions to make. She trusted his clarity of breaking things into a "this is right; this is wrong" analysis—even when the outcome had cost her.

A snuffle escaped. Several heads turned in her direction since no one else was crying. She sniffed hard but surrendered to scrounging in the gym bag at her feet for the pack of tissues. With a fresh tissue in hand, she closed her eyes against the bright sun and listened to the eulogy that captured the essence of Hal. Though not a perfect man, a decorated soldier. One who gave of himself far beyond the service required. She drew comfort from the accurate description of the man who sought no glory for his actions.

With her heart rate and breathing almost normal, she relaxed a bit on the folding chair. Though it had been years since she'd lived in Hal's home here in Fayetteville, North Carolina, she searched for familiar faces around her. She recognized a blonde seated in the front row, but the woman likely wouldn't remember her. Then she picked out the woman's bear of a husband standing at parade rest with the honor-guard detail. He met her eyes and gave her a slight nod. She returned a wavering smile, trying to recall their names.

Another pallbearer, a younger man with a strong jaw and well-defined cheekbones, stared at her. His narrowed eyes and the stern set of his mouth made her shift her gaze back to the chaplain and sit straighter to keep from squirming in her seat.

EVEN WITH HER hair pulled up, AJ recognized the runner. She'd changed into a black dress—where?—and sat in the back row, a seat apart from everyone else. What the …? Another thing about this day that made no sense to him. The chaplain's voice carried through the still air. AJ's gaze shifted to the tissue wadded up in the young woman's hand. He tamped down the irritation in his gut, determined not to let her arrival distract him further.

When the chaplain concluded, Chief Lundgren assumed his position at the head of the grave. AJ and the other pallbearers came to attention. The funeral director asked the mourners to stand for the rendering of honors.

AJ had attended over a dozen military funerals since enlisting—too many thanks to Iraq and Afghanistan; however, the protocol still moved him.

"*Pre*-sent arms!"

Seven rifle bolts slid into place with one metallic click.

"Ready! Aim! Fire!"

The expected crack of rifle fire still made his body jerk. The sliding of the bolt to chamber the next round preceded the second call to aim, fire, then the simultaneous volley of shots. By the third round, the instinctive jerk became a mere twitch.

The bugler began playing *Taps*. Sunlight glinted off the gleaming brass instrument. How could anyone here not feel the honor that accompanied the solemn ceremony? No matter what anyone said, AJ was damned proud of his service. What he did. Sure, sometimes it meant doing ugly things to prevent others from perpetrating cruelties and injustices, but, as Hal pointed out, where would the world be without men like them to ensure balance and justice? He and his team were part of that equalizing force. Raining down bad karma on those who deserved it. He stood straighter—if that was possible—his eyes fixed on the coffin.

The last strains of *Taps* faded. AJ and the detail took their positions alongside the casket. Lundgren nodded. They took hold of the corners of the flag, gently lifted it from the coffin, and pulled it taut. They folded it in half lengthwise, then again before turning it on the triangle. The fold man tucked in the end and inspected it to ensure no red showed. As the casket team leader, AJ ran his hands over the edges to "bless off" on the corners and squeezed the flag tight to his chest before bringing it down to hand back to the fold man— another Special Forces member Hal had mentored.

The men passed the flag down the line of pallbearers to Chief Lundgren, the presentation man. After the three-second salute, Lundgren turned the flag, preparing it for presentation.

AJ tried to swallow the hard lump in his throat. It stuck like a wad of chewing gum. Normally, the flag would be handed to family. A spouse. A child. Parents. A sibling. Hal had none of those. He had family forged by blood, sweat, and gunfire.

I want that flag. It means more to me than anyone else.

Lundgren had been silent on the subject of disposition of

the flag. He turned on his heel and walked toward the seated mourners. AJ ground his teeth. Lundgren strode past those seated in the front row, then turned and proceeded down the aisle. AJ squinted into the sunshine. At the last row, Lundgren dropped to one knee—beside the redhead.

What. The. Hell?

TWO

THE MOMENT the soldier carrying the flag turned down the aisle, the jitters hit Cassidy's stomach. Hard. Why was the one soldier who recognized her also responsible for handing off the flag? Everyone turned in their seats to observe the presentation. She sure couldn't fly under the radar now. *Crudola.*

When he knelt in front of her to recite the speech, she read the man's name tag. It surprised her that Chief Lundgren remembered her from a visit to Hal's several years ago. And though Hal had been the only father figure in her life, she wasn't real family. She hadn't expected the honor of receiving the flag that had covered his coffin.

"Thank you," she managed. Tears spilled over and dripped onto the flag in her lap.

He rose, saluted the flag, did an about-face, and walked away with the same precisely measured steps. Slowly, heads turned away. The first screechy notes the bagpiper played turned into "Amazing Grace." It fit Hal perfectly and buoyed her spirits despite the lingering self-consciousness.

With the official service concluded, the aura changed. A

handful of people departed, but the majority of men lingered. Chief Lundgren—Ray, that was his name—produced a whiskey bottle. He pulled a shot glass from his pocket, then poured.

"To Hal Boswell. I'd follow you to the gates of hell wearing gasoline-soaked chaps."

She chuckled. She couldn't help it, hearing the chief use Hal's unique compliment regarding trust.

Ray downed the shot and set the empty glass on top of the casket. The other men filed up, each producing their own shot glass. Soon, a row of glasses lined the lid of the coffin.

The men's words swelled her heart with pride, even as grief tried to wring the life out of it. The broad backs of the men surrounded the coffin, all but blocking her view. When one of the women joined the men and made a toast, Cassidy couldn't stay in her seat any longer. Clutching the flag to her chest, she made her way forward.

"May I?" She motioned to the nearly empty bottle.

"Of course," Ray answered.

A glass was passed to her. Whether it was clean was the least of her worries. She poured a splash, then raised it. "To Hal. Thank you for everything you taught me. And for being there when you didn't have to be. You were more than a stepfather. You were my hero."

The liquid fire seared her throat. Somehow, she swallowed without choking. She set the glass at the end of the row with a *thunk*.

"Hooah!" Ray's deep voice carried to the heavens.

"Hooah!" a chorus repeated.

After the toasts, several men offered her their condolences. She edged out of the group, poised to retreat and retrieve her gym bag, except Ray Lundgren and his wife blocked her path.

"Cassidy, glad you were able to make it." Ray extended a hand, enveloping hers in his. "When I spoke with your mother, she said she'd try to get in touch with you. You remember my wife, Stephanie?"

The becoming blonde bypassed Cassidy's hand to give her a sympathetic embrace. "I didn't see you before the service, though I may not have recognized you." Stephanie eyed her hair, which was now several shades darker than when they'd met.

"I didn't get here until it was starting."

Stephanie touched Cassidy's arm. "We're having people over to the house later. Please come."

"Oh, um." She stalled while panic spiked then dropped like an EKG reading. "Thanks for the invite, but I drove through the night and need to get some sleep so I can drive back for work."

"Do you need a place to stay?" Stephanie persisted.

"That's sweet, but I'm set." At least, she planned to crash at Hal's to get enough sleep to make the trip back before her absence caused problems. Big problems. Marshal DeLong would sedate, restrain, and post a guard on her if he found out she'd gone MIA. She understood the rules of the witness protection program were in place to protect her, but her mother and Hal had been divorced three times longer than they'd been married. *Nobody* expected her to be here. She'd made it, paid her respects—despite the damn tire blowing. Now it was time to vanish—again.

"Are you still in Chicago? That's a heckuva drive." Ray's lips tightened in a contemplative frown. "Hal bragged about you working trauma at a major hospital there."

"He was my biggest supporter. I wouldn't have gotten my nursing degree without his help." It was true. Though she'd only seen Hal a half dozen times in the decade since she left for college, they'd talked regularly until two years ago. His loss reopened the hole in her heart and life—one only he had ever filled.

"You're welcome to come if you change your mind." Stephanie wrote in a small notebook, then tore out the paper and pressed it into Cassidy's hand. "It's not a big get-together, but there'll be plenty of food."

"And likely a number of somewhat-classified stories." A grin turned up the corners of Ray's mouth. "It'll be interesting."

Cassidy bent to retrieve her gym bag. The idea of hearing stories about Hal tugged at her. She had a general idea of what he'd done in the Army, but he rarely spoke about it. On the occasions the men or families from his unit got together, there might be veiled references, but she'd never been given a clear picture into his world. It involved important, often dangerous, work. It also necessitated his being gone for achingly long stretches. What she did understand was that he was a part of a special breed of men. Men worthy of respect and honor.

Maybe one day, when it was safe, she'd come back and learn more about what shaped Hal Boswell into the warrior, patient teacher, and supportive stepdad.

She debated what to do next. Several uniformed men stood in a cluster. The same soldier who'd stared at her earlier met her eyes. The corners of his mouth turned down, and his eyebrows dipped as he headed in her direction with a determined stride.

"You plan to jog out of here in those shoes?" he asked.

Her chest, neck, and face heated. And it wasn't because he looked sexy as all get-out in his dress uniform. "I thought I'd walk." She flashed what she hoped was a disarming smile.

He just stood there. His drill-sergeant stare added to her need to escape.

She sighed. *Okay.* He obviously cared about Hal. It wouldn't hurt her to explain. "I blew a tire just down the road. I figured I could make it here in time if I ran rather than wait for triple A."

"Maybe you should have allowed more time to get here."

Her lips twitched. *Maybe you should mind your own damn business.* "I'll keep that in mind." Her voice dripped with sweetness so artificial it could cause cancer. He raised his brow. Heck, this guy—Rozanski, according to the name tag across from an impressive rack of service ribbons and medals—didn't need to hear what she'd done to get here.

He frowned in the direction she'd come. "You came in the back *road*?"

"Yeah." It hardly qualified as a road, but it'd looked to be the shorter route on the GPS. Except when the tire blew, there'd been no traffic. No one to stop. Not that she would have tried to hitch a ride. Hal would have been furious.

"I'll give you a ride back." It came out more order than offering.

Her mouth opened to tell him she didn't need his help. But—*damn*—a ride would beat the hell out of walking two miles in the heat. Exhaustion had sapped nearly all her energy. Plus, he'd offered. It's not like she'd asked or expected someone to bail her out.

"I'd appreciate that." The words would have been easier to say if they didn't sound just like her mother. "I'm Cassidy." She shifted the folded flag to the crook of her left arm to shake his hand.

His mouth gaped open, and his eyes widened as he looked her over. "I'm AJ. AJ Rozanski."

She jolted. *AJ*. A name Hal had mentioned in more than one conversation.

He released her hand, though his eyes remained fixed on the flag until he pivoted on his heel and led her back to the graveside. She paused a moment to lay a hand on the casket for a final whispered thanks and choked goodbye, then she followed AJ to a black Mustang parked in the shade of the towering pines.

While he shucked his hat and jacket, she climbed in. No fast-food wrappers or receipts. No dust on the dash. Hal had cared for his vehicle like this, too.

After sliding into the driver's seat, AJ started the car and cranked up the air conditioner. When he put on sunglasses, Cassidy discreetly studied his profile. His closely cropped, light-brown hair looked as though it might curl if it grew out. Tanned skin showed he spent a lot of time outdoors. He had great bone structure with a straight nose and perfectly shaped lips. Not model material, but the classic, clean-cut kind of handsome that stayed with you.

He navigated the car through the cemetery, grumbling when he took a wrong turn before finding the back exit. Neither spoke on the short drive down the country lane. He slowed the car, then stopped nose to nose with her abandoned vehicle.

He glanced from the jacked-up car to her. "You were going to change it yourself?"

"Hal taught me how to drive. Said every driver should know the basics. How to pump gas. Add washer fluid. Check the oil. Jump-start a battery. And how to change a tire. Only I couldn't get the lug nuts off."

"Service centers use a power torque wrench." AJ's head bobbed, a slight smile finally appearing on his face. "Hal teach you to hot-wire a car, too?" He turned to study her, his smile broadening.

She laughed. "No. You?"

"He offered. I already knew how."

"Really?"

"I hung out with a few questionable friends in high school." He shrugged.

"I guess he didn't think I'd need that skill."

AJ opened his door. "This will just take a few minutes."

"If you could loosen the lug nuts for me, I can…"

AJ cocked his head and laughed, then stared at her. "If Hal were here, what would he do?"

"He'd … he'd order you to change it for me." She'd seen Hal's chivalrous side enough to know that's exactly what he would do. Except she wasn't a helpless female. She was not like her mother.

"Yes, ma'am. I got this."

"I get you're a rule follower, and Hal and the Army have plenty of rules, but I don't want you to do that in your dress uniform. I'm capable. I'm already sweaty and—"

"You're not the only one with a change of clothes handy." He stepped out of the car. "Stay here in the air-conditioning. This won't take long."

Cassidy's hand edged to the door handle. A protest formed on her lips, then died when it hit her that getting out would mean watching him change clothes. That didn't faze her—she was used to seeing half-dressed and naked people all the time in the hospital—but better not to give this guy the wrong idea. Let him play hero, rescue the damsel in distress. His type lived for this stuff.

"Thank you." Handing over her key, she refrained from batting her eyelashes until he was out of sight.

He opened his trunk. In the side-view mirror, she caught a

glimpse of arms moving, then his white shirt sliding off. She leaned further right in her seat, getting an eyeful of skin, muscled arms, and well-toned abdomen. She averted her gaze. Better not to get caught gawking.

When AJ strode past wearing a gray Army T-shirt and shorts, she opened her heavy eyelids fully to admire his strong legs and nicely rounded butt. Damn, it'd been way too long since she'd been with a man.

The jury might be out on whether she and AJ liked each other, but that didn't stop her from imagining his sinewy arms around her as he twisted the wrench and overcame the first stubborn lug nut. For two years, all she'd done was follow the rules and avoid personal relationships. So for a few seconds, she let her guard down, and instead of worrying about watching her back, she checked out his.

THREE

HAL'S STEPDAUGHTER. Guess he shouldn't be mad that the chief had given her the flag. He hadn't recognized Cassidy from the photo he'd seen at Hal's. She'd been younger, and a shapeless graduation gown had covered her now very adult curves. He'd swear her hair had been more of a light red, too. Yeah, the red worked. Matched the temper that flashed in her eyes. Even with little makeup and dark smudges under her eyes, Cassidy warranted a second look. Not surprising that Hal hadn't shown her off to the young soldiers he mentored.

AJ grimaced as he strained to power the second lug nut free. No wonder she couldn't get them off. He shifted his leg to get better leverage and stole a glance at his idling car. Cassidy's head lolled to the side, her eyes closed. After another attempt, he stood, and since she didn't appear to be watching, he resorted to stepping on the wrench. The nut budged. He used the same technique to remove the rest, then wrestled the tire off.

The blown tire was so flat it wouldn't roll. He carried it around to the back and unlocked the trunk.

Inside was a dinky, sorry excuse for a spare. "Shit. Seriously?" He removed the tire, then checked out the car's license plate. No way would she make it back to New York on this thing. He'd fulfill this duty, then insist she get a replacement tire before hitting the highway.

It only took a few minutes to get the donut spare on. The full-size tire wouldn't fit in the well, so he stowed the jack and hefted the tire into the trunk, where it took up most of the space.

He pulled a pair of pale blue scrub pants and a floral-print top from under the edge of the dirty tire, wiping at the smudge of grime on the fabric. *My bad.* When he refolded the top, the ID badge clipped to the hem flopped over. He started to lay the clothes down, but something pinged his brain and made him flip the badge back over. The picture was Cassidy, dark red hair and placid expression, but the name on the badge said Fiona. Fiona Liddell.

Still holding the top, AJ peered over her car into his own. Cassidy's head listed further to the side. Her lips parted in the respite of sleep. Okay, no big deal. Maybe she went by her middle name. It wasn't like he told people his full name: Andrzejek Jedrus Rozanski. Growing up in an area of Ohio with a heavy concentration of Polish families, Rozanski was enough to identify him. By third grade, he'd decided to go by AJ.

He closed the trunk, ambled over to the passenger side of his car, and rapped on the window, startling Cassidy awake.

"All done." He opened the door, and the cool air rushed past him.

She ran a hand over her face. "Thanks. I …" She blinked against the sunlight before letting out a series of dainty sneezes.

"Bless you. You'll need to get a full-size tire before you head home."

"What?" She shot out of his car and released an aggravated sigh as she glared at the temporary tire. "Okay."

Her icy tone didn't assure him she'd take his advice. "If you want, you can follow me toward town. There are a couple tire stores we'll pass."

She continued to gape at the car as if the tire might magically transform. "Fine. I'll follow you. I appreciate it."

AJ didn't know which service she was thanking him for, but she returned to her car, and he got in his. Once she was behind him, he set a slow pace on the potholed road. He kept it at the recommended speed for the donut tire after they hit the main road. Watching the way the spare wobbled in his rearview mirror, he turned into the first tire store on their path.

Cassidy pulled in behind him. He opened his door when she approached. Though he wanted to maintain this connection to Hal, would he offend her if he offered more assistance?

"Thanks for the escort. Hal thought a lot of you."

"I thought even more of him," he replied. "I'm glad you made it. Sorry for the death stare"—*Crap. Poor word choice*—"back at the cemetery. I thought—I didn't know you knew Hal."

"I get it. I didn't make a traditional entrance."

"Not hardly." He had to admit she had grit.

"Take care." She gave him a weak smile.

"Be careful driving back." *How lame.* But what else could he say? She didn't want his help. Duty served.

AJ made it half a mile down the road before he pulled into a fast-food restaurant, grumbling to himself.

IN THE WAITING ROOM, Cassidy had chosen the seat furthest from the television. Still, the change in the news anchor's pitch pecked through the exhausted fog of her mind. The few minutes of sleep in AJ's cushy passenger seat made her want more. Except the noise and hard plastic chairs of the tire store didn't make for comfortable rest. Neither did the loud growl or cramping in her belly. The older gentleman seated across from her glanced over and smiled.

Well, if she wasn't going to catch some z's, she should attend to another primal need. She fished her wallet out of her purse as she crossed to the snack machine. The machine inhaled the dollar bill and she settled on a pack of peanut butter crackers. Surely, Hal's kitchen had food he wouldn't be needing.

She sighed at the idea of cleaning out his fridge. Did she have time for that? She could leave it to whoever handles his estate. *Please let him have updated his will.* Surely, after all these years, he'd named someone other than Mom as his beneficiary. Tiffany would burn through whatever he'd left like it was her God-given right—like she had when they were married.

The cracker stuck in Cassidy's parched throat. Though the fizz of a cold, caffeinated soda called to her like a siren's song, she settled for a cup of water from the cooler. Back in her seat, her gaze shot to the television when the field reporter announced a massive bust in the Chicago area. Her lungs stopped working as she listened.

"Thirteen people were caught in a sting operation for smuggling cigarettes," the announcer reported. The captive air escaped in a slow, steady, reluctant release. Her lungs drew in fresh oxygen because that's what bodies do.

Breathe in. Breathe out. You couldn't stop the natural process for more than a few seconds—not without intervention.

Dammit. She turned from the television and reached for another cracker. The door's entry alert chimed as warm air swept inside. Sneakered feet and muscular legs entered her field of vision.

Cassidy's gaze darted up. "What are you doing back?"

"I thought you might be hungry." AJ's hand clutched a white take-out bag.

"I'm not some damsel who needs rescuing."

"I know." AJ threw out his hands in a defensive pose, the bag swinging. "It's just a sandwich and fries. I was trying to do something nice is all."

I can take care of myself. I'm not my mother. Not that he'd know about that. "I'm sorry. I'm overly tired." Which wasn't an excuse for being a bitch. With crackers in hand, denying she needed something to eat wouldn't carry much weight.

"Everyone needs help now and then."

She heard Hal's voice in his words. "Hal teach you that?"

AJ opened the bag and handed her a chicken sandwich. "I kinda had it figured out already. It's why I took Hal up on his offer to help me through Selection. I passed the second time —thanks to him." He set the fries on top of the bag on the seat between them.

She chewed a bite of the sandwich. AJ felt he owed Hal, and helping her was his way of clearing his debt. Fine, she'd eat the food, so he could go back to his life with a clean conscience.

A service technician approached. "Ma'am?"

Wow, that was fast. "Yes." She folded the wrapper around the sandwich.

"We can put the tire on, but you've got a broken strut."

"And that's bad?" She'd hit a pothole. Surely the car was still drivable.

"Uh, yeah. You could drive on it for a short distance, but it's part of the suspension. The ride would be rough, and since it's what keeps the tire on the road, it's a safety issue."

"He's right. It needs to be fixed," AJ chimed in.

Cassidy exhaled loudly—okay, it was more like a huff—then closed her eyes and clamped her mouth shut to refrain from swearing. "Fine." She opened her eyes, ignoring AJ. "Go ahead and fix it."

"We don't do that here."

"Seriously?"

"We only do tires. There's a dealership down the road that can do it. Would you like us to go ahead and put the new tire on?"

"Don't bother. They'd have to take it right back off to fix the strut," AJ answered for her.

Her jaw locked like a deadbolt, but she nodded at the tech.

"We'll have it down from the lift in a minute." The young man ambled back to the garage.

Cassidy took a generous bite of her sandwich. Chewing kept her from swearing, and she refused to whine.

Without another word, AJ wrapped up his food. When the tech pulled her car up front, he handed her the bag.

She headed to her car with AJ close on her heels.

"The dealership is down about two miles on your left." AJ pointed. "Huge American flag. You can't miss it."

"Thanks for the ride—and lunch." She climbed in her car and closed the door. *Dismissed, soldier. I can handle this. I have to.*

On high, the air conditioner cooled her but not her irritation. A blown tire and a broken strut? *No good deed goes unpunished.* "Arghh!"

Maybe she should have let the marshals know about the funeral, but the idea of them putting the kibosh on her plans trumped the need to keep them informed. *Shit.* What were the chances Marshal DeLong would find out if she had to take another day off? It wasn't like she had to check in every day. What good was it to be kept safe and alive if she had no freedom?

She turned into the dealership determined not to let karma screw up her plan to quietly slip away to pay her respects. At least she hadn't exposed anything damning to Ray Lundgren or AJ—even if he was harder to get rid of than the frequent-flyer drug-seekers who showed up in the ER hoping for a narcotics fix.

Inside the intake bay, a bald man wearing glasses and a blue polo shirt approached her vehicle. He made notes on his clipboard, then led her to a workstation.

"What name is your appointment under?" The man peered over his glasses at her.

"I don't have an appointment. The tire blew, and the strut broke according to the guy at the tire place."

The man consulted his computer. "We've got the part and a tire. But we're booked solid for today. We have appointments tomorrow—"

"I'm just in town for a funeral. I have to leave tonight. Is there *any* way you could fit me in?" She played the sympathy card. God, she needed a break.

"Sorry to hear that. We'll do our best to work you in."

"I would *really* appreciate it."

He placed a form on the counter. "Sign here."

"Would a twenty ensure it gets done today?" No response. She signed and pushed the paper back to him. "There's an extra twenty for whoever does the work, too," she added to let him know she was dead-as-a-zombie serious.

He chuckled but made a point of withdrawing his hand rather than holding it out for the money. "What number can we reach you at when it's ready?"

"I'm going to wait here." She smiled sweetly.

The service advisor's gaze flicked left, then back to her face. "Oh-kay."

When she turned, she practically bowled into the person behind her. A hand under her elbow steadied her. AJ.

Again.

"What the …? Why are you …?" Where had he come from?

"Come on. I'll give you a lift wherever you need to go." He steered her to the exit.

She tugged her arm free. "I'm staying here. Put pressure on them to get it fixed today."

"Between your bribe and flirting, you should be good without glaring from the waiting room. And it won't do you much good if the car's fixed, but you're too tired to drive."

Had he been standing there the whole time? *Stealthy bastard.* Heat crept up her neck. She bit down rather than deny she hadn't poured on the sweetness to get what she wanted. It probably looked that way to him.

He made a good point, though. Between the television shows to entertain the masses and equally inevitable individuals talking too loud on their cell phones, rest would be out of the question.

None of this was AJ's fault. Maybe Hal sent him to watch over her in his place; that'd be just like him. Though she'd appreciate it more if AJ didn't treat her like some needy female.

Guess Hal couldn't communicate that from beyond the

grave. And she couldn't stand in the middle of the service bay debating all afternoon.

The promise of sleep won out. "Let me grab my bag."

Her concession brought a smug curve to the corners of his mouth. "Where can I take you?" He started his car after she settled in the passenger seat.

"I planned to crash at Hal's. I figured if no one would mind."

AJ turned to face her for a second. Then, wordlessly, he turned on the blinker and pulled out of the lot. It made sense he knew the way. How many times had Hal invited young soldiers over to impart his vast wealth of knowledge?

"My buddy Devin's been keeping Champ at his place. Since we get called out on short notice a lot, he can't keep him, though. He's trying to find him a permanent home, if you're a dog person and would be interested."

How did I forget about Champ? She'd only been to Hal's once since he adopted the retired service dog, but to forget Hal's constant companion? The idea of taking Champ swirled in her brain. Champ would be a connection to Hal, and he'd bring a level of security and peace to her life that was sure as hell missing right now. An almost giddy sensation washed over her arms and bubbled up in her chest. "I'd be happy to give him a home."

A muscle in AJ's cheek twitched. "'Kay. I'll call Dev and see if I can pick up Champ before I come back to get you."

"How did he die?" Her mother hadn't said. Probably hadn't asked. The obituary hadn't given a cause of death either.

"They're not sure yet. When I found him, he—"

"*You* found him?"

"Yeah." AJ took his eyes off the road to shoot a pained look her way. "He'd been at his cabin over the weekend. Left me a message Sunday night saying he caught a bunch of trout and to stop by and get some. He didn't answer when I called, but after a few days, I stopped by after work. His truck was there, and Champ started barking like crazy. When Hal didn't come to the door, well, it was unlocked, so I went in. He was in the hallway to the bedrooms."

AJ turned into Hal's neighborhood. "The coroner estimated he'd been gone for a few days. Probably a heart attack. I never expected he'd go that way."

"Me, either." She stared out the window at the familiar homes. They passed Lisa Morales's old blue clapboard. How many nights had she and her childhood best friend had sleepovers, talking about boys half the night?

Lisa would want to know about Hal's death. Except Cassidy couldn't call her friend, thanks to protective custody safeguards. Only a handful of people were aware of her situation, and she couldn't endanger anyone else by telling them there were people who'd kill to keep her from testifying against an enforcer for a powerful arms cartel.

AJ pulled into Hal's driveway. The house looked the same. A nondescript brick ranch with Army green shutters—Hal's nod to camouflage. At the front corners, the roses provided a pop of color. Her mother made him plant those bushes to give the house a friendlier appearance.

Cassidy didn't move. She gripped the handle but couldn't open the door.

"Do you want me to go in with you?" AJ interrupted the flood of memories.

"I need to do this myself."

"The dealership closes at six. I'll pick you up at five thirty."

"Can you make it earlier? Say five eighteen?"

"Five eighteen?" Amusement laced AJ's voice. "I know

you got that from Hal. *Three miles! You've got twenty-two minutes and eighteen seconds!"*

She laughed at his impersonation of Hal barking orders. Including Hal's quirk of throwing out odd increments of time brought back more memories.

"What are you waiting for? Go!"

It was easy to see the love and respect AJ had for Hal. In another setting, she could see herself wanting to hang out—or more—with AJ. Maybe she could let her guard down to build this connection. After all, he'd gone out of his way to help her. "He set my curfew at ten forty-two. He said an odd time had more impact."

AJ grinned. "It keep you from being late?"

"Yup. We might have exceeded the speed limit to get back, but if Hal was in town, I was home by ten forty-two. Usually earlier. Don't *you* be late."

"Yes, ma'am."

Steeling herself, she got out of the car. She still had a key since Hal insisted that she was welcome anytime. Inside, she let the familiarity seep into her pores. Sunlight filtered through the wooden blinds. The tan carpet she stepped onto hadn't been replaced in over a decade. The brown suede couch sat in the same spot, though it faced a larger, newer flat-screen television. The faint aroma of cigar smoke lingered. What she wouldn't give to see Hal's face with an unlit cigar clamped between his teeth while her mother threatened him if he lit it inside the house.

In the kitchen, she ran her fingertips over the ring-stained oak table. She'd never met her birth father, but here, in these pressed-back chairs with carved designs, she'd learned what family was supposed to look like. The definition of Dad. Learned what she wanted from a man. More than a financial provider. Someone who invested himself in others. A mate.

But, currently, those things and the future she'd planned were out of reach.

She found Hal's cigar box and placed it by the front door, then went to the bathroom. Once the water warmed, she stepped into the shower's spray. The water washed away the stickiness. It washed away the stink. It washed away the tears that streamed down her face.

FOUR

Cassidy closed the refrigerator and tied the trash bag tight. She'd fixed a sandwich for the road, though neither the bread nor meat were exactly fresh. There hadn't been a lot in there, typical of Hal, but stench of rotten fish prompted her to bag it and the moldy strawberries and other perishables to toss before they got worse.

A car pulling up to the house made Cassidy glance at the microwave clock. 5:13. If it was AJ, he'd arrived early. If it wasn't… Blood pumped faster and harder through her veins.

She set the trash by the door and peeked through a crack in the living room blinds, careful not to move them. The tension dissipated upon seeing AJ's Mustang.

She was just unnerved from being in the house where Hal died. Sure, she'd witnessed patients die and seen far more dead bodies than the average person, but she hadn't shaken the sensation that something was off in the house.

A tan blur shot past AJ. Champ barked excitedly at the front door, tugging at her heart.

She opened the front door before AJ could ring the bell. Champ nearly knocked her over when he charged past. AJ stood with a bag of dog food balanced on his shoulder while Champ dashed through the family room to the kitchen. After lapping the table, he disappeared down the hallway.

The dog's search for his beloved companion, made tears burn her eyes again. AJ's expression mirrored her sadness. This sucked.

AJ whistled through his teeth, and the dog returned. "Sit."

Champ obeyed. Cassidy extended her hand for the dog to sniff before she spoke soothingly. "Do you remember me, huh, Champ?" She scratched him behind his ear, and he rubbed his head against her leg. "Do you want me to put this in the kitchen or leave it here by the door?" AJ indicated the dog food.

"Can we take it?"

"To the dealership?" He eyed the duffel bag along with the other items she'd placed by the door.

"I'm going to head out from there."

"You can't drive to New York tonight. You need more sleep."

"I won't be able to sleep right away. I should get halfway, then I can stop somewhere." The rest, coffee, energy drinks, and blasting the AC should get her through the drive tonight and work tomorrow.

He nodded as if buying that, then pointed to the trash and other items by the door. "This all go?"

"That bag needs to go in the garbage. It stinks. And I thought you guys might like the beer and these." She picked up the cigar box. "Though smoking these things goes against everything I know as a nurse, I gave these to Hal for his birthday. He didn't make gift-giving easy. Ammo or his stogies. I thought you and the guys could smoke these in his memory."

"Thanks. We'd be honored." He looped a finger through

the empty ring of the six pack and also grabbed the trash. "Come on, Champ."

AJ headed out, but she scanned the street. Two doors down a neighbor watered her flowers around her mailbox. The only other movement was a white sedan crawling down the street. She stayed in the shadow of the doorway until the car passed, then stepped out and locked up.

Champ tagged after AJ as he loaded the car then tossed the garbage in the can on the side of the house. Only the dog stopped between the house and car and whined, facing the front door.

She went to him, dropping to one knee to rub the lab's neck. "I know. I miss him, too. Since he's not coming back, will you give me a chance? I'm not the same, but I'll do my best."

Champ licked her cheek, then followed her to the car. Two heartbroken souls in need of a friend.

"I'D RATHER NOT TAKE Champ in the bay. Will you stay with him while I check out and pay?" Cassidy broke the silence once they arrived at the dealership.

"Sure." AJ parked in one of the available spaces beside the service department and opened the windows. Champ stuck his head out one side, then switched to the other, watching as Cassidy disappeared inside. "You'll follow a pretty girl anywhere, huh, boy? Bet she won't take you fishing, though." Champ seemed to like Cassidy, and dogs were supposed to have the innate ability to judge people.

He wasn't quite ready to see her go. Maybe it was her elusiveness and defensive responses that made her a bit of a mystery. A few years back, Hal had mentioned plans for

Cassidy to visit. Then she hadn't come—something about her boyfriend. He'd started dating Jess around that time, and Hal hadn't brought up Cassidy after that. Hal playing matchmaker? He mulled over that possibility.

Champ abandoned his post at the window and stuck his head between the seats. He stilled briefly before pacing across the back seat, adding to AJ's restlessness.

He popped the trunk. After he got the leash, he clipped it on and let Champ out.

"You might as well take care of business before you guys hit the road." He walked to the grassy strip that separated the car lot from the restaurant next door.

"Oh shit." The words slipped out when he spotted her car, spare still on, in the row of cars to be serviced. Right now, the service rep was likely learning a new definition of earful—or witnessing an emotionally overloaded nuclear meltdown.

After Champ selected a spot to mark as territory, AJ shortened the leash and headed into the service bay. He eased behind Cassidy while she spoke to the tech.

"But I needed to leave tonight." Her fist rapped the countertop, and her desperate tone added to the urgency of her words.

"Rick mentioned that before he left, ma'am. We're trying to get the work done for the folks who *have* appointments. We open at seven and should have you done and out by nine. I'm sorry, but that's the best we can do." He dropped his gaze to the computer screen.

Champ let out a short yap, and Cassidy swiveled, defeat written on her face.

AJ followed her outside. "They didn't call to say it was ready?"

"No," she snapped and massaged a finger over her left eyebrow. "I didn't leave a number since I'd planned to stay."

My bad. He'd kinda slipped up on that. "So, you leave first thing in the morning instead. You want me to take you back to Hal's or …?" Should he offer dinner, or would that make her defensive again?

"You've got things to do. I can call for a cab."

His gruff laugh startled Champ. "Yeah, a cab for you and the dog and his food and bed. Look, it's not a big deal. The get-together at the Lundgren's just started."

"Oh." Her scowl melted into a wistful expression. Those brown eyes ringed with fire shifted left to right as she debated her options.

"Do you want to go?"

"What about Champ?"

"We can take him." Weight slipped from his shoulders at finally hitting on something going her way. "Come on." Champ followed, which left Cassidy little choice than to do likewise.

Since it was either ride in silence or talk to the dog, AJ searched for a safe topic of conversation once they left the dealership. Work beat religion, politics, and relationships. "What kind of work do you do in New York?"

"I'm a nurse."

"What kind of nurse?"

"I'm, uh, working at a nursing home."

She didn't elaborate, or sound enthused. He pictured Cassidy in a more active role than giving out meds, changing bedpans, and chasing down wandering patients and denture stealers.

"You can take Champ to visit the patients. That's become a big thing."

"Patients do like visits from therapy dogs. Do you think Hal's old teammates will be at Lundgren's or mostly guys from his training job?"

"Likely both from the teams and the training cadre." He noted the change of topic from her work. When he threw out a few names of who'd been at the funeral, she didn't respond to any of them. He turned up the radio to fill the silence and refrained from singing along to the eighties rock.

Cars lined the street in front of the Lundgren's house. Up ahead, he spotted Tony Vincenti and his girlfriend, Angela Hoffman, in Mack Hanlon's driveway. Tony took two camp chairs from the back of his SUV, then pointed to the vacant space beside his car. He did a double take when he saw Cassidy in the passenger seat.

"Where are they going?" Cassidy watched them cross the street.

"Lundgren's live across the street. This is Mack and Kristie's house. He's on the team, too. Here." He handed her Champ's leash, then got out and wrestled his hunting stool out from under the dog bed in the trunk.

The mix of voices carried from the backyard as they walked up the driveway. In the partial shade from the hardwoods that lined the back of the yard, chairs formed two circles on the grass. People talked and ate from plates loaded with barbecue, beans, potato salad, and fruit balanced on their laps.

Stephanie Lundgren popped to her feet, eyeing Cassidy at AJ's side. "Cassidy! I'm glad you made it. The food's in the kitchen. Let's go get you a plate." She ushered Cassidy inside while he found a vacant space to set his chair, greeting his team before he headed in, too. When he came back out, Cassidy was seated beside Stephanie.

"Of course, the guys in Seventh Group adamantly denied it," Walt Shuler was saying when AJ stopped to fill a cup from the keg on the patio.

Oh, Lord. Of all stories to share, Shuler had to rehash

Hal's story about a Special Forces team inadvertently hooking up with transvestites at a bar in Panama City. What would Cassidy think?

"They'd been in Honduras for six months," Ray Lundgren added. "Copious amounts of alcohol had already been consumed. I can see how anything in a skirt passed for female."

"Too bad that was before camera phones, or there'd be proof to back him up. Hal would've loved to have that for blackmail, even if they were Army and not SEALS or Marines." Mack Hanlon took a swig of beer.

AJ had to agree. Hal would have wrangled that into free drinks way beyond that night.

"How about the time Shuler rode that bucking tapir in Colombia?" An evil grin turned up the corners of Lundgren's mouth.

"Damn, I knew someone would bring that up." Shuler avoided eye contact with his teammates. "That thing was the size of a horse!"

"Horse?" Lundgren snorted. "More like a petting-zoo pony."

"It might look like a pony to someone seven-feet tall."

"Closer to six-and-a-half feet," Lundgren corrected, his grin broadening.

"Damn ugly creatures. Came charging out of the jungle at Hal and me."

"As I recall, you were trying to round up what was probably her baby while talking about a barbecue. Tapirs are like bears—protective of their young."

Shuler scowled at Lundgren. "He looked like a pig. I didn't know they got that huge. Hal jumped clear. I grabbed hold to keep from getting trampled."

"Rode him about ten whole feet." Lundgren nearly choked from laughing.

AJ and the others all smiled or laughed—except Cassidy, who sat forward and listened, neglecting the plate of food in her lap.

"Dislocated my shoulder when I landed. Damn near broke my collarbone. 'Bout had to cancel that mission. And the barbecue was Hal's damn brilliant idea," Shuler concluded and finished off his beer.

"Better to encounter an unexpected mother tapir than a jaguar or, say a dozen cartel gunmen," Mack pointed out.

"Amen." Tony rubbed his left bicep while staring past Mack.

"What is it with you guys and Colombia? Are you cursed or something?" Kristie Hanlon stared at her husband.

"Last time went smooth as Tennessee whiskey. Before that, the mission tanked, but something really good came out of it." Mack wrapped an arm around his wife's shoulder, and the two came together for a kiss.

"Ahh, gag me," Shuler said, then got punched in the arm by his wife.

"I want to know what happened there and how you two met. You know, on that scenic flight." Stephanie's finger swept back and forth, pointing at Mack and Kristie. Her eyes narrowed as she leaned forward in her chair.

"It's classified." Tony slouched in his seat, looking to several of the team who shook their heads to agree.

"*Hmmph*," Stephanie grumbled and carried her plate to the garbage.

"I have security clearance," Angela purred and ran a fingertip over the scar on Tony's bicep.

Tony returned her smoldering gaze but didn't say anymore.

His buddies' relationships twisted AJ's gut. He'd expected to be the one about to go down the aisle. Except after his last deployment to Afghanistan, Jess returned his ring. Everyone knows words can cut like a knife. Hell, he'd been shot a few weeks ago, and that hadn't hurt as much as Jess's statement—which he remembered word for word.

I don't want to spend half my life like I'm still single, or worse, become a single mom because you're deployed for six months every time I turn around.

But AJ wasn't going to give up the job he loved in hopes it would appease Jess. No, he'd find a woman who'd support him and respect what he did. Someone like Stephanie Lundgren. Or Kristie Hanlon.

It might have taken Mack a second time to find the right woman, but he had with Kristie, as evidenced by Mack's wickedly proud grin whenever Kristie rested a hand on her slight bulge of her stomach. You didn't have to hang an "I'm so freaking in love with this woman" sign around Tony's neck, either. Watch him with Angela for ten seconds and you'd know his bachelor days were O-V-E-R.

"Maybe I need to get a job with classified security clearance." Stephanie slid her arms over her husband's shoulders from behind and placed her cheek to his.

Chief Lundgren's eyes bulged into a rare picture of panic. "Uh, no!"

"Trust me, you'll sleep better not knowing certain things," Angela backed up the chief, turning Stephanie's coy smile to a resigned expression.

FIVE

Cassidy soaked up every word of every story about Hal. Seated next to her, retired operator Mike Barden took a cigar from the humidor AJ held in front of him. The movement stretched the tattoo on Mike's arm into a screaming eagle.

He ran the cigar across his thick mustache, taking in the tobacco's aroma. "Hal didn't have many vices, but he did have a weakness for aged Tennessee whiskey and a good smoke."

"He had another weakness," Cassidy said, and several pairs of eyes locked on her. "A woman in need."

Mike's head bobbed, and a smile rolled across his face. "True. True. I remember more than once Hal pulling over to help some damsel in distress. Fix her car or change a tire. Carry something heavy for a lady."

She couldn't help but glance at AJ's back while he continued to pass out cigars to the men gathered in the circle. "He liked being a knight in shining—no, camouflaged armor."

"You nailed it. Thought he could fix anything," Mike said.

"And if it wasn't an easy fix, he'd marry her," she replied without thinking.

Mike's belly laugh resonated through her. "I told him it was cheaper and less heartache if he'd just find a woman he hated and buy her a house."

Several men laughed, and Mike's expression showed slight remorse. "Sorry, I probably shouldn't say that."

"It's okay." Cassidy waved it off. "With my mother, it was probably true." Too true. She'd have taken the house. And Tiffany would've wanted him to provide a cook and maid to go along with it.

"He was married to her longer than the others, as I recall." Mike took a puff on his cigar, then blew out a curl of smoke.

"Really?" If so, it was due to Hal waiting until she'd left for college to file for separation. If Tiffany had been honest with him, Hal would have realized earlier that she didn't—and never would—fit into his world. She never went to any of his team get-togethers or associated with the other wives like the women here tonight. Her mother never supported or gave back to Hal even half of what he'd given to their family. While he'd drawn the short straw in that relationship, it'd been the biggest blessing in Cassidy's life.

Hal loved to impart his wisdom and experience, whether to young soldiers or loved ones. While Tiffany hadn't been an enthusiastic participant, Cassidy learned essential life skills like how to cook, balance a checkbook, and maintain a car from him so she'd never *have to* depend on others like her mother.

Hal was her go-to guy on the rare times she needed help. She trusted his advice. Like what to do when your patient confesses he's killed people.

Random sparkles of light dotted the darkness blanketing the sky as lightning bugs blinked to each other on the edges of the yard. The operators hadn't run out of stories, but sleep deprivation numbed Cassidy's mind and weighted her body. A hand on her forearm chased away the lethargy cocooning her. She turned her head and met AJ's gaze.

"I'll give you a ride back whenever you're ready. No rush."

The way his hand rested on the bare skin of her arm made her reluctant to move and lose the human contact. Several silent seconds must have passed before she pushed up from the chair to face him. "Stephanie invited me to stay here tonight. Rather than inconvenience you …"

"It's not a problem. Though, I know firsthand she can be hard to say no to—even if I don't have to take orders from her."

She chuckled. "I did try. She'll drive me to the dealership. I need to get my and Champ's things from your car."

"All right." He looked and sounded less relieved to be off the hook than she expected.

"Thanks for the stories, guys." She forced the words through her tight throat without choking up too badly.

AJ trailed her around to the front of the house. Champ appeared and loped alongside them.

Ever the gentleman, AJ carried the bag of food and dog bed across the street and deposited them at the Lundgren's. He knelt and scratched Champ behind the ears. "I'm sorry about Hal. He was unique. For someone who never tried to attract attention, he left quite an impression. I'm gonna miss the hell out of him."

"Me, too," she echoed, noting the shine of moisture in AJ's eyes and catch in his voice.

"I'm glad I got to meet you. Let me give you my number in case you come back this way sometime or need anything."

"I doubt I'll be back—with Hal gone." She hated to rebuff his offer, saw the dull pain of rejection in his eyes, but he might ask for her number. Then what? *Sorry, you can't call me. See, I'm in witness protection, but after I testify and have a life, I'll call you.*

"I guess not." He stroked the dog's head one last time. "You two take care of each other." He backed away, holding up a hand signaling for Champ to stay.

She nodded, straining to hold back the overflow of dammed emotions.

Though his departure ended the potential awkwardness of a goodbye, it left Cassidy in the same isolation that had become her norm for the past two years. She longed to take a sledgehammer to the icy walls meant to protect her. Walls that had become her prison.

SIX

WHILE CASSIDY READ over patient notes on her tablet, she made a note to check on Mrs. McCarthy's wounds following her below-the-knee amputation.

"You need to take the east wing, Fiona." Jason sidled up beside Cassidy and her aide, Nidia, at the nurse's station desk.

Back to being Fiona and the joys that came with this job —all thanks to protective custody. She sighed while groaning inside. "Why's that?" Cassidy discreetly cut her eyes to Nidia, who kept her head down, making notes, though a grin twitched her lips.

"Because if I have to deal with Mrs. Simpson and her mouth today, I swear I might go off on her."

"What happened this time?"

"She called me a drama queen." Jason waved his hand across his chest with a flourish.

"To your face?" Cassidy tried to sound surprised. She was more surprised he didn't take it as a compliment. While no one apparently said it *to* him, Jason's antics had earned him that moniker from the staff, a majority of the residents, and a number of their family members.

"She doesn't have the nerve to say it to me directly, but Mrs. Nelson overheard her."

"There you go," Nidia interjected. "I wouldn't believe everything coming out of Bessie Nelson's mouth. Talk about a drama queen. That woman likes to be the center of attention and stir things up. Not always in a good way."

Jason's mouth pursed as he contemplated. He peered at them through his thick glasses with volatile, wild eyes that tended to unnerve Cassidy.

"I'm more inclined to believe Mrs. Nelson. She doesn't intentionally antagonize me." He defended the older woman who treated him like her lap dog—or purse puppy. "But Mrs. Simpson, on the other hand … I'm done ignoring her prejudiced little jabs at me. She likes you, Fiona. Can't you rein her in?"

"Sorry. I don't have a magic wand," Cassidy said. "And Mrs. Simpson *may* 'like' me because I don't antagonize her, but she scares me a little. Okay, maybe a lot. I recommend trying not to get on her bad side."

"Too late, honey. If she keeps it up, then you're going to have to report her to the director before I call her out in front of her friends, so they see her true nature." Jason sauntered down the hall to begin collecting the morning's breakfast trays.

Nidia waited until he was out of earshot before she rolled her eyes. "*So,* are you going to say something to Mrs. Simpson or the director?"

"Sure. Right after you tell me how I can come out ahead, trying to mediate between them."

"There is not a universe that exists where you can come out ahead—not in a battle between those two. You're better off keeping a safe distance and waiting for one of them to blow up or implode."

"Amen." It sounded like what Hal might advise. Though he also wasn't afraid to mix things up—or blow things up. Managing staff-patient relations was not part of her job duties. No way would she jump into *that* battle. Being the middleman between people at odds had already cost her her freedom.

THE EXTENDED BRIEFING on the depressing state of the world had AJ ready to get to the fun stuff. A few hours in the shooting house might improve his morning.

Lundgren moved on to an update on the deteriorating situation in Russia. *Great.* Add them back to the list of unstable countries with even more unstable leaders who had access to a cache of nukes.

The conference room door opened. When Colonel Mahinis stuck his head in, Lundgren stopped mid-sentence. Nine pairs of eyes locked on the colonel. The colonel's gaze shifted from Lundgren, roved over Tony and Mack, and landed on AJ.

And didn't deviate.

AJ held his head up rather than shrinking into his seat.

The colonel straightened to his standard ramrod posture. "Rozanski, there's a detective here to speak to you." A crook of his index finger ordered AJ to rise.

AJ sat in the crosshairs of nine sets of eyes. His core jerked like the recoil of a twelve-gauge shotgun. The colonel stepped out of sight.

Juan leaned on one elbow. "What's that about?"

Hell if he knew.

AJ followed the colonel to the entry area of the command post. A man in a basic suit and tie studied the wall filled with pictures of heroes who sacrificed their lives for their families. For their country. For their brothers. The detective tore his gaze away as they approached.

"Sergeant Rozanski? I'm Detective Price." Instead of extending his hand, he pulled a notepad from his jacket pocket. "You found Hal Boswell's body?"

"Yes, sir." A detective asking about Hal? AJ's thoughts slammed on the brakes and left skid marks on his brain.

"What were you doing *in* his home?"

"I stopped by to pick up some fish he caught over the weekend. He didn't answer when I knocked, but Champ, his dog, barked and scratched at the door. It wasn't locked, so I went in. Why is—"

"Did you know Mr. Boswell suffered from a bee-venom allergy?"

"Uh, yeah. A severe allergy. *Master Sergeant* Boswell," AJ corrected the detective, "kept an EpiPen with him. Why are *you* asking about his allergy?" The alarm in his head that blared like a warning of incoming mortars told him he was not going to like what was coming.

AJ escorted Detective Price out of the command center ten minutes later. Ten minutes in which the detective's questions basically ripped out his internal organs, except for his brain, which pounded against his skull. His upper body swayed, but his combat boots melded to the floor.

The sound of automatic-weapons fire infiltrated the building. Training going on. Soldiers carrying on with their duty. Carrying on with their lives. AJ filled his lungs with a deep draw of air, then pushed his legs across the floor to find his team. Nothing he passed registered.

The men lingered in small groups inside the conference room.

"What'd a detective want with you?" Juan blurted out the

second AJ walked into the room. Mack backhanded Juan's arm.

AJ sank into the nearest chair, his gaze flicking across the curious expressions of his friends' faces. His limbs still undulated like ocean waves. He exhaled in a huff. The team edged closer while he collected his thoughts. "The medical examiner found high levels of bee venom in Hal's blood."

"I thought the paramedics said he died of a heart attack," Lundgren said.

"That's what they *suspected*."

"Damn. A heart attack killing him is bad enough, but a bee sting? Shit." Vincenti shook his head.

"Why would a detective investigate if Hal died from a bee sting?" Dev mused.

AJ met Devin's eyes, then looked at his team leader. Lundgren cocked his head to the left, his lips puckered into a crooked line.

"The amount of venom equaled dozens of stings." AJ witnessed Mack shudder and Tony wince. "Except the ME didn't find any welts on Hal's body. Which is why they didn't suspect anything until they finally got the toxicology report back."

"Huh? How's that?" Juan asked.

"They don't think he was stung. They think it was injected, or he ingested it."

"You mean murdered," Lundgren stated. It wasn't a question.

"Yeah."

Jaws locked, and the men donned their battle faces.

"I can't see anyone wrestling Master Sergeant Boswell down to give him an injection," Juan said.

"The detective have any idea why? Or who?" Mack asked.

"No. He did ask about any enemies Hal had."

Tony snorted. "You tell him he had a few? Like a dozen cartel leaders in South America and most terrorist groups in the Middle East?"

"Those didn't concern him. He asked me what I was doing at Hal's. He can investigate me all he wants. I'd never hurt Hal. I'd kill anyone who did."

Lundgren nodded.

"But …" AJ stopped. Guilt stabbed him repeatedly, telling him to fess up.

"What?" Juan leaned forward, his eyes widening.

"He asked about Hal's ex-wives and if anyone else had been in the house. I kind of told him Cassidy had been there, that she had a key, and she's a nurse." *Who would know how to give an injection.* Lundgren's heavy stare weighed on him. He shrank into the chair a bit. He hadn't meant to push the detective's spotlight onto Cassidy—he just answered his questions. Shit, he should've thought it through. "I should probably give her a heads-up that he'll want to talk to her. You have her number?"

"No," the chief said. "Her mom's was listed in Hal's file. Hal would have Cassidy's somewhere at the house."

"Uh, the house is now a crime scene." AJ shook his head as paralysis threatened to stop his breathing.

"I had trouble getting her mom to call me back, but Cassidy works at one of the big hospitals in Chicago. I'm sure we can track her down with a few calls."

"Her car had New York plates, and she told me she's working at a nursing home." As AJ said it, the impression something was off about Cassidy returned and waved a crimson-red warning flag.

Lundgren frowned. "That's odd. She didn't correct me when I mentioned Chicago."

"I saw her work ID badge. Something Manor."

"Does sound more like a retirement home," Lundgren admitted.

"Googling it," Dev said, his fingers already tapping his tablet. "Got several hundred in New York. Remember anything else to narrow it down?"

"Think there was a city or tree name in it." Damn, he should have paid more attention. Seconds later, Dev rattled off names. AJ closed his eyes to envision the name badge he'd glimpsed. "Wait. What was that last one?"

"Elmwood Manor. It's in Schenectady, New York."

AJ could visualize the name. "I'm pretty sure that's it."

Thankfully, Chief Lundgren pulled out his phone and punched in the number Dev called out. AJ didn't want to be the one to hit her up with the news Hal had been murdered, and she was the prime suspect.

Lundgren put the call on speakerphone. "I need to speak to Cassidy O'Shea."

"I don't have any residents here by that name," a bored male voice replied.

Cassidy O'Shea. AJ repeated the name in his mind. O'Shea. That was not the name on the badge. "Ask for Fiona," he said, trying to remember the last name on the ID.

"Sorry, Fiona. She's a nurse." Lundgren's tone wavered, and confusion distorted his features.

"Fiona's making patient rounds. Can I take a message?"

"It's imperative that I speak with her. Now." Lundgren's authoritative edge returned.

"Hold then," came the response with an audible air of annoyance.

"Certainly. Thank you." Instrumental music signaled they were on hold. The chief fixated on AJ. "Who's Fiona?"

"That was the name on the badge. I thought it could be

her given name. But the last name wasn't O'Shea. Maybe she got married recently." She hadn't worn a wedding ring; he would have noticed. Divorced? That could explain it. Maybe.

"I don't think so," Lundgren stated. "Hal would have mentioned it."

A full minute passed as the men stood and stared at the walls, at the floor, at each other as the music played in the background.

"Fiona Liddell." The name rolled with the hint of a Scottish lilt from the vaguely familiar voice.

"Cassidy? This is Master Sergeant Ray Lundgren."

"How … how did you get this number?"

"Sergeant Rozanski saw your work ID card in your vehicle. The reason I'm calling is that we've received information we wanted to pass along. Did you know Hal had a bee-sting allergy?"

"Of course. I learned how to administer a dose of epinephrine when I was in high school," she prattled. "I don't understand. Why is that important?"

Though he couldn't see her face, the note of panic in her voice mirrored AJ's reaction to the identical question.

"A detective questioned Sergeant Rozanski about Hal's death."

"A detective?"

"The preliminary cause of death may be inaccurate. Hal's system showed a high level of venom."

"But if he were stung, he'd use his EpiPen," she stated emphatically.

"The detective left the impression that Hal may have—" Lundgren exhaled. "That somehow he may have been injected or even ingested it. That's why he's investigating. I wanted you to hear it from me before someone questioned you."

"Me? Wait." The panicked volume of Cassidy's voice cranked up a few notches. "Did you give him this number or any info?"

Conflicted emotions prompted AJ to speak up. "No. I mentioned you'd been here, but I didn't even have your last name."

"Are you sure he was a detective? Did you check with the department?"

What the ...? "He got on post. And past the colonel. I didn't see a need to check his badge." Where was she going with this?

"Please, don't tell him anything about me. I can't explain. I'm sorry. I ... I wish I could, but I can't. I ... I just can't." Cassidy ended the call.

"What the hell?" Lundgren stared at his phone.

AJ met his teammates' confused expressions. Suspicion seeped through his skin, into his veins, and spread throughout his body.

Cassidy sank into the rolling chair behind the nurses' station. Her entire body trembled. This didn't make sense. Hal poisoned by bee venom? The detective had to be lying.

What if he weren't a real detective?

There was another possibility, one she didn't want to contemplate. And the possibility slowed the blood rushing through her arteries as though her heart had flatlined.

Jason headed toward the desk from the west-wing corridor. *Crap. Not now.* She couldn't put her thoughts together, and he'd surely ask about the man who demanded to talk to her.

Ignoring his approach, she rose on legs that still threatened to collapse under her and headed for the privacy of the break room. She peeked back before she ducked into the room to make sure he didn't follow her.

The lock worked, fortunately. She'd never had a reason to use it in the year and eight months she'd been here, but she had to call Flint. Whether the reason the detective was checking on Hal's death lay behind door number one, door number two, or door number three, all possibilities ended with the same grand prize: she was so screwed.

She had to fess up and deal with the consequences. God, this was going to be fun.

It took a second—not enough time to come up with a justifiable explanation—to scroll through her limited contacts and find the name she'd used to store the number for the U.S. Marshals Service. She stared at the number and overrode her finger's resistance to initiate the call. The slightest touch committed her.

"Marshal DeLong, please." She almost hung up before the operator responded.

"Marshal DeLong is out of the office on his honeymoon."

Hang up. Hang up!

But she couldn't.

"This is Cassidy O'Shea. My identity and location may have been compromised."

SEVEN

Colonel Mahinis showed up as the team was about to roll out for lunch. "Conference room," he directed them.

AJ glanced at Lundgren, who appeared as curious as the rest.

The colonel stood by the door as the team filed past. While some took seats, Lundgren and Mack remained standing, and AJ and Dev perched on tabletops. After Juan entered, the colonel trailed in, closing the door behind him.

"The detective was legit," the colonel relayed. "However, I just got off the phone with U.S. Marshal Valone. Turns out Hal Boswell's stepdaughter, Cassidy O'Shea, is in the Witness Protection Program."

"Damn. What'd she do?" Juan asked the question that nearly erupted from AJ's mouth.

"She's a witness. The *only* witness in a federal case against an enforcer for Felix Avila's gun-running operation. With the suspicious nature of Hal's death, the marshals are concerned Avila could have been trying to get a lead on Ms. O'Shea's whereabouts."

Avila? Crap. The pieces finally locked with the right fit, so AJ could see the completed puzzle that was Cassidy.

"They're concerned enough that they want to relocate her," the colonel stated.

A tingle crab-walked a few hesitant steps up AJ's spine. He knew more than he wanted about Felix Avila and his organization.

"They need to put her in temporary custody while they set up a new identity. However, with what's happened, Ms. O'Shea is threatening to back out of testifying."

"Wouldn't she be safer staying in protective custody?" Dev asked.

"Fear doesn't make for rational thinking," Lundgren pointed out.

"She admitted to coming here for Hal's funeral, and she apparently mentioned Hal's position on the teams," the colonel continued. "The marshal assigned to her is currently out of the country, and Marshal Valone thinks having familiar faces might calm her down. Someone who can convince her to testify. Since everyone in our unit has marshal credentials, he asked if we would provide a three-man detail until they can relocate her. This is a voluntary assignment, but I thought you might have a personal interest. Lundgren?"

"I'm taking Stephanie on a cruise starting Friday, but …"

"You cancel that, your wife may kill you." Mack trumped the chief's hesitation. "Kristie's got an ultrasound tomorrow, or I'd volunteer."

"Rozanski, what'd the detective say about further questions for you?" Lundgren asked.

"He didn't explicitly tell me not to leave town." The idea that Hal had been murdered seemed a solid possibility if it meant protecting the interests of a major gun-running cartel. God, he'd given Cassidy the benefit of the doubt being Hal's stepdaughter, but how had she gotten mixed up in this? Money? A guy? And now she wanted to back out of doing the right thing by not testifying?

"Considering your relationship with Hal, how about taking lead on this?" Lundgren asked.

Take lead? He'd been waiting to head an op, but this? Babysitting Hal's stubborn stepdaughter? The same woman who may be the reason Hal was dead. *No way.* "I'm supposed to be in Ohio for the big anniversary party my brother is throwing our parents." AJ seized the convenient out. Let Tony intimidate Cassidy to do the right thing.

"Family party? You have a flight booked?" Lundgren didn't let him off the hook that easily.

AJ looked at his hands resting on his thighs. His parents would rehash their disappointment over his broken engagement and claim if he had a different job—one outside the military—he could find a wife and a big house like the new home Damien would be showing off. Like those things and sitting in an office all day would make him happy.

His parents would gush over whatever fabulous gift Karolina brought them from her trip to Italy. He'd given his mom a pretty scarf in her favorite shade of blue, and his dad a hand-carved wooden box after his last tour in Afghanistan. Gifts he hadn't seen worn or displayed anywhere. It was the best he could do. Not like Kandahar was known for its great shopping.

He scratched at the dried mud on his pants. Would he rather have his teeth pulled out or his fingernails torn off? His fingernails would grow back. His family would be family forever. You didn't get to pick them. "I was gonna drive—"

"Congrats, you landed your first mission as team leader. You need two more."

Lundgren shot down his hope of getting off the hook on

this one, but he had lead. Fine. He'd make sure as hell Cassidy did the right thing. Good thing he'd have someone there to keep him from going off on her while holed up in some hotel room for a few days. He rose from the table. Shoulders back, he scanned the faces of the team.

Lundgren and Mack were out. Tony outranked him.

Devin's arms were crossed over his chest, but he wasn't staring at the floor like Linc Porter, who avoided meeting his eyes, sending the come-on-man-I-have-plans-with-my-lady signal.

"Dev, you in?"

Dev gave an affirmative nod.

"I'll have to cancel a date or two, but I'll be your number three," Juan volunteered.

"Don't want to put you out," AJ said, giving Kyle Liu a help-me-out-here look.

Kyle helplessly turned up his hands. That left AJ stuck with the prospect of keeping Juan on task and not letting him turn this assignment into an attempt to hook-up with Hal's stepdaughter. She might be enticing on the outside, but Juan might want to steer clear if she was tied to someone in Avila's organization.

Whatever his personal feelings about Cassidy, he'd do the right thing. He couldn't afford to screw this up.

EIGHT

"You guys are armed, right?" the marshal asked as he led the suit-clad men out of the baggage claim area of the small airport.

"We packed them to get through security and make the flight," AJ answered over Juan's "Duh!" response. He took the question as a warning of the danger associated with anyone who might be after Cassidy.

The taillights on a sleek black SUV with dark-tinted windows flashed when the marshal approached. Another marshal emerged from a second vehicle. Juan opened the tailgate and hefted his suitcase inside. He slipped out of his suit jacket, fastened his holster, and unlocked his handgun case.

"I need to see your IDs," the marshal said.

AJ and Dev handed over their military IDs and U.S. Marshals credentials before retrieving their weapons and stowing their suitcases.

"You need to sign for this." Extending a clipboard, the marshal waved a sealed yellow envelope.

AJ scribbled his signature, then exchanged the clipboard for the envelope.

"Our witness is under the name of Fiona Liddell."

"Is anyone with her?" AJ unsealed the envelope.

"We were on our way to get her when we were told to get another vehicle and pick you up instead. There's not an immediate threat and she's someplace safe. Valone said you know her." The marshal looked them over like they were citizen's patrol instead of an elite Special Forces team.

"Friends with her stepfather," AJ kept the explanation simple.

"She was told it would be your team and is *supposed* to be waiting for you." Irritation punctuated his words. She seemed to have that effect on people. "Address for her place of employment is inside. Her home address is in there, too."

The second marshal held out the car keys.

Juan snatched the keys, leering at the shiny SUV. Considering Juan's beat-up, piece-of-shit car, AJ wasn't going to fight him over who drove.

"Listen." The marshal's eyes scanned left to right, verifying no one else was close. "Cassidy O'Shea is the only witness the U.S. Attorney has to prosecute Reynaldo Flores. If she doesn't testify, he's free with no incentive to give state's evidence on Felix Avila. His organization is responsible for nearly a quarter of the illegal arms entering the States and getting them into the hands of street gangs in half the major cities. Avila's group is also believed to be behind the murder of those two border agents last spring. O'Shea is the key to taking down Avila and his organization."

"We get it. Protect her and convince her to testify," AJ recited. If Cassidy's involvement with someone in Avila's organization led to Hal's death, the least she could do is testify. And if Avila had Hal murdered, he needed his ass in jail, or better yet, in the lethal-injection room.

"Address for where you'll take her is in there along with

cash for expenses. Keep the receipts. Vehicle has GPS. Marshal DeLong is back in the office Tuesday. We anticipate being ready for a pickup to relocate her then. Take a look and let me know if you have any questions."

Juan typed the address into the GPS and adjusted the driver's seat. While Dev asked the marshal about the timing for the trial, AJ sat on the edge of the passenger's seat and went through the envelope. A wave of emotion crashed down on him as he stared at Cassidy's picture. How was she involved in all this? Had she known at the funeral she played a part in Hal's death? It didn't seem so, but how could she have not known? Soon, AJ would be face-to-face with Cassidy again and looking at her from a new perspective—the cause of his mentor's death.

"YOU WANT TO GET DINNER?" Juan braked for the light and peered out the windshield at the businesses lining the boulevard.

"After we collect our package, we can pick up food." AJ wasn't going to screw around because Juan wanted burgers.

In minutes, they were away from the main business district of Schenectady, passing through a more suburban part of town. The sun slipped lower, disappearing, then reappearing in flashes through the treetops.

Juan turned in at the bright white sign with Elmwood Manor in dark green letters. A white wooden fence surrounded the one-story brick building.

"Cruise through the lot, then circle the building," AJ ordered.

There were no occupied vehicles as they navigated the half-empty rows of cars. A service drive ran behind the building. There was a door marked Emergency Exit, a set of double doors, which he guessed was the kitchen because of the dumpsters, and another emergency exit.

"Drop us off at the front, but we'll try to come out the back. I'll call you."

Juan looped around, coming to a stop under the covered entrance.

AJ and Dev stepped through the automatic doors onto faded flecked-tile flooring. Past the foyer, a nurse's station guarded access to two wings of patient rooms. A woman in patterned scrubs with purple streaks in her brunette hair studied them over her glasses. "Can I help you, gentlemen?" Her gaze flicked back and forth between him and Dev, settling on Dev with an inviting smile.

"We're here to speak with Fiona Liddell." The name sounded foreign coming out of his mouth, but he got it right—though that wouldn't matter in a few minutes.

"Fiona's shift ended a few hours ago. Can I help you instead?"

Shit! The marshals told her to stay put. Why the hell would she leave? Why hadn't he thought to check the parking lot for her car?

"She was expecting us. Are you sure she left?" Dev asked in his smooth voice of utter calm and charm.

AJ would swear the nurse swooned from infatuation, staring into Dev's eyes.

"I can check. Hang on." She groped for the radio lying on the counter. "Terry, has Fiona left for the day?"

"She was here half an hour ago, reading to Mrs. Singer in her room."

The volcanic frustration sputtering up from AJ's stomach subsided when he heard the update.

"You're in luck. Follow me." The nurse rolled the chair back, then led them down the hall, sashaying her hips.

Devin's eyes locked on the nurse's moving-target ass, but to his credit, he kept his tongue in his mouth. A couple of days sequestered in a hotel room with Juan's suggestive comments and stares and Cassidy falling for Dev's boy-next-door charm—AJ could hardly wait.

The nurse stopped outside a room. She pushed open the door, giving him a clear line of sight to Cassidy seated at the side of the bed, reading to an older woman.

Cassidy's head jerked up, and she fumbled with the book. Her lips closed from an alarmed oval to breathe a sigh while her wide eyes closed, and her shoulders dropped.

"Sorry to stop mid-scene, Mrs. Singer"—Cassidy set the book on the nightstand—"but these gentlemen are here for me."

"Just when you're getting to the good part. Can they be convinced to stick around for the big love scene?" The woman adjusted her light-blue nightgown, studying them. "I saw that look." She wagged a finger in their direction. "Don't judge me. Even old women like to believe in romance."

"Afraid we don't have time for that, ma'am." AJ didn't need to listen to Cassidy read some trashy romance—not that Jess breaking up with him had soured his outlook on love —*much*. Now just wasn't the time in his life. And certainly not on this mission.

"We'll pick up tomorrow, dear." The woman shot them a disapproving look. Well, at him. She smiled at Dev.

"Don't wait on me." Cassidy touched the old woman's arm. She picked up a bag from the floor and eased away from the bed.

The purple-haired nurse stepped out of the way. "Are you guys detectives?"

"Why would you think that?" Dev asked in return.

"The suits. It wouldn't surprise me if you were looking into Mr. Holt's death. He had dementia, and physically he was in good shape—alive one day. Dead the next. His daughter wanted to know who'd visited him. She's not above accusing her stepfamily to get them cut out of his will. If you need to talk to someone else, let me know."

"We'll come find you if we have more questions." Dev flashed his you'll-do-whatever-I-suggest smile to tactfully dismiss her.

It worked. She gave Cassidy an envious departing glance and strolled back down the hall, looking over her shoulder at them halfway.

"You need to get anything else?" AJ asked Cassidy.

"This is it. I cleaned out my locker." She kept her voice low.

"Can we get out there?" He pointed to the emergency-exit door.

"Uh, it sounds an alarm if opened. It's to keep the ambulatory patients from wandering off."

"What about the kitchen doors? Can you access them?"

"Yeah." Cassidy nodded, her eyes widening.

"Meet us in back at the double doors in one." He sent a voice-to-text message to Juan. Cassidy kept pace with them as they passed patient rooms. The flirty nurse lingered at the corner of the station, but they proceeded by without speaking. Better to let her think they were going to the dining area to talk. She'd figure it out later.

Cassidy navigated around the tables and chairs to the back set of doors.

He waited to hear the crunch of loose gravel under tires before stepping out first. Once he opened the back passenger-side door, he signaled. Cassidy ducked inside and slid over to allow Dev to slide in beside her.

"I need you to stay down and out of sight until we're away from the facility," AJ instructed her.

Despite her panicked look, she complied, leaning forward to become invisible from the outside once he shut the door. He appreciated that she didn't question him. Juan accelerated the second AJ closed his door.

"Normal speed," he warned, bracing a hand on the dash as Juan hit the brakes. "You can do evasive maneuvers once we're out of the lot."

"Where to?"

"Cassidy, do you need anything from your home?" AJ asked without turning around.

"I need to get Champ. Some clothes would be good."

Champ. Shit. He didn't know how long it would be until the marshals collected her things. They couldn't leave Champ behind.

He nodded confirmation to Juan, then programmed the GPS with the address the marshals had provided for Cassidy's residence. "Dev, you have a hat or hoodie for camouflage?"

"On it." Dev twisted over the back seat to the stashed luggage.

Juan waited at the stop sign for a good half-minute before pulling out of the nursing home lot.

"You can sit up." AJ turned to study Cassidy. "When we get to your place, you'll have eight and a half minutes to pack up what you need and what the three of us can carry down in one trip." He pointed to Dev's backside, Cassidy, and himself. "Are we clear?"

Cassidy nodded, a quick, sharp acknowledgment.

"Here." Dev plopped back down. "It'll be kinda big, but it'll cover up the scrub top, and you can pull the hood up."

Juan ignored the GPS and turned randomly, always checking the mirror before he finally followed the directions to Cassidy's apartment complex. She directed him to her building.

"Stay with the vehicle. We won't be long," AJ said more to remind Cassidy than to inform Juan.

Keys jangled in Cassidy's hand as they hustled up the concrete walk to the front of the building. Dev took point while AJ covered her rear—*her very nice rear*—though he quickly shifted his gaze to scan the stand of pines near the adjoining building. Anyone looking for her would be more likely to stake out her home than work.

Upstairs, Dev claimed the keys. Champ's bark greeted them as soon as the keys grated against the lock. Dev pushed open the door only to be charged by the dog that stood on his hind legs with his paws on Dev's chest. Champ got in a few licks, then set down on all fours and circled Cassidy's legs, emitting an urgent whine.

"I need to take him out. I haven't been home since this morning."

"Dev, take him down to do his business. You pack." AJ herded Cassidy into the apartment.

Cassidy went straight to the cramped kitchen and opened the door to a tiny pantry. She grabbed a leash and lugged a bag of dog food toward the front door until he took it from her. She disappeared into her bedroom, then emerged seconds later with Champ's bed. He reached to take it from her, too. That she took care of the dog first, Hal's dog, swept away some of AJ's resentment that had piled up since learning of her possible tie to Hal's death.

He wrestled with the resentment and attraction that

swirled inside his head and chest. Emotions that, like oil and water, didn't mix and blend, but stayed separate.

Dev stepped back inside, interrupting AJ's attempt to pin down his feelings. "I left Champ with Juan. She need help?"

Banging and slamming emitted from the bedroom. "I guess so."

Partially closed dresser drawers explained the noise. A suitcase lay on the bed, and beside it sat a pile of clothes. Juan's sweatshirt draped off the side of the bed. Cassidy had discarded her scrub top to the floor, and she'd changed into a navy long-sleeved T-shirt.

"How can we help?" Dev asked.

AJ moved to the window and turned the blinds closed.

"See how much of this you can fit in here." Cassidy pointed to the clothes beside the suitcase. "Oh, and these need to go in." She tossed a pair of sneakers on the bed, spun around, and disappeared into the bathroom.

With glass and metal clanking in the next room, Devin stuffed socks into the running shoes. AJ picked up a stack of shirts and packed them in the suitcase. He stared at her lacy bras, one in hot pink and another in royal blue, both with matching underwear. He figured she'd rather not leave behind her expensive lingerie, so he grabbed them and the two athletic bras, stuffed them in, then covered them with jeans and workout pants. Dev grinned at him. At least Juan wasn't here to make a crack about what they'd look like on.

She wouldn't need her scrubs for the next few days, which was good since the suitcase wouldn't hold everything she'd pulled out. He and Dev crammed in what they could and forced the zipper around.

Cassidy reemerged with a large tote bag in hand. She edged by them to the nightstand for the e-reader she tucked in her bag. Then, with her back to them, she removed a few items from the drawer and quickly shoved them in the bag.

"Ready." Her assertive tone delivered an I-have-time-to-spare message.

"I got this. You get Champ's bed and food." AJ hoisted the suitcase off the bed, not bothering to wheel it across the floor.

Cassidy trailed Dev out the front door. "Should I lock it?"

"Definitely," AJ and Dev said at the same time. AJ stepped aside to let her engage the deadbolt. No point in giving anyone easy access to see she'd fled or scrounge up anything on her, her family, or friends.

They went down the stairs with Cassidy sandwiched between them.

"What the …?" She hesitated, staring at where Juan parked the SUV, tires in the grass on both sides of the walkway, a few feet from the front of the building.

Dev loaded Champ's items and turned to take Cassidy's tote. By the time AJ stowed Cassidy's suitcase, she and Dev were in their seats and buckled.

Juan eased the massive SUV over the curb, then stepped on the gas. AJ kept his mouth shut. Her home held a higher threat level than her workplace. He wanted out of here. Turning enough to put Cassidy in his peripheral vision, he noted her fingers dug into Champ's fur. She stared straight ahead.

"Did you already eat or need us to pick you up something?" Juan asked after a few minutes.

"I'm not hungry."

Cassidy's voice sounded flat and far away, making AJ wonder what she thought about all of this—though he didn't plan to ask. "We'll get something to eat at the lodge." He hoped that would pacify Juan, who turned on the GPS screen and followed the directions.

Ever the Boy Scout, Dev passed around energy bars to tide them over for the drive.

No one spoke as they left the city behind. Juan turned on the radio and sang along to the tunes playing as darkness settled in on the cloudless night. The half-moon hung low in the sky.

As they neared their destination, AJ zoomed in the GPS screen. Near the intersection of two rural highways, the lodge didn't appear to have much around it, making it an ideal location to keep Cassidy sequestered.

Juan pulled into the lot under a partially lit neon sign that proclaimed vacancies.

"You gotta be shitting me," Dev complained. "Sorry."

AJ assumed Dev directed the apology to Cassidy. This was no resort lodge—more like a clichéd version of a run-down, one-story motel from a horror movie. At the end of the building, a blue plastic tarp covered a sagging portion of the roof, where a fallen pine tree blocked two parking spaces. He could count the number of cars in the lot on one hand, with a finger leftover.

"Pine View Lodge. It's a damn motel."

"Not up to your five-star standards, Dev?" Juan remarked.

"I've stayed in worse, but I was thinking of her." Dev jerked a thumb toward Cassidy. "And, FYI, there's no restaurant."

Juan grumbled.

AJ growled, agreeing with Dev's point. The marshals wanted to convince Cassidy to stay in protective custody, yet they sent them to this rodent motel? Unfortunately, they were in the right place, but the Marshals Service was sure as hell going to hear about it.

"It's not what I'd pick either, but this is my fault. Sorry, guys." Cassidy looked at them instead of the motel.

"Crap, either a possum or a damn big rat just took cover under the wooden decking."

"I'll go check-in." AJ had no illusions that he'd be told there was no room at the inn.

"I say we need a plan B." Juan hadn't turned off the engine yet.

"I'm on it." Dev already had his phone out and to his ear.

"Who are you—"

"Hi, Mom," Dev spoke over AJ. "I'm good. I was wondering if anyone was using the mountain cabin now through the weekend?"

Crap. What is he thinking? AJ slashed a hand across his throat in a signal to Dev to nix giving out info.

Dev flashed the *OK* sign and kept talking. "It'd be me and a couple of the guys. Yeah, well, it's work-related, so that wouldn't be a good idea this time. I'll come visit soon, though."

Dev pocketed his phone and opened the driver-side door. "Going with plan B. I'll drive."

"Wait, wait, wait." AJ stopped him. "We aren't going anywhere. We need to call the marshals."

"Screw that. They sent us here. Forgiveness over permission," Dev reasoned.

The rule-following angel on AJ's right shoulder said: Stick with the designated plan. Don't blow this. Cassidy violated protocol, and she should suck it up.

The little devil on his other shoulder spoke in Devin's refined New England accent, saying it'd be easier to accomplish this mission if they weren't holed up in a motel one step up from a campground. "How secure is this other location?"

"Beats this place hands down. High ground surrounded by

forest. And no one is gonna know where she is. I'll have to navigate," Dev said like this was a done deal.

The voices in his head countered each other. Yes. No. Stay. Go.

"I'm driving." Juan gripped the wheel, refusing to relinquish his spot, but clearly in favor of plan B.

AJ took another hard look at the Pine View Lodge. There were lights on in the office and in two rooms—one had two cars parked out front—probably for a different kind of covert mission.

He opened his door and motioned for Dev to take the front passenger seat. "How far?"

"Maybe an hour." Dev changed spots with AJ. He punched the address into the GPS, and Juan backed up the SUV before AJ could change his mind.

The "lodge" disappeared seconds later. Inside the vehicle, a group sigh cleansed the charged atmosphere.

NINE

Cassidy scratched behind Champ's ears. Curled between her and AJ, the dog lay on the seat, his head on her lap. The silence in the car allowed Cassidy to try and process what she'd learned today.

She'd worried about Flores trying to get to her—that was a one hundred and fourteen percent given—but he was in custody. Despite the marshal's assurances that her family would be safe, she worried about her mom. About her sister, Sherri. About her niece and nephew. But Cassidy hadn't worried about Hal. He wasn't real family—at least not to someone who didn't know her. And if anyone could take care of themselves, Hal could.

Ice water trickled down her spine, one vertebra at a time. Whoever killed Hal—*killed Hal*—that scenario settled like a crushing weight in her chest—had spent time getting to know her. She had no idea how they'd dug up information on her relationship with Hal, but they'd dug deep and struck gold.

Was it worth it? By trying to do the right thing and bring a killer to justice, it had resulted in another death. A death that mattered to her. The marshals needed her to testify, or they couldn't hold Flores. But at what cost?

She'd lost two years of her life already. Now Hal. What would stop whoever killed Hal from targeting the rest of her family? If she didn't testify, she'd be out of Witness Protection—then what? Would Flores leave her and her family alone? Could she have a life, or would she be trapped in this cell of fear, watching her back forever?

Her thoughts spiraled in an endless circle of what-ifs that never reached a conclusion. It didn't help that rancor rolled off AJ's body toward her in rushing waves. She couldn't condemn him for blaming her for Hal's death—she blamed herself. Her brain throbbed behind her eyes like the beat of a song with the bass cranked to the max.

"Up on the right is the closest grocery to get decent provisions."

"Thank God. I'm starving." Juan slowed, then whipped the vehicle into the mostly empty lot.

"It'll be safer to stay at the cabin than go out or even get delivery, so stock up a few days' worth," AJ said.

"No one delivers all the way up to the cabin," Devin replied. He and Juan were the first out and headed inside the store. Champ raised his head and emitted a hungry whine.

"I need to feed him." Cassidy looked to AJ.

AJ nodded, which she interpreted as permission to get out of the vehicle. He also got out.

Champ stuck close to her side while she opened the bag of food and filled a bowl. AJ produced a half-full bottle of water and poured it into another bowl.

"He's gonna need more water. Let's go help with the shopping. Here, boy." AJ put the bowls on the floor of the SUV. Champ climbed back in.

Inside the grocery, AJ grabbed a cart. She followed him past aisles until they found Devin and Juan.

"Seriously? That's what you're planning to eat for five days?" The words blurted out, and her bowels blocked just looking at the frozen pizzas and dinners in Juan's cart.

Juan shrugged, adding in a bag of frozen fries.

"Does the cabin have a stove and cookware?" she asked Devin, cooking up an idea. If they had to be cooped up, she could do her part to make the next few days more palatable.

"It's a second home. There are pots, pans, spices, and stuff. No perishables. Oh, and a nice gas grill."

The prospect of cooking for someone other than herself for the first time in two years made her giddy. God, she'd missed this feeling. "Any food allergies?" she asked, taking over AJ's empty cart.

"I hate brussels sprouts and liver. And cubed steaks." Juan's features scrunched in distaste.

"I promise not to serve liver if you put most of those back."

Juan hesitated and studied her dubiously.

"I'll take care of the menu and cooking." She dug in her purse for scrap paper and a pen. "Go ahead and get whatever snack items you want."

"No alcohol."

Juan waggled his head and grumbled at AJ's mandate, but he and Devin moved off as Cassidy scribbled out meal ideas. Beside her, AJ exhaled loudly. She ignored him and kept writing, recalling some of Hal's favorite meals. Once she had a menu drafted, she headed to the meat department. AJ stayed one step behind like a sentry while she shopped.

"Can we hurry this up any?" AJ said after about his tenth exasperated sigh.

She gripped the shopping cart tighter, but she picked up

her pace and gritted her teeth to keep from asking if he'd prefer to make multiple trips. Finally, Juan and Devin showed up, both munching on apples. In addition to the opened bag of fruit, their cart held chips, dip, cereal, Pop-Tarts, and at least two partially hidden frozen pizzas.

Juan eyed her cart. Cassidy pushed aside the bagged lettuce, revealing the packages of steaks, shrimp, and chicken, which earned smiles and nods from both men. AJ cleared his throat.

"Why don't you go and get anything else you want and leave these two as my protection detail?" she suggested.

AJ hesitated. She nearly gave him the "Go!" order to see if he'd obey. Fortunately, with another overdramatic sigh, he left the trio behind.

"Is he always this uptight?" she asked once he was out of earshot. She selected a package of rice noodles.

"AJ? He's usually the most laid-back guy on the team," Devin said.

"After Liu, you mean," Juan added.

"True. Forgot him. My bad."

"Great. It's me, then." She didn't know why that revelation made her feel unworthy.

"Don't take it personally. Hal's death hit him hard, and he's taking being in charge seriously."

"Too seriously," Juan piped in, pulling a bottle of hot sauce from the top shelf and adding it to his cart.

Devin flashed a smile. "He'll chill."

Shopping alongside Devin and Juan proved more relaxing than AJ stalking her. She grabbed two bottles of wine. The guys might be on orders, but a glass or two could be required for her to chill out.

AJ returned with a bag of trail mix and a container of mint chocolate chip ice cream. Cassidy's stomach rumbled by the time they'd checked out, bagged, and loaded all the groceries into the back of the SUV. Driving to the cabin, she heard the guys' stomachs growling, too.

"The driveway is on the left, up around this bend. It's hard to see, so slow down," Devin cautioned.

Juan nearly overshot the drive camouflaged by trees. The GPS warned they were entering an unverified area. Branches brushed the sides of the vehicle. Taller trees blocked much of the moonlight.

"Stay right at the fork ahead," Devin instructed.

After several minutes of climbing the twisting black sliver of asphalt, a two-story log home with an expanse of windows stood in a cleared area.

"Shit. That's the *cabin*? How fucking loaded is your family, Dev?" Juan rolled to a stop.

"Language." Devin opened his door.

"Seriously? This is not a vacation cabin. I'd love to see your parent's main house. It must be an effing mansion."

"It's not what you think. Dad bought it out of foreclosure."

Cassidy got out on her side and went to the back of the SUV. AJ stared at the impressive house, then scoped out the dark woods.

Everyone grabbed bags of groceries and followed Devin to the covered front door. He punched a code into the lock, then stepped into the great room and flipped on the lights. The stereotypical mounted deer head hung over the massive stone fireplace.

A modern galley kitchen lined the left side of the cabin, extending to the back wall that was almost all glass.

"Give me a tour of the place." AJ set his armload of groceries on the granite countertop. "Juan, bring the other groceries and bags up, and I'll assign places."

Juan grunted, but set down his bags and headed out. Devin and AJ disappeared down a flight of stairs. A devoted Champ padded after the pair, despite the lure of food.

To get the lay of the kitchen, Cassidy emptied bags and stowed food in the cabinets and nearly empty fridge. She found the cookware and filled a large pot with water, then scrounged up a frying pan. Juan deposited more groceries, spun, and tromped back out. Devin and AJ reemerged and checked out the remainder of the main floor. When Devin opened the glass doors to the deck, a cool, fresh breeze stirred the air. As they headed upstairs, Champ joined them in exploring.

She sliced the ingredients for dinner as Juan dropped the last load of suitcases inside the front door.

"Need any help?" He stepped to her side and sniffed the air, then peered at the rice noodles soaking in the pot.

"Can you get plates? I think they were over there." She pointed to the cabinet over the dishwasher.

He set the plates on the counter about the time Champ bounded down the stairs. AJ followed. He paused at the foot of the steps, eyeing Juan at her side.

"Dinner will be ready in about twelve minutes." She added garlic, ginger, green onions, and finely chopped chilies to the frying pan. AJ's left eyebrow quirked up as the food sizzled in the hot oil. "Hal's Pad Thai recipe, though not as spicy as he liked it, but you can add more red chilies." She added shrimp to the stir-fry and basked in the mouthwatering smiles.

"Dev will take the master on the main floor since it's his place. Downstairs, there's air hockey, pool, and Ping-Pong tables," AJ started.

"*Loaded*," Juan coughed out.

She suppressed a chuckle as Devin rolled his eyes and crossed his arms over his chest.

"There's a full bath and bedroom down there. Juan, that's where you'll bunk.

Devin did a double take at AJ, who ignored him and continued.

"Cassidy, I want you upstairs in the back-left bedroom."

She nodded, adding sauce to the stir fry.

"I'll take the other upstairs bedroom, and there's a shared bath," AJ continued. "We'll take eight-hour shifts. Juan, you'll take zero hundred to oh eight hundred."

"Why do I get stuck with graveyard and—"

"I've got my reasons. Dev and I will run a perimeter check in the morning. I'll take oh eight hundred to sixteen hundred, and Dev has third shift."

Cassidy picked up that the men were friends, but AJ was clearly the alpha dog while they were assigned to watch over her—though it seemed a bit overkill, considering their location. Stirring in the noodles, she half listened as they discussed details of their assignment.

Being here, doing something as simple as cooking a meal for them, restored a sense of normalcy missing from her life the past two years. They knew her name—her real name—and just hearing it made her feel like herself. Gave her hope for having her own life again. She couldn't help but smile at the men staring at the food like a pack of ravenous wolves.

Though they probably didn't care about presentation, she took her time mixing in the bean sprouts. She served up generous portions of the Pad Thai with a sprinkling of crushed peanuts.

None of the men spoke as they shoveled in food, chewed, swallowed, made *mmm* sounds, and repeated.

Juan added more chilies to his serving, then reached for his water after two bites. "This is excellent," he proclaimed.

"Better than frozen pizzas?" she teased.

"Way better. Sorry. My exes couldn't cook, so I don't expect much."

Cooking. Another life skill Hal taught her. She'd never expected to enjoy cooking since her mother made it out to be a drudgery. But they were different people. Thank God. Maybe the nurturing gene skipped a generation.

"So, how did you end up in Witness Protection?" Juan asked between mouthfuls.

The few bites of pasta suddenly filled her stomach. *How?* The better question was why. She'd asked herself that and called fate a bitch, and worse, at least every other day. All three men were silent. Juan and Devin's eyes fixed on her face. AJ pushed food around with his fork, then his gaze flicked to her.

She consciously drew in air, then slowly exhaled before beginning. "I was working an early morning shift when we got a call that medics were transporting a patient who'd requested a priest. It happens occasionally. Sometimes they want a prayer or blessing. Sometimes they want to confess. Sometimes they want last rites—thinking they can cheat hell." Which sure seemed to be the case with Flores. "If their injuries aren't life-threatening, we try to accommodate their request since it gives them peace and improves their chance of survival. Anyway, this guy was adamant about needing a priest when the medics were bringing him in. He'd been pinned in his car, and his left leg was mangled. There was a real possibility he could lose the leg, and he had severe internal injuries. I began prepping him for surgery, but when the priest walked in, the patient blurted out, "Forgive me, Father, for I have sinned. I've killed people."

"Seriously?" Juan's eyes widened.

Devin and AJ's mouths hung open.

"It was in Spanish, *pero yo hablo español*. Maybe he didn't think I'd understand. Or he had enough pain meds in him that his inhibitions were down or needed absolution because he thought karma was catching up for payback and owned his ass."

Juan snorted and looked to his teammates. "Karma's a bitch."

"Before I could get out of the room, he confessed he was an enforcer for the Avalia cartel—"

"It's Avila. Felix Avila," AJ spat out.

"Yeah, that sounds right. The patient, Reynaldo Flores, said he killed one of the smugglers who betrayed them, someone named Luz, that morning. He named other names."

"What did you do?" Devin's food sat forgotten on his plate.

"I got out of there as fast as I could to give him and the priest privacy."

"A little late for that." Devin shook his head.

"The priest came out afterward and told me we were both bound by his deathbed confession."

"Seal of the confessional," Juan corrected her.

"I'm not Catholic!" And she didn't feel bound by someone else's beliefs.

"Did anyone else hear him confess?" AJ asked.

She shook her head, wishing to hell someone had. Like the surgeon. In shock, she'd kept her mouth shut—hoping it *would* turn out to be a deathbed confession.

Only Flores didn't die.

"The next day, I got word Flores wanted to see me. Called me the strawberry-blonde angel." She shivered like an arctic blast of air penetrated her skin to her very core. "Not my real hair color." She ran a thick lock of hair between two fingers in response to the confused looks of the men.

"Did you go?" Devin asked in a rush.

"I put it off. I doubted it was to thank me for helping save his life. Then I saw a story on the news about a car explosion. A woman and her young son died in the explosion. Her name was Luz."

Several seconds passed with no one speaking or eating.

"I kept thinking about what the priest said, but dammit! I. Am. Not. Catholic. How many other people had he killed? Would he kill again?" She stabbed the air with her fork. "Even if I kept dodging him in the hospital, he knew my name and where I worked. I couldn't sleep."

"So, you went to the police." AJ nodded, conveying he agreed with that decision.

The decision that she hadn't initially had the courage to make. Her boyfriend, Parks, had been out of town on business, and problem-solving had never been her mother's forte —Tiffany's self-preservation method depended on finding someone to take care of her. She hadn't wanted to involve her sister since Sherri had two young kids.

"I called Hal." Her throat constricted as she confessed. Long after the divorce, he'd still been her go-to guy. Strong, level-headed Hal. Capable of handling the worst bad guys on the planet. Someone she didn't need to worry about protecting. "Told him everything to see what he'd say."

Had she underestimated her enemy?

"And he told you to go to the police." AJ's words were spoken clearly and slowly, as if each were a puzzle piece being put into place.

"Yes. Oh God. You don't think someone killed Hal because they found out I told him?" Her body trembled, and her throat tightened to the point she could hardly swallow or breathe. She shrank into the wooden chair.

"I'm sure there are other possibilities," Devin started, "but they could have accessed your phone records and made the connection. His testimony would be hearsay and wouldn't stand up in court, though, so it's more likely they used him to draw you out. You're the threat."

"I worried about them going after my boyfriend or my mom or sister, but not my *ex*-stepfather."

"They'd be too obvious," Devin kept talking. "Marshals would never let you show up if they died under suspicious circumstances. I'm surprised they didn't send a marshal with you to Hal's funeral."

Another slab of guilt crashed down, crushing her body. "I didn't tell them. I was kind of AWOL."

Silence.

"I only found out he died the night before the funeral," she explained. "I was afraid they wouldn't let me go. I had to be there. I had to. It's been two years. How would they know I'd show up for his funeral?"

"If they did access your phone records, they might deduce you were close, despite the divorce. They took a shot. If I were an assassin, that's how I'd do it." Devin's eyes narrowed. "Lure you out with something personal, but enough distance that you'd feel safe. He knew there'd be a bunch of special ops guys at the funeral, plus he thought you'd have protection, so he wouldn't try anything there. He might have been there or watching Hal's place, though. Plan to track you rather than ambush you."

"Course, Dev here is a genius, so he's smarter than most assassins." Juan resumed eating.

"Don't underestimate them. A good assassin is smart. Methodical. Has to be to not get caught. Flores is probably more of a thug type. A car bomb's crude. But if someone went to the trouble to kill Hal …" Devin hesitated. "Where it wouldn't raise suspicion, and almost didn't, that's who you need to watch out for."

"Enough, Dev. Jeez." AJ looked helplessly at her while she absorbed everything his teammate had suggested.

Her head pounded. She'd never stopped to think like an assassin—her mission revolved around saving lives. With the flat tire and staying at Lundgren's, she might have dodged a very real bullet.

Devin's reasoning attacked her body like being stung by an army of angry fire ants. "I didn't know." She sniffed. "I didn't think …" She couldn't finish as her body hiccupped. She couldn't stop the tears.

"You weren't supposed to suspect anything. That's the point." Devin's attempt to reassure her did little to alleviate her self-condemnation or fear they hated her for putting Hal in jeopardy.

Juan finished his helping of Pad Thai and went for seconds, possibly to escape her snuffling. "Anyone else want more?"

The uneaten food on her plate no longer held any appeal. "Help yourselves. I'm going to get settled in." She carried her plate to the kitchen, then trudged upstairs to the bedroom where her suitcase sat on a bed covered with a patchwork quilt. Up here, her tears wouldn't mortify the guys.

TEN

THE MORNING SUNLIGHT streamed through the wall of windows, but instead of enjoying the view and sounds of nature, AJ sat mere feet from Cassidy, killing time reading the news on his laptop. When Cassidy rose from the couch, Champ tagged after her into the kitchen. She set her coffee mug in the sink, then stood silently staring out the window. After what felt like ten minutes, though in actuality was probably less than two, she turned and headed up the stairs carrying her e-reader.

He breathed easier when she disappeared from view. She had to know he'd heard her crying after she'd gone to bed last night. Had she expected him to do something? To try and talk or comfort her? But he didn't know what to say or do. Crying women was not his field of expertise. So, he'd lain in bed listening to her sniffles and sobs and Champ's occasional sympathetic whimper. The dog probably knew what to do better than he did.

Her story. Whoa. So, she wasn't culpable even if Hal's death was related to why she was in protective custody, though now she probably blamed herself. It punched through the barrier wall that had dropped into place when he suspected she could have played a part. If Hal's death was murder, anyone involved was going to have some seriously bad karma raining down on them.

AJ drained the last of his coffee and went to refill his mug. It'd taken him a while to fall asleep after she finally quieted. She could take a nap, but he needed to remain alert for the next six and a half hours.

He turned on the television, rethinking his decision to put Juan in the basement. Not smart since it meant they couldn't use any of the game tables with Juan coming off watch and over twenty-four hours without sleep. AJ'd planned to stay down there so they all could entertain themselves during the day shifts. But seeing Juan standing beside Cassidy in the kitchen hijacked that plan.

They were here to protect Cassidy. He owed it to Hal to make sure Juan treated her with respect—not exactly Juan's strong suit. Women constantly fell for his dark Latin looks and trace of an accent, which he turned up to his advantage. And it worked. Maybe it was his whole bad-boy appeal. Not that he promised them anything.

AJ had started going out with the guys again after Jess ended things between them. Juan offered to play wingman and gave him unsolicited tips. Juan's moves worked about as well for him as a Navy submariner flying an Army Apache helicopter. Fail. He might not have Dev or Juan's looks or self-confidence, but he did all right on his own approach. One more selective than Juan's.

With her looks and college degree, Cassidy was out of AJ's league, but she was out of Juan's, too. He could see her falling for Dev with his looks, manners, and off-the-charts intelligence. Dev had women proposing marriage thirty-four minutes after an introduction, though he seemed to like more of a challenge.

AJ wasn't the only one on the team to wonder if Dev was too perfect to be real at times. This house confirmed the privileged upbringing he tried to deny. The way Dev's eyes targeted on a generously endowed chest and nicely shaped ass screamed heterosexual, high-octane-testosterone male. He drew a whole bevy of options with a flash of his smile, but damn if AJ could figure out Dev's strategy when it came to women. He only knew Dev had no plans to settle down soon. As soon as the M-word came up, he managed to extract himself in a manner that left his girlfriend-of-the-moment disappointed, but not crushed. *Hmm.* Maybe he told them he was gay.

Well, he couldn't help it if Cassidy succumbed to Dev's all-American charm, but it was too late now to switch Dev to the night shift. He shouldn't have to worry about Dev sidling up to rub a hip against Cassidy. More like the other way around.

Damn, why did that unsettle his stomach as much as the idea of Juan's hands on her? He shook off that entire track of thinking. Why the hell was he obsessing about this?

Protect Cassidy for a few days. Convince her to testify against some asshole responsible for a good man, a true hero, being dead. Hal had encouraged Cassidy to go to authorities —the irony pierced him like a saber sliding through his rib cage. If someone had the balls to confront Hal or use death threats to request he persuade Cassidy not to turn in the assassin, Hal still would have told her to do it. That's the kind of integrity Hal demonstrated in everything he did. If Avila's guy had confronted Hal, it would have given him a chance, a damn good one—instead of a cowardly assault by poisoning an unsuspecting man.

Flipping through the channels, AJ skipped past comedies, game shows, news, animated children's shows, ridiculous court TV, and tabloid talk shows with whiny humans griping about problems of their own making. *You make stupid decisions and screw up your life, take the consequences like a man.* God, he was so fucking tired of people not taking responsibility.

Flores.

Avila.

Those idiots who go on tabloid TV to tell the world about their sorry excuse of a "relationship" gone Chernobyl toxic. Trying to convince strangers it was all someone else's fault.

AJ switched channels, refusing to get sucked into the train-wreck drama of love, or lust, turned to hate, contempt, and malice.

"Just walk away," he said to empty air. Sometimes life wasn't fair. Sometimes it plain sucked. Screwing up someone else's life didn't make yours better. Just bitter. Most things in life didn't go as planned. Wallowing didn't change it. Stand up, shake off the dust, and move forward. Another of Hal's great, hard-learned life experiences he'd passed along. Could explain why Hal hadn't soured on the idea of relationships after three failed marriages. Though, Hal's epiphany that dogs were more loyal and a helluva lot cheaper than a wife might account for his contented singleness in the time AJ had known him.

He found his go-to channels on the satellite channel guide. A commercial played on A&E, so he flipped to the History Channel, where a melodic, deep southern drawl gave a blow-by-blow on the current battle between a team of gator hunters and a ferocious monster. He set the remote on the armrest.

The patio door opened, and Dev strolled in from the deck carrying his tablet.

"You want more?" Dev held up the nearly empty coffee pot before filling his mug.

"I'm good."

Dev perched on the arm at the far end of the couch and stared at the television. "We ought to do that sometime." Adrenaline-fueled fire lit up his face.

"Hunt gators?" He could see Dev giving it a go.

"Yeah. I've hunted deer, wild boar, turkeys, ducks. There's lots of coyotes and even black bears around here, but alligators would be awesome."

He looked to see if Dev had drool running down his chin.

"Gotta have a partner. You in?"

AJ laughed. "*If* I go gator hunting, first time, I'm going with someone who knows what the hell they're doing. Not some rookie. See the teeth on those things?"

"Probably a good idea. I bet we could hire a guide."

AJ would put money on Dev planning a trip to the Louisiana bayou next gator season. He watched the screen, debating the appeal of hunting in a bug- and vermin-infested swamp to bag an alligator. Add that to his bucket list. He'd let Dev make the arrangements, though. Dev tended to keep things interesting.

The jangle of metal on metal preceded Champ bounding down the stairs and into the room. Cassidy followed, wearing running shoes and warm-ups, with her hair in a high ponytail.

So much for his deduction of her napping or reading someplace alone. It could be a long day.

"I'm going to take Champ out for a run." She headed for the door.

"Okay." He rose. "Give me a minute to get changed."

"You don't have to come," Cassidy started.

"You do not step out of this house without one of us with you." He jerked his thumb to Dev and then himself. "We're here to protect you." Shoulders back, he leaned forward and maintained eye contact.

"Fine. I understand. However, you hadn't communicated that." Cassidy leaned forward, too, delivering the last part with a slight in-your-face head waggle. "Whenever you're ready."

AJ broke eye contact first. Then he tromped up the stairs.

In his room, he stripped down and changed back into his sweatshirt and PT shorts that were slightly damp from this morning's perimeter run with Dev.

Okay, he hadn't spelled it out, but it should have been obvious. Or maybe she hoped Dev would join her. If so, she'd know for next time to wait until the afternoon shift. Guess he'd see how long this run lasted.

Didn't communicate. Ouch. He'd heard that before from Jess. She'd blamed his lack of communication for making her feel isolated and alone when he was deployed. *Hello, I was in a combat outpost in Kandahar, Afghanistan, with shitty internet, without the bandwidth for Skype, no phones, no post offices.* It's not like he didn't email practically every day.

Hal pointed out it wasn't him. It was Jess's inability to deal with the realities of his job and the separation that led to their breakup. Hal told him he got lucky finding out before he got hooked for alimony. He didn't feel lucky.

Running into Jess on a date with the dad of one of her students two weeks after the breakup hadn't made him feel lucky, either. She'd listened to that guy with the same rapt interest and engaging smile that had made AJ want to spend the rest of his life with her. Those things were gone now. Hadn't survived their first deployment together.

He shoved his feet into his running shoes. Thinking about

Jess worsened his mood. Yeah, he should probably apologize to Cassidy for barking at her for not reading his mind. Two words that, according to the late Hal Boswell, could end an argument, save you a shitload of grief, and get you naked for fantastic make-up sex. *I'm sorry.* One of the hardest phrases known to man. He doubted Hal would have approved of his associating them with Cassidy and the idea of sex, though.

As he rushed down the steps, his heel slipped off the edge. He grabbed hold of the banister in time to keep from bumping down on his ass, but his heart pounded as he managed to hit the last three steps in an upright position. He came to a complete stop.

The great room was empty.

Cassidy was gone.

Dammit. Did she not listen? Did she not care? It was her ass they were here to protect.

He jerked open the front door, ready to—what? Scream her name?

She stood fifty feet away, talking with Dev, who gestured toward the woods.

His body temperature dropped as the flames searing his common sense tampered out. Fresh, crisp mountain air filled his lungs. Inhale. Exhale. Inhale. Exhale. He crossed the gravel drive at a leisurely pace, watching the two.

Cassidy jogged in place and rolled her head. She did a double take, her gaze lingering on his shoulder holster that held his service revolver.

Protection. That's what I'm here for, he said with his eyes.

She released a soft sigh, then closed her mouth without speaking.

"No chasing squirrels, Champ." She ruffled the fur on the dog's neck. Without preamble, she started jogging down the road that led up to the cabin.

Her quick start meant trailing behind her, but when he began to pull alongside, she accelerated. If she thought she could outrun him, she had better think again. She'd wear herself out, especially at this altitude. He backed off a bit. He didn't have to prove anything. If she wanted the dog as her running companion and him trailing, fine. He'd stay behind and enjoy the view of shapely calves, toned thighs, and a bouncing booty.

Over half a mile down, Cassidy veered off the road onto the rutted dirt trail that Dev had led him down that morning. Her pace slowed, traversing the uneven ground. An occasional stump lined the winding path that cut through the forest. They ran past a hunter's blind, which overlooked a small clearing with a stream running through it.

She pulled up short, and Champ ran on a few steps while AJ ducked off the path to keep from plowing over her.

"What the—" he sputtered, awkwardly high-stepping through the knee-high undergrowth back to the dirt path.

"This isn't working." Cassidy pressed her fists against her hips and shook her head in a frustrated manner.

"What?" he asked, clueless.

"Thinking through this witness-protection crap." She huffed an angry sigh. "Running usually helps me think." Her fiery eyes settled on him.

He threw out his arms, palms up.

"It's not you. Well, you tagging my heels isn't exactly helping. God, I want to talk to Hal." Her voice squeaked as her pitch rose. She turned up her face to peer at the leaves.

Helplessness suffocated AJ. He glanced around. Should he give her space to think? He grasped at an idea. "Follow me. I want to show you something."

She met his gaze with all the enthusiasm of a prisoner walking to the gas chamber, but he heard her footsteps behind him as he maintained a brisk clip and projected false confidence, though he couldn't recall how far it was or know if it would even impact her.

He spotted the foot trail to his left and whistled to Champ, who trotted back to join them. He ducked under low-lying limbs. Before he reached the outcropping of rocks, he stepped aside. Holding a branch back, he waved her past him.

He paused next to where she stood, a few feet from the ledge jutting out from the side of the mountain.

Her head moved as she took in the view. At the base of the mountain, a small lake sparkled. Splashes of yellow, orange, and red mixed with the predominant green on the range of the adjoining mountains. Wisps of clouds streaked the baby-blue sky. Better yet, Cassidy's mouth curved into a contented smile, softening her features.

"Wow. How'd you find this spot?"

"Dev showed me this morning when we scouted the area."

"It's gorgeous. Not sure how it helps, though."

"Talk to me. Use me as a sounding board." He could take a stab at channeling Hal. "What would you say to him?"

"I'd tell him I was sorry. If I'd done the right thing, he'd still be alive."

"What makes you think you didn't do the right thing?"

"I shouldn't have involved him. I should have gone to the police right away."

"Look, there's no solid evidence to prove Hal was poisoned because of you."

"No? Do you have any other suspects or theories? Because I'd love to hear them."

"Hal knew you were in danger either way. He wanted you protected. That's why he told you to turn the guy in. If he thought they'd come after him, he would still have told you the same thing. It's not your fault."

Cassidy sank to sit on the flat surface of a rock. She wrapped her arms around her knees, hugging them to her chest. "If they could kill Hal, what's to stop them from going after my mom or my sister or her family?"

"If they wanted to send you a signal not to testify, they would have gone after them first. They would have made a statement. Not made it look like a natural death. They wanted to draw you out."

"Flores is in custody. So, he didn't kill Hal. If I don't testify …"

"He goes free. They win, *and* they come after you because you're still a threat."

"That means I'm screwed if I do and equally screwed if I don't testify." She half groaned, half sighed. "Do you think the police will find who killed Hal?"

AJ stared at the valley rather than meet her hopeful expression. The garbage bag of food from Hal's fridge and kitchen were long gone. There were other possibilities. Toothpaste. Mouthwash. The beers the men drank and cigars they had smoked after the funeral. He presumed bee venom wouldn't affect someone without that allergy. Everything screamed professional hit. Someone who wouldn't leave fingerprints.

"I take it that's your version of no," she said in response to his silence. "What are the chances Flores will name the guy he hired?" She stared into the distance as if not expecting him to answer that, either.

Something clicked in his brain. The realization lit up his horizon like a sunrise. Flores hadn't hired some thug to eliminate Cassidy or go after Hal. This went beyond his skill and pay level. Felix Avila—he had the incentive to keep her from testifying.

Shit. All this time, Cassidy's been a pawn in the Feds' case. The Feds wanted Avila to the point that Flores might never go to prison—if the Feds were offering Flores a deal. And they surely were. But they wouldn't tell Cassidy that because she wouldn't have the motivation to testify.

"Let's head back." AJ extended a hand to pull her up. While she wouldn't kill the messenger, whoever was the bearer of that news better protect his junk. And he sure wasn't telling her while on the edge of a cliff.

ELEVEN

"I'm going to have to do extra PT after this." Devin laid his fork on the empty dinner plate and leaned back.

A flush heated Cassidy's face at the compliment.

"Sorry I ever doubted your skills in the kitchen," Juan chimed in. "Definitely worth getting up for."

"Dude, you slept over ten hours," AJ said.

"Give me a break. I'd been up over twenty-seven hours. You all got your beauty sleep."

"He wanted you up so we could shoot pool," Devin said.

"That would not have been cool while I was sleeping." Juan scowled as if trying to intimidate them from considering it.

AJ cleared his plate and reached for hers. "You cooked. We'll do KP duty. That is, if I'm allowed in the kitchen now." He grinned.

"Cooking gives me something to do." Okay, she probably shouldn't have told him he could stay out of her way when he'd offered to help with dinner. But, she'd said it with a smile.

For AJ's eight-hour shift, he'd been tethered to her to the

point she'd retreated to her bedroom to read and think without the distraction of his scrutiny. Try as she might, she couldn't get her thoughts through the maze in her brain.

The idea of Flores sending someone after her family scared the hell out of her. What were her options? If there was evidence Hal had been killed because of what she knew, then surely the Marshals Service would protect her family. Would they agree to go into the program, though? Give up their lives?

Could she subject them to witness protection until the trial was over? Better that than dead. She kept circling back to the alternative of not testifying. But that would mean she was letting killer off the hook. Hal's killer, too. AJ had said that she was still a threat. *Screwed if she did, equally screwed if she didn't.*

She reached for the bottle of wine none of the guys had touched over dinner and refilled her glass.

"After we clean up, we're going to shoot pool. Cassidy, you want to play?" Devin asked as he moved to help AJ.

"Say that again," she requested.

"What?" Devin's eyes narrowed, and his brows dipped.

"Say my name. You don't know how good it is to hear my real name."

"We might need to cut off her wine." Juan pointed at her glass. "You are a lightweight."

"I haven't had any alcohol in two years."

"Two years?" Juan asked incredulously. "Are you in AA?"

"No. I'm in witness protection. There are a lot of things you don't do in the program. You don't go by your real name. You don't call your family because someone might trace the call if it's from your number. You don't write because they might manage to see the postmark. You don't email because they might trace the ISP. You certainly don't drink because you might slip and say something you shouldn't. You don't get close to people because they might get suspicious when you can't answer questions, or worse, you could put them in danger."

None of the guys spoke a word while she poured out her woes, but their gazes shifted from her to one another in a form of silent conversation she wasn't privy to.

She'd lived in danger ever since Flores rolled into the ER. These guys understood. They lived it, too, with their deployments and missions. Here, with them, she felt safe for the first time in months. Longer. Two years.

Rather than keep trying to figure out what she should do, tonight she was going to shoot pool—probably badly—and pretend she was a normal person, living a normal life, having a normal night with friends.

Once downstairs, Devin handed her a pool cue. "Um, teams?" He stepped toward AJ.

"Fine. But we aren't playing for money." Juan moved to her side. "Dev's kind of competitive. Takes all the fun out of it because he has the angles down, too. Would serve him right if you were a pool shark. Are you?"

"Not hardly."

"Oh well. At least let someone else shoot for the break," Juan said, scooting around Devin to the far end of the table.

"So, did you get to pick your new name and where you wanted to live when they put you in witness protection?" Juan chatted her up while AJ chalked his stick.

She stared at Juan, speechless.

"Ignore him. With two ex-wives and his reputation with women, getting a chance to go into hiding and start over would probably be a good thing." AJ's authoritative tone didn't quell her irritation with Juan's naive view on her life being royally screwed.

"Being in the witness protection program doesn't exactly rank up there with taking a singles cruise. They gave me a name. Put me in a city I had never been to. Where I knew no one. Clary, with the Attorney General's office, said it'd be six to nine months before I'd have to testify. *I* figured nine months to a year."

"Smart," Devin agreed.

"I thought I'd be able to go back to my life. My job. My friends." She shook her head; the harsh movement made her dizzy. "It's been two years. And still no trial date. I had a boyfriend when I went into the program. We hadn't been together long, and I couldn't ask Parks to go into protection custody—or to wait." He hadn't suggested it either. A sign he wasn't the one.

"I had a job I loved. Where I made a difference. But I had to take a job I'm way overqualified for because no one can verify my background. I was a trauma nurse. I dealt with knife and gunshot wounds. Overdoses. Car accidents. I saved lives every single shift. For the last two years, the most traumatic thing I've dealt with is chasing down Ms. Drake to see if she stole Mrs. Nelson's teeth again. I haven't seen my mother, my sister, my niece, or nephew in two years. I get to talk to them every two weeks on a secure call my handler sets up. No video chat because that might give some clues.

"If you think witness protection is cool or fun, or a chance for a fresh start, think again. It's more like low-security prison, only, in my case, the whole I'm-not-guilty bit is true."

Juan stood there, his mouth clamped shut, his eyes wide and wary, as if waiting for his buddies to rescue him. Neither AJ nor Devin threw him a lifeline.

"You can shoot the break," he muttered.

She shot with enough force to create a satisfying *crack* and scatter the balls, sinking one. Thankfully, not the eight ball.

Cassidy moved the Ping-Pong paddle in front of her chest, deflecting the ball. The ball flew off the table, giving Juan another point in the battle-to-the-death game. He may not hesitate to flirt and make sexual innuendos, but he didn't cut her slack for being a female to get kiss-ass points, either. She wasn't doing much better at Ping-Pong than pool.

While she stooped to retrieve the ball, she eyed AJ, who'd retreated out to the lower deck after he'd gotten a call. His back faced her, but the defeated slump of his shoulders and the grip of his left hand on the wooden railing made her curious.

She waited until Devin sank his pool shot to ask: "Do you know who he's talking to?"

He glanced out the sliding glass door at AJ. "Pretty sure it's Colonel Mahinis." He lined up his next shot.

Since Devin didn't seem worried, she tried to focus on the game with Juan. However, the moment AJ came back in, Devin stepped away from the table. "Colonel smooth things over with the marshals about the change of location?"

"Yeah." AJ's serious demeanor was back in spades.

"What's up, then?" Devin leaned on his pool stick.

"The colonel called to pass along what he found out from the local detective. They got the autopsy report. It showed he died from an allergic reaction after *ingesting* bee venom," he said in a tone devoid of life, making eye contact with Champ, who raised his head at Hal's name.

She'd managed to cling to the flotsam of hope that Hal's

death had been natural. A bee *sting.* A heart attack. A blood clot. The reality it was something far more heinous took over her thoughts.

"How would someone get hold of bee venom to do shit like that?" Juan asked.

"Easy enough to steal it from an allergist's office," Devin pondered aloud.

She shook her head numbly, knowing that was true.

"They found a used EpiPen on the counter in the master bathroom, but according to the blood work, Hal didn't have epinephrine in his system. Son of a bitch must have discharged it"

She hadn't even gone in the master bedroom or bath in the few hours she'd been there. Standing suddenly required an effort and rigidity Cassidy's legs no longer possessed. She leaned against the pool table. The image of Hal struggling for breath, panic building at finding his lifesaver had been sabotaged, made her want to retch. Who was so evil they would do that to a person?

"There's a chance his murder wasn't related to her potential testimony," Juan said. "Maybe he messed around with the wrong woman—someone with a jealous husband or ex?"

"That's never been his style. It went against his principles." AJ was adamant.

She looked to AJ, hoping he'd offer a reason. Any reason. A rejected recruit? Wouldn't that go against the honor they aimed for? Though that would explain keeping someone out of Special Forces.

She grasped at possibilities that slipped through her fingers. There might not be solid proof, but the guilt poured over her like a ton of wet cement. If only the floor would open and swallow her up.

"They're sweeping your car for tracking devices and

checking your apartment for anything suspicious. So far, everything's clean, but we don't want to take any chances. One of us is your shadow twenty-four seven until the pickup team arrives. Got it?"

She got it. "I'm sorry." She whispered the words to Hal's spirit. To Champ. To AJ.

"Don't!" AJ snapped.

"But—"

"It's not your fault." His eyes drilled into her and didn't soften.

Wasn't it? AJ, Juan, and Devin might try to spare her feelings by not saying it, but their silence didn't ease her self-condemnation.

She'd never wished a patient dead before, but if Flores hadn't pulled through, this wouldn't be happening. She'd have a life, and Hal would be alive.

TWELVE

Cassidy had surprised AJ by asking him to go on a late-morning jog rather than wait until Dev's shift. The exercise suited him and helped fill the time. Instead of trying to outrun her demons today, she maintained a steady pace on the slow jog toward the lake.

Champ happily romped ahead, as though leading a mission. He broke into a run once the lake came into view, heading in to splash in the shallow water. Memories of trips to Hal's lake cottage constricted AJ's throat.

Cassidy slipped off the backpack that she'd insisted on carrying and scrounged inside. When she tossed a tennis ball into the water, Champ charged in and swam to retrieve the ball.

"Stay. Shake," Cassidy commanded when Champ surged back to shore.

Water showered in a circle as the dog complied before he approached and deposited the ball at her feet.

After several rounds, Cassidy left AJ to toss the ball while she spread a blanket on a flat, mossy expanse of ground.

When he looked back, she'd spread out food and attempted to set up two bottles of water, finally laying them on their sides.

Once Champ slowed down, AJ joined Cassidy, stretching out his legs on the blanket.

"Thought you might enjoy getting out instead of being cooped up in the cabin all day." She handed him a sandwich.

"Thanks." He angled to face the water rather than her—less temptation for him to forget why he was here.

Champ sniffed around, settling in at the foot of the blanket between him and Cassidy, who poured out a baggie filled with dog food. AJ watched a hawk float lazily over the lake and listened to the peaceful sound of the water lapping at the shoreline. This beat him sitting in the cabin for sure. It's like she got him—or maybe they shared similar interests. Either way, it felt good and helped drop the tension between them a few levels.

"How long did you know Hal?" she asked, having waited a full minute longer than he expected before breaking the silence. At least she picked an easy intro.

"Couple of years. We met the first time I went through Special Forces Selection."

"You didn't make it through the first time?"

He stuffed down his pride rather than justify his failure by rattling off the statistics on how few candidates ever make it through, much less the first time. "No. About two-thirds through, I got sidelined because of a stress fracture in my third metatarsal."

"You would have tried to finish with the fracture?"

"Probably." He flexed his right foot. He'd sure tried to keep going. "A while after it healed, I went out to dinner with buddies, including another guy who washed out before me. Coming out of the restaurant were four members of the Selection Cadre."

"Hal?"

He nodded. "They recognized Adam and me and started giving us shit. Asking if we 'pansy asses' planned to waste their time trying again."

"No sympathy for your injury, huh?"

"Hardly," he grunted, noticing the teasing smile that lit up Cassidy's alluring features. He leaned back on his elbows. "Anyway, Adam's all 'No way, Master Sergeant.' But when Hal looked at me, I'm like fu … eff this. I stared him straight in the eye and said: 'Yes, Master Sergeant. I plan to go through, but I sure as heaven and hell don't plan to waste your time.' And that wicked smile Hal gets—got—when he heard something he liked slowly appeared." AJ smiled himself at the memory of Hal's reaction. That was the moment he'd committed to making it happen no matter how many times it took. "Then Hal tells me he helps train prospective candidates at the park on Saturday mornings. At oh four fifty-eight. Not oh five hundred."

Cassidy's melodic laugh wrapped around him, letting his guarded nature stand down.

"Then Adam said maybe he'd come and try again." Cassidy's wary expression told AJ that Hal's response wouldn't shock her. "Hal told him not to bother. That he didn't have what it took to be an Operator. He didn't want someone who'd quit on himself or his team. He pointed at me and said *I* had what it took." Emotion caught in the back of his throat, refusing to let air pass for several agonizing seconds. That vote of confidence, that respect, had changed his life. For the first time he could recall, he hadn't felt second or third best. Someone had truly believed he was capable of greatness.

Now, Cassidy's approving smile ratcheted that high up a level.

"I showed up at oh four forty-five that Saturday."

"Was Hal waiting?"

"Nope. He showed up about oh five seventeen."

Her brows furrowed, and her mouth gaped in disbelief.

"I think he was in some concealed spot watching me the whole time. To see what I'd do. If I'd stay."

"Which you did."

"I had my doubts for a bit, but I'd already decided I'd give him until oh seven hundred before I'd leave. Two other guys showed up just before oh five thirty." The real designated start time.

"So, you passed his first test."

"Guess so. Usually two or three other guys would show up Saturday mornings. Some only came once. The guys who stayed with it got invited to go through Selection again. Special Forces takes a combination of skills. You gotta have drive and heart, but 'heart doesn't carry a ruck. Legs do.'"

Cassidy chuckled when he did his best impression of Hal.

"You have to think outside the box of normal Army training. Be able to solve problems on the fly, or on the run, or under fire. It's survival, but it can't be all about your own survival. The guys who know that going in are the ones who usually make it through. The ones who go into Selection with cocky attitudes rarely make it to the end. Hal became more than a mentor to get me into Special Forces."

Cassidy sighed. "It's a shame he never had kids of his own."

"He never thought his lifestyle was conducive—being away so often. He filled the father gap for a lot of guys, though." Would he miss his own father as much as he'd miss Hal?

"Not just guys." Her soft voice cracked.

"How did he and your mom meet?" AJ hoped a change of topic might keep her from breaking down and crying again.

She thought for a moment, then laughed. A smile broke out, and she wet her lips with a quick roll of her tongue. "He helped her with her car." Her head bobbed as she stared at him.

The similarity made him grin, and a seed of connection sprouted. "Was it a flat tire she tried to change herself, too?"

"Oh, hells to the bells, no! My mother can put gas in, but that's where her car know-how stops. I think she had a dead battery. I remember Hal teasing about her leaving her lights on intentionally, so he'd come to her rescue."

"He might have met two of his wives by coming to their rescue after car trouble." He laughed despite a mouthful of sandwich.

"Knowing my mother, he might have been right about that. She's the type who always depends on others to do things for her."

"So, Hal enrolled her in his necessary-life-skills-for-the-damsel-in-distress class until she didn't need him anymore?" How many times had Hal found a woman to care for and then fixed her to the point that she didn't need him? At least the partings seemed amicable.

"No. But not for lack of trying. My mother, uh, to put it delicately, was an only child who grew up with the American-princess syndrome. I guess it's not totally her fault. Her parents didn't do her any favors by never expecting her to do anything for herself. It's all she knew."

Cassidy pulled a piece of meat from her sandwich and fed it to Champ. "When the men in her life get fed up with the one-sided relationship and her unwillingness to try, they throw in the unwashed towel, and she goes on the hunt to find someone else to take care of her. With her looks and shameless flirting ability, she usually has men offering to do whatever before it's time to unload the dishwasher."

The resigned disapproval in her voice turned on the light of understanding. "So, you swing to the side of the non-dependent spectrum." He couldn't help but grin, especially when she gave a guilty shrug.

"Kind of."

He laughed at the understatement.

"Give me a break." She backhanded him on the arm.

He fought not to laugh louder. It did explain a lot—especially her resistance to ask for help. "Okay, going forward, I'll try not to take it personally."

"People don't mind helping someone out, but it gets old fast. And it gets embarrassing as a kid. Not to mention the lack of stability."

"I get it. That why you went into nursing?" AJ could see her wanting to be the one on the giving end for a change.

"Indirectly. Hal got stung by a bee while pruning mom's rose bushes. He rushed in, yelling for his EpiPen. His face had turned all red. He was making this horrendous gasping noise because he couldn't breathe, and his hand was swelling up. Mom found the EpiPen, and Hal tried telling her what to do, but he could barely speak before he passed out. Mom went into full-on panic mode. Called nine-one-one. I thought he was going to die right in front of me."

She shivered and closed her eyes, then took a long, slow breath, triggering his own fear at finding his larger-than-life mentor lying motionless, face down on the floor.

"I did what he'd said and jammed it in his leg. In seconds, he started breathing—and so did I."

AJ hadn't been so lucky. Nor had Hal this time.

"It was kind of a rush. That feeling of saving a life. It was Hal who suggested going into medicine and pointed out it was a career where I would always be able to find a job. His support made me work harder in school and believe I could get into college. He paid my deposit the day I decided to go to UNC-Greensboro, even after the signs of their relationship limping toward his 'I'm finished' line. I'd seen it before."

Anguish punctuated her words. She peeled a banana, offering a piece to Champ.

"A month after I started college, they split up. It was pretty obvious he let her stay that long because of me."

"Hal Boswell was no sucker. No one made him do anything he didn't want to do."

"No, but he had a soft spot for females in need. He didn't have to, but he paid my second-semester tuition, too. I worked and took out loans, but he sent money to help out the next three years, always saying he owed me for saving his life. All I did was stab him in the leg with a needle. It wasn't anything heroic. He was the hero." Tears moistened her eyes.

Champ raised his head, then crawled forward to rest his head on her leg. She scratched behind his ears with her watery gaze fixed on some distant object and took a series of ragged breaths.

She didn't say it, but AJ would bet a month's pay she still blamed herself for Hal being dead, all because she called him for advice after overhearing Flores. He kept his mouth shut rather than point out there was no way to anticipate that her phone call would make him a target, too. It's not like there were indicators she and Hal were related, and it had been two years since the confession.

"That's why I became a nurse." The words flowed out as if she simply answered his question without the extra, very personal history thrown in. "And what about you? Did you follow family footsteps into the military?"

"God, no. Well, I had a great-great-uncle who served in

the Polish Army in the beginning of World War II," he clarified. "He and about twenty thousand other Polish military and intelligence officers and police were killed by Russian military in the Katyn Forest Massacre."

"What?" she gasped. "Twenty *thousand*?"

"It's not a highlight in history class. Wasn't in the books at all until about eighty-nine when Gorbachev admitted Stalin had the Soviet Army kill somewhere between sixty and a hundred thousand Poles in the name of ethnic cleansing, too. A lot of Poles still have a distrust of military. My *babcia*—grandmother—was a girl then, and to her, all soldiers were killers and rapists."

"Ouch. I guess your family was a little shocked at your career choice."

A little shocked didn't adequately describe their reaction. He cringed at the memory of the words they'd used. The pleading to change his mind.

"My parents wanted me to go to college, like my brother and sister. Except I wasn't the honor student that they'd been. They would say I didn't put forth the effort. In high school, my English teacher got me tested, and I found out I have dyslexia." It would have been nice to know that earlier rather than struggle with reading for a decade. "My parents enrolled me in therapy, which helped. Knowing the reason helped, too, but by then, I hated going to school where teachers compared me to Damien and Karolina. Ironically, when I'd get in trouble over grades or cutting class, my parents would threaten to send me to military school."

"Is that how you ended up in the Army?"

"No. Though to me, that sounded good rather than like punishment. I like being outdoors, and I knew I could excel at something I cared about. I thought I could make my family proud of me. I thought I could make them see serving our country as an honorable profession. I thought wrong."

"*They're* the ones who are wrong."

Cassidy's authoritative tone amplified her words. They parted the shroud of doubt his family's disapproval created. He met her eyes, and what he saw on her face melted the top layer of steel surrounding his heart.

"You can't judge everyone in that occupation on the actions of a few," she continued. "It's a different time and place. Our men and women serve by choice. They have honor and integrity. Sure, there are going to be a few assholes in every profession, but they aren't the norm. Teachers and religious leaders get caught in sex scandals. Accountants and financial advisors embezzle or use insider information. Cops and politicians take bribes. Okay, I'd like to think they're the exception, but I might have to give in on the politicians."

AJ grunted in agreement.

"Doctors get hooked on pills. Hell, there are even nurses who wish certain patients wouldn't survive." She gave a weak, hollow laugh. "You don't want the least common denominator in society making up our military. We need men like Hal. Like you. Men who'll stand up for what's right, and will fight to protect our lives and freedom so that atrocities like what happened in the Holocaust, which still go on in some third-world countries, don't happen here. They should give you the respect you deserve because you sure don't serve for the pay."

AJ stopped himself in time from leaning in to kiss her. *Protect her. Protect her!*

He wanted to kiss her. Hell, he wanted to take her home to meet his family so she could repeat her impassioned speech to them. She wouldn't side with them as Jess had. Or try to change or *improve* him. Why hadn't he seen it with

Jess? Or stood up for himself when she talked about other career options or getting a college degree—like he had to have one for them to be equals?

A one-minute speech and his whole perspective on dating relationships shifted. His job was a part of him, and anyone he was with was going to have to accept that. He and Jess had seen things differently when it came to his job. He let the weight of guilt slip off his shoulders as he sat with his back straighter, his face tilted up to bask in the sunlight and warmth of Cassidy's respect. Damn, he really did want to kiss her.

Minutes passed in comfortable silence as they finished the food, with Champ happily accepting any shared treats.

Though several homes built on the mountainside peeked through the green, they were all alone here. Colorful fall leaves were beginning to pop around the small lake. The tranquil view contributed to him letting his guard down with Cassidy as much as her connection to Hal.

She tucked a wisp of hair behind her ear when the breeze kept blowing it in her face. Her fingers brushed against his leg when she set her hand back down to support herself.

He imagined her hand doing more—for about five seconds before he jerked his leg a few inches away. Hal would kick his ass if he put his rusty moves on Cassidy instead of doing his job. The *"protect her"* mantra played through his head, in addition to the fact she was Hal's stepdaughter, which hung as a flashing neon off-limits sign around her neck.

Plus, in two or three days, she'd disappear back into witness protection, despite her hopes of testifying and getting her life back. He had serious doubts that would happen soon—if ever. Envisioning something between them beyond protection detail could seriously derail this mission. Hell, the temptation to tell her to screw testifying already threatened to override his orders. He rose to his feet, putting space between them.

Except Cassidy held out her hand to him. He helped her to her feet, pulling her close to his body. She didn't release his hand or break eye contact or move away. Her head tilted to the side. Her face angled up, coming closer.

AJ dropped her hand and stepped aside. Bending down to grab hold of the blanket, he drew in a breath and held it long enough to refresh his lungs. Keeping his back to her, he folded the blanket with military precision and put it in the backpack with the empty water bottles and trash.

Cassidy stepped to the water's edge. Her arms folded across her chest as she stared out over the water. "Hal would have loved this place. The water. The mountains. The trees. Fishing." Her soft, sad voice interjected a lighter tone on the last word before she sighed.

"It's not your fault he's dead." Her pain drew the words out of him.

"You keep saying that and maybe, eventually, we'll both start to believe it." She ended with an anguished grunt. "Look, I get it. If it were the other way around, I'd probably be furious with you, too."

"I'm pissed about this whole situation, but not *at* you. You didn't cause any of this."

"Really? Because you can't look at me, much less stand touching me." She turned to face him, hurt haunting her features, then stepped closer.

He took a step back. She kept coming at him to prove her point.

"Trust me, it's not that I don't *want* to touch you." He retreated another step.

"No? Because I'm feeling kinda like a leper here. If you don't blame me, what is it then?"

He swallowed. If he took hold of her to comfort her, it would be all too obvious what he was feeling. He wanted to turn away from her eyes, eyes that demanded answers, and lips that tempted him more each minute he spent with her. "I need to keep you safe—that's it. I can't afford to be distracted."

"Dis—" She stopped. Her features scrunched in the perfect picture of thoroughly perplexed.

Crap. Why did I say that? He didn't risk opening his mouth to give away anything else. Heat seared his trunk and arms as though she'd lit a gas burner. He refused to flinch when her head cocked to the other side. Her lips turned up in a smile that became more alluring the bigger it got.

"Really? So, you don't hate me. You might even kinda like me, huh?" Southern sass worked its way into her voice.

"No. I don't hate you."

"Then maybe you shouldn't work so hard at pretending you do." She leaned forward, invading his bubble.

His hands went toward her on their own accord. Except she veered to his left. Her shoulder nudged him as she slipped by. Based on her smile, he was in trouble. The kind of trouble that made his body tingle in what were usually all the right places.

He slung the backpack over his shoulder and headed after her but kept a pace or two behind. Champ bounded ahead of them on his way to the trail. What were the chances she'd let what just happened drop? In a different circumstance, their mutual attraction would be a good thing. Talk about the wrong time, the wrong place, and the wrong woman. *Rozanski, don't fuck this up.*

Two more days. He'd need to find an excuse not to be alone with her. With any luck, it'd rain tomorrow.

What'd I do to deserve this?

What had Cassidy done to deserve this?

Damn, trying to do the right thing wasn't working well for either of them.

He trudged up the dirt path, evaluating his options, when Cassidy's arms shot out, and her body went off-kilter. He managed to steady her with an arm around her waist.

"You all right?" Adrenaline, mixed with the sexual energy of having her in his arms, surged.

"Yeah. Just rolled my ankle a bit. Stupid root," she grumbled and maintained a hold on his arm, tentatively putting weight on her left foot. "It's okay." Her hand slipped into his. She resumed walking, keeping an eye on the path.

They strolled with their fingers intertwined in a firm, pleasant grip, though she didn't limp. He increased his pace and loosened his grip. She matched his steps but didn't relinquish his hand. He stared at their joined hands.

"What? We're just holding hands. It's *safe*." She wore a teasing smile and squeezed his fingers. "No risk of communicable diseases or pregnancy."

"But—"

"I swear if you say you're supposed to be 'protecting me,' I'm going to start making you pay me five dollars per utterance or turn it into a drinking game. If all I wanted was to get laid, I'd invite Juan for a romp in the woods."

"Jeez, Cassidy!" Maybe his fear over her being more attracted to Dev or Juan was grounded in reality after all.

"He's not my type. And that's not what I want." She came to a stop. "I don't want to be a sex object. I don't want to be *the witness*. I *just* want to be a human. You keep saying you're here to keep me safe. Well, I'm asking you to keep me *sane*. Let me feel like I have a normal life, mixed with a little fantasy, to hold on to once I go back into witness protection. Can you give me that?" Hopelessness shone in Cassidy's eyes, and her lips quivered.

I'd-rather-die-than-ask-for-help Cassidy O'Shea had shown her vulnerability and asked him for something. Something simple. Some humanity. Human touch.

How could he say no? He wasn't a heartless bastard. He knew from his longer deployments how the deprivation of human contact affected him. She'd been in the witness protection program for two years. Two years of isolation and living a lie.

He gripped her hand. A lifeline to hold to while he tried to hold on to his own heart instead of putting it in her hands.

It took several minutes before he dismissed the fear about what Dev or Juan might think or say if they saw them now. Once he relaxed, he enjoyed the colors and peace of his surroundings. And just being with Cassidy.

He could get used to this. Being out here, in his element, hiking with a dog and a beautiful woman. She'd said Juan wasn't her type, but she'd picked him not Dev, with his upper-class manners and most-likely-to-have-girls-fall-at-his-prom-king-feet quality, for *her fantasy*. This is what it felt like to not be runner-up.

Hal told him to shoot for the top rather than settle for good enough. It had motivated him to make it through Selection his second time. But he didn't have to *be* the best at everything; he only had to *give* his best effort. What if he wasn't the best looking or smoothest guy on the team? It didn't matter to Cassidy.

He wanted to earn his family's approval and respect. But he didn't need to *outdo* Damien or Karolina. He didn't need to outdo Juan or Dev. He didn't need to outdo anyone. What he did need to do was keep himself from getting caught up in his own fantasies about Cassidy—no matter how she made him feel.

Champ halted a few feet in front of them. He stared into the woods, not moving. A low growl emitted from the dog's throat, and the fur on his neck bristled before he charged off through the forest.

AJ's right arm drew up, instinctively reaching for his weapon, except Cassidy's hold on his hand stopped him halfway there.

"Champ! Come back here. Leave the squirrels or rabbits alone." The dog stopped, and she gave a light laugh while shaking her head.

AJ positioned his body between her and the path to the unmoving dog. He'd seen Champ chase squirrels plenty of times at the lake with Hal. There'd been plenty of barking, but Champ never growled at a squirrel. A squirrel didn't represent any threat.

Champ remained in place, a good thirty yards away, amidst the forest's undergrowth of ferns and plants. He raised his nose and sniffed the air, cautiously moving a step forward.

"Champ, stay." AJ resisted the urge to draw his weapon. There was no definable danger, and he didn't want to alarm Cassidy. He didn't want to take chances, either. Not when a tremor rippled through his limbs, and a cold tingle made the hair stand up on his arms and scalp.

"I don't think he's after a squirrel. Dev mentioned there being coyotes and bears around here."

"Bears?" Her pitch rose. She gripped his hand tighter, and her body edged close enough to make contact with his. "Okay, now I'm glad you have a gun."

"I don't have a bear hunting license"—he worked to keep

his tone nonchalant—"so let's pick up the pace and get back." *To safety.*

She nodded, her eyes roving over the vegetation and through the trees beyond Champ. "Come here, boy!"

A nudge set her in motion. Champ hesitated a few seconds before AJ's whistle prompted the dog to bound after them. He trusted the canine's innate ability to detect things a human couldn't smell or hear. *I wish you could tell me what's making your fur stand on end, buddy.*

As they maintained a slow uphill run, he snuck several glances back and kept surveillance of anything in his field of vision. The rhythm of his and Cassidy's feet pounding the ground and his own steady breathing blocked out most other sounds. He heard an occasional bird, especially when they startled one with their presence, but nothing out of the ordinary. He prayed Champ would alert him to any perceptions of danger.

Cassidy slowed to a jog, then a brisk walk when the house came into view. Perspiration dotted her hairline and upper lip. Though she breathed hard, a light smile played on her mouth and around her eyes. "Nice run. We safe from big, bad bears now?" She stroked Champ's head. He barked in answer, his fur no longer bristling.

AJ took a last look over the woods. The mix of emotions and the run sapped his strength as he strode up the steep drive.

THIRTEEN

A sound perforated AJ's bubble of sleep, jerking him awake. Not a loud sound, but something muted. Stealthy. Champ? No, he was downstairs with Dev. Did the dog change his mind or …?

No. Not now.

He threw off the blanket and swiped his 9mm off the nightstand. Another faint creak came from outside on the balcony. Through the crack of space in the blinds, he made out a bulky, shrouded figure near the railing.

How the hell did someone get up here? Had Juan heard it? If not, sending out an SOS would kill any element of surprise. He took a deep breath to steady his hand. Gripping the doorknob, he turned it slowly, his gaze fixed on the little he could see of the barely moving figure. When the knob no longer turned, he swung the door open and surged outside, training his weapon on the person who spun to face him.

"Don't move," he said at the same time that Cassidy shrieked and reared back. The dark blanket slipped off her shoulders.

His arm dropped, pointing his weapon at the deck. His

lungs released air in a whoosh, and the frenetic energy flowing through his veins poured out of his body.

"Are you okay?"

"I was—until you pointed a gun at me." She exhaled, her wide eyes blinked, then her body shuddered.

"What are you doing out here?" He moved closer, surveying the dark woods behind the house for any movement.

"I couldn't sleep. Thought I'd come out to get some fresh air. I've never been any place where you could see so many stars." She pulled up the blanket to cover her shoulders and leaned against the railing.

"Let's get you inside." He put a hand on her back.

"If you're cold, you go inside. I want to enjoy my last night of freedom a little longer."

It wasn't that he only wore a pair of lightweight sleep pants that made the hair on his bare arms stand up. The remote places where he'd seen a sky devoid of light pollution like this were typically places you didn't let your guard down to enjoy the beauty and peacefulness. "Please don't fight me on this. I don't want to take any chances."

"Seriously? You're worried someone could find me *here*? Because if I'm not safe here, where the hell am I going to be safe? What's the point of all this? Let them kill me now rather than keep prolonging this bullshit."

"You don't mean that. You don't want to die." He herded her into her room.

"No. But I don't want to live like this, either, because it's not living."

Crap. He had no idea what to say. It's not like he could put Avila on trial and his ass in prison.

"What kind of life am I going to have? Am I going to be working in nursing homes where the most exciting use of my nursing skills is doing wound care on diabetics after an amputation or when a ninety-year-old's heart stops beating? Why do I have to give up on having a husband and family?"

"You don't."

"No? So, when do you recommend I tell a guy I'm in witness protection? After I've been lying to him about who I am for a few months or right up front? Save us both some time and misery. Maybe have him turn me over for the payoff?"

He couldn't deny she had a point. Not unlike what Tony Vincenti and Angela had been through. Hell, the contract on Angela's life kept her from marrying Tony because the Vasquez family might find out she was still alive.

"Hell, you know I'm in witness protection and look how it affects you. You're this superhero warrior, and you may like me, but you're too scared to kiss me. What hope do I have of finding someone willing to step into this mess? This danger?"

Okay, that was a low shot. "It's not that I'm afraid." Her loneliness didn't give him permission to take advantage of her.

"It wouldn't be fair to have kids and subject them to this. At best, I'm looking at an occasional hook-up. Maybe I *should* go down and find Juan."

"Don't do that." He put out a hand in case she tried to leave the room. He had no right to stop her. No right to tell her what she could and could not do with her body. But the thought of Juan, or anyone for that matter, putting their hands on her made his gut clench.

"Why not? What does it matter?" She didn't move to the door, just stared at him in hopeless brokenness.

It did matter. She wasn't saying it to hurt him, but Juan? Sleeping with Juan wouldn't give her what she wanted. What she needed, either. She needed more than sexual satisfaction. She'd told AJ exactly what she needed: hope for some kind of normalcy.

He gripped her upper arm so suddenly that the blanket fell to the floor, and her mouth gaped, making for an awkward first meeting of mouths. She didn't try to pull free or rear back. Not in the least.

Her lips pressed to his, and her body melted against his torso.

He released the hold on her arm to bury his fingers into her silky hair. The faint taste of mint toothpaste lingered as the kiss intensified to a hot, open-mouthed tangle of tongues.

His arm snaked around her waist, holding her close. The 9mm in his hand kept him from grabbing her ass a few inches south of his fingertips to mold her to him. He also feared that any second Cassidy would come to her senses and push him away. Instead, her hips pressed into him.

He silenced all his objections and excuses and worries to hear her delicious murmurs as he ground his aroused body against hers.

An anguished groan rose in his throat when she finally pulled away. *Oh, shit.*

"Condoms?"

"What?" If his sex-fueled brain heard her right, she wasn't stopping after all.

"Condoms? If you don't have any, I'm clean." She kissed him through her words. "And I have an IUD." Her hands locked behind his shoulders.

She took away his last rational thought of stopping. The absolute worst thing he could say to her now was that he wanted to protect her. She'd take his weapon and use it on him. "In my wallet."

He wasn't sure who steered who as they moved toward

the connecting bath. Then, step-by-step, they kissed and bumped their way into his bedroom.

He set his weapon on the dresser and fumbled blindly for his wallet. Once located, he freed his hand from Cassidy's hair to find the condoms, lonely and neglected the past few months. Not any longer. He pulled them out as Cassidy boldly pulled the strings on his pants and untied the knot.

She hooked her fingers into his waistband and tugged him with her as she stepped from the bed and backed against an expanse of bare wall. Her sultry smile and mischievous heat in her eyes conveyed her intentions.

Oh, this was going to be good.

First, it was time for her to get naked, and he wanted to do the honors. He placed the condoms within reach on the dresser and took hold of her T-shirt. He teased it up below her breasts, kissing her while bare abdomen to matching bare stomach touched. Her right leg lifted to wrap around his thigh, and her foot hooked over his calf. His cock throbbed against her, ready for a reward, except more delayed gratification was in order. His thumbs rubbed over her skin, moving under the shirt to glide over the mounds of her breasts. She gasped as his fingers flicked over her tits, then as they circled with increased pressure.

Her mouth left his, and her head lolled back against the wall. Even her barely open lids didn't hide the passion burning inside those fiery eyes, stoking his own fire and need.

He hauled her from the wall to slip the shirt over her shoulders and off. His hands held hers captive over her head as he leaned into her again. Kissing her mouth, her cheek, her neck. She struggled to free her hands. He released them so he could sculpt and caress her perfect breasts. He wanted to taste and tease her hard, raised tits.

Cassidy's hands roamed over his back. Warm fingers dug

into his muscles. Her hips rocked into his, withdrew, and thrust again and again. Only two layers of fabric stood in their way. It was time for those obstacles to go.

He dragged his hands from her breasts and slid them slowly down her sides until they encountered the top of her pink pajama shorts. She unwrapped her leg as he eased the shorts past her hips to her thighs, after which they dropped to the floor, and she kicked them free. Breathing heavily, she reciprocated, and his sleep pants joined the heap on the floor.

An urgent smile spread over her face, then their needy mouths united. Heat from bare flesh on bare flesh spread as they touched in new places, their bodies molding against each other, but not yet joined.

Both his hands slid around to cup her firm, shapely ass, pressing intimately against her.

Crap. The condom.

He stopped before pushing inside her. She moaned as he snatched a condom off the dresser and tore it open, losing precious seconds of bodily contact while he rolled it on.

Now, Cassidy's eyes begged.

His body stroked hers, lubricating him as she pulsed against him. Her arms draped over his shoulders.

Holding her under the curve of her butt, he lifted her. With her back pressed against the wall so she could wrap her legs around his waist, he pressed into her warm depths. He lifted her higher and went deeper, making her gasp. Her arms tightened around his shoulders as he thrust in, eased almost out of her, then thrust again, faster and harder, until he went over the edge, coming in a satisfying rush.

Except she hadn't come—yet.

Supporting her weight against him, he turned their joined bodies and carried her to the bed, carefully setting her down on its edge. The bed was high, but not quite high enough. He grabbed a pillow, disengaging their bodies to prop up her hips.

The lure of her breasts created a lust for a second pair of hands so he could fondle them, too. For now, he spread her legs to drape over his hips. She scooted closer, giving him total access as he delved inside her, his hands lifting and pulling her up to meet him. Her feet braced against the dresser behind him, raising her to the perfect angle based on her increasingly rapid and ragged breaths and how her hands twisted into the sheets.

When she took hold of his hips to anchor him inside her, he slid a hand from underneath her ass and trailed it over her quivering thigh to touch her where their bodies meshed. His fingers worked their way between them to stroke the slick, velvety folds. Her body pulsed and clenched with the contact of his fingers, which delivered the final, necessary touch. A that's-what-I'm-talking-about orgasm rocketed through her, and she constricted around him in pure mutual ecstasy. Neither moved as the pleasure lapped over them like waves breaking consistently against the shore.

Cassidy's frame sagged, and her hips collapsed to the bed. She gave a blissful sigh, then breathed deeply, her limbs trembling under his touch. He didn't want to let go of her. He wanted to envelop her. To taste her. As if she read his mind, she pushed up to her elbow and scooched further back on the bed. She swung her legs over to make room for him to join her.

He held and kissed her, working to impart without words that this was more than a physical act. And that, despite the sucky reality that brought them together for the night, he cared about her. Once she disappeared back into witness protection, maybe she'd have hope to get her through the ordeal.

Their mouths separated as they lay together. Her fingers brushed up and down his arm. "Don't take this the wrong way," she said, her voice somewhat husky, but her preface immobilized him, "but that was freaking amazing."

The temporary tension vanished. "Why would I take *that* the wrong way?"

"I don't know. I guess because guys want to hear that, whether it's true or not, and tend to think as long as they come, they're great, but you went the extra mile. There's something to be said for all the PT and strength training," she purred, resting her palm on his bicep.

Damn, he was going to get a big head. Her initiative and adventurousness played a huge part in the payoff, too. "I wanted to make it memorable."

"You definitely succeeded, then." She giggled, sounding more relaxed after intimacy than he expected. She snuggled to a comfortable position, then jerked her head back to meet his gaze. "Is it okay if I stay here—with you—tonight?" Her tone and eyes pleaded desperately.

"Absolutely." He told her what she needed to hear, and what he wanted, even if it ranked low on the best-ideas-ever list.

Panic faded into a relieved smile, and she rested against him. "What's your favorite sport?"

"Huh? To watch or play?" The change of topics batted away sleep.

"Both."

"Um, I like to hunt, but I guess I'd have to say I like to play baseball. If you mean organized sports, I'll watch about anything. Football. Soccer. Basketball. But I don't get the appeal of watching golf. It's boring."

"Yet you fish," she teased.

"That's different." His eyes drifted closed. "What about

you?" he asked, though perplexed about her sudden interest in sports.

"I played soccer in high school. I used to watch football with Hal. I like playing softball and volleyball. Movies or TV?"

He opened an eye. "Are we playing twenty questions?"

"Maybe."

Some fairy godmother with Hal's voice jabbed him awake and said: *Connection. Communication.* They had one night before reality crashed back down on her, and sleeping obviously wasn't how she wanted to spend that time. Rather than grumble about his body's rightful need to sleep, he propped himself against the backboard and opened his arms in invitation. She cuddled up and repeated her question.

"Movies," he answered, settling in for a blizzard of postcoital getting-to-know-you questions.

CASSIDY WOKE SOMEWHAT disoriented in AJ's bed. Alone. Sunlight illuminated the room. Not surprising since the sun had begun to chase the darkness by the time she stopped coming up with semi-coherent questions, and they'd lain back down. AJ had spooned her body against his before he quickly fell asleep.

She stretched. His side of the bed was warm. The comfort of the bed called her back to sleep, but the drum of water started in the bathroom. The lure of AJ, his arms wrapped around her, his naked body touching hers one more time made her throw off the covers and cross the chilly wooden floor to the bathroom.

AJ draped a towel over the glass, his back to her. Then he

opened the shower and stuck in his hand to test the water temperature.

She moved closer.

God, she wasn't usually this bold, but last night she'd been broken, or nearly so. She'd basically offered herself up for one night of no-strings-attached-you-never-have-to-see-me-again sex. She hoped that having brief control of one aspect of her life could keep her sane. AJ saved her.

Maybe he felt sorry for her. But it sure felt like more than pity sex. He'd read her every desire like she had "touch me there" or "kiss me here" painted on her body in flashing neon colors. But things didn't end after they climaxed. After the first few questions, the answers came easier, not forced conversation, more natural, deeper. Maybe the idea of never seeing each other after today allowed them to open up, be honest, even a little silly, the sleepier they got.

She could carry that fantasy with her, but she had one more opportunity to live out that daydream.

AJ stepped in but caught sight of her before closing the door. His eyes scanned her naked body.

A niggle of doubt kept her frozen in place.

His lips formed a smile, and his eyebrows quirked up as if asking, "Want to join me?" His *it's-morning* erection rose higher in invitation.

She smiled.

He gave a nod, then stepped in, leaving the door open for her.

AFTER THE STEAMY romp in the shower, AJ slipped downstairs to relieve Juan. Cassidy still tingled as she dried her hair. She dressed hurriedly, desperate for more time with AJ.

When she came downstairs, she headed straight for the coffee maker. The strong aroma perked up her other senses before the first sip of caffeine hit her veins.

AJ planted himself inches away, topping off his mug. "He knows," he said out of the corner of his mouth.

"Hmm?" She followed his gaze to Juan, who sat at the table, not bothering to suppress a knowing grin while he watched them.

"I don't care," she said loud enough for Juan to hear. "I'm not embarrassed. We're two consenting adults. Was it the afterglow that gave us away?"

"Tip," Juan said. "If you don't want people to know you're showering together, you shouldn't take such a long, continuous one. You turn the water off for a few minutes to give the impression of separate showers."

Okay, maybe she was a teeny bit embarrassed, but not having to act like nothing happened came as a relief.

"I heard you outside on the deck last night, too," Juan continued.

"At least you didn't point your gun at me." She shot AJ a sideways glance.

"Not directly, but only because he got to you first, and I heard your voice," Juan admitted.

"Sorry. I didn't mean to alarm everyone. How about I whip up omelets to make it up to you?"

"Oh, I think you already made it up to AJ." Juan's grin grew bigger.

AJ choked on a swig of coffee, his neck and face reddening.

"Ham, cheese, onions, and peppers with hot sauce. Please," Juan added.

She fixed Juan's omelet first, delivering it up without direct eye contact. *Yup, that's all you get, dude.*

"Good morning," Devin greeted them on coming in the front door from a run with Champ while she cooked up AJ's omelet. An amused grin played on his face while he ruffled Champ's fur.

Okay, so he knew, too. At least he downplayed it.

"Can I fix you an omelet?"

He dropped into a chair at the table. "That'd be great."

She caught the conspiratorial look between Devin and Juan. When she served AJ his bacon and cheese omelet, she served it up with a kiss to his cheek. Why the hell not?

"Thanks." AJ's eyes met hers.

"What time are the marshals due in?" Juan's question burst her daydream bubble.

"Between fourteen and fifteen hundred." AJ's tone matched the ache in her chest.

"Then I'm going to crash for a few hours before lunch." Juan carried his plate to the kitchen. "Give you some alone time," he whispered once he was close to her.

She shot Juan a mock scowl, which had no impact on him. He disappeared down the stairs, whistling an upbeat tune.

AJ began cleaning up once she finished cooking. She wished he'd have stayed at the table with her while she ate. They could clean up together. Side by side. Making excuses to bump into or touch each other.

Devin went to shower, leaving her alone with Champ. She picked up her e-reader and settled on the couch while AJ wiped down the counters and table. An awkward, how-do-I-act-now silence filled the room. She held her breath when he finished and waited to see if he'd sit in the chair opposite her or join her on the couch.

He sank to the cushion beside her. Right beside her.

She smiled and leaned into him, a pleasant quiver

building in her chest. "Wanna watch a movie?" She set down the e-reader and handed him the remote.

For the next hour and a half, they watched TV. Holding hands, with Champ at their feet, she was almost able to believe she had a normal life.

Once she testified, she could have a life again. Could get back into a trauma department or at least an ER. She could see her family. Date.

She cut her gaze to AJ's profile. He angled to grin at her, setting off those butterflies in her stomach. Or more like dragonflies. No harm in daydreaming instead of thinking how this was the final hours before the big goodbye.

AFTER TV, she'd fixed lunch—the last meal she'd probably get to prepare for someone other than herself for a while—then they'd all cleaned up and packed. AJ carried her suitcase down the stairs with his and set them by the door.

"Ping-Pong or pool?" he asked as if knowing she needed a distraction until the marshals arrived.

"Ping-Pong." More action, less time to think.

Being here, hanging out with these three, had beat the heck out of being sequestered at that crappy motel with uptight marshals. As much as it sucked to move and start over with a new name, a new job, and more waiting, these few days had given her a needed reprieve and more motivation to endure and get justice for the people Flores had killed. If their suspicions Hal was murdered in hopes of finding her or scaring her out of testifying against Flores were on target, she had to do the right thing more than ever. Hal's death wouldn't be in vain.

She ended up paired with Devin in a surprisingly competitive match. They were staging a comeback rally when Champ barked and surged to his feet, startling Cassidy. When he stopped barking, a car door slammed, confirming the arrival of the marshals.

"Game point?" Devin waited to serve.

"We might do sudden death if it was a tie game," Juan protested. "Just concede already."

"Game point." The authoritative edge of AJ's voice shut down Juan's protests.

"I concede. Sorry, Devin." Cassidy laid down her paddle. The expected arrival killed the mood and the game.

AJ nodded. He and Devin traipsed up the stairs behind Champ, but she lingered, fighting the crushing pressure in her chest. Could she do this? Did she have a choice? If she refused to go back to witness protection, it's not like she could stay here forever. It'd been a nice respite, but the guys had lives and work to get back to. She owed it to Hal to see this through. If she left, the marshals wouldn't do anything to protect her family, either. This wasn't some game she could concede. There was too much on the line.

She climbed the stairs, feeling like she was the one entering a prison's gates.

"Nice place," she heard one of the marshals say as AJ let them in the Grant family's mountain home. The marshal looked around the room with a wide-eyed, mouth-gaping expression. "You know you had a budget for accommodations, which is—"

"Why you made reservations at the Bates Motel." Devin let go of Champ's collar.

"It's not the Embassy Suites, but that place is clean. It's well-located, got adjoining rooms, and—" Flint DeLong started.

"And rats or raccoons living there and a tree through the roof." Devin wore a don't-shit-me face.

Flint's face turned the shade of his red hair. "I didn't know that. I was out of town. Enjoying my honeymoon *until* this came up. I left it to the team covering to choose a safe house." His eyes didn't blink, but his Adam's apple bobbed, and his jaw shifted.

The second marshal, a younger male, whose hard-eyed stare reminded her of Hal, diverted his gaze to study the floor, not saying a word.

"Don't worry, all you have to pay is the cleaning fee. I took the money for that out of the *excess* we had for food." AJ handed over the envelope with a smug air.

"You guys aren't squatting here, I hope." A third marshal, who Cassidy had never met, continued to check out the house, his mouth still open. Three marshals felt like overkill —or intimidation. *All right. I screwed up.* She couldn't change it and didn't regret it.

Neither AJ nor Devin answered him, though AJ's smile formed as all three marshals stilled, their eyes darting back and forth from Devin to AJ.

"We have the owner's permission." AJ's smirk didn't seem to set the marshals at ease. It was the same kind of response she imagined Hal would have given them.

Juan hauled his bag up the stairs. "Ready to roll?"

AJ nodded and handed Cassidy's suitcase to Flint. "Here. I'll grab the dog bed and bag of dog food—"

"Wait. Wait! The dog is coming with us?" the new marshal sputtered.

"Yes. Champ is my dog now. My protection. He comes with me," she said adamantly.

"A dog is probably a good idea," Flint conceded. "We'll

have to find pet-friendly housing for your new location, though."

"Do you know where I'm going?"

"We have some details to work out." Flint's eyes darted to AJ, Juan, and Devin, which told her he damn well knew but planned to keep it quiet. He headed out the door with her suitcase, preventing any further attempts to get information from him.

The marshals loaded her things in one SUV while the guys loaded their luggage in the other. She waited, a heavy void expanding from her stomach to her chest and limbs.

Devin dropped to one knee to scratch Champ behind both ears and let the dog lick his face. "You two take care." He rose and gave her a half hug and brushed a kiss to her cheek.

"Thanks for bringing me here. It definitely made things easier."

"No problem." Devin's eyes flicked to AJ as Juan edged him out of the way.

"Thanks for cooking. Sorry I doubted your skills in the kitchen."

"You're welcome. It helped fill the time." She accepted his brief hug.

It was AJ's turn to say goodbye. She wanted to bury herself in his arms. Kiss him in a way that ensured he'd never forget her. Instead, she memorized the strong angles of his face. The depth of caring in his eyes.

He moved within reach, patted Champ on the head, stared into her eyes, then took hold of her hand.

"I'm sorry about Hal, but it was not your fault." He punctuated each word. She melted into his chest. He wrapped an arm around her and stroked her back. "You're strong. You can do this."

I don't want to, she wailed in her head. But she had to—

because it was the best solution for everyone else. She took a deep breath.

AJ freed one hand, then slipped something into hers. "Call me if you ever need anything. Or after this is over."

She folded her fingers over the black business card with the Army logo. A lifeline to hope. She swallowed the emotion choking her. Her lips pressed against his despite the five pairs of watchful eyes.

"Thank you—for everything," she whispered, then put space between their bodies. "I wish things could be different."

He nodded in agreement.

"Hal did good with you." She managed a smile. "Don't let him down. Stay safe, but don't wait for me." Though the words tasted rancid, they had to be said.

The muscles in his cheek twitched, and he swallowed. "Be careful."

"No more going AWOL, but I don't regret it," she added fiercely.

A resigned smile broke across his face. A face she would dream about. He lowered his head, their foreheads and noses touched, while they ignored the others for a few more seconds.

One of the marshals cleared his throat. She and AJ sighed in unison before their lips touched one last time—there were no words left to say. After a final squeeze, AJ let her go. She climbed into the middle row of the SUV with Champ. Flint closed the door before she could reach for it. Then he and the other marshal slid in their seats, silent and stony-faced as the vehicle gained speed over the gravel.

"You know you can't call him." Flint turned in the passenger seat before they hit the end of the drive.

"I know."

Flint held out his hand, presumably for the business card with AJ's name and number. "The Marshals Service has never lost a witness who stayed within the parameters of the program."

She understood. Only the "parameters" were so damn suffocating. She gripped the card tighter. "How many who broke the rules have you lost?"

Flint stared for several seconds. "A significant portion."

The deep freeze of his words made her fear she'd see her breath. She tucked the card into the back pocket of her jeans. "I won't call him while I'm in the program," she reassured him.

"We can't keep relocating you because you take chances like skipping out instead of coming to us to make a plan to protect you."

Jeez. It was one freaking time. "I found out about the funeral the night before. There wasn't time." Especially with him out of town. They wouldn't have let her go. In hindsight, maybe it was risky, but she hadn't thought they'd know about her connection to Hal.

She had to quit kicking herself. "What about my mom and sister?"

"You haven't contacted them, have you?" Flint's voice rose.

The marshal driving shot her a look via the rearview mirror.

"No. Only the biweekly secure call through the service before the funeral."

Flint breathed audibly.

"But what's to stop them from being targeted next?" she asked.

"It wouldn't be a smart move strategically. Too risky.

Without a direct threat, we can't justify the expense of putting them in witness protection."

"Do you know the trial date yet? Because your six- to nine-month estimate is whacked. What the hell are we waiting for?" *And don't give me shit about cost when I wanted to testify and get this over with way back when I first went to authorities.*

"That's the District Attorney's department." Flint evaded again.

"So you have *no* idea? Who do I need to talk to?" She'd had enough of this bullshit. Of having no power.

"I think the problem is getting Avila into custody," the marshal driving contributed, earning him a death stare from Flint.

"What do you mean?"

"The case can't go to trial until they get Avila in custody. Mexican authorities haven't been able to locate him to extradite him. Probably has a third of the Mexican police on his payroll."

"What the hell does that have to do with me testifying against Flores?" As she asked, realization dawned on her like a blinding nuclear explosion.

The marshal shut his mouth, giving Flint an apologetic look.

"They're offering Flores a deal to testify against Avila?" The dots connected to give her a more complete picture. "Where is he?"

"He's in custody."

"Protective custody?" Just like her. "What kind of deal?"

Silence.

Her stomach clenched, sending pain knifing through her. "Are you telling me that Flores isn't and won't be going to jail?" She felt dizzy. And nauseous. And cheated. Oh, so cheated.

She'd spent two years hiding, living in a different kind of prison, and Flores wouldn't even be punished? Somehow, she doubted witness protection seemed like a prison to him, considering the alternative for multiple murders. If she'd been driving, this vehicle would be grinding to a halt, so she could get out and scream until she was voiceless. So she could hit or kick or throw things. She could get into the other vehicle with AJ. Into the shelter of his arms.

"Stop the car! Stop the car," she demanded, weaker the second time.

Flint shook his head. The vehicle didn't slow. Her fingers toyed with the door handle, but she didn't have the courage to jump out at this speed. She wasn't suicidal. Though it felt like all remaining life had been sucked from her veins.

FOURTEEN

"Let's stand a little further back," Lundgren ordered after watching Linc and Dev set up the explosives for the training exercise.

"Three, two, one," Linc counted.

Paakow! The explosion threw AJ off balance. He closed his eyes against the cloud of dust carried through the air.

"Jeez. A little less boom-boom next time, Porter." Tony Vincenti coughed.

"My bad. I didn't know it'd be so strong. But look at that. There's nothing left." Linc Porter closed in to inspect the bent rebars where the cement-block wall stood a minute ago.

"I don't need to look. We're wearing it." Mack Hanlon brushed dust off his pants, his red hair now camouflaged to chalky grey.

"I calculated how much you needed. But you said, 'Let's go with more'" Dev shook his head, but his smile confirmed he was as amped about the power of the new explosive compound as Linc.

AJ shifted his jaw, trying to pop his ears.

"Reset the wall, then we're done for the day." Chief

Lundgren kicked a chunk of concrete with his boot, crumbling it further.

"Rebar?" Tony asked.

"Of course. We'll return the favor to Alpha team." Lundgren cocked his head, wearing a wicked grin.

The team cleared any debris they could pick up, then laid out the base layer of blocks before they jammed rebar through the holes and into the ground to reinforce the wall. Next came the tedious process of layering rows of blocks to form a six-foot-high wall. They had it down to a system now.

"We going to dinner before we head to Jumpy's?" Dev handed a block to Juan.

"No, man. I gotta save some bills in case I need to spring for some lady's drink." Juan passed a block into AJ's waiting hands.

"Kyle, AJ?" Dev asked.

"Beats cooking," Kyle said.

"I got plans." AJ passed the next block to Tony to slide down over the rebar.

"What kind of plans?" Juan asked.

"Plans."

"You aren't even going with us?" Dev kept the blocks flowing.

"Not tonight."

"That sounds like plans with a lady. Who is it? That Rebecca chick you were chatting up last week?" Juan pressed for details.

"I was only chatting her up because you were trying to pick up her friend. She was not my type." He'd tried to keep an open mind, but a couple of drinks in and Rebecca let it slip that she kind of had a boyfriend who was deployed for a few more months. Whether she was lonely or leading him on hoping for free drinks, he'd shut things down pronto.

"Who?" Juan persisted.

"I met her at the bookstore."

"Bookstore? Are you taking dating advice from the Boy Scout?" Juan slapped Dev on the back.

"Maybe I am." AJ shut Juan up with that but didn't share that she'd hit on him, writing her number on his receipt.

The first two weeks after the marshals took Cassidy away, he'd blown off his buddy's invites to hit Jumpy's Place. Going to a bar, even a team hangout, hadn't felt right. Not with the news from Detective Price that they had no leads or evidence in the investigation of Hal's death—*uh, murder*—and then thinking about Cassidy.

They'd only been together a few days and one night. That was all they got; they'd both known it. Her situation sucked and wasn't likely to change anytime soon. He needed to quit wishing Hal introduced them before this shit with Flores went down.

Everything about Hal's death pointed to someone higher up than Flores. Like Avila wrapping up loose ends. Drawing her out with a professional hit that didn't look like murder. It would have been easy enough for the killer to find out the details of the funeral and plan to look for her there, then track her.

AJ had driven out to the cemetery last week. He'd scouted the area and found several high-ground areas where someone could conceal themselves. Not that he'd found any indicators or proof. It'd been too long for the grass to be matted or show footprints. A real pro would ruck out his trash. Leave no evidence behind.

He thought of how Cassidy had nearly disappeared. If he hadn't seen her work ID …

It was like Hal was still watching over Cassidy with her getting a flat that dealt some bad karma to somebody's plan.

Where was she now? Maine? Florida? The marshals could have her anywhere. He sighed so loud that Dev met AJ's eyes as he handed another block to Juan.

"Sorry. I thought getting you out might be a good thing to, uh, you know." Dev gave a quick glance up to Tony.

The rest of the team didn't know about what went down between him and Cassidy. He'd been worried about what Hal would have thought, but the chief might not look favorably upon him sleeping with the woman he was there to protect, either.

"If tonight bombs, I'll show up for a beer." Better to go home on a high note than another implosion.

FIFTEEN

CASSIDY PICKED up the form at the reception desk and opened the door to the pediatric practice's waiting area. "James." No one moved. "Jimmy?"

By this late in the day, Dr. Greene was usually running a little behind due to the amount of time he spent with each patient, but surely a ten- or fifteen-minute wait wouldn't make a parent leave. Maybe they'd gone to the bathroom.

"James Shand," she called.

A man with black-framed glasses tucked his phone away and rose. The boy beside him, absorbed in a handheld gaming device, didn't budge.

"Come on, JJ." The man touched the boy's arm.

JJ.

The similar name slammed her like stumbling into a closed glass door. It'd been four weeks since she left the mountains, but even here, things reminded her of AJ. Except he wasn't part of her new identity—or life.

The boy scowled at his dad before he got to his feet and trudged toward Cassidy, shifting the scowl to her.

"I'm Teresa. I'll be your nurse today." She led them to the scale. "Step on up for me, JJ."

"I'm not getting any shots!" he said fiercely, finishing with a growl.

"We just need to see how tall you are and how much you weigh." She recorded his measurements. No change since his last visit—only two weeks ago. She scanned the notes on his last visit. Ah, back for a second attempt at immunizations required for school. Yup, he was getting shots today, like it or not. "We'll be in exam room number eight." She pointed to her left.

"Teresa." Charlie, one of the nursing assistants, flagged her down before she followed them into the room. "Call me before you give him the shots, and I'll help. Last time, he nearly kicked Gloria in the head. After the first shot, there was no holding him down for the other, without traumatizing him." His eyes said: *good luck, sucker*.

Great, give me the shot-traumatized kid. Well, time for a different, gentler approach.

"I'm not getting any shots!" JJ repeated when she entered the room.

"Sorry." The dad looked like he wanted to crawl under the exam table.

"It's okay. You don't have to," she added in a cheery tone.

"But—" JJ's dad started before catching the discreet I've-got-this hand signal she gave him.

"I am going to take your temperature, though. Okay?"

JJ nodded with a stubborn gleam in his eyes, opening his mouth for the probe.

"Which of the turtles is that on your shirt?"

"Raphael." He gripped the hem of his shirt and pulled it out to look. The hostility downgraded a notch.

"Is he your favorite?"

He nodded. She pulled out the thermometer when it beeped.

"What are the other turtles' names? I can't remember who wore which color mask."

"Leonardo wears the blue mask, Michelangelo the orange one, and Donatello the purple."

"And who was the one with the yellow mask?"

"There isn't a yellow one," JJ said with all the knowledge of a five-year-old cartoon addict.

"There used to be. You probably haven't seen those old episodes from when I was a kid. I think his name was Geraldo."

"Why isn't he on the show now?" JJ leaned forward to ask.

"He didn't like shots any more than you. Sadly, he didn't get his vaccinations, and he got whooping cough. The turtles were on a mission, and because Geraldo started coughing, the bad guys caught them. Which didn't go well. After that, Geraldo had to turn in his superhero mask and leave the turtle's team." She gave a sympathetic pout.

"Is he a bad guy now?"

"No. Last I heard, he's working at a school in Hoboken, New Jersey." She had to improvise fast.

"Teaching fighting?"

"No. Working in the cafeteria, making sure the kids eat all their veggies. It's too bad. We use new, better needles now. He might have gotten shots and stayed on the team."

JJ's mouth scrunched, and his eyes narrowed. "Do the new needles not hurt?"

"Well, they hurt a little bit. But I'm sure he's brave enough that he could get one or two shots to stay a superhero."

"Do *you* have the new needles?"

"We got some in this week."

"What do you think, buddy? Are you willing to give it a try?" JJ's dad latched on to the opening. "We'll get milkshakes afterward. How's that sound?"

"I think you can do it. You're more like Raphael and Michelangelo than a Geraldo," Cassidy encouraged him when his bottom lip rolled under.

"If you promise it won't hurt a lot."

"I'm kind of an expert at this. Be right back." She grabbed the syringe and vial before he lost his superhero nerve.

"Here's what we'll do. Dad is going to hold your hand for you to squeeze if you want to. You're going to close your eyes." She swabbed his arm with an alcohol pad. "And you're going to say 'I'm doing this for you, Raphael, Michelangelo, um, Don—'"

"Donatello and Leonardo!"

"That's it. Ready?"

JJ gripped his dad's hand, squeezed his eyes shut, and began his brief monologue, wincing when she stuck the needle into his shoulder muscle. She slowly injected the vaccine, then pulled out the needle.

"All done," she proclaimed before he got through all the turtles' names. "You were very brave, JJ."

"Like a real superhero." The boy broke into a huge smile and looked up at his dad, who wore a matching smile.

She affixed a Spiderman bandage, since they didn't have any with the Turtles, and gave his dad the vaccine information sheet. They followed her out of the exam room to the surprised look of two of the nurses.

"Do I get a sticker?" JJ asked.

"Sure. Pick any two you want."

"You're a lifesaver," JJ's dad said while his son dug through the selection of stickers.

"No." Vaccines did save lives, but this wasn't on the same level as working a trauma case. "I got lucky with him wearing that shirt. Tried a tactic I'd seen where I worked before. Sorry I had to lie to him, though." Her life was one big lie these days.

"Don't worry about it. You were great. My ex said I had to bring him after the fit he threw last time. Can I take you to dinner to say thanks?"

"Not necessary. Just doing my job."

"I still, um, wouldn't mind taking you to dinner." His voice dropped in volume. His gaze fell from her face to her hands before darting to JJ, now debating over several stickers, then back to her again.

Oh. He was serious. And nice looking with short, dark hair and neat beard. He wore khakis and a light-blue button-down shirt and came off as a pretty decent guy. "Thanks, but I, uh …"

"You're seeing someone. Sorry. I didn't see a ring. Thought it was worth a shot."

"No ring yet." Or ever, if her current luck held. At one time, she would have been interested, but a man with a child was too risky. "JJ, you were so brave today, you can take all four of those stickers."

"For real?" JJ pulled his sticker-filled hands to his chest.

"See what happens when you're brave? We'll ask for Ms. Teresa next time we come. After today, my ex will likely have me bring him in for future visits," he added while JJ affixed a sticker to his shirt.

"You can take all the credit. I won't tell."

Cassidy slipped back into the exam room to prep for the next patient after they left.

"I didn't know you had a boyfriend." Gloria hung in the doorway, fixing her with a curious stare. "You should invite him to come bowling with us next time."

"Not exactly a boyfriend. I was letting the guy down easy." She might fantasize about a future with AJ, but that'd be stretching things by a few miles. Like three hundred miles to Fayetteville.

"That's the second guy you've turned down for a date in the three weeks you've been here—that I know of." Gloria stepped inside and closed the door behind her. "I think I've figured it out."

"Figured what out?"

"Your history."

Panic surfed through Cassidy's veins like it rode a killer wave. "My history?" She laughed, wadding up the paper covering the table and stuffing it in the trash with her back to Gloria. She couldn't possibly know.

"I figure it's either a stalker or an abusive ex."

"How'd you know?" Relief calmed the waves. She went with the marshal's advice to go with someone's assumption because that was easier than selling a lie.

"Either would explain your move here and taking a job you're obviously overqualified for. Turning down dates. Not wanting your picture taken. It adds up. I'm sorry you had to deal with that. Which was it?"

Last week, when she shied away from pictures while bowling with a few coworkers, she feared it might raise a red flag. However, she couldn't come right out and tell them her picture on social media would necessitate relocation again—or could be a death sentence—if Marshal DeLong didn't kill her first. Maybe this would explain her behavior and need for privacy without making them more suspicious. "I had a former patient who became obsessed with me." She stuck close to the truth.

"So, you had to move? Couldn't the police deal with him?"

"I went to the authorities, but there's only so much they can do. I had to do what was best for my safety and my family's. I'd really rather not rehash details. You know?"

"Yeah. I can't imagine. I hope things will be different here." Gloria gave her a sympathetic smile.

Different? She wanted different, too. She wanted this all to come to an end so she could have control of her life again. Except, no matter how she looked at it, she was stuck in protective custody because the DA didn't give a damn about her testimony. She was merely being used to get Flores to testify against Avila. The more she thought it through, the less likely it appeared that would ever happen.

SIXTEEN

AJ TOOK a deep breath before knocking on Lexie's door. She was pretty, employed, and seemed nice enough. She'd even made a supportive comment about the Army leadership book he'd bought. Spending time with her should beat sitting home on a Friday night.

"Wow, you look nice," he complimented her when she stepped out.

"Thank you." Lexie gave a sultry smile and dip of one bare shoulder, then did a little spin, making the dress flare out around her thighs, and her long, light-brown hair swish like a scene in a shampoo commercial.

He had suggested dinner and a movie—a safe first date. Except her three-inch heels, heavy makeup, and flirty dress that showed a generous amount of cleavage looked more suited for an extravagant night out. He better up his game for a nicer dinner.

"You look good yourself." Her gaze roved from his face down to his shoes—then she laughed. "Are those boat shoes?"

"What?"

"Isn't that what they call that kind of shoes?"

"I have no idea."

"I read an article from Cosmo that said you can tell what kind of boyfriend a guy will be by his shoes. It also said most guys who wear them never set foot on a boat," she said playfully, then lifted one foot and gave a turn of her ankle. "I thought I'd go all out for you."

A pair of shoes were supposed to be an indicator of what kind of boyfriend—and wasn't that jumping ahead—he was? What the hell? And what did her unpractical high heels say about her? He didn't ask as he walked her to his car and resisted saying he usually wore combat boots.

"I'm more of a fishing boat than a yacht kind of guy." At least he had been when Hal was alive. The ache pinged around his chest. "Would you like Mexican or Italian for dinner?"

"Italian, but with gluten-free options." She rattled off the names of two restaurants to avoid before naming a place she loved as he opened the door for her.

On the drive there, he bit his tongue as she gave him turn-by-turn directions, even after he'd told her it was near the Cineplex. Cassidy had been independent, but she hadn't been bossy or a control freak. Oops. Probably shouldn't be thinking about her. This date was supposed to help him *not* think about her.

They'd just been seated when his phone vibrated.

"Who's that?" Lexie tried to see his screen when he checked the message.

"Friend from my team." He swiped to prevent her from seeing Juan's text that said if he needed to bail, he could come to Jumpy's. He put his phone on "Do Not Disturb" mode. "They're hitting a bar and invited me."

"Dancing sounds fun, and I could meet your friends."

"It's not that kind of place. Besides, I see them all week." He kept his tone light, but no way in hell was he introducing her to his team on a first date.

He tried to stay positive when she asked him to order his barbecue chicken pizza on the cauliflower crust so she could try a piece, but she crossed the line when she also asked the server to hold the onions and cilantro—on his pizza—then made the server wait while she made sure they held the onions on her salad because one time they hadn't.

One time. *Let it go. And quit messing with my food.*

Champ's welcome-home bark made Cassidy chuckle. She'd never had pets before. Never thought she was a dog person, but already she couldn't picture coming home to an empty house.

Tonight, he sounded especially excited to see her. She unlocked the door, then braced herself to avoid being knocked down.

"What the hell, Champ?" The dog circled her legs as she stood, feet glued to the laminate flooring, and took in the chaos that had transformed her family room into the aftermath of a natural disaster. Champ didn't even have the grace to act guilty. He nudged her toward the door.

She moved past him to pick up the lamp and pushed the end table back into place. Glass from the broken bulb slid out of the cracked shade to the floor. The blinds hung askew, with several of the wooden slats broken. Wasn't that just great? "And here I was thinking how glad I am to have you and you go and do something like this. No treat for you tonight."

At the word 'treat,' Champ ran to the kitchen.

"Hey, what did I say? *No* treats." She followed him when she heard him pawing at wood. "Stop that!"

Instead of trying to get in the pantry, Champ scratched at the back door, where the paint was scraped off. "I let you out at lunch. You can't have to go out that bad." Or maybe he did. She was still learning about dogs, but a bathroom emergency could have caused Champ's abnormal behavior.

"Okay, fine." She grabbed the leash and latched it on his collar before she opened the back door.

Champ dashed outside, jerking her arm as he pulled her with him.

She growled. "Don't tell me you wanted out to hunt down a squirrel. If it was a damn squirrel, I'm going after him with you."

Champ didn't head to his usual bathroom spot but dragged her to the bump-out for the gas fireplace. His nose bumped the exhaust vent's protective wire cover that hung loose and barked more.

"What is up with you, Champ?" She looked inside and saw what looked like a bird's nest blocking the vent opening. "It was birds freaking you out? Seriously?"

Champ stared back at her and whined. He never barked at birds.

Her mind whirled and stomach muscles clenched. The shivers shooting from her spine weren't from the autumn chill in the Virginia air. She would have noticed the cover being off earlier. Birds couldn't build a nest in an afternoon.

She looked closer. The pine needles and twigs formation cracked, not newly made. Maybe birds had gotten in before she moved here.

Was she being paranoid?

She took a step back and took in the grass—muddy and recently trampled.

SEVENTEEN

BY THE TIME they finished eating, he knew more about Lexie than he ever needed. She was still taking college courses after changing her major like four times. He'd lost track. The girl seemed to be a magnet for drama—or maybe it was her own creation since she tended to look for, and find, things to complain about.

When he got the check, Lexie tried to tell him how much to tip the guy since her water glass wasn't kept full enough for her liking. AJ filled in the amount tempted to write "First date. Last date with her." on the receipt to the patient server. He'd probably get it.

"Did you have a preference for any of the movies I texted about?" he asked, as they headed to his car.

"Well," she drawled, "there were one or two that looked okay, but I had another idea."

Oh Lord. AJ swallowed the words and braced.

"Some of my friends were going clubbing. Maybe we can meet up, and you can invite your friends to join us."

He stopped himself before suggesting next time since he wasn't planning on a next time. "I'm gonna pass on that tonight. But if you want to go dancing with your friends, we can skip the movie. It's okay. I had a long week." He gave her an out, hoping she'd pick up that this wasn't going great.

"Oh, no. I wouldn't ditch you, I just thought it'd be more interactive than sitting in a theater."

She had a point, and her pout made him feel like a heel. It'd be harsh to bail on her, but for now he stuck with the movie plan, letting her pick to appease her.

Once the theater went dark, Lexie placed her hand within reach on the armrest, her fingertips dangling just above his leg. Maybe if he weren't hung up on Cassidy, he'd have slipped his hand over hers, but he couldn't do it. He couldn't lead her on or use her when he didn't see it going anywhere after tonight.

THEY FUNNELED out of the theater with the crowd into the brisk fall air. Lexie shivered and came chest-to-chest with him when they got to his car. "Do you want to grab a drink? We could join your friends or mine, or go back to my place."

He opened her door to buy a few seconds to think because he didn't want any of those options. "If you want to check that your friends are still there, we can swing over, and maybe one can give you a lift home if you want to stay awhile." He closed the door before she could reply, but he caught her crestfallen expression.

He checked the time on his phone. There were two more texts from Juan and a missed call from a number he didn't recognize. The voice mail notification blinked. Though the message was probably a robocall about a special credit card offer or extended warranty on his car—he hoped there was a special hell for spammers—he swiped the screen and connected as he walked around the car.

He was about to delete the message until he recognized the panicked voice. *Cassidy's* panicked voice. His stomach lurched, and he leaned against the driver's door, restarting the message and straining to make out her words.

"AJ, they found me. I don't know how, but they did. What looked like a bird's nest was crammed in the gas fireplace vent. Only birds remove the wire. And there were footprints in the mud. AJ, I'm not crazy."

Holy shit.

"I was going to go to the marshal's office, but I swear I haven't done anything—nothing—to give away my location. I know this isn't your problem, and you never expected to hear from me again, but I don't know who else to trust. You said to call you. Oh God, you might not even be in the country. I'll … I'll figure this out."

There were several seconds where the only thing he heard was Cassidy's gasping breath. His mind reeled.

Crap. Lexie.

He ignored her stare as he buckled up. "I need to take you home or to the club. Whichever is closer."

"What was that call about?"

"I can't say."

"You expect me to buy that 'If I tell you, I'd have to kill you' macho bullshit?"

"No." He started navigating out of the lot. "I wouldn't have to *kill* you, but if I told you, it could put you in serious danger." Like Cassidy was.

"*Right.* That was a woman's voice, not Army stuff."

"It is work-related." Maybe not officially. "She's a friend, and she's in danger. That's all I can say."

Since she hadn't said where the club was or if she'd have

a ride, home it was. He pressed the accelerator, running through a traffic light somewhere between amber yellow and "my bad" red. Lexie grunted her disapproval, though he didn't look her way. His need to talk to Cassidy went beyond any debt to Hal, and he couldn't call her with his date in the car.

AJ remembered to make the turns to take Lexie home since, this time, she didn't give directions or say anything else to him. The silence suited him as he replayed Cassidy's message in his head.

"Well, this was fun." Sarcasm oozed from her voice and into her expression. "Let's *not* do it again sometime."

"Sorry," he said as she got out. He half meant it.

She slammed the door so hard the car shook. He waited until she got inside her apartment before he pulled away, then he drove out of sight before parking his car and calling Cassidy.

He put the pieces together as he listened to her. Sneaky son of a bitch. Just like the damned insurgents who placed IEDs then ran and hid. Poison Hal with bee venom. Carbon monoxide to kill Cassidy.

He, or she—AJ couldn't rule that out—would be long gone before Cassidy turned on the fireplace.

His blood boiled, and his hands itched to wrap around the throat of the animal who killed Hal. Who'd failed to kill Cassidy—thank God. After talking with Cassidy, he'd need to call in the calvary. The kind of calvary he trusted to pay back some karma. Bad karma.

EIGHTEEN

"There it is." Just like AJ said. "Almost there, bud." Cassidy rubbed Champ's head and checked her rearview mirror for the one hundred and seventy-second time before she got in the exit lane for the rest stop. "We aren't going to be alone in this." Relief rushed through her and made her rigid arms relax and quiver.

She parked several spaces away from others after making sure no cars followed her. Her fingers drummed on the steering wheel within seconds. "You want out?" That would give her something to do for a minute.

While Champ sniffed around, and around some more, then marked his territory, she tried to work out the knots from her shoulders and neck.

Headlights washed over them as a car backed out, then rolled past. At this time of night, there were only a few vehicles at the rest area. Enough people that she didn't feel overly nervous, but not safe, either. The rumble of the diesel engines from the semis in the designated truck lot carried across the grassy expanse.

More headlights shone as two cars pulled into the rest

area. They passed the vacant spots in the front of the building and cruised her way. The Mustang's emblem made her knees buckle—even if this wasn't the way she envisioned seeing AJ again.

AJ parked on one side and the charcoal-gray Charger parked on the other.

Champ barked while AJ made his way to them. AJ ignored him, and in a few long strides, he was face-to-face with her. Her control crumbled. He lifted his arms, making space for her as she buried herself against his chest. His arms wrapped around her, and she held on to him as if her life and sanity depended on it—they did.

"Thanks for coming," she choked out.

"Of course." He kissed her forehead.

She tilted her face up, melting into him as his lips met hers.

"Just like old times," Juan greeted her.

"Hey, Cassidy." Devin petted Champ as the dog jumped up on him.

She shifted to face them, glad for the continued connection as AJ held her to his side. He didn't question her SOS, and not only did he come, but he brought the cavalry, or infantry—or, better yet, Delta Force. Whoever hoped to kill her better bring their A game, because the odds were in her favor now.

"First thing, I need you to take a deep breath. Okay. You're sure the covering on the fireplace hasn't been loose for a while?" AJ's tone batted away the instinct to defend her assumption.

She'd been over it at least fourteen times since she grabbed her pre-packed go-bag and fled with Champ. Was she being overly fearful—seeing threats that weren't there?

The deep breaths gave her the focus to relate what she'd

discovered. The three men listened and asked questions, especially about whether she'd used the gas fireplace. Their grim expressions and head nods solidified her worst-case fears.

"He was probably watching a few days to check out your patterns and routines," Devin began his expert analysis. "He knew you used the fireplace in the evenings. Carbon monoxide would build up quickly. Look natural. Waited until you were at work to come and block the vent because he knew, either way, Champ would sound an alarm. Right, buddy? You're a hero, boy. Yes, you are." Champ licked Devin's hand.

"You saved my life, Champ." God, what if she'd stuck with her squirrel assumption? She and Champ would be dead —if not tonight, the next time she used the fireplace for any length of time. A shudder shook her body.

"Why take the chance, though? He could have shot her at the funeral. Broken into her place and killed her to be sure the job was done." Juan shook his head the whole time he talked.

"Would you shoot someone at a funeral attended by over a dozen Special Forces Operators?" AJ asked.

"Fuck, no," Juan said without pause.

"Didn't think so. He knew who Hal was."

"From what you said about your patient, he sounds like the thug type of enforcer," Devin said. "I can't say for sure, but my guess is this bastard is a pro."

"As in professional assassin?" Cassidy asked. "I thought that was only in the movies."

"Afraid it's real. People will do crazy shit for money," Juan stated.

"Or revenge," AJ added.

"This guy thinks he's smarter than everyone and can get away with murder. Which he almost did with Hal. Maybe poison is his preferred method. Less evidence. Can't trace it to a weapon." Devin made good points.

"And he's long gone before authorities start looking into what could be a natural or accidental death," AJ added.

"You did call the marshals, right?" Juan asked.

"No." She stared at the ground. "I started to call them to check it out, but I knew they would figure I screwed up and gave away my location, and I haven't. I have followed *every* protocol to the letter. No phone calls. No letters. No emails. No pictures on social media. No slip up about who I am or where I'm from. I haven't done anything that could expose me or blow my identity. That's why I'm afraid there's a leak in the Marshals Service."

"I know TV and movies make it look like corrupt marshals are always selling out the people they're supposed to protect, but it really doesn't happen," Devin stated with authority.

"I hate when shows portray ex-SF guys as going bad or psycho," she countered.

"Sadly, that's probably more accurate," AJ interrupted her.

"He's right. We had a former member who went darkside. I wouldn't worry about anyone on our team now, though," Juan said. "Don't want to totally burst your romanticized image of us." He winked.

"Let's check her car for tracking devices." AJ got them back on track. "Do you keep your car locked?" He put his hand on the driver's-side handle.

"Always." A habit Hal had instilled in her. She unlocked the doors with the key fob.

"Is this the same car you had when you came to the funeral?" Devin asked.

She nodded. "Because I got the flat and didn't have the

car at the cemetery or Hal's house, Marshal DeLong thought it safe for me keep it."

AJ opened the door and popped the hood as Devin searched the interior. Juan squatted next to a tire, using his cell phone's flashlight.

"Bingo! Got a napkin or tissue?" Juan asked.

Cassidy grabbed one from the console.

Juan popped to his feet. "That was easy."

"Too easy." AJ carefully took the matchbox-sized device Juan held and examined it. "Has anybody had access to your car?"

"Just the dealership when they fixed the strut, and the marshals when they brought my car from the nursing home."

"Keep looking." He went to his car, returning with a flashlight.

As if finding a tracking device weren't enough to make Cassidy light-headed, AJ's tone and demeanor made her want to curl into the fetal position. She was sick to her stomach while she waited and watched them inspect her car.

Devin requested her keys and pried out her stereo. Juan inched his way down the underside of her car.

"Nothing wired in here." Devin re-inserted the stereo. At least it looked like he knew what he was doing.

"Cassidy, did you buy the car new?"

"Yes." She came around to the front, where AJ had pulled out the battery.

"Do you remember if it had an anti-theft device?"

She shook her head. "I don't remember that being a standard option."

AJ set a metal box the size of a deck of cards on the car's frame and continued to poke around.

"Son of a bitch," Juan grunted from underneath the car, nearly disappearing from view.

"Inside's clean," Devin proclaimed when he got out of the car. He picked up the device AJ had removed and studied it.

A minute later, AJ reconnected the battery and closed the hood. Juan wiggled out, holding a tracking unit identical to the first he'd found. Grease and dirt streaked his shirt and covered his hands.

"What's this mean?" she asked.

Juan gave a gruff laugh. "Somebody, or *somebodies*, want to know where you're at."

That much she knew. "Who? You think all three were …" Holy freaking cow. Three tracking devices on her car. She took a deep breath. "That all three were put there by the same person or …?"

"These two are identical. Easy to get. Using two is smart," Devin said.

"First was well hidden. I mean, you had to be looking for it, which I was, but the one underneath the car, you *really* had to be looking." Juan didn't brag when he said it.

"Same with that one." AJ pointed to the larger device.

"These have about a two-week battery life." AJ and Juan nodded, agreeing with Devin's assessment. "Probably put them on her car this week. Backup, in case …" Devin stopped. "Anyway, you don't have to subscribe to an account to trace them, and they can send updates via text message or email."

"So, he could know where I'm at right now." Could this get any worse? She could be putting them all in danger. "Do we take them to the police?"

AJ sighed heavily. "We will, but since they didn't find any prints at Hal's, I'm betting they won't find any prints on these, either.

"What do we do?" Where could she go if, instead of finding a haven, she'd laid out a welcome mat to an assassin?

"We're going to let them work for us." AJ turned to observe the truck parking area. He held out the tracking units to his teammates. "Find these a new home. Preferably with someone heading far south if you can, but be careful not to give out any information."

AJ opened the trunk of her car after Juan and Devin headed toward the welcome center. "This all you brought?" He removed the bag she'd hastily thrown in.

"Yeah. I didn't want to look like I was skipping town in case I was being watched. Are we leaving my car here?"

"No. There could be another tracker we didn't find in the dark. We'll take it someplace safe where we can check it out, and no one can get to it. Hopefully, it'll look you made a pit stop here, then kept on going." He put her bag in his trunk.

"Do you think I should contact the marshals?" Maybe she'd been wrong about a leak. Had she blown it by running away?

"Not yet."

"Then what's our next step?"

"I'm not sure," he admitted. "But we'll work out a plan." He held her near, but not long enough before he let go to type a text message.

Juan and Devin came back, beaming like two teenage boys who'd gotten away with some minor crime.

"Done. They're on a truck headed to south Florida."

"Perfect." AJ tossed her car keys to Juan. "Meet up at the storage building, east side of the training compound."

Half an hour later, after explaining her presence to the guards at the secure part of Fort Bragg, AJ parked in a remote lot adjacent to a small corrugated-metal warehouse. He led her and Champ in, then opened a bay door for Juan to drive her vehicle inside.

Despite being late Friday night, Ray and the redheaded

soldier she remembered from the Lundgren's get-together were waiting inside, along with a younger man she hadn't met.

Ray gave her a comforting embrace before introducing her to Mack and Kyle Liu. "Anybody heard from Shuler, Vincenti, or Porter?" He motioned for her to take a seat at the scarred wooden table

"Shuler's out of town. Vincenti's on his way." Mack checked his phone. "Porter hasn't responded yet."

"We'll fill them in. Cassidy, bring us up to speed."

Surrounded by all these capable warriors, she soaked up their strength, their confidence. She sighed, then recounted Champ's uncharacteristic behavior and what she'd discovered in the fireplace exhaust vent.

Tony Vincenti slipped in shortly after AJ began filling in the details about the tracking devices. She remembered him, his cannoli, and the heat between him and the stunning brunette he'd been with.

Juan stared across the table at Tony. "You've got bed head. Well, sex hair."

"I'm here." Tony shrugged and ran a hand through his hair.

Devin described his conversation with the trucker while Juan planted the trackers.

"Vincenti, you might have competition for those undercover roles." Mack gave a laugh.

Tony crossed his impressive arms over his equally muscled chest. "Fine by me."

"Tracing the serial numbers is a long shot, but worth a try." Ray passed around AJ's phone with the pictures of the GPS devices. "I'd bet money on it being the same person."

"The anti-theft unit—" Devin displayed a picture of the larger device AJ had found "—uses the battery as a power source. Better long-term option. More the caliber of what we'd use *if* we you have access to get under the hood for a few minutes. The Marshals Service had her car after we picked her up in New York; they might have installed it after she went AWOL."

"Or it could be the same guy who put the other two on. Extra insurance," Mack reasoned.

"It leaves the problem of how someone found her in the first place." AJ took things back a step.

"Are you suggesting the marshals leaked her location?" Tony asked.

No one said anything. Some of the men cast discreet looks her way. A few openly stared, as if waiting for her to confess to screwing up. Devin rubbed Champ's ears, then his belly when the dog lay on his back.

"I swear I haven't contacted anyone or done anything to give my new identity or location away," she reiterated for the newcomers. "I didn't even tell my mother I'd moved or changed jobs."

"We need evidence before accusing the marshals." Ray's tone insinuated the possibility had some merit.

"Other than the tracking device?" AJ went to bat for her.

The chief huffed. "We'd need to know who to go to at the—"

"Holy eureka!" Devin's exclamation garnered snickers from Tony and Juan. His fingers continued to run through Champ's coat. "Champ's a retired military dog. They put tracking chips in service dogs. Not the kind the vet can scan, but ones where someone can pinpoint the animal's location with an access code." Devin talked faster. "We know somebody had to be in Hal's home and spend enough time to find out about his allergy. What if … what if they knew a way to locate Champ?"

"They wouldn't know Champ would end up with Cassidy after Hal died, though." Mack played devil's advocate.

"It wouldn't be a sure thing, but they might consider that possibility. We should consider it," Kyle agreed.

A chill seeped through her skin and into her bones. She tapped AJ's arm. "When you brought Champ to me at Hal's, do you remember a white car, a mid-sized four-door, driving past?"

"No."

"It was driving really slow. I remember because the driver stared at the house. Us. It felt off, but I dismissed it as a curious neighbor wondering who was there."

"Whoever killed Hal would sure as hell stake out his house and the cemetery to see if she showed," Ray agreed.

AJ's head nodded slowly. "Except the flat tire and broken strut made the chance they could get to her car pretty damn slim. Plus, the marshals would have swept the car before bringing it back to her."

Who would have thought a flat tire could end up being a lifesaving blessing? Maybe Hal had already been watching over her.

Ray pointed to AJ, Devin, Juan, and her. "You four go to Hal's house and see if you can find anything that would allow someone to locate the dog. We'll do another sweep on the car."

"Is the house still considered a crime scene?" Juan asked.

"Does it matter? This may be the break to get a lead on who killed Hal. Just preserve any evidence," Ray advised.

Outside, a car door closed. Before the four of them got to the entrance, the warehouse door opened.

"Nice of you to show up, Porter." Juan breezed past the new arrival.

"I wasn't checking my phone for nine-one-one messages.

AJ's not the only one who had a date tonight." Porter studied her with open curiosity. "You telling me I came out here and now you're leaving?"

Date? Cassidy nearly laughed. Porter had an odd sense of humor calling *this* a date.

"Field trip. They'll be back. We need you." Tony set down several cinder blocks near the back tires of her car. Mack followed him, carrying more blocks.

Devin averted his gaze and hurried out of the building after Juan. She glanced at AJ. He evaded her eyes, too, but the red tingeing his cheeks and ears corrected her misunderstanding. *Duh. Friday night.* Porter hadn't meant *her* when he said AJ had a date.

A stab of jealousy, and guilt, pierced her rib cage. He hadn't returned her call for over two hours. Still, he hadn't hesitated to tell her to come here, though she'd already headed this way instinctively.

"I'll drive," AJ stated when Devin headed to his own car.

Great. Now he didn't want to be alone with her. Devin opened the passenger door but grumbled under his breath before squeezing into the back seat.

Had AJ kissed her, or had she initiated it?

It didn't matter. She'd pretty much begged, offering him one night of no-strings-attached-because-you-never-have-to-see-me-again sex. Then she called tonight, and he dropped everything to help her. Probably because of his commitment to Hal. AJ wasn't some player. He deserved a life. A wife. Things she couldn't offer him.

Despite the ache in her heart, she didn't—couldn't—expect AJ to wait around. It wasn't fair. She needed to reassure him of that. Only Juan and Devin were in the back seat, discussing the possibility that an assassin might have found them at the mountain house.

Oh, to hell with it. They already knew AJ slept with her. It's not like this would get more awkward.

"I'm sorry I ruined your date. I understand you weren't supposed to have to see me again—but I appreciate your help."

"Not supposed to?" AJ braked to a stop in the middle of the deserted road. He turned to face her. "More like I didn't think I'd ever *get* to see you again. You didn't ruin my date. There wasn't going to be a second, anyway. I kept thinking of you. I'm where I want to be. With you. And we are going to find the son of a bitch who tried to hurt you and shut him down. Then we're going after the guy who hired him. Whatever it takes. Do you believe me?"

She nodded. The suffocating fear of the past few hours let up, and she could breathe because of AJ's promise.

His hand wrapped around the back of her neck, pulling her head toward him. She didn't resist when he kissed her. And she kissed him. Sweet, yet hot kisses full of promises.

"Uh, don't forget we're back here, and that we're supposed to be on a mission," Juan interrupted from the back seat.

AJ kept kissing her, and she didn't want to stop kissing him. He'd been thinking of her, just like she couldn't forget him.

His hand dropped to her arm, gave her a gentle squeeze. "This isn't over."

NINETEEN

"Good, no crime-scene tape," Juan said in relief as AJ parked in Hal's drive.

"You still have a key?" AJ asked Cassidy while Juan and Dev climbed out of the backseat.

She nodded and dug it out from her purse.

AJ unlocked the door, but Cassidy didn't move to go in. Instead, she stood looking down the street.

"You okay?" he asked her.

"Trying to remember the car and driver."

He vaguely remembered her being distracted when he came to pick her up and take her to her car, except he hadn't paid attention to it at the time. "You said a white sedan? What do you remember about the driver?"

"White male." She closed her eyes, her features scrunching in concentration. "He wore a hat."

"Ball cap? Knit cap?"

"Too square to be a ball cap. I think you call it a patrol cap."

"Camouflage?" That wouldn't stand out around here.

"The digital pattern. Clean-shaven."

Again, nothing unique near a military base.

Her hand touched the back of her head. "Darkish hair. Longer than standard Army cut."

"How old?"

"I don't know. Maybe late thirties?" She sighed and opened her eyes. "He was too far away to see his face."

"You did great remembering that much considering it was a month ago. We'll check the street before we leave to see if you recognize the car. Might rule something out." He opened the front door.

"What are we looking for?" Juan asked once they were inside.

"Files or anything that would relate to Champ and info on his tracking chip. Where should we start?"

Instead of answering, Cassidy studied the room with narrowed eyes and tightly closed mouth.

"What is it?" AJ asked her.

"Something's off."

"The police have been here. They likely moved things around." He tried to calm her nerves. Even he didn't want to think about Hal's killer being here twice—or more. That realization probably affected her more than it did him, considering she was already spooked about someone trying to kill her. He gave her a few more seconds.

"Hal kept folders related to the house in the kitchen desk. And there's a file cabinet in one of the bedrooms."

AJ headed to the kitchen, guiding Cassidy along with him while Juan and Dev went to the bedrooms.

Cassidy opened the bottom drawer of the built-in kitchen desk. A row of hanging file folders was labeled in Hal's bold scrawl. She combed through them, reading off the headings.

"What was that last one?" He stopped her.

"MWD something." She tried deciphering the writing. "Adapt lion?"

"That's it. MWD. Military working dog," he explained.

She handed the file to him. There were a few sheets inside, but the third page was the one he needed.

"Got it!" he yelled to Juan and Dev. He read over the information, then handed the page to Dev. He turned on Hal's desktop computer and flipped through the pages again while waiting for the computer to boot up.

Dev tapped him on the shoulder and edged in to take the seat in front of the computer.

"Password? Bad karma?" Dev said, typing.

"We didn't have that name when he was on the team," AJ reminded him.

"Bravo company. Nope. Course he was probably in every one of them at some point. Cassidy. Nope. S-F-O—"

"Try fishing." Cassidy and AJ said in unison.

Dev grinned up at them as the screen changed to a picture of a tree-lined lake. He pulled up the history. "Last log-in was the sixth."

AJ checked the calendar tacked over the desk. "Friday before he went to the lake."

Dev opened another screen and scrolled through. "Someone tried to log in on the fifteenth. Didn't guess the password and got locked out."

"That could have been the police." AJ ignored the prickling at the back of his neck.

Dev opened Hal's bookmarked sites before he typed in the web address listed on the MWD-adoption sheet. "Hal didn't write down a password. Maybe he had it on autosave. Nope."

A round of unsuccessful attempts to guess Hal's username and password followed before they were locked out.

"Crud. Let's take this back to the compound then," Dev suggested.

Cassidy's head bobbed when Dev spoke. Seated at the kitchen table, she got to her feet, not able to squelch a yawn.

"Need some coffee?" AJ asked.

"I will if we're going to pull an all-nighter."

"We'll cruise the block. That won't take long. Then we'll head to the compound."

AJ drove down Hal's street in the direction she'd watched the car go that evening. After checking out all the surrounding streets, with no luck, they called it quits. The chances of Cassidy recognizing the car were slim anyway.

AJ let her doze on the drive back. He figured that beat her rethinking everything that happened today. He wished he could do the same. If it was Champ's chip that led an assassin to her, planting the tracking devices on the semi-truck might let him know they were on to him. That could be a big mistake. Or could he make this work for them?

When they walked into the storage building at the compound, Cassidy pulled up short and eyed her car up on cinder blocks. The tires and a few parts were on the ground around the vehicle.

"Didn't find anything else," Tony informed them while mounting a rear tire. "Rotated your tires for you, though."

"Thanks. You change the oil, too?" She attempted a smile as Champ padded over to her.

"Nah, didn't have oil on hand. You due for a change? Cuz if you take it into a dealership, they usually put your VIN number in their records. Now that he found your car, he might have the VIN to track it."

"Seriously? I give up. I just give up." Her shoulders sagged, and her head dropped. "I need to go to some remote island and get a bike. But I'm not trading you for a goldfish, boy." She ran a hand through Champ's fur.

"Tell me you were successful." Lundgren's eyes locked on the file in AJ's hand.

"Got the info but got locked out of the system when we didn't get the password." Why hadn't Hal picked something as easily decodable as his computer password?

"You call the company?" Lundgren took the folder.

"It's after midnight," Dev started.

"You don't think Kandahar calls between nine and five, do you?" Lundgren said.

"Duh. We didn't even try." Dev slapped his own head while AJ slapped his mentally.

Lundgren went to the table and spread out the file contents, tapping the number he found onto his phone. "Airman Sieber, this is *Chief* Lundgren, Fort Bragg." He listened, putting it on speaker for the team. "Are you able to ascertain if someone logged in to check on the location of one of your adopted animals?"

"Yes, sir. The system keeps a log of that."

"Here's the ID number." The chief read it off.

"Master Sergeant Boswell recently called because of a forgotten password, but the account hadn't been activated. He pinged the location on the twenty-second of September and again on the sixteenth of this month."

Lundgren jotted down the dates and slid the paper to Cassidy. "Where?" he mouthed.

"He must have forgotten the password again because he tried to log in a little while ago, and the account is temporarily locked," the airman continued.

"Master Sergeant Boswell died in September. Under questionable circumstances. The person who called may have had something to do with his death."

"Do you need me to permanently block the account?" The airman's pitch rose.

"No. I have reason to believe he'll try to access it again soon, and we don't want him knowing we're suspicious. Can you notify me if it's pinged again?"

"It can be set to send you a text message automatically, but I'll need to pass you along to my captain for authorization."

"Whatever is fastest. This is a matter of life—and potentially *more* death."

The team remained silent while the chief was transferred and repeated the request. "I'll need the phone number or IP address for the computer used, too," he told the captain before wrapping up.

"What next?" Mack asked. "Call in the detective or the marshals?"

"We've got more of a vested interest in finding who killed Hal and wants to find Cassidy." The chief chewed on the inside of his lower lip. He stared past the men, then dropped his gaze to Cassidy.

Yes. AJ did a mental fist pump. They weren't passing this off to *the proper authorities.* The idea of the Bad Karma team working to find who killed Hal and protect Cassidy infused AJ with the same confidence he experienced when they embarked on any dangerous mission.

"We'll get sleep and meet back here tomorrow to brainstorm," Lundgren declared. "Champ, you're going to have to spend the night here. What to do with you?" He drummed his fingertips on the tabletop while regarding Cassidy. "Let's assume this guy is as good as we are."

Somebody snorted.

"Hotels have security cameras and clerks who can be bribed into giving away her location. They're out," the chief continued. "Let's also assume he had eyes on her while here for the funeral. Anyone with her, any place she was, they're out, too."

AJ squelched the protest about to roll off his tongue. If an assassin saw her get in his car at the cemetery or was the man in that white car when he picked up Cassidy at Hal's, he could have identified AJ. It was one night, and the chances were slim, but Cassidy's safety took priority.

"She was at my house after the funeral." Lundgren sighed.

Mack threw up a hand and opened his mouth to speak. "I parked in your drive," AJ interjected.

"The twenty-second, you were at the safe-house location, he might have seen Grant and Dominguez if he went straight there. I doubt he'd be able to ID them, but let's not go there. That means we're down to Porter, Liu, or Vincenti." Lundgren eyed the three men.

"I've got a guest room," Tony offered.

"What about Ang?"

"She won't mind. She knows security and is good with a gun," Tony answered Lundgren with a wicked grin.

"All right. Everyone be back here at ten hundred hours."

"Champ, let's take care of business," Cassidy called. "We need to get his food and bed."

"I'll take him. Come on, buddy." Dev used his talk-to-the-dog voice.

Linc rapped AJ's arm once Dev and Cassidy stepped out. "There something going on with you and her?"

"Uh, well, complicated." AJ turned his hands up. "As long as she's in protective custody." Hell, he didn't know how to describe it. If they could track down the assassin, and get this trial over with, maybe they could have a real relationship. Or would she disappear into the Witness

Protection Program forever? For now, he needed to keep her safe.

"Sorry for bringing up your date in front of her. Didn't know."

"Not your fault. We discussed it, and it's all good."

Linc gave a relieved nod.

"You coming with?" Tony asked AJ, holding his keys as Cassidy got Champ settled in for the night.

"Yeah." It looked like Linc wasn't the only one who picked up that there was something between him and Cassidy.

"Ride with them then," Lundgren said. "Don't want your car spotted at his house. We're in this together. Whatever it takes."

The reassurance from his boss formed a lump of emotion in his windpipe, so, again, he only nodded.

This devil holding Cassidy prisoner better get ready for a battle between good and evil—with a lot of bad karma thrown in.

When Tony pulled into his driveway, it jarred Cassidy out of her dozing state. Lights lit up the area around the front door and garage.

AJ had her door open before she'd unbuckled, then got her few things out of the back. The house reminded her of Hal's. A small brick ranch with a neutral-color door and shutters. Neatly maintained yard. On the porch, a terra-cotta planter popped with ornamental cabbage and yellow and purple pansies.

The interior displayed a decidedly masculine vibe. A recliner, couch, and end table were the only furniture in the family room dominated by an enormous flat-screen TV. Certainly, not a setup for entertaining the masses.

Tony didn't speak, just proceeded down a hallway. He flipped on the overhead light in a bedroom-turned-office, then pushed the desk chair into a corner. In seconds, he'd pulled down the Murphy bed concealed in a wall unit.

"You, uh, staying in here or need pillow and blanket for the couch? Or should I ask her that?" Tony perused them both.

"Will you stay here with me?" Cassidy didn't want to spend the one night they had with AJ sleeping on the couch while she wanted to be in his arms. Who knew how long they'd have together?

"Bathroom's right next door. See you in the morning." Tony disappeared as thanks left her mouth.

After she brushed her teeth, she pulled running shorts and a T-shirt from her go-bag. She should have put in pajamas. Not like she'd anticipated ending up in a near stranger's home. And thinking on it on, the two thousand dollars she'd stashed wouldn't last a month if she had to hide out on her own. She'd made the right decision to call AJ and come here —even if she were wrong about a leak in the marshals.

AJ was already under the covers, wearing a T-shirt—*too bad*. She turned off the light, then slid between the sheets. It was a heavenly respite to snuggle next to him.

He turned to his side and spooned her yet maintained space between their bodies. When she inched closer, his impressive erection poked her right in the ass.

"Sorry." He scooted his hips back. "I know you're tired and not in the mood after all you've been through, but I can't exactly help it. Just ignore me."

She laughed. "That's hard to do." She flipped to face him. The earlier fear of discovery had faded and simply being alive put her "in the mood." Memories of what transpired at the mountain house didn't hurt, either.

AJ's slow, even breaths were the only sound in the room. Her eyes hadn't adjusted to the darkness yet, but she could make out the outline of his face until she closed her eyes and kissed him. The solid length of him pressed into her belly, but he made no move, other than continuing to kiss her. She slipped her hand down, then wrapped it around him.

A pleasured groan ruminated from his throat. "You don't have to."

"What if I said I could use something to take my mind off everything that happened tonight?"

"I'd say, I hope you aren't wanting to read a book."

"*Not* what I had in mind." Not after he ditched a date to rally the team after her frantic SOS call. And not when he worked so hard at being a gentleman, despite his body's response to them being back in bed together. He was a guy with physical needs. She had a few needs of her own. Needs he created and could satisfy. But their connection went deeper than sex. She wanted him, even if they only got a few days or just tonight, she'd take what she could get because her future was out of her control.

TWENTY

CASSIDY WOKE ALONE. The sheets on AJ's side of the bed were cool, and the clothes he'd laid over the back of the chair last night were MIA. Based on the light streaming in through the cracks in the blinds, the sun came up hours ago.

She hurriedly dressed, then brushed her hair and clipped it up. AJ and Tony's voices told her they hadn't left yet as she made her way toward the delicious aroma coming from the kitchen.

"Morning," Tony greeted her, an empty plate in front of him. "Cassidy, this is Angela."

"Welcome." The striking brunette Cassidy remembered from the Lundgren's got up from the small kitchen table.

"Thanks for letting us crash here last night."

"No problem. I was asleep." Angela laughed. "Coffee?"

"Please."

"What else can I get you? Eggs, bacon, French toast?"

"Don't we have to get out to meet up with the others?" Cassidy didn't want them to be late because of her.

"We got time. Sit. Eat," Tony ordered. "Might be a long day."

She obediently sat under the weight of Tony's words and stare.

"You don't need to go to any trouble. A piece of fruit or yogurt is fine." Cassidy caught AJ's grin. Some habits, like being self-sufficient, were hard to break.

"It's no trouble." Angela handed Cassidy a coffee mug and waved a hand toward the counter. "I already prepped, and Tony told me about your situation—because of Felix Avila. You can have whatever you want for breakfast."

"He told you?" She looked from Angela to Tony. Why would he involve her?

"It's okay," Tony reassured her. "Ang works with us in Joint Special Ops Command. She's former FBI and won't say a thing."

"I also know who Avila is from my days with the CIA, and I can relate to a cartel wanting you dead. So, how do you like your eggs? Do you want sausage or bacon?" Angela smiled as if she were an innocent Army wife.

Last night when Tony said Angela could handle a gun, Cassidy thought he meant he'd taken her to a firing range. She tried to visualize Angela as a spy or undercover agent but didn't dare ask the bad-ass woman fixing her breakfast how she'd come to work for both the CIA and FBI and made enemies of a dangerous cartel, too.

"Told ya," AJ commented as Tony wheeled into the storage building's lot.

"Don't sweat it. It's not even ten yet." Tony remained completely unfazed that, based on the cars already there, they were the last to arrive.

Dev and Kyle tossed a tennis ball to Champ on the green

expanse between the building and the wooded area. The dog raced over to Cassidy.

"Hey, boy. Sorry we had to leave you." She stroked his head.

"I already fed him, and we gave him a little workout," Dev said as they headed inside.

The men gathered around the table were unusually quiet. AJ's stomach constricted. "Did I screw up putting the trackers on another vehicle?" Would it blow any chance at finding Hal's killer? Keep Cassidy in the kill zone?

"By letting the guy know we found him?" Tony asked.

AJ nodded weakly, prepared for the team to crucify him.

"I don't think it's going to be news to the tango someone's onto him," Lundgren said. "Especially with Cassidy pulling the pin on his attempt to eliminate her. He doesn't know we're involved. My money is on him thinking the marshals found those GPS units and are trying to throw him off. It may make him overconfident. I doubt he knows we're onto him tracking her through Champ. Now, if this little pep talk is over, we're going to do things differently today."

The weight of I-totally-fucked-this-up slipped from AJ's shoulders like dropping a forty-pound rucksack after a twenty-mile march. Encouraged, he took a seat. Notecards and pens laid at the center of the table. *What's up with that?*

"Don't want to scare Ms. Cassidy with our usual brainstorming techniques. And language," Lundgren stressed, inciting a few snickers as she slipped into the empty chair next to AJ. "Any questions, or is everyone up to speed on the situation?"

Heads bobbed.

"If you have ideas, write them down. Star your top choice." Lundgren slid paper to each team member.

AJ scribbled down the idea that woke him after a few

hours of sleep and kept him awake, plotting it out. Cassidy peeked at what he wrote as he slid his paper over. Tony and Mack followed suit with their ideas.

Once Chief Lundgren had everyone's paper, he picked one out and read it: "Set a trap."

"That's mine," Tony claimed.

"Let him come to us and take him down." Lundgren laid another note card on top of the first. "Set a trap for the son of a bitch."

"Actually, *that* was mine. I had the son-of-a-bitch part." Tony pointed to himself. His mouth turned up in a brief, and fake, toothless smile.

Kyle snagged a note card from the chief's pile and crumpled it up. "Those are better than mine," he muttered.

The chief read another. "Can't repeat this one in mixed company, but it's the same gist."

"She lived with Hal." AJ shrugged. "She surely heard worse come out of his mouth."

"He did a good job moderating his language at home." Unless her mom had thoroughly pissed him off—again.

"Anyone not on board with this?"

No one objected.

"That was the easiest brainstorming session in like—"

"Ever," Mack finished for Tony, who gave a gruff laugh of agreement.

"We've got the general what. Let's talk where." Lundgren moved on.

"After L.A. this summer and then D.C., no residential areas, please!" Tony grimaced.

"Agreed. We want someplace not totally remote, but where we can control the AO."

"The what?"

Cassidy's question confirmed she was paying attention

even though she appeared absorbed in petting Champ. "Area of operation," AJ clarified for her.

"We can go back to my parents' mountain place," Dev offered.

"That was a sweet setup," Juan said.

"No." AJ had a better idea to lead into. "He may know we—or Champ and Cassidy were there. We don't know for sure he went there."

"We wouldn't want to go someplace he knows about, right?" Cassidy asked.

"Actually, in most cases, circling back is a good idea, but this time we *do* want our tango coming to us," Lundgren said.

"Then …" Cassidy shook her head. "I'm lost."

Several of the men grinned—not *exactly* laughing at her confusion.

"Think of it like playing hide-and-seek when you were a kid," AJ explained. "I would hide in the shower in the hall bath. After my brother checked the linen closet and went into our parent's bedroom, I'd sneak out of the shower and hide in the closet—where he'd already looked for me—because he'd eliminated that as a place I'd be. You see?"

"I think so." Her voice didn't ring with certainty.

"Trust us." Lundgren used his ultra-calm, we-got-this voice. "Obviously, we can't use here since we don't want the tango knowing we're involved."

"He may be good, but he's not stupid," Mack concurred.

"Hal's fishing cabin." AJ crossed his arms over his chest, replicating Lundgren's this-is-how-it's-going-down pose. Probably didn't have the same impact with his less-than-intimidating size and slighter build. "It's close, but far enough not to scream Fort Bragg. Not heavily populated. We can use the other cabins for surveillance. Cabin itself is manageable size."

Heads nodded as he poured out the ideas he'd come up with as the sun rose.

"It is an ideal location and setup," Lundgren agreed. "Has everybody been there?"

"Not me." Dev's mouth twisted into a pout.

"Sorry, newbie." Tony chuckled.

"Once was enough," Juan said. "Fishing is boring."

"That's because you weren't doing it right." Mack grinned at Juan.

"It's because there weren't babes in bikinis for him to hit on." Kyle's quiet humor peeked out.

"All right, before this jumps the rails, we have the where checked off, but who? We gotta have Champ there—and get him there ASAP."

"If this guy is thorough, he'll have night-vision equipment. Can't rule out thermal imaging, either," Linc said.

"That means he could distinguish gender," Dev added.

"I'm not strapping on a bra and fake boobs," Juan cracked in response to Dev's targeted gaze. "Won't hide the real heat." He gestured to his pelvis with a flourish.

"I—" Cassidy started.

"Give us all a break, Dominguez." Tony drowned out Cassidy.

"Get a female marshal?" Dev suggested.

"That means including them in the plan," Lundgren countered.

True. Not ideal. What if the marshals moved Cassidy again, and they went back to the starting line? AJ wanted to keep Cassidy safe, but they had to make the bait look real. There was a flaw in his plan.

"How long can we keep the marshals in the dark?" the chief asked.

"I check in weekly, or as needed," Cassidy answered. "And I—"

"You could pretend everything is normal. Let's not get hung up on that now." Lundgren talked over Cassidy.

"Ang could do it. She's close enough in size and build and—"

"No," Cassidy cut Tony off. "I'm not putting your wife in danger for me."

"Girlfriend," Juan corrected her, drawing an eat-shit-and-die glare from Tony.

"Whatever." Cassidy sighed out the word. "The woman he loves. It has to be me—I have to be the bait."

"But she's trained in self-defense, offense, and can handle a weapon," Tony explained.

"I don't care. It's hard enough to think of you guys risking your lives for me."

"Yeah, but—"

"I know," she interrupted Lundgren, drawing surprised looks from several of the team. "You're trained. You can take care of yourselves. I'm not going to stop you since it's probably Hal's killer, but at this point, I don't have a life. I'm not going to let someone else take my place. Period."

Cassidy had no clue how easily they could cut her out of the process, but AJ understood how she felt. She needed this. To ease her guilt over Hal's death. To have a shot at a normal future. "She's in. She's the bait."

"All right." The chief gave a resigned nod of approval. "We need to get Champ out there ASAP. We'll see what we need to set up. There's no security system at the cabin as I recall."

"Hardly," AJ snorted. Hal left the door unlocked for any hunter or fisherman to use.

"Who else knows the way out there?" Lundgren's gaze

roamed over the men. Mack's index finger went up. "Perfect. You drop Cassidy off back at Vincenti's and meet us there."

"Wait. I'm not going?" Cassidy stared at the chief.

"Not yet. We'll get you out there after we get an idea when he's coming. It could be hours, days, weeks before he pings Champ's GPS again. Or maybe not at all," Lundgren reasoned.

"You can't leave Champ out there alone," she protested.

"We could remove the chip and leave it there, though," Juan said.

Dev whistled to Champ. "Should be easy enough to take out. Local anesthesia, small cut, and a few stitches."

"You want to cut Champ open?" Cassidy drew the dog to her side rather than let him go to Dev.

"He's a medic. He knows what he's doing," Juan assured her.

She continued shaking her head.

"Problem with removing the chip is that technology is so dead-on, our guy may notice the GPS is stationary and get suspicious. Could backfire and blow our shot at him," Porter spoke up.

"For now, Cassidy can go home. No need for you to be out at the cabin while we're working. We'll take Champ out with us and on of one of us stay out there," Lundgren said.

"Home?" Cassidy sounded defeated as she apparently accepted Lundgren's statement as an order.

"I've got a better plan than you hanging out with us. You get to have a girls' day having lunch and shopping with the most awesome women on the planet." Mack pulled out his phone. "My wife needs to get some maternity clothes."

"Don't you need more clothes?" AJ asked, relieved that Mack intuitively picked up on Cassidy's homeless dilemma.

"I have a change in my bag. I don't want to put your wife in danger," she added.

"No worries. Ang is meeting Kristie and Stephanie. I'll make sure she's carrying." Tony pulled out his phone, and he and Mack punched numbers and made plans to include her.

"You need money for shopping?" AJ pulled out his wallet. He could see her fitting in with the women in the unit in a way Jess never did.

"I have money in my bag at Tony's."

Her tone raised the flag that warned him he might be treading on her stubborn independence. Now wasn't the time or place or audience to have a showdown about the difference between needing help and taking advantage. "Good planning." He pulled his hand from his wallet.

"Thank you for offering." Her tone softened.

Despite her need to be self-sufficient, each thing he did do for her made him see how they could work together as a team. As a couple—if only it weren't for an assassin and the complication of witness protection.

TWENTY-ONE

PULLING up to Hal's fishing cabin, the emptiness in AJ's core expanded. He'd never again sit in a boat with the man who'd believed in him. Inspired him. Poured his vast array of knowledge and experience into him.

What started out as protecting the stepdaughter who'd meant so much to his mentor was so much more personal now. He'd bring Hal's killer to justice for both of them to get closure.

Everyone piled out of their vehicles before AJ opened his door.

Champ bounded up the steps; Lundgren followed. "Let's start with the cabin interior."

The eight men filled the snug cabin. Each man walked through the rooms to commit the layout to memory, which only took a few minutes in the small space.

"The master closet will work as a safe room. Be cramped, but not like we're talking anything long term," Tony began. "Line all three walls with steel plates. We'll need to set a door plate with hinges. Weld a slide bolt to lock it from the inside."

Lundgren nodded approval. "How long?"

"I'll get measurements and use the shop to cut the plates and mount the hinges. Then we'll need to transport here and assemble. Few hours, tops."

"Let's move to the exterior." Lundgren led them outside.

"I'm thinking we put a thermal-imaging camera on the roof. Stream live feed into the cabin." Dev rose on tiptoes to peer at the roof. "Put it on a rotating platform and mount it on the chimney to sweep and get three-hundred-sixty-degree coverage."

That idea hadn't occurred to AJ. Setting up motion sensors around the cabin would definitely give them the drop on anyone breaching their perimeter, but thermal imaging would eliminate false alarms from the abundant wildlife filling the surrounding woods.

The daggers of doubt still digging away at his confidence dissipated.

"How's it coming in here?" Chief Lundgren's voice startled AJ. His boss filled the doorframe of the cabin's master bedroom.

"Almost there. Just gotta get the door piece installed and make sure the inside bolt lines up. You want a plate to cover the top?" Tony pointed to the small metal sheet leaning against the wall behind AJ.

"Since you have it. Better safe than regrets. But we're on a time crunch now." Lundgren held up the cell phone clutched in his hand. "Got a text from Lackland. Champ's GPS got pinged."

The air in the small room became oppressively heavy; no one spoke immediately.

"They trace the ISP?" AJ found his voice.

"They're working on that. The ISPs from the two prior pings were to coffee-shop servers. They're trying to get any footage to ID him, but I doubt he went inside."

"At least knowing when will help us gauge how much time we've got," Tony said.

"I'm banking on him driving—less of a trail. My guess is he'll ping again later to make sure the signal is stationary, but he may head this way as a starting point. With her leaving Virginia, I'm thinking he's gonna be on the desperate side. Don't count on his typical MO. Rozanski, I want you and Grant to go pick up supplies and Cassidy. I want her out here tonight. We're going to hunker down as if he'll be sniffing around in hours."

"Get my go-bag when you pick up Cassidy's things." Tony fished his keys out of his jean's pocket. "Door key, closet key. Bag's on the floor of the hall closet. Ghillie suit and cover are in the garage. I'll need those, too."

The keys Tony gave him were heavy in AJ's hand.

"Good idea," Lundgren agreed. "I'll stay here to help you finish. Have Mack grab my bag."

AJ should be happy. This was what they wanted. No waiting around. Instead, his stomach felt like he'd eaten a live scorpion—an experience he never planned to repeat.

"Cassidy doesn't know the area, so I'll call Ang and see where they are." Tony touched his phone's screen.

"You don't think they're back yet?" AJ asked.

"Yeah, right. Four women shopping for maternity and baby stuff, and yours has one change of clothes?" Tony gave a coarse laugh. "Hey, babe. How's it going?" He nodded in told-you-so triumph. "Then you're still at the mall? Okay. AJ's gonna be there to pick Cassidy up in about an hour. Keep her busy until then. Oh, and where's your vest? Yeah, that one. Thought we'd borrow it just in case." Tony's gaze darted around.

AJ swallowed. Damn, this shit got real.

NONE of the men on Ray's team had complained about the emergency call summoning them on a Friday night. Or giving up their weekend. It showed their respect for Hal, but they also wanted justice.

The women rallying around her touched Cassidy in a different way. From the moment Mack dropped Cassidy back at Tony's, Angela, then Stephanie and Kristie, included her rather than making her feel like a tagalong.

The women's bond was nearly as tight as the men on the team. Growing up, it'd been her and her sister, Sherri. She'd had friends in college, and at work—before Flores. But the past two years, cut off from everyone she'd known and afraid to involve anyone in her life, had been the loneliest.

Her mother had only had a few close female friends—and those usually didn't last long. Tiffany had never connected with the wives on Hal's team. She'd gone to one or two get-togethers or events, then complained the other wives didn't like her. That could have been true, even likely if Tiffany had flirted with the other men on Hal's team.

In two hours at the mall, they'd checked out the maternity shop for Kristie, and Cassidy had picked up some clothes and sleepwear. Before hitting another department store, Stephanie insisted on skipping the food court for soup and salads at a nearby bakery café.

This was the kind of life Cassidy had always wanted. Friends. Loving marriages. Kids.

Maybe one day. Maybe. *Please*, she prayed as they approached the children's clothing section.

"Oh, look. This reminds me of one of the outfits I had for Alexis." Stephanie Lundgren detoured to the rack of toddler clothing and held up a little purple romper with big, bright flowers.

"That is too precious," Kristie Hanlon cooed. "Only we don't know *for sure* it's a girl."

"Statistically, guys who serve in Special Ops are five times more likely to have daughters than sons. If you don't have a girl, *someone* else will."

Cassidy picked up on the glance that Stephanie sent Angela's way.

"Don't look at me." Angela held up her free hand. "We are not there yet."

"*We?* I don't think you can say that for Tony. And you know he'll be a great dad," Stephanie continued.

"You should have seen him at Darcy's birthday party," Kristie said to Cassidy.

"I kinda think us being invited to her party was a setup." Angela's eyes narrowed with good-natured suspicion.

"Trust me, that was all Darcy. Mack tried to talk her out of inviting Uncle Tony and Uncle Ray. Told her he didn't want the rest of the team to be jealous. I also think he didn't want to feed them." Kristie laughed.

"She's how old?" Cassidy tried to envision AJ and the guys from his team at a kid's birthday party.

"Eight, going on twelve."

"She's utterly adorable. However, Tony and I've only been together a few months, and there're still unresolved issues," Angela said cryptically. "We're enjoying things, but we're not in a rush."

"Fair enough," Stephanie agreed. "I'm glad you found

each other, though, because he's never been happier. With what these guys do, they need a reason to come home. I have a vested interest in seeing more of the team married or in solid relationships."

Stephanie's gaze roved from Kristie to Angela and even toward Cassidy.

"Come on." Kristie grinned and looped her arm through Cassidy's. "She can't help it. It's her mothering nature."

"You and Mack can make me and Ray godparents as thanks." Stephanie turned her attention back to sifting through the clearance racks of baby clothes.

"We'll be over in the maternity section." Kristie chuckled as they walked away.

As Cassidy studied the racks of clothes, the ache in her chest grew heavier. She missed having close friends she could confide in. Share inside jokes with. Missed being part of a group. Missed the life she'd had.

After Kristie went into the dressing room, Cassidy worked up her nerve, waiting until she could look Angela in the eye. "This morning, you mentioned a cartel wanting you dead …" She didn't know exactly what to ask.

Angela nodded. "It was a different circumstance than you. I was working for the CIA in South America. The players there didn't know my real identity. After they put a hit on me—or my alias—the agency reassigned me to the Middle East. All was good until someone I trusted recently decided to cash in on the contract."

Cassidy closed her mouth once she became aware of it hanging open. "So, now everything is … it's over? You're safe?"

Instead of the relieved smile she expected, Angela shook her head and sighed. "We faked my death, and the cartel family did buy it enough to pay out, but we don't know for sure what information was given to them. They could know the name I go by, so I can't rule out the possibility they could ID me someday. But I'm starting a new life here, with Tony, and we're hoping that it's over."

If not, she'd have Tony to protect her. What would that mean for them, though? Disappearing? Him leaving his job?

"That looks great on you," Angela said when Kristie emerged in a dark teal boatneck top with slits in the sides over tan pixie pants.

"It does," Cassidy seconded. Not only the clothes but the happy glow she exuded.

"I love the top. The pants are a little big." Kristie pulled up the top to show them. "But that'll change soon enough, and they'll go with a lot of stuff."

"That's a keeper." Stephanie joined them with another shopping bag. "What else did I miss?"

"This is the first one I came out in. The navy dress made me look eight-months pregnant already. Pass. Be back in a flash." Kristie disappeared back into the dressing room.

"You're not getting teary, are you?" Angela asked.

"Maybe a little. But it's good. She deserves this second chance. Sorry, Kristie's first husband was killed in action," Stephanie explained to Cassidy. "It wasn't an easy road for her and Mack to get together, but I knew they'd be perfect for one another. It's my superpower. I can tell if a couple will make it. Well, if they're in the Special Ops community."

"Oh, really?" Angela remarked with an amused grin.

"It's true. First time I saw Tony with you, I knew it was meant to be," Stephanie said smugly.

"My mom and Hal?" Cassidy asked.

Stephanie shook her head. "To be honest, I'm surprised that lasted as long as it did. And I knew Jess wasn't the right woman for AJ. Now, the only time I've seen you with AJ was at my house after Hal's funeral. Can't judge on that."

Head flooded to Cassidy's face. "Um, we're just …" How did she explain that her situation was too damned complicated for a relationship right now? Even if there was something nearly perfect about being with AJ.

"I know it's soon. But you're back here, and I like you and your attitude. I'll have to see you two together again before I know."

Kristie emerged and ran a hand over the small bulge of her stomach. "What do you think?"

"That's really cute on you, too," Angela said.

"I like the stripes now, but … you know what, I don't even care if they make me look huge later. I'm having a baby." Kristie beamed as she turned and went back into the dressing room to the amused chuckles of her friends.

While Kristie continued trying on outfits, Angela answered her cell. "Guys are on the way to pick you up," she told Cassidy. "Anything else you need to get? We've got ten minutes."

"No, I'm good." Other than having this outing end and not knowing if she'd see these new friends again.

"I pray this all works out. I'd love to see you again," Stephanie added.

"Glad you joined us," Kristie said when Cassidy said her goodbyes. "You're invited to the baby shower. We've got a few months until then."

"Thanks. That would be great." After the trial, she would be free, but how long would that take? She couldn't expect AJ to wait indefinitely. What if he were seeing someone? Not just a date, but a relationship by then? She had to accept that possibility was likely reality.

Angela walked her to the front of the store—a reminder to Cassidy she was still on temporary protection detail.

"That's them." Angela motioned to a black Jeep that stopped at the curb. AJ waved from the passenger seat.

"How's it coming?" Angela asked AJ and Devin as Cassidy climbed in.

"Security at the cabin is almost complete," Devin said.

"Good. Be careful. And take care of Cassidy. We like her." Angela winked at the group, then stepped back.

"We will." AJ turned and grinned at Cassidy as Devin pulled away. "That all you bought?" He nodded toward the shopping bags she'd set on the floor.

"It's enough." If they were stuck at the cabin for a while, there'd be plenty of free time to wash clothes.

"Not going to show me?"

"Nothing exciting. Jeans, running pants, and a sweatshirt." She patted the large shopping bag, then opened the smaller bag and showed him the deep blue sweater.

"That's a good color on you." He stared at her for a few moments. "You sure you want to do this?"

What were the chances whoever killed Hal would show up? Considering the debris crammed in the fireplace vent, darn good. But if they caught this guy, what would it mean? Would it speed up the case against Avila? Would it bring an end to this purgatory?

She nodded. "I need to."

"Okay." He nodded, not smiling, but not trying to talk her out of it. He reached back, and she put her hand in his. He gave hers a comforting squeeze, his eyes still locked on her even after he let go.

"This your undercover vehicle?" She ran her hand over the Jeep's plush interior as Devin headed out of the parking lot.

"I thought it would work for us being rednecks. Camping out. Off-roading around the lake. Fishing. It's not deep-sea fishing, but it'll do." Devin tossed a boyish grin over his shoulder at her.

"You as a redneck?" Not the impression she'd gotten of Devin.

"He can be when he wants." AJ laughed. "This Jeep will be covered in mud. Trust me. He'll drive it around post that way—for about two days—before he washes it, even under the hood. Only single guy on the team who needs a three-car garage. Car. Jeep. Bike," AJ said.

"I'm not gonna let it sit in the garage caked in mud for weeks."

Probably a good thing Juan wasn't here to give Devin a hard time again about coming from money. She'd experienced both and knew money didn't always make life happier.

The Army, especially Special Ops, didn't get many upper-class recruits from her limited experience. The pay wouldn't keep him in the style of life in which he'd obviously grown up. He seemed pretty balanced, though. Good thing because, in her mind, entitlement was a dangerous trap. It led to people like Avila, thinking they could do whatever to whomever because they had money. They didn't see *it* controlled them. Trying to make and keep a fortune led to bad choices. She was praying karma was going to bite Avila in the ass—or put a combat boot up it.

The marshals had kept her safe—so far, but AJ and his team gave her hope. A hope that built while they picked up the things from Tony's, while they shopped for groceries for the stay at the lake, and while they drove out to Hal's cabin.

Hope could be a wonderful, yet dangerous, emotion.

Hal's weathered fishing cabin didn't pack the same punch to Cassidy's heart as going to his home. She could picture him in a worn flannel shirt and camouflage boonie hat, fishing rod in hand, coming out the front door. Tony and Ray lounged on the front steps. Tony's black SUV was parked beside a white SUV that had been at the storage building last night.

For the sixty-eighth time, she strained to conjure up the memory of the driver of the white car. Something made it stick in her head. Had the driver been Hal's killer? Had he been watching for her? What if she'd gone back to Hal's after her car hadn't been ready?

Champ left the porch and loped to her side as she carried an armful of groceries across the hardpacked ground toward the cabin.

"*They* got beer," Devin grumbled.

Tony grinned, then raised the bottle in a mock toast.

"Yeah, well … there's worse things than no beer," AJ said.

"Mack bought our groceries," Ray explained. "Gotta make it look real."

"Besides, we've been working hard at home improvements." Tony took a swig from his bottle.

"There's more in the fridge." Ray jerked a thumb giving them the go-ahead. "But just one."

"You get a location off the ISP?" AJ asked.

"Bagel shop in Charlottesville, Virginia."

Air rushed from Cassidy's lungs, and her body jolted in a shiver that registered on the Richter scale. She'd driven through Charlottesville coming to Fayetteville. How many close calls could she dodge before her luck ran out?

Part of her wanted to shut this down now. Before anyone else got hurt. Or worse. Let the marshals stash her someplace safe. Stop involving AJ's team. Except they had their own motivation for wanting to find this guy. What would Hal have done if it had been one of his teammates targeted? Or to protect her?

"Come on in." Ray rose to his full height, like some Norse god of protection. Tony stood at his side—a dark, sexy, mafioso-like enforcer. Thank goodness they were on her side because she wouldn't want them coming after her.

She trampled on the hesitancy that fell around her feet. *Time to get this guy.*

The cabin's interior looked like she remembered. She set the groceries on the kitchen countertop, taking in the faint aroma of Hal's cigars, fish, and the oil used to fry it, all absorbed by the wood-paneled walls.

AJ carried her bag to the larger of the two bedrooms. Hal's bedroom. She followed behind Ray and Tony, who strode to the closet. Instead of the wooden door, a solid sheet of metal stood in its place. Tony opened it with a flourish. Gone was the hanging bar, and the interior walls were now cold dull steel.

They'd mentioned a safe room, but the possibility of being stashed in there made this even more terrifying. Cassidy wrapped her arms around her body, trying to ward off the fear breathing down the back of her neck.

Tony proceeded to demonstrate the slide bolt—like locking herself in a two-by-three-foot prison.

"Dominguez and Porter are going to pose as marshals and be with you twenty-four seven." Ray pointed to the other bedroom and led the group back into the main living area of the cabin. "Mack and I will be in the cabin two down. We'll be on the lake fishing during the day. We have surveillance equipment set up on the roof feeding to both cabins. Grant and Rozanski will be camping about a mile down the shore with a good view this way."

"And tooling around the lake," Devin added, carrying in groceries.

She wasn't surprised Ray didn't have AJ in the cabin with her and she understood why, but the disappointment still hit her. What she wouldn't give to not live in hiding again.

"Yes. They will." Ray gave a slight eye roll and released a resigned breath. "Liu and Vincenti will be in the woods doing surveillance. You won't see them, but they'll be there."

The implication took several seconds to set in. "So, you drew the short straw, huh?" She aimed a sympathetic smile at Tony.

"Naw. I don't mind. Done worse than hiding in the woods. You're the one who drew the short straw."

A wry, emotionally painful grunt escaped her lungs.

"Same security procedures as with the marshals. Do. As. They. Say. Any questions before we go set up?" Lundgren drilled her with his stare.

"Can I have a minute with AJ?"

"Sure." Ray's gentle smile eased the tension steeped into her bones.

She left the men in the living area, and AJ followed her into the bedroom, closing the door behind him.

"You okay? You can change your mind anytime. You don't have to do this."

"Yes. I do." If she was going to have any control over her life, she had to do this.

"We're doing everything we can, but we can't guarantee your safety." He swallowed visibly.

"I know. I trust you guys. This is my best shot." She edged closer, and his arms slid around her. "Promise me you'll be careful."

"You don't have to worry about us. We kn—"

"Not true. This guy killed Hal. You have numbers, but he's not some untrained thug with a gun."

"Yes, this guy is a pro. He's smart. He's sneaky. He's also a coward, and he's met his match. He's due some bad-karma payback."

What AJ had told her about his family's negative view of his career swirled around her consciousness. She wanted this over, except she couldn't let him torture or kill on her behalf. To be a vigilante and live with that choice. "You want him as much as I do, but your mission is not to exact your own justice."

"Message received." AJ stared into her eyes—his were unreadable.

She didn't know what to hope or pray for as he left with barely a squeeze of her hand.

TWENTY-TWO

Cassidy chopped peppers and onion for the omelets, still groggy after tossing and turning most of the night. With no television or internet at the cabin, the evening had been quiet and long, but the night was longer. Lying in bed, listening to sounds, thinking about the men out there—AJ, the men on his team, and somewhere, a killer.

"Mornin', Chief," Juan spoke into his phone. "You called it. Same ISP?" He huffed out a sigh listening to whatever update Ray gave him. "Figured, but worth asking." He made a hand motion to Linc, communicating something she wasn't privy to. "We're on it."

He didn't explain anything after he hung up or when he retrieved several water bottles from the case in the corner of the kitchen. Out of the corner of her eye, she saw him enter her bedroom. She followed, chef's knife in hand, Champ on her heels.

"What are you doing?" she asked when she found him in her closet-turned-safe-room.

He startled, then straightened, revealing the upholstered storage ottoman relocated from the main room.

"Jeez. Put the knife down," he requested. "I put some comfort items in the cube. While I'm not banking on you being in here long—if at all—thought it should be more comfortable than sitting on the floor against cold metal." He stepped out and closed the door behind him.

She hoped he was right about her not staying in there. Though she wasn't sure she wanted to know what made him think of putting the items in there. "Thanks. That's ... very thoughtful of you." And a different side of him than she'd seen. Had Ray suggested that? Why? What had he told Juan?

"No biggie. Breakfast smells good." He eyed the knife as if to use mind control to send her back to the kitchen. They were on the same side, she went.

"WHOA!" Dev whipped the steering wheel, and the Jeep bounced off the crumbling edge of the asphalt.

AJ clung to the roll bar to keep himself inside the doorless vehicle as they nearly sideswiped a tree to avoid the gray sedan.

Dev slowed, gently veering back onto the road.

AJ barely had time to get a glimpse of the license plate before the sedan disappeared around the bend. "Only got a partial." He resisted grumbling about the near collision. He hadn't expected the car, either. They'd encountered two other vehicles, both trucks, while driving around the lake for hours. *Damn.* It had lulled them into a lower state of readiness.

"Want me to turn around?"

"Naw. *If* that was our guy, that might make him suspicious."

"Not if we give him hell about running us off the road."

Dev had a point. They'd get eyes on the guy. Get a look-see in his vehicle. If it had been a white sedan with Florida plates, it'd be a no-brainer. They were on their first day, and the chance of an assassin making it easy was too good to be true. "We'll see if we run into him again." He wrote down what he'd caught of the plate in his notebook.

"Figuratively, not literally," Dev added.

They spent the next hour driving around the lake, looking for anything that raised a red flag. Or even a yellow caution flag.

The longer they drove, the more he got in his own head about how he'd left things with Cassidy yesterday. It wasn't a fight, but he'd shut her out after she basically told him not to go vigilante on Hal's killer. Maybe he'd flashed back to Jess's complaints, but Cassidy was different.

It wasn't that she didn't respect him and what he did. No. She'd wanted to protect his honor.

He owed her an apology—even if he would do anything to protect her. And not just because Hal would want him to, but because of how she made him feel. Worthy. Wanted.

It might be crazy to fall so hard for a woman in Cassidy's uncertain circumstances, but he couldn't help it. They didn't have a shot if he couldn't get her out of an assassin's sights.

Cassidy clicked her tongue against the roof of her mouth. Champ's head lifted to fix her with hopeful eyes.

"You need to go out, boy?"

Champ's nails scratched against the wood floor as he scrambled up.

"Can I take him out? I need some fresh air."

"Just for a minute. We gotta stay close." Linc rose, abandoning Juan and their card game. His gaze went to the vest hanging on a pegged coatrack by the door.

She wiggled into the protective vest, then pulled her coat on over it. Champ nuzzled at the door.

It'd been a long day cooped up in the small cabin. Juan's restlessness had crossed from distracting to downright annoying. She got it. These guys liked action. It was the same way she felt about working in a nursing home or pediatric office versus a trauma department.

As soon as Linc opened the door, Champ shot outside and down the steps. He pulled up short and sniffed the cool air, his head turned, scanning the tree line to their right.

Linc led her out, standing between her and the cabins on her right. In the darkness, Cassidy couldn't make out much other than the surface of the lake, contrasting against the light-colored shoreline that bled into the shadows of the dense forest.

"Do your business, Champ."

The dog didn't respond. She wrapped her arms around her body to keep from shivering.

"Champ!" Her sharper tone got the dog's attention, and he moved to the patch of clover he'd marked as his spot. It took a conscious effort for Cassidy not to search for signs of Tony or Kyle—she knew she wouldn't see them—hidden out there, keeping watch.

Throughout the day, she'd heard Devin and AJ as they spun the Jeep around the woods. Dancing flames glowed, and a plume of smoke marked their campsite further down the shoreline. She raised her hand in a very subtle wave in the event AJ or Devin had binoculars on her. Just act natural. Well, as natural as she'd be if it were just her and Champ here, protected by "Marshals Juan and Linc."

Champ sniffed the air again before returning to her side.

She wanted to believe he picked up the scent of one of the men. Or perhaps the aroma of fish cooking from Ray and Mack's cabin two doors down. She'd seen them bring in a string of fish from their day tooling around the lake to keep an eye on things.

Though she knew the team was watching her, it didn't account for the prickle at the base of her skull that made her hair stand on end.

Inside, she shrugged out of her coat while Juan shuffled cards at the kitchen table. "Wanna play?" he asked her as Linc rejoined him.

"Sure." She'd spent most of the day reading. Time for another form of entertainment.

"We're playing poker. Regular, but we can switch to strip." Juan flashed a devilish grin at her and dealt the cards.

"I don't need to see that." She dismissed his comment with an eye roll.

"You sure?" He pulled up his T-shirt to display his abs.

She just shook her head and looked at her cards. "Pass. I'll take two." She slid him two cards.

He lowered his shirt and shrugged.

"I'll take one." Linc traded in a card.

Juan dropped the innuendos. Linc cleaned up in cards. And they killed two hours with her still completely dressed and wondering how good AJ was at poker and thinking about his abs.

TWENTY-THREE

FROM ACROSS THE LAKE, AJ made out the familiar bark. He picked up the binoculars, scanning until he landed on the right cabin. Cassidy, with Juan at her side for protection, looked toward their campsite and gave the slightest wave.

The simple gesture told him she was thinking of him and renewed AJ's resolve to put an end to the threats against her. Give her a life—hopefully, one with him in it.

Last night had been uneventful. Nothing stuck out today. Not on their surveillance run this morning, nor the chief and Mack's after lunch. Cassidy was still safe, but the team was no closer to catching whoever had tried to kill her. Hard as it was, he and Dev stayed put, fishing for another hour before climbing into the Jeep to make rounds.

They took the long way around the lake, checking out several side roads. Dev braked to a halt. "Is that the car that ran us off the road yesterday?" He backed up to get a better view of the sedan parked beside a run-down cabin.

"Pretty sure." AJ had only gotten a glimpse of it yesterday. It'd been nondescript enough to not stand out. From the lake, Mack had seen a gray sedan drive past the cabins shortly after that. Though they'd looked for it, neither group had spotted it since. "I say we go check the plate and run it."

"You want me to park a ways down? Sundown's in half an hour. Provide us some cover to poke around."

Dev's plan made sense, but something about the picture before him didn't feel like a scene out of a Norman Rockwell painting. "What do you notice about the car?"

"Those bushes provide natural camouflage. It's backed in, so we can't see the plate. And that makes for a quick getaway."

AJ nodded in agreement. "If someone comes out, we can use them running us off the road as a cover story. Block him in." He transferred his weapon from the ankle holster to his waistband when he got out of the Jeep.

With one eye on the cabin, they approached the car. AJ laid a hand on the hood. The cool metal did nothing to fight the chill bumps creeping from his wrists up to his neck.

Had they missed seeing the car here on their last lap? Dammit. They were only half a mile from Hal's cabin. Plenty of time to get close. And this spot? Close proximity to the main road. All pointed to a fast escape.

"No power." Dev pointed to the wires dangling from the electrical box on the side of the cabin.

AJ tried the driver's-side door and then the back, finding both locked. He peered through the window at the immaculate interior. Not even an empty coffee cup to provide a clue or DNA. Dev tried the doors on the passenger side with no success, either. He rounded the vehicle and was already on the phone, calling in the plate number.

They didn't have a strong reason to break into the car—but the temptation waged a battle with AJ's judgment. "There a keyed lock on the trunk?" he asked, almost certain of the answer based on the recent model of the car.

"Nope." Dev checked, phone to his ear. "What's that? The car is?" His head jerked, and his eyes widened like he'd eaten a three-alarm chili pepper. "Just the plate?"

His head nodded in an excited rhythm as he pushed past AJ and looked at the dash by the driver's window. "Shit. The VIN number window was painted over." He pulled his knife out, then scraped the blade over the glass. "From the inside. Someone went to a lot of trouble. I'll call you back if we get it." He pocketed his phone. "Plate was reported stolen. Yesterday. From another gray Hyundai," he passed along.

"This has to be our guy." Certainty acted like a power source, sending high-voltage charges through every artery of AJ's body. "Let's check the house." He drew his weapon.

Though there were no signs of recent entry via the front porch, they stood with weapons ready. AJ tried the knob, and it came off in his hand.

A thunk sounded when the other half hit the floor. No other sound came from inside. No bullets pierced the door. No explosion blasted out the windows.

Mess with the lock or kick it in? At this point, he doubted anyone would care about a busted door. Not that he'd bet a nickel on someone being in there.

He clued Dev to his plan to kick it in. The door's lock gave way so easily that AJ fell to his knee. Dust swirled up from the floor in the empty room. No footprints marred the layer of dust. They still spent a precious minute to check the abandoned cabin.

"Let's call this in."

Lundgren answered before the second ring. AJ did his best to give a calm, unbiased summation of what they'd found.

The chief cut him off. "He's out here somewhere." It

wasn't a question. "Get the drone up. I'll let Porter and Dominguez know."

"Boss wants us to launch the Raven," AJ relayed to Dev as they stepped out into the twilight.

Dev headed to the sedan and knelt beside the front tire. He turned his knife in his hand, but he unscrewed the cap on the valve stem and proceeded to let out the air. "In case we're wrong."

Ever the Boy Scout. AJ shook his head. "Come on."

While Dev made sure the tire wouldn't roll, AJ flashed back to changing Cassidy's tire. That flat may have saved her life. This flat gave them the lug-nut up—this guy wasn't getting away. *It's called karma, you prick. Bad Karma, to be exact.*

They sped off in the Jeep. It only took a few minutes to get to the small clearing they'd scoped out earlier. AJ and Dev put on their communication headsets to loop in with the entire team.

Devin unpacked and assembled the drone. AJ removed the controller with display for the unmanned aerial system (UAS) and booted it up. With Dev's football-style forward pass, the UAS took flight. AJ flew it away from the lake, letting it gain enough altitude to silently patrol the area below. Once he had his bearings, he navigated the craft over the lake. The heat signatures of three humans and one large dog identified Cassidy and his teammates, then two more in the cabin occupied by Mack and the chief. Not detecting any other heat sources in the immediate vicinity, AJ drew in a full breath.

He expanded the craft's flight-path circle and picked out a figure near Kyle Liu's overwatch position. The drone climbed higher to encompass a wider view. Several smaller dots showed through the canopy of trees and foliage, but none large enough to be a human.

Then, he saw a prone outline. Tony? He had to be sure.

"Liu, Vincenti, give a wave to mark your positions."

"Mark my position? I'm not a dog?" Liu huffed.

Tony laughed. "That would be Dominguez."

The left arms of both bodies moved out—possibly flipping AJ off. Confirmation of his buddies' locations didn't make him drop from alert-to-readiness status. He flew the drone in larger circles. Dev's and his heat signatures showed up, then individuals in homes in the small neighborhood being built on the far side of the lake.

"Anything?" Lundgren radioed in.

"Nothing out of the ordinary in a two-plus-mile radius." No lone folks out walking in the woods—or lying prone. "I'm going to fly it over the woods again." Where was the driver of the gray sedan?

"Bring it in after that to save resources. We can relaunch in an hour for another surveillance search."

Ten minutes later, AJ brought the drone in for a bounce landing.

Dev retrieved the drone. "You want to stay here, cruise around, or head back to the campsite?"

AJ debated a moment. If the guy was lurking somewhere, they weren't likely see him once darkness engulfed the forest, and they might spook him if they drove around for a few hours. It might be easier to draw him out if he thought they were settled in for the night. "Let's head back to camp and keep up appearances."

"Great. We get to drink more water out of beer bottles."

"I'll buy you a case when this is over." *God, I want this to be over and get the guy that killed Hal. And I want Cassidy safe. She doesn't deserve this.*

From his position resting on the floor, Champ rose, his head high and alert.

Cassidy looked up from her e-reader. "You need to go out again, boy?" He didn't give any of his usual signs, but she got to her feet.

The dog faced the door, the fur on his neck bristling. A growl rumbled in his throat and stopped Cassidy mid-stride.

Juan scrambled to his feet. Linc quickly followed.

"Don't open it." Juan pulled her back.

Linc swiped the radio from the table. "Rozanski, Hanlon, you seeing anything out there?"

"Nothing."

"I've got nothing on my screen," Mack echoed AJ.

Linc sat at his laptop and watched the display as the camera on the roof panned the area.

Champ stepped closer to the door, his nose raised to sniff the air. Then the threatening barking began—and the hair on Cassidy's arms stood up.

"Quiet, boy."

Champ quieted at Juan's command, though the growl returned. Juan hovered between her and the dog, weapon in hand. His eyes cut from Linc to the master bedroom.

Linc's hands turned up while his lips clamped. His head shook in frustration.

"Shit. Nothing is showing up, but Champ is growling like nobody's business," Juan said into the radio.

"You can circumvent all this technology easier than a dog," Ray Lundgren's deep voice rumbled over the radio. "Stash Cassidy. Rozanski, Grant, head this way. When I give the word, let Champ out."

She stood frozen by the men's orders and the edge to Ray's voice. A deep freeze seeped through her skin and into the marrow of her bones. "No. You can't send Champ …"

"He's a military working dog. This is the kind of thing he's trained for," Linc said.

Juan wrapped an arm around her waist and pulled her toward the bedroom. He didn't slow when she tripped over her feet and wasn't exactly gentle in forcing her into the closet.

"Lock it, and don't come out until you hear one of us give the all clear and safe word."

She whirled to face him. "Safe word? What safe word?"

"Karma, baby." Juan threw out a nefarious grin before he closed the door, leaving her in utter darkness.

"Be careful," she whispered through a breath.

God, why had she agreed to this? She groped for the ottoman, pulled the top off, and rummaged inside. Two room-temperature water bottles rolled on top of a flannel blanket. Her fingers found the hard, plastic cylinder of a flashlight. The beam illuminated the closet, giving her back an iota of power as she plunked down on the ottoman and prayed and rocked and waited.

If anything happened to one of these guys or Champ because of her, it was over. Done. No more witness protection. No more testifying. She'd given up enough of her life. Of her soul. Of her usefulness. She *could* go to some third-world country with an aid organization and save lives. It would be rewarding. She'd be safe. Her family would be safe.

Flores might go free, might kill again, but she refused to put more people at risk. Sorry, rest of the world. Sorry, Mr. U.S. District Attorney, who couldn't get his big barracuda without Flores. He hadn't managed to get him with her, either.

She heard low voices, then the front door scraped open against the wood floor. The new quiet unsettled her even more than the darkness had.

The silence was broken by a faint, hissing pop and then a high-pitched whelp. *Champ!*

She shot to her feet. She stopped with one hand on the slide bolt and the other flat against the metal-plate door.

What could she do? She had no weapon. No way to help. But she could be a target. It was her the guy wanted. Juan's order resounded in her head. Her hands dropped, and she rested her forehead against the cold steel.

"Oh, Champ," she whimpered, fighting tears.

Seconds passed before another pop and crack of wood splintering mixed with the men's voices. Despite her ingrained inability to sit on the sidelines, she had to trust these men and their plan.

She pressed her ear to the door, desperate to get some idea of what was happening. To find out if Champ was okay. She made out the strain of voices but couldn't decipher the words or who spoke. Why hadn't they put a surveillance monitor in here?

Seconds turned to minutes—minutes that transformed the meaning of time.

Finally, Devin's Jeep rumbled up, then cut off as voices grew louder, closer. She recognized AJ and Devin's anxious tones before the front door slammed against the cabin wall. Champ's whine sliced away a piece of her heart.

"It'll be okay. We got you." Devin's gentle tone didn't soothe her.

Come. Give me the safe word. No one came. Other voices, mainly Ray's deep rumble, faded again outside.

What the hell was happening?

Another eternity passed before she pounded on the door. "Hello!" What could it hurt?

"Shit! Be right back." It sounded like AJ. "You have to unlock it from the inside."

Duh. She knew that. "What's the safe word?" She'd followed protocol so far, might as well not abandon ship now.

"Safe word? Um ... Oh. Karma!"

Close enough. Juan's added "baby" was probably not part of it anyway. It took two hands to slide the metal bolt free and pull open the heavy door.

Her knees buckled at the sight of blood covering AJ's sweatshirt. She grabbed his arms to keep from falling. "Oh God! What happened?" She went into triage mode and scanned his body for wounds. "Where are you hurt?"

"What? No, it's not my blood. It's Champ's."

Her own blood stopped moving, just like a rush-hour traffic jam. "How bad?" She skirted AJ and bolted out of the bedroom. Dev's body blocked her view of an unmoving Champ, laid out on the kitchen counter. "Is he ...?" She couldn't say it. "Please tell me he's alive."

"Yeah. I sedated him. He's hit in the right shoulder. Found the exit wound." He used the hand sprayer to gently irrigate the wound. "Hand me that gauze to pack it."

She did as he instructed, despite the less than prime or sterile surgical conditions.

"Bullet didn't hit vital organs. He's going to be okay."

She didn't know veterinary medicine but wanted to believe Devin's attempt to reassure her.

Her mind moved past Champ to the cause of his injury. "Did you get him?" *God, please let them have the son of a bitch.* Victorious relief surged through her when AJ nodded. "Where is he?"

"They took him to the other cabin for now."

"That should do until we get him to a vet," Devin proclaimed after he wrapped the wound. "He'll need a drain and antibiotics."

"You two take him to the emergency animal clinic," AJ said.

She hesitated, torn between taking care of Champ and the need to face the man who likely killed Hal. "But …"

"Let us take care of things here. Champ needs you," AJ said as if reading her mind.

"Promise to tell me what you find out. Because if he killed Hal, I need to …" What? She didn't know exactly.

"Get a blanket and help me load him up," Devin said.

She hurried to get the blanket from her bed, interrupting whatever AJ was quietly telling Devin as she returned.

She climbed into the back seat, and they laid Champ next to her. "I'm sorry, boy, but he's not going to get away with this." She ran a hand over the silky fur on his head, and a few tears escaped.

"Text me after you're done at the animal hospital. Then Dev's gonna take you to Vincenti's to stay with Angela tonight. Get some sleep."

Devin pulled away before she could make AJ promise to let her come back.

AJ WAITED until Dev's Jeep disappeared into the darkness before rejoining the team. He reached for the knob and stepped into the light.

The team surrounded an unimposing male, seated on one of the kitchen chairs with his hands flex-cuffed behind his back. The chief stood less than three feet in front of the guy, who didn't attempt to look up at Lundgren's face. His gaze darted around the room, avoiding direct eye contact.

"No ID on him." Kyle finished searching the pockets of a camouflage hooded jacket and dropped it on the back of a kitchen chair. A set of keys, several energy bars, a water bottle, and an ammo clip were spread out on the table.

"There's no reason to haul me in here, cuff, and interrogate me. I was just hunting," he protested.

"At night? With an assault rifle, a thermal scope, and a suppressor? Nice equipment to leave behind. Why don't you tell me what you're hunting?" Mack aimed the M-4 with a 300 Blackout suppressor toward their captive. The thermal blanket the guy had been hiding under draped over the chair next to him. "This kind of hunting the law calls murder."

"I didn't kill anyone. Now, *this* is unlawful detainment."

"You shot a dog," Mack said.

"I thought it was a coyote coming at me."

"You shot at me, too," Porter countered. "Good thing you're not a very good shot or have an M203 grenade launcher."

"True." The guy smirked and gave a slight shrug.

Damn. Had he tried to get that kind of weapon? AJ's heart pounded. If he'd managed that, Cassidy, Linc, Juan, Champ—they could all be dead.

"Shooting isn't your MO You usually prefer a more subtle approach," Lundgren said. "Bee venom. Carbon monoxide. Guess you didn't care about making it look like an accident this time."

"I have no idea what you're talking about. If you think I'm guilty of something beyond not being a good hunter, go ahead and turn me over to the local police."

"I don't think we need to involve the authorities. We're quite capable of handling this—our own way." Lundgren's voice rained down on the man.

The oh-fuck-I'm-screwed registered on his face and gave AJ a major twist of satisfaction. *That's right, asshole, you came expecting two U.S. marshals, and you're getting a whole team of whoop-ass.* And AJ didn't feel like playing by the rules.

"Want to give us your name?" Lundgren asked.

"John. John Smith."

Tony gave a gruff laugh.

"That was it says on your hunting license?" Lundgren moved a few inches closer. "Where's that?"

"Must have left that in my car."

"Of course, you did. Boy Scout with Champ?" Lundgren asked AJ.

"Taking him to the vet." AJ noted Lundgren wasn't going to reveal the real names of the team, either.

"You and Lucky Dragon go check our friend's car, gray sedan, right? See if you find that hunting license. Want to make sure you're in compliance with the law." Lundgren gave AJ his keys along with Smith's.

"You've got no reason to search my vehicle," Smith said as Kyle pick up his keys from the table.

AJ drove to where the sedan was still parked with its deflated tires. While Kyle checked the inside, AJ opened the trunk. The case for the rifle was there. He poked through a bag of food items, then rummaged through a suitcase. Nothing but clothes and toiletries.

"Car's a rental. Registration won't help." In the passenger seat, Kyle held up a small piece of paper. "Bingo!" he exclaimed.

AJ slammed the trunk shut.

"Three phones in this hidden compartment under the armrest. Wallet with two IDs. Credit cards in both names." Kyle scooped up their haul.

"No hunting license?" AJ asked dryly.

Back at the cabin, they handed the wallet to Lundgren.

"Cheap burner phones. All passcode protected," AJ laid them on the table.

Lundgren's mouth shifted to a scowl while he studied the IDs. "You must be confused, Mr. Smith, or Sean Curry, or Richard Johnson. We should run your prints."

The man Smith gave a nonchalant shrug.

Tony rummaged in the kitchen cabinets, coming back with two bowls, a drinking glass, and a box of cornstarch. "Lighter?"

AJ fished a lighter out of his pocket and took the bowl from Tony, then held the flame under the bowl until a layer of black soot formed.

Lundgren wiped the glass clean, then pressed Smith's fingers to the exterior without him resisting.

AJ scraped the soot into the cornstarch Tony had poured in the other bowl. After mixing the two, AJ dusted it over the glass, blowing away the excess powder. He clung to the remote hope this guy's prints were on record somewhere, despite his cavalier attitude.

Juan picked up one of the phones from the kitchen table, then the other two. "There's letters written in Sharpie on each. C.B., N.D., and A.R."

A.R.?

The room went silent again. A tremor swept through AJ's body. Was he next on this asshole's list? Did he know about him and Cassidy? "Were you coming after me?"

"Maybe." Smith's left eye narrowed in an honest telling of confusion, but his mouth turned up in an arrogant bluff.

Tony gave a forceful shake of his head, clearly annoyed with the guy's bullshit, yet reassuring AJ that the initials weren't connected to him.

"Where's Avila?"

"Who?" Smith's head snapped left from the slap to the

side of his skull. He glared up at Lundgren. "That's your plan? To beat or torture it out of me? I can't tell you what I don't know."

"Tell us which of these phones is the one to contact him and how to unlock it. We can do the rest." Lundgren's demeanor mellowed to good-guy cop.

"Pass. You got nothing on me."

"You put a lock on the outside of the closet?" Lundgren's gaze went to Tony, who gave an affirmative nod.

"How long do you think you can keep me here?"

"As long as we need. Something tells me no one is gonna miss you." Tony hauled Smith up from the chair by his bound hands, making him grunt in pain. "What was it Hal used to say? You need to know where to hide the body before you need to hide the body?"

Smith's head jerked up as he searched the men's faces. His countenance wavered.

Yeah, the son of a bitch had a lot to think about.

Lundgren led them outside. Tony manhandled Smith with AJ and Juan following at their heels.

Smith in Hal's cabin evoked a fresh surge of rage for AJ to tamp down. Despite the implied threats, he wanted this asshole locked up for life. A quick, painless death meant giving him the easy way out.

"Hang on a second." Juan cut in front of Smith before Tony could shove him in the closet. Juan pulled out the ottoman. "Don't want to make it too comfortable for him."

"Right." Smith's lip curled.

"We plan to be nice." Tony cut the flex-cuffs to free Smith's hand from behind his back, only to secure his hands together in front of him.

"We'll even give you a drink." Juan opened the ottoman and removed a water bottle.

"Gee, thanks. Do I get bathroom breaks every three hours, too?" Smith's sarcastic bite pushed another button on AJ's reasons-to-peel-off-the-guy's-fingernails list.

"That's what the bottle's for." Tony forced Smith inside. "If you need anything else, knock, and I'll be right here to ignore you." He closed the door and dropped the metal bar into the latch.

Sleep tight, asshole.

TWENTY-FOUR

"How's Champ?" AJ was at Cassidy's side as soon as she got out of Devin's Jeep.

"He was happy to see us this morning. The vet wanted to keep him at the animal hospital today and tonight to monitor him, but he said he'll make a full recovery."

"You get some sleep?"

"Some. You?"

"About the same." He glanced Devin's way before he leaned in to kiss her.

"Did you learn anything from the guy?"

"Not yet. We'll see if we get any hits from prints or facial recognition." AJ's tone didn't burst with confidence.

"And if you don't …?"

"He might be afraid of Avila, but we're the ones in his face and crawling up his ass. He'll crack. But you don't have to be here. You can wait in the other cabin."

"By myself, or are you willing to be with me while your team deals with this guy?"

AJ gave a tell-tale swallow. "I'll go with you. Whatever you want."

"I need to see him."

He gave her hand a squeeze. It was the fortification she needed before she faced the man inside. She wasn't alone. She was safe.

In Hal's cabin, a wooden chair sat in the middle of the room. The rest of the team stood around, all focused on Ray on the phone.

"It's time." He set his coffee mug on the kitchen counter after ending his call, but the once-over he gave her was enough to clue her in that he'd prefer she wasn't there.

"My pleasure." Tony pushed off the counter and disappeared into the main bedroom. "Rise and shine!" He pounded on the metal door. "Up."

Tony led in the man with cuffed hands. He didn't look like she expected. No more than late thirties, he looked more accountant than killer. The type to hold open the door for a woman in hopes of getting noticed and a smile. No one you'd cross the street to avoid. Except, his eyes absorbed all light into their black-hole depths.

From the way he looked at her, she could practically feel his hands around her throat. She met his gaze dead on, her eyes filled with hate. *You lose, asshole.*

"Good news, John Smith. Johnson. Curry. We've solved your identity crisis." Ray paused. "Facial recognition matched you to a driver's license. A few years back, but it's a definite match, Daniel Kraus. And you sell life insurance. Isn't that interesting?"

Kraus's chest sucked inward before he let out a steady breath. He watched Ray pick up his coffee mug and take a swig, probably salivating for a strong cup of java. Tony blew on his own steaming cup, sending the aroma Kraus's way.

"Then you know I don't have a record. You're casting wild accusations at an innocent man."

"True. No criminal *record. However,*" Ray drew out the words, "they got a hit on your prints."

Kraus's head angled up cautiously, betraying nothing.

Cassidy prayed the chief had solid intel versus bluffing him into a confession.

"Your prints match those in the files for an unsolved murder of a call girl in the D.C. area. A Wendy Michaels. Ring any bells?" Ray leaned over Kraus, who shrank back against the chair, his focus locked on a spot on the floor. An inaudible *Shit!* played out on his now pale face.

"She was strangled. A pretty different MO. I'd bet she was your first kill. Am I right?"

No answer. No claims of innocence.

More of a resignation that life as he knew it was O-V-E-R. Cassidy cast a smile AJ's way. He smiled right back, giving her another hit of hope.

"A call girl? Why'd you kill her?" Tony asked. "You wanted a *Pretty Woman* moment, and she wouldn't give up other guys?"

"My money's on you not satisfying her. She make fun of the size of your package?" Juan taunted.

Kraus lurched forward, but his butt didn't leave the chair—and he didn't make any retorts.

"She steal something? Try blackmailing you?" Ray took a stab. "You like things rough and went too far?"

Kraus's jaw shifted, and his gaze dropped again.

What would this sick bastard have done if he'd gotten her alone? Cassidy shivered at the thought.

"Was it the thrill of the kill or getting away with it that got ya?" Ray pressed on. "Couldn't stand not being able to brag to anyone, so you had to do it again?"

A cocky smirk flitted over the asshole's face at Ray's suggestion. "What'll it take to let me go?"

"Five to ten thousand feet between you and the ground."

Kraus's head jerked back as Ray's threat became clear.

"You killed Master Sergeant Boswell. Went after her family to draw her out."

"Who?" Kraus continued to play innocent.

Though Ray's arm flexed like he wanted to punch Kraus, he held back.

Cassidy eyed AJ. His fists were clenched at his sides, and the way his lips curled, she knew he wanted to inflict some physical pain on the asshole. She wanted to join that party herself.

"He was part of our family. You made it personal. That was your mistake."

"You've got nothing but speculation."

"We've got you. After looking for her for two years, you were so close. How's it feel?" Ray asked him.

"I haven't been looking that long. Whoever Avila had looking for her didn't get the job done. He made it an open contract. Do what you want to me, but it won't put an end to the contract."

Tony's scowl deepened, and she'd swear AJ growled.

Goosebumps broke out on Cassidy's arms. She wanted Kraus to be bluffing about the open contract, but if Avila was worried that his thugs hadn't found her, it made sense he might put out a professional contract.

Why after so long, someone had been desperate enough to find her connection to Hal.

Even Ray didn't say anything for a few seconds, but the muscle in his cheek twitched as he stepped closer.

"Now, if it appears the job's been done …" Kraus started.

"You're not walking away free."

"Then what are you offering?"

"Your life, not in chronic pain, with all your anatomy

intact." Ray crossed his arms in front of his chest in a relaxed pose.

"Darn." Tony turned it into a two-syllable word as he ran a finger along the blade of the combat knife in his hand.

"What do you want?" Kraus spat out the words when no one else spoke, and only the occasional happy twitter of birds broke the silence.

"Avila," Ray said in a way that sent chills down Cassidy's spine.

"I don't know where he is," Kraus insisted.

"But you have a number. A way to reach him. Give that to us. We'll do the rest. He won't know it came from you."

Kraus's eyes narrowed. His mouth stayed sealed in a tight line, then he exhaled testily through his nose. His lips parted, huffing out another annoyed-sounding breath. "Stored in the phone."

"Which one, and what's the passcode?"

Kraus hesitated. "The one with the A.R. initials."

Cassidy gasped, hearing AJ's initials. Had Kraus found out about them? Was he targeting AJ like he had Hal?

"You trust him?" Mack asked.

Ray picked up the first phone. "C.B. Who's that?"

"Not important."

"It is to somebody," Ray countered. "Let's call it a test. What's the security code to unlock it?" He kicked the chair when Kraus didn't answer.

"C-B-0-8-2-9-T-B."

Ray's mouth morphed into a frown. "All right. Who's your contact?"

Kraus shrugged. "I don't ask."

"See what you can find out." Ray handed the phone to Linc, who settled at the laptop on the kitchen table.

In under ten minutes, they knew the sole number stored in

the phone belonged to Taryn Brooker, a woman in her midthirties married to a guy a decade older who'd made a fortune with discount hair salons.

"Hospital records for a few ER visits for Taryn, including a broken wrist and a dislocated elbow. No obituary for her husband popped up. Sorry, Taryn, looks like you'll have to settle for divorce and alimony," Linc said.

"That's a big step from taking out a spouse to accepting a contract offered by one of the biggest gunrunners in the hemisphere," Ray said.

"Big money."

"The letters …?" Ray probed, picking up the two remaining burner phones.

"Initials. My way of keeping them straight. And discreet."

"Taryn Brooker would be T.B. Her husband's Ron. C.B.?"

"Someone famous in the past for being beating on women."

Around the room, heads tilted as they caught on to his system.

"And A.R.?"

"Anastasia Romanov. Redheaded Russian princess who disappeared to keep from being killed." The glower he fixed on Cassidy could peel the paint off a house.

"What's the passcode?" Ray's finger poised over the screen.

"A-R-0-9-1-7-F-A."

"The numbers. That's my birthday." This guy knew her birthdate, making her feel violated, but at least A.R. was her and not AJ.

"Asshole," Juan muttered.

"Check Ron Brooker's birthday," Ray instructed Linc.

"Numbers in the passcode match his birthdate," Linc confirmed quickly.

"Told you. I'm trying to be cooperative."

Based on the men's expressions, no one in the room bought Kraus's reformed performance.

"There's no contacts." Ray's slow, low enunciation silenced the room.

"Downloads."

Ray tapped on the screen. His annoyed sigh lasted several seconds. "Same password?"

"No. I'll type it in."

Gruff laughs echoed in the small room.

"Don't think so."

Unrelenting, Kraus met Ray's gaze. "I can't tell you."

"Because …?"

"Just let me."

Lundgren nodded to Tony, who moved closer, wearing the kind of malevolent smile that would make a normal person head in another direction—if he weren't bound and surrounded.

"All right," Kraus conceded. "C-L-0-5-1-8."

"Which is …?"

"The password." Kraus's lips sealed shut.

Ray's finger touched the screen, one hesitant tap at a time. His mouth pursed; his steely gaze fixed on Kraus. "You were watching the funeral. See if she showed?"

Kraus didn't confirm and wouldn't make eye contact.

"Hal and Champ." Ray flashed the phone her way, and she glimpsed a picture of Hal and Champ outside his house. "Pretty substantial evidence." He flicked through several more pictures. "Who's this?"

The corners of Kraus's mouth drew up in a tense, telling manner. His eyes closed as tight as his mouth, his head sinking a few more degrees.

Ray warily turned the phone to show Cassidy.

"That's my mom," she stuttered, frantically grabbing the phone from his hand. "And my sister. And ... you son of a bitch!" The phone fell and bounced on the floor as she lunged for Kraus, getting in one wildly aimed, but solid, smack to the side of his skull before Devin intervened and pulled her away.

Ray retrieved the phone and concentrated on the screen. He whistled through his teeth. "It's the contract information."

"The file confirms what he said about it being an open contract. We can turn him over, but there's no telling who else is looking to find her. Get command to trace this number, and we need to get everything we can on Avila."

"I'll see what JSOC can dig up." Tony already had his phone out. From his greeting and tone, he had to be talking to Angela.

Voices became a buzz as her mind spun like it'd been caught in a whirlpool, sucking her thoughts into the dark waters. Going after Hal had been bad enough, but seeing Brodie and Aidan's pictures on an assassin's phone ... would this ever end?

"Give him an energy bar and put him back in the closet," Ray ordered.

"I'm cooperating," Kraus protested.

"Cooperating?" Cassidy snapped out of her fog. "You killed my stepfather. Tried to kill me. Shot my dog. And had pictures of my nephew and niece, my sister and mom. They're putting you in there to keep me from slicing your fucking throat."

Dead silence.

"You wouldn't," Kraus called her bluff.

"Not before I saw those pictures."

They let him sweat a minute in the men's silence before Mack led him away.

"Damn. That was impressive." AJ slipped an arm over her shoulders and pressed a kiss to her temple.

"And a little scary," Juan added.

She released a long breath once Kraus was out of sight. Still, with what he'd said about the contract, this wasn't over.

Avila. This went back to him. He wanted *her* dead.

She wanted Kraus to pay. She also wanted to have a life again. One without looking over her shoulder, watching every word, or analyzing each new person she met.

What where the chances AJ's team could find and get to Avila when authorities had failed? If they couldn't, there was only one other option.

Refuse to testify.

Letting Avila and Flores walk might be the only way to keep her and the people she cared about alive.

TWENTY-FIVE

Tony made for the window of the borrowed cabin before Cassidy heard the car stop. Even though the guys assured her assassins almost always worked alone, and they'd found nothing to indicate Kraus had a partner, he peeked through the blinds.

"It's Ang." He smiled and tucked his weapon back in his holster.

The afternoon had stretched into a non-productive, almost outlandish series of plans to locate and nab Avila. Other than the planning, the guys had been quiet, but the looks and few snatches of conversation she'd overheard told her the sum Avila offered went beyond substantial.

Unfortunately, the guys had little intel on the man himself. Angela Hoffman, however, had something she'd gotten from her contacts. Enough to warrant bringing it out herself. The team let Tony have a minute alone with Angela rather than follow him outside.

"Do you know how much I love this woman?" Tony carried in four pizza boxes, Angela right behind him with an armful of file folders.

"I think that's going to be unanimous love," Mack agreed, grabbing plates out of the drying rack.

AJ tugged on Cassidy's hand, wordlessly urging her to eat something.

"This is better than pizza." Angela spread several files on the table. "It's everything the CIA, ATF, DEA, Homeland Security, NSA, the SEC, and FBI have on Felix Avila."

"Holy shit!" came out of AJ's mouth.

"I can relate to your situation." Angela regarded Cassidy sympathetically, strengthening the connection she already felt to Tony's girlfriend. "I cashed in a few favors, owe one, and, well, I'm not above a little blackmail."

"That's why you couldn't email it." Tony bit into a fragrant slice covered with pepperoni, sausage, onions, and extra cheese.

"Exactly. But I also brought a flash drive with the files to do searches like you asked." She tossed the USB drive to Devin.

Though GPS coordinates placed Avila in the Riviera Maya area, she couldn't get her hopes up yet. That info was just step one. Hopefully, one of the agencies had intel the team could use to get close enough to locate him.

"Somebody want to tell the chief dinner's on, and we got files?"

"Not before I get some food." Kyle loaded up a plate.

"Four extra-large pizzas? Should be plenty. Even he can't eat half." Angela jerked a thumb at Tony.

"You haven't seen the chief after three days of our cooking." Mack laughed and grabbed another piece.

"Guess we should feed Kraus something," Kyle said. The rest of the team grunted or ignored his statement.

"We've got leftover pork and beans you can give Kraus."

Mack pointed toward the fridge when Kyle picked up an extra plate.

"That'll do. Pizza's too good for him." Tony grabbed another slice.

"I'll take it over and tell the chief," Devin volunteered. He found the container of leftovers in the fridge, tucked it under his arm, and loaded nearly half a pizza onto two plates before heading out the door to Hal's cabin.

Cassidy nibbled on her slice, with her eyes locked on the stack of files.

They were down to one pizza when Ray hustled in a few minutes later. "You are an angel," he said to Angela, picking up a slice of pizza. A third of it disappeared in one bite. "Whatcha got?"

Angela ticked off the list of agencies she'd contacted while Ray finished off that piece and reached for another, using a plate this time.

"Other than the CIA file, most of them came in late this afternoon. I've only had a chance to glance through them. ATF didn't arrive until after sixteen hundred hours, so I only skimmed it while I made copies."

"Impressive work," Ray said after swallowing.

"Thanks. You guys are also on the hook to let some NSA guys train with you for two days—and it doesn't look like they had much useful intel, but I wanted to cover all the bases." She pushed files to each of the guys. "What have you got so far?"

"Got a phone number that command was able to trace and get a location for. Now that we know where he is, we need to plan how to get him and bring him in for trial," AJ answered.

Angela's mouth opened. Her gaze swept the men's faces before words finally spilled out. "I hate to tell you this, but I wouldn't bank on that being his location." She reached for the file labeled ATF and flipped through it.

"What do you mean?" AJ frowned, delivering another blow to Cassidy's hopes.

"Avila doesn't use just one phone." Angela ran her finger down a page in the file. "ATF has a dozen numbers associated with him. He rotates the phones between his lieutenants so they're in use, but it's like musical chairs with phones."

"You gotta be fucking kidding me," AJ blurted out.

"You didn't expect Avila to make it easy, did you? There's a reason he's been able to avoid ATF and every other agency that wants him."

"In addition to half the Mexican authorities accepting enough *dinero* to look the other way, we got this. Shit. Shit. Shit!" Tony groused.

Cassidy closed her eyes. The pizza she'd eaten bubbled up to burn the back of her throat before she swallowed it back down. She tucked her hair behind her ear to discreetly brush away a tear.

"What the hell do we do? Get UAVs and surveillance teams on all his phones at once to pinpoint him?" AJ clearly wasn't giving up despite the overwhelming odds.

"It won't be a layup, but any information here helps us narrow down the odds," Ray said as Cassidy stepped back and slipped out of the circle.

She needed air, fresh air to cleanse her lungs, clear her mind. To feel free instead of trapped in a glass cage where everyone stared at her.

She opened the cabin door and quickly closed it behind her. The cold, crisp air filled her lungs but didn't change the bleak outlook of her circumstances. Those men were doing everything they could think of, even putting their lives in jeopardy for her, but it wasn't enough.

Where had doing the right thing gotten her? Her whole life was turned upside down, inside out, and spun in circles. Maybe it was time to concede. Send these guys home to their wives and families. This wasn't their battle. Kraus had killed Hal. He could be tried.

Let someone else deal with Avila. How many times had Hal walked away rather than fight with her mother? He'd told her more than once that sometimes it wasn't about winning or losing, but surviving.

The idea that everyone would be better off if she disappeared had more merit than trying to do what multiple government agencies had been unable to do.

AJ joined her at the porch railing. "You okay?" His voice had returned to a more mellow state.

"I should have known better than to get my hopes up. Every time I do, the earth opens up to swallow them whole."

"Don't wave the white flag yet. Let us have a crack at Avila."

"It's not just Avila. It's … I don't know. All I've ever wanted was stability. A non-dysfunctional family. A father figure. When Mom married her second husband, I thought we'd have this fairy-tale life. We lived in a fabulous house, didn't want for anything materially. Sherri and I were part of the package deal, but it never felt like a family.

"Then Hal came along. It was perfect for the first nine months or so. I had a dad. Someone to teach me, protect me, love me. Then he deployed for six months. Six long, lonely months. Things were great when he came back, but that only lasted until his next deployment. Mom didn't understand why he couldn't stay. Things kept going downhill until there was no joy or hope left." She'd taken it harder than her mom.

"But I powered through. Got a degree, a job, a boyfriend. Then Reynaldo Flores decides to unburden his soul in front of me and, poof, there went all my hope for a future. It's the suck-ass story of my life. Why should this be any different?"

Why should she put these guys in danger? Risk destroying their families?

"It's different because we're here. And it's time for karma to catch up with Felix Avila. Don't give up—we aren't." AJ wrapped his arms around her and pulled her to his chest.

He stroked her back, his hands and body heat keeping the last ember of hope from completely dying out.

"Let's go inside and see what we can dig up for his grave."

She gave a weak nod. AJ might be unwilling to give up and accept her fate, but the rest of the team would help him see this was a battle they couldn't win.

Inside the cabin, energy thrummed as the men poured over files.

"Here. You want to help?" Angela slid a file folder in her direction. What looked to be one of the thinnest files, with a label reading: FBI.

Better than sitting around being useless. Cassidy opened the file. "SECRET" in bold red capital letters above Felix Avila's name stopped her. "Are you sure I'm allowed to read this?"

"You're his target. I think it's allowed. Just don't go posting it on social media." Angela winked.

Cassidy didn't know what she was looking for, though what she read painted a horrific picture of a cruel and dangerous man behind an international gun-smuggling cartel.

"Says here Avila took over his father's share of the business after Gerardo Avila was arrested and went to prison—where he died," Mack read from a report in his file.

"Mexican prisons suck," Ray said.

"This CIA report alludes to Gerardo's younger brother,

Ignacio, ratting him out. Felix Avila ran things with his Uncle Ignacio, but after Gerardo died, they battled for control until Ignacio was eliminated in a drive-by assassination."

Tony shook his head. "Nothing like family feuds."

"You got family in the mafia, don't ya, Vincenti?" Juan said with a straight face.

"Yeah. All Italians do, asshole. Like all Hispanics run drugs or arms." Tony rolled his eyes at Juan.

"Let's stay focused. So, we know he's competitive, and with his dad dying in prison, he's even more motivated to avoid being locked up. That's nothing we didn't already know," Ray said.

"This is interesting." Angela's eyes lit up. "Page four of the CIA dossier. Avila's married, but he cheats."

"Again, no big surprise," Ray interjected. "Does he have a steady mistress we can track?"

"No such luck, however, he has some *unusual* interests," Angela hinted.

"Like *Fifty Shades* interests?" Tony grinned.

Angela shrugged. "Haven't read it. Not going to. Avila likes swinging and threesomes. And, apparently, he doesn't care if it's two women or a male and female."

"I am so not doing that!" Juan spoke up first.

"His wife involved in that?" Linc asked.

Cassidy didn't like where this was going.

Angela ran a finger back and forth across the lines of text. "Occasionally, they think. When it's two females."

"I can see Avila not wanting another *guy* doing his wife," Tony started.

"Yeah, but what about him?" Kyle's face mimicked a child's who'd sucked on a lemon.

"Possibly a power-trip thing more than a sexual turn-on," Tony speculated. "Don't look at me that way, cuz no!"

"You're the one who brought it up, dude," Juan goaded.

"Might be time for Grant to get undercover experience," Tony offered.

"You guys know I'm one-hundred-percent straight, right?" Devin protested.

"*Sure,* we do," Juan taunted Devin now. "That's why three dates and you drop a chick—like every time."

"Let's stay focused on the task at hand." Ray shook his head like the parent of spatting siblings and left Devin with his mouth open but unable to refute the charge. "Besides, you can't exactly walk up to the guy and say you hear he likes a ménage and offer to go home with him. We'll keep it in mind, though."

"DAMN, Avila has two to six armed guards with him at all times." Linc stared at the photos spread out in front of him. "One could be his double, too."

"Probably intentional." Mack looked over Linc's shoulder.

"But Viviana doesn't have bodyguards on her," AJ said. The realization dawned on him like a light switched on. He dug back through his file folder to the pictures of Viviana Avila.

"Man, she's smoking hot." Juan took the photo from AJ's hand only to have Angela claim it.

"He's right. We've been going at this all wrong." Angela turned pages in the DEA folder, going quiet as she read. "Viviana is the way to get in striking distance of Avila. He's always got his guard up and guards around him. But the right person could get close to Viviana without being perceived as a threat. What's her background?"

AJ skipped ahead to the notes in the CIA file on her. "Daughter of one of Ignacio's lieutenants. Three brothers. Mother died shortly after she turned sixteen. Married Felix when she turned eighteen."

Angela gathered the pictures of Viviana from her file and lined them up with his as AJ talked. "Notice anything in these?"

"No bodyguards?" He'd already pointed that out, though.

"Look what she's holding."

"Shopping bags," AJ said.

Lundgren crowded closer.

"Looks like the same store logo, though based on what she's wearing, these were clearly taken on different days. What do women with too much money and too much time do? They shop." Angela gave a confident smile. "She may have a favorite store. Let's see if we can identify the logo and match it to a location."

"It's a starting point. What are you proposing?" Lundgren's voice held that this-mission's-going-down confidence AJ had come to know and trust over their years together.

"The key is Viviana. She makes a friend while shopping. She invites the new friend to do something, maybe get the couples together, and you've got an in. Trust me. It works. It's how I ended up as Elena Vasquez's nanny."

"We'll need a female operative then," Lundgren mused.

"I volunteer." Angela raised a hand.

"Not happening." Tony's tone was one hundred twelve percent don't-mess-with-me.

"Why not?" Angela didn't blink as she met Tony's gaze dead on.

"That's not your job."

"My *job* is to keep your team safe."

"Back at JSOC. Not in the field where Avila can get his … No."

"You'd rather take your chances with an unknown asset than someone who can read you like a picture book and who you read just as easily?"

"That's not fair. You're every bit as sexy as his wife. I don't want to risk you getting in a compromising position with a perv like Avila."

"It could end up being you instead. Come on, you've already seen that I can handle myself." She winked at Tony, but his stern expression didn't waver. Not even an iota. She turned to Lundgren. "You tell him I'm in."

"I'm staying out of this. Vincenti's call."

Angela's eyes narrowed, and she huffed out a sigh.

AJ could understand Tony not wanting to put the woman he was head over freakin' heels in love with in danger, but she had a point.

"Look, if anyone understands the predicament Cassidy's in, it's me," Angela tried again. "I want to help. I can do this. And I don't want to see you cozy up with a CIA operative who doesn't have your back like I would."

"Cozy up?"

"You're going to have to put on a bit of a show to fuel Avila's imagination and get him where you want him. Then, *bam!*" Angela clapped her hands. "You close the trap."

"I thought Grant was going undercover on this," Tony rumbled.

"I'd do it for Cassidy," Dev volunteered.

Dev was an adrenaline junkie, a risk-taker, but it was the compassion for the woman AJ cared about that played on Dev's face, bonding them tighter than brothers.

Lundgren shook his head. "On this, with Avila, it's gotta be Vincenti. We need the powerful intimidation factor."

"This your way of making me let her get her way?" Tony asked.

"Thinking of the best plan for overall success of the mission." Lundgren finished his statement with a hint of a smile.

Tony heaved a long, drawn-out sigh that told AJ they were moving ahead.

Cassidy stood, shaking her head. "I can't ask you to do this. There're too many ways this could go wrong. I already have to live with Hal being murdered because of me—"

"You couldn't control that." Lundgren attempted to reassure her.

"No, and I can't change what happened, but this I can control."

"So, you'd give up? Spend the rest of your life in witness protection? Unable to see your family, the people you care about?" *Including me.* AJ knew it was a low blow, but he didn't want Cassidy to give up hope on a future. Not since she revived his dreams of a wife and family. What they could have went beyond comfort sex when she needed a lifeline. He needed her to see that, to trust him. To trust this team.

She had to let them give this a shot. Then, if they couldn't get Avila, he had one option left to be with her: Leave the team and go with her to keep her safe.

"That's not what I want. It's just—"

"Give us a chance. It's what Hal would want." Lundgren once again attempted to overcome her objections.

"I need you to promise you won't do anything you'll regret later." Cassidy looked directly at AJ.

"Trust me, there's nothing that could happen to Avila that I'd regret," AJ assured her.

"Can you really say that? Maybe you think if he's dead, it will solve my problems. Maybe give you a sense of justice about Hal's murder. But Avila didn't put a hit on Hal. From those pictures, that was probably Kraus's own idea."

"But Avila did put a hit on you." AJ was not backing down.

"Yes, but I'm alive. That doesn't make it an eye for an eye or a life for a life. You can't be posse, jury, judge, and executioner. That's not your job and—"

"Well, in some ca—" Juan started.

"Shut up, Juan," Cassidy cut him off. "It goes against the Army values of honor and integrity."

Damn. AJ squirmed. Did Hal have that printed on a T-shirt or teach her that, too?

"If you can't promise me, you guys need to call this whole thing off because you aren't going after Avila for the right reasons."

"She's right," Angela chimed in. "This is about getting Avila in custody and to trial."

"Can you promise me?"

"Yes," AJ answered half-heartedly.

"Say it." She called him out. Her eyes didn't waver from his face.

"I won't assassinate Avila." That much he could likely promise. Mack might be on the other end of the sniper rifle, though.

Her head cocked to the side as if reading his mind. Her eyes narrowed, and the left side of her mouth shifted in exasperation. She extended a fist with her pinkie finger extended. "Pinkie swear?"

Was she freakin' kidding him? "I'm U.S. Army Special Forces. I don't pinkie swear. My word is my bond." He covered her hand with his and slid his other hand to her lower back. "I'll seal it with a kiss."

Cassidy turned her face to offer up her cheek instead of

her lips. He pressed a kiss to the warm skin. "I mean it," she whispered. "You can't let this fulfill your parent's prophecy. Do not sacrifice your honor over Avila."

He inhaled her scent, let her words swirl around his brain, then travel down to rap on his heart's door. For years, he'd done everything he could to prove himself to his family on his terms. He might never get their respect. But if he lost Cassidy's respect ...

That. Would. Kill. Him.

TWENTY-SIX

"Damn. How many boats has Avila had?"

Cassidy looked up from her file when Linc broke the silence engulfing the group.

"He's into offshore sport fishing. ATF's tried tracking his boat, but he apparently has it swept regularly because the GPS trackers go MIA every time." Ray frowned in frustration.

"That would be ideal—let the Navy pick him up without him surrounded by a dozen armed bodyguards." Linc turned another page in his file.

"Is he trading boats trying to throw them off? That doesn't make sense," Mack said.

"Hang on." Linc tapped on his laptop keyboard. "Looks like he keeps getting bigger ones."

"Instead of penis envy, this guy has boat envy and wants the biggest vessel to catch the biggest fish?" Loathing laced AJ's statement, but Cassidy smiled at how his comment sounded like something Hal would have said.

"We might be able to use this," Lundgren mused. "Catch his interest with a luxurious yacht."

"Luxury being key because showing up with a Coast Guard or Navy cutter might spoil the element of surprise," Mack pointed out.

"What's the length of Avila's current fishing boat?" Devin asked.

"It's a fifty-four-footer. Three cabins."

"Shit. Are you gonna tell me your folks have a big-ass boat, too, Dev?" Juan started in.

"No. Not my parents."

"What? Grandparents? Uncle?"

"Dad of a girl I used to date."

"A girl with Daddy Bigbucks, yet you didn't marry her, either?" Juan persisted.

"Her idea of an adrenaline rush was getting all dressed up for charity events in hopes of getting her picture in the paper. You can only expect a guy to wear a tux so many times a month."

"A *month*?" Mack snickered.

"I hope you aren't planning to steal your ex's father's boat." Cassidy could see this plan going up in flames, and the team, not Avila, in prison.

"No." Devin whipped his phone out. "He likes me. I'll ask to borrow it."

"Shit. You gotta be kidding me." Juan grunted an unbelieving laugh. "My exes' dads might lend me a sinking canoe, but a multimillion-dollar yacht?"

"Grant's every parent's dream son-in-law." Tony sounded slightly envious.

"We haven't discussed this." Ray fixed Devin with a dubious look. "We don't know timing. Logistics."

"Let the kid see if it's even an option," Mack said.

"Mr. Ryan, it's Devin Grant." He already had the man on the phone, halting all other talk. "Yes, sir. I'm at Fort Bragg now. Yes, sir. Home of the 82nd Airborne and the Green Berets," he continued. "Well, Delta *Force* only exists in the movies." He rolled his eyes. "I wish I could, but most everything is classified, so I'm not privy to details. However, there is something we're working on, which is why I'm calling. Do you still own the *Fine Print*?"

"Ask him if his daughter's single," Juan whispered.

Devin held up a hand to silence Juan before stepping into the bedroom and closing the door on everyone.

"Had to go there, didn't ya, Dominguez?" Tony glared at Juan.

Cassidy tried concentrating on her file again as Devin's muffled voice leaked from the bedroom. Based on the men's restlessness, she wasn't the only one in standby mode. Tony scrounged up the last slice of pizza, then added the box to the pile of empties.

He hadn't quite finished eating when Devin burst out of the bedroom.

"The boat is in the Florida Keys. Mr. Ryan's going to let the captain know we'll be contacting him. He can send him toward Mexico, so we'll be set whenever."

"Seriously? Just like that, he gives you his yacht?" Juan threw his hands out in the same disbelief Cassidy

"There were a few conditions. He'd prefer there not be a bunch of holes in it when we're done. Although, he does have it well insured and was thinking of going smaller." Devin's animated grin brought to mind images of explosions and sinking ships. "And I promised exclusive details and a photo of Avila's arrest for his paper."

"I can't believe I'm saying this, but sounds like Grant's plan is a go," Ray said.

TWENTY-SEVEN

WHILE ANGELA and the team worked on their mission plan, Cassidy cleaned out the perishables from the cabin's refrigerator. After bagging the last of the items, she slipped outside with her phone.

When AJ joined her, she held up a finger while she finished. "Thank you so much. I'll see you tomorrow."

"Checking on Champ?"

"Yeah. The tech said he's doing great. Even put some weight on his front leg."

"Good." AJ put his arms around her, and she snuggled into his warm embrace. "Chief voluntold Juan and Linc to hang out until authorities pick up Kraus."

"With the way you caught him, there's no way he's going to get off, right?" What if authorities couldn't press charges because of a technicality, or they didn't process evidence the right way, or he got out on bail?

"We aren't going to let that happen," AJ assured her. "The chief has connections. And the colonel. Not to brag, but I think the president has him on speed dial."

She pulled back to study his face. "*The* president? That

sounds like a Hal kind of tale."

"Hal did meet one. I'm not at liberty to give details."

"Even now? Come on. Which one? W?" she guessed.

"Like I said …"

"Is there photographic evidence?"

"I'll show you someday."

"I'd like that." Learning more about Hal. Seeing AJ again. She turned her face up. His lips met hers.

They only shared a few kisses before sounds from inside signaled they were about to have company.

"I, ah, came out to ask if you wanted to go back to my place for tonight. Dev can drop us off, and I'll take you to get Champ in the morning. Then we can hang out until the marshals come to get you."

"What are my other options?"

"You … could stay at Vincenti's," he said hesitantly.

"No. I'm not staying at Tony's." She laughed and took hold of the flannel shirt he wore over a Henley. "I'm spending the night with you. I meant about contacting the marshals." The team and Angela were needed elsewhere, so she had no choice other than to return to protection custody. "Is it too much to ask for another day? You and me taking care of Champ before I have to fess up to Marshal DeLong." She pressed her forehead to his chest.

"Then I have good news and bad news. Chief talked to Colonel Mahinis. He's contacting Valone, big honcho at the Marshals Service, in the morning to smooth things over."

"Really? Whew."

AJ chuckled at her. "Don't know how fast they can make arrangements, but we're going to be pulling out for Mexico as soon as we have things in place. I'm not leaving you unprotected, so it'll be tomorrow. And with what we learned about the contract Avila offered, the marshals are going to be wrapping you up tight."

That wasn't going to be fun, but no point wasting the limited time they had left by complaining.

The front door scraped open. Angela and Tony walked out.

"You good?" Tony asked, keys in hand.

"Yeah. We'll ride with Dev."

Tony gave AJ a fist bump. "Hang in there," he told Cassidy, giving her a quick embrace. Angela followed with a longer one.

"Be careful—"

"We got this," Angela gave a confident wink. "We'll see you."

Devin came out with Kyle and Mack.

"Packed up the campsite this morning, just gotta load it up. Let me grab her bag," AJ said to Devin.

It only took a few minutes to drive over. She stayed inside the car while the guys loaded up the tent, chairs, and gear. AJ packed two large duffel bags in the front seat, then climbed in next to her. His grin did things to her insides that she hadn't felt in years.

"Come here," she gave a little tug on his shirt.

"Hi. I'm Dev. Apparently, I'll be your driver tonight," he cracked, sliding behind the wheel.

Like a good chauffeur, he ignored them on the drive. She recognized the shopping center they passed about forty-five minutes into the trip, and the road to AJ's apartment complex was familiar despite the time she'd been away.

Devin parked next to AJ's Mustang, and AJ handed her his keys.

"This stuff goes in the storage closet out back. Will you

take my bag upstairs?" With a smile, he handed her a duffle from the front seat and went to help Devin.

Cassidy retrieved her bag. She found the light switch and checked out the living room. The gray couch and black recliner strategically faced the flat-screen television. AJ's laptop and a book sat on the modern glass coffee table. There were even coasters. It was cleaner than she expected for a single guy's place, though he did keep his car immaculate.

Upstairs, she set the bags on the bed, then dug out her toothbrush. Her reflection in the mirror revealed dark circles under her eyes and wild wisps of hair that escaped the braid. She needed more than minty-fresh breath.

Freeing her hair, she ran her fingers through it to tame the waves. She applied a touch of foundation and eyeliner, then frowned at her sweatshirt.

She stripped down to the gray long-sleeved T-shirt underneath. It'd been fine for her role at the cabin, but, dammit, she wanted to look pretty for AJ. She didn't have anything close to sexy. At least her new sweater was feminine. It'd have to do—for a few minutes.

AJ walked in on her packing the sweatshirt away. "It looks good on you." He gave her a puzzled once-over.

"Thanks."

"Were you planning something other than going to bed? I thought you might be tired."

"I am. But not as tired as we're going to be when we're done." She pulled back the spread.

At AJ's throaty laugh, she peeled off her top. He was out of both his flannel shirt and Henley in seconds.

"Wait. Let me do that." He closed in on her with the stealth of a panther before she had her jeans unzipped.

They had one night for the foreseeable future, and she intended to make it memorable.

When the stereotypical black SUV pulled up in front of AJ's, Cassidy exhaled deeply. They exchanged a sorrowful look, and AJ gave her a hand a reassuring squeeze.

She could do this. Spend a few more weeks, or more likely months, sequestered away before they went to trial, then Flores would go to prison, and she went back to being Cassidy O'Shea.

After picking up Champ, AJ had gotten the call from his colonel, giving them the ETA of the marshals. They'd spent a quiet morning making sure Champ rested. While AJ had packed, she'd fixed them lunch. And then they'd talked a little about the future.

Her plan had been to go back to Chicago. Her sister was there with her family. Her old friends. The Cubs. Her job. But after two years, it wouldn't be the same. If she had to start over again, she wanted to do it here—with AJ. It'd give them a better shot than trying to do it long distance.

No point making decisions until she had a future outside of protective custody, though. She had to hold on to AJ's confidence that his team could succeed where everyone else had failed.

Champ raised his head at the solid rap on the door.

"Stay," Cassidy ordered as they got to their feet.

AJ opened the door to Flint and another marshal she remembered from New York. They wore equally disgruntled expressions.

Flint threw an I-knew-it glance from AJ to her. "Good to see you're okay, but you should have called *us*."

"I'd followed every protocol, so I didn't know how he'd found me." Chill bumps broke out on her arms, just thinking of that night. "I thought maybe … maybe … you had a leak or mole, or whatever you call it in the marshal service," she admitted.

Flint shook his head. "It wasn't us."

"It's over," AJ cut Flint off. "You can see how she might think of it coming from inside. At least she came to us, and it all worked out. She's safe. Kraus is in custody. Did they find anything when they checked out her place?"

"The fireplace vent was deliberately blocked," Flint acknowledged. "We did get a partial print from a plastic bag in the debris used that matches to Kraus."

"Good. That'll motivate him to testify for some leniency. We've got a bead on Avila. It worked out pretty damn good how I see it, so she doesn't need you giving her shit."

AJ's warrior-mode defense of her nearly made her shout, "Hooah!" Other than Hal, no man had ever defended her this way. Everything about him made her feel protected and cared for—but not like she was weak or needy. She wanted to throw her arms over AJ's shoulders and show her appreciation in a very public display of you're-my-hero affection. Only she refrained so as not to diminish his power in this face-off.

"All you have to do is keep her safe until we have him." AJ picked up her bag and handed it to Flint.

"Okay, Champ. Our ride's here. Let's take care of business."

Flint held up his hands. "The dog is not coming with us this time."

"Yes, he is. Champ's the reason we found out Kraus tampered with the fireplace vent. And he was shot protecting me."

"My understanding is that he tracked you through the dog's GPS chip," Flint protested.

"We've taken care of that. It won't happen again. We both go, or we both stay right here."

Flint's eyes closed, and he sighed like he wanted to say something but finally nodded.

"I need to be added to her authorized calling list," AJ said.

The muscle in Flint's cheek twitched. "You'll have to follow proper procedures for security."

"I have no problem with operational security." AJ's tone kept them on the same power level as he extended Flint a card identical to the one he'd given her before leaving the mountains.

Flint took his time accepting the card, then slipped it into his shirt pocket after a cursory glance. "I'll see that security procedures are emailed to you."

"Load her bag, and we'll be out in a minute."

The second marshal's head drew back, and Flint's mouth opened, then clamped shut, but they followed orders and stepped out.

"Remember what you promised me about not taking matters in your own hands with Avila."

"We've already discussed this."

"Yes, but you train over and over, so the repetition becomes ingrained." She invaded his space. "So, I'm repeating it to make sure it penetrates any selective hearing, and my voice is in your head if you—"

"I will use lethal force to protect myself and my team if warranted," he said without blinking.

"I understand." Though she prayed that AJ wouldn't be the one who had to pull the trigger if it came to that. She couldn't risk him doubting whether it'd been necessary and have that eating away at him—at his relationship with his family. Or her. "Your word is your bond."

"Yes, and you already have my word. I need your promise you'll behave and let the marshals keep you safe until this is over."

"No more running away. I promise." She held up her fist with her pinkie extended, getting the crack of a smile she'd hoped for.

AJ and the team already caught one killer. They had a plan for getting Avila and had the buy-in from other agencies. They could do this. She had to see the light at the end of the WITSEC tunnel. The light she'd been assured of when she first went to the authorities.

AJ hooked her pinkie finger with his long, slender, calloused finger and pulled her close. "Call me. And when this is all over, we'll have a real date."

"I'll hold you to that."

A minute later, she climbed into the back seat of the SUV with the hope of the Bad Karma team buoying her spirits.

TWENTY-EIGHT

After two days of a late-season tropical storm dumping rain across the Yucatan Peninsula, the sun shone in a cloudless blue sky, and gentle waves lapped against the hull as AJ debated his next move in the Risk game with Linc, Tony, and Dev.

Tony cleared his throat, then his gaze shifted from the board to Dev.

"I know you're all aligning against me," Dev said.

"It's because they can't beat you in poker." Angela grinned from her seat on the sofa before she resumed reading.

Linc snickered, and Tony shrugged.

"Alberta is attacking Ontario." AJ passed two dice to Dev.

They were docked. Waiting. The luxury yacht had drawn a few curious onlookers, but no one they could tie to Avila. Last night, Angela and Tony had dined at one of the most upscale restaurants to establish their presence. The chief, Mack, Juan, and Kyle had eyes on the villa—the heavily guarded villa—pinpointed by the GPS on the phone number they had.

So far, no eyes on the man and no one had left the villa grounds. They weren't going anywhere, either. Hopefully, now that the weather had cleared, Avila would decide to do some deep-sea fishing or take a cruise out to international waters.

Despite the alliance, Dev had nearly knocked AJ out of the game when Tony's distinctive ringtone bounced off the glass windows of the yacht's salon.

Tony swiped up the phone and automatically put it on speaker mode.

"Solo female just got in a blue Beemer and is leaving," Mack reported.

"What's she wearing?" Angela asked.

"Wearing? Um, a dress and heels. I think," he answered.

"Not a trip to the grocery. Time to shop." She crooked a finger at AJ, then slipped into designer sandals before picking up a large leather handbag with gold metal initials and donning a pair of oversized sunglasses.

Dev, dressed in a uniform of khaki shorts and a white polo shirt—he probably would love to have a shirt with epaulets and a captain's hat—went out and let down the ramp.

AJ put on his suit jacket to conceal his Glock.

"Damn. You look like a million bucks." Tony admired Angela in the dress with a plunging neckline.

"That's the idea." She kissed him.

He held onto her arm a second before letting her go, his gaze shifting to AJ. "Take care of her."

Message received. AJ snagged the rental car keys and followed Angela onto the deck. He drove her the short route to the Rodeo Drive of Playa Riviera.

"Beemer is headed your way now," Lundgren relayed from his position in the tail vehicle.

Angela's mouth turned up. "And who says women are unpredictable."

He parked on the street a few shops down from the one Viviana frequented. Angela waited for him to open the car door.

Inside the boutique, a sales associate issued a greeting while hanging up clothes. Angela browsed the racks, pulling dresses and handing several to him to hold. He was no fashion expert, but the material felt expensive and luxurious in his hands. A dress hanging on the wall was a similar bright blue shade as the sweater Cassidy had changed into—briefly—just a few nights ago.

AJ's phone dinged. He checked the text from Juan. *Crap.* "She went into the jewelry store down the street."

"Ask if she's shopping the cases or at the customer-service counter." Angela ignored AJ's let's-go eye signal and continued to browse.

With one arm loaded down, he dialed up Juan as she handed him two identical dresses.

"At the register. Guy went in back," AJ relayed Juan's answer.

"Give it a minute." Angela remained calm. She'd selected several more dresses by the time Juan began a blow-by-blow account of Viviana accepting a package, exiting, and pausing outside the jewelers before heading to the boutique.

"Would you like me to start a dressing room?" The sales-clerk cast an appraising look at the armful of clothes Angela had selected.

"*Si. Gracias.*" Angela waved her hand, with the ginor-mous—and fake—diamond ring, in front of the woman, then dismissively turned to continue perusing the selection.

AJ unloaded the items into the woman's arms. She let out

an *oomph,* then headed to the dressing rooms, which flanked a three-sided mirror with two posh armchairs.

When Viviana Avila breezed through the front door, blood flowed through his veins like the sluiceway of a dam had opened. Sales associates in Mexico must work on commission based on the way the two clerks beelined toward her. The woman manning the register won out. The younger associate made sure to greet Viviana before returning to her task of hanging up items.

"Send me pictures of what she selects to try on." Angela selected a pair of pants, then turned on her heel and headed to the dressing room.

He ignored the little niggle that came with giving up control. Though technically not part of the team, he knew Angela outranked him on this, and he'd better follow any orders she issued, especially considering she didn't have to volunteer for this.

The associate led Viviana to a rack within earshot of his position and pulled out a colorful floral-print dress.

"I bought that weeks ago." Viviana dismissed the selection.

"This came in this week." The associate held up a dark dress.

Viviana's fingers glided over the fabric, then she glanced at the tag. "Do you have it in a size smaller?"

AJ edged closer as the associate scanned the tags of the dresses identical to one, or maybe the pair, Angela had taken. She came up empty-handed before she asked the younger associate about the dress.

"I think someone is trying it on."

Under Viviana's gaze, the associate sorted through the dresses again. "I don't see another. Would you like to try this one?"

Viviana gave a bored nod. AJ managed to snap a picture of the dress before the associate draped it over her arm.

The two moved to a rack near the back of the store where Viviana chose a flowing light-orange dress.

Angela emerged from the dressing room in the same black dress the associate had pulled for Viviana. As Angela turned and checked out the dress in front of the mirror, he caught a glimpse of Viviana's face. *Shit!* Angela was supposed to be making friends, not pissing Viviana off. What the hell was she doing?

Completely ignoring Viviana, Angela ducked back into the dressing room. Next, she came out in the same orange dress Viviana had picked out. Seconds later, Viviana appeared in the same dress. From ten feet away, Viviana's wide eyes fired daggers at Angela.

WTF, he typed in a text to Angela. He sure as hell wasn't going to send pictures of anything else Viviana picked if Angela intended to keep making her jealous.

"We have the same tastes." Angela slightly mispronounced the words with an Italian lilt, even though she could speak Spanish like a native.

Nice touch. He clamped his jaw shut and didn't send the text. Not yet. He had to trust her experience. He'd let this play out.

Viviana aimed a tight, totally fake smile at Angela.

"This color looks fabulous with your skin tone and hair." Angela moved a step closer to Viviana yet maintained enough distance to not invade the woman's space. Viviana preened, turning to see herself from several angles in the mirror.

"You don't think it's too much? Or actually too little?" Viviana gestured to the plunging neckline and almost hip-high slit.

Angela gave a sexy, throaty laugh. She took hold of

Viviana's wrist and indicated her wedding ring. "It's good to show our men their money is well spent."

This could take a while. Instead of using the chair, AJ channeled Tony. He crossed his arms over his chest in his best bodyguard impression and scanned the store, rather than focus on the modeling. At least Viviana had only picked two dresses, though the saleswoman circled racks in what looked to him to be a concerted effort to find something for Viviana to buy.

Kill me now.

Angela quickly made as if heading to her dressing room when Viviana made her next entrance in the same black dress Angela had first worn. Viviana's mouth scrunched in disappointment.

Angela spun on her high-heeled sandal. "You need a size smaller," she declared.

"They didn't have one," Viviana said like a child cheated out of the last cookie.

"*Un momento.*" Angela flashed a smile, then flung open her dressing room door.

Viviana peered inside, cocking her head at what AJ could deduce as surprise at the number of dresses Angela had greedily chosen. When Angela offered her the black dress, Viviana's guarded expression dissipated. "You aren't buying this one?"

"It didn't fit right."

"Your accent. Where are you from?" Viviana asked.

"Southern Italy." Angela kept her answer somewhat vague, ducking into her dressing room.

The conversation continued as the women changed. Viviana appeared first, striking a pose in front of the mirrors. He'd bet a six-pack of German beer Angela kept her waiting on purpose.

"I love it. It fits you just right," Angela proclaimed, stepping right up to Viviana. He didn't know if she referred to the dress or the boob job, as Viviana clearly had implants. Her breasts were too large for her slight frame, far too round, too high, and too perky to be real. Maybe that's what Avila liked, but AJ was more of a natural guy. Cassidy's were just right.

Angela touched the fabric at Viviana's shoulder and then ran the back of her fingers down the inside of her arm. *Holy shit.* He caught both women checking each other out only slightly more discreetly than a guy would. He started getting a hard-on watching them.

The sales associate interrupted the chitchat to show Viviana two other dresses. She half-heartedly took one of the dresses. Then, before things got too heated, Angela slipped back into her dressing room with Viviana watching her go.

Okay, maybe Angela did know what the hell she was doing while working Viviana. When Angela came out in yet another expensive-looking dress, she gave him a slight, but satisfied, I-told-you-to-trust-me smile as she did a slow turn in front of the mirror.

"I love that print." Viviana watched Angela almost hungrily.

"It's a bit conservative, don't you think?"

"You should ask your husband." Viviana motioned his way.

"He's not my husband." Angela gave another throaty chuckle. "He's my bodyguard."

"Bodyguard?" Viviana's voice dropped lower.

"My lover is a very powerful man. Powerful men make powerful enemies." She touched the bullet wound on her shoulder, effectively drawing Viviana's attention there before she tugged the material to cover the scar.

A gasp slipped through Viviana's lips. "Someone shot you?" Horror infused her voice.

"I got in the way." Angela sounded amazingly blasé. "But the man who did this will never hurt anyone again." Her tone hardened as she stuck close to the truth of what actually happened. "My lover brought me on this trip to make up for it after I recovered. Though, I think he wanted to check out a silly boat as much as make up for what happened."

"What is it with men and their boats?"

"Well, it's more of a yacht, but still for fishing. Though it is quite luxurious."

"Are you staying on the yacht?"

"Yes, down at the marina." Angela shook her head, wrinkling her nose as she studied the dress she wore.

Viviana glanced in AJ's direction again. "Does he go everywhere with you?"

"He lets me go to the bathroom by myself." She gave a flippant head toss.

AJ could practically see the thought bubble in Viviana's head as she wondered why Avila didn't have someone protecting her.

"And your lover isn't worried about you and he *together*?"

"Togeth—oh, no. He doesn't need to be, especially since I don't have the right *thing* for him to be interested." Angela added a light laugh and head wiggle in AJ's direction.

Jeez. Thanks, Angela. His neck and face heated, and he fought to maintain a placid expression.

"Oh." Viviana looked his way. "Was he worried you'd cheat or …?"

"No." Angela ignored Viviana's lead-in, but he could read the question on her face as Angela talked over her. "My lover isn't the jealous type. He's very generous." Her lips turned into a lusty grin, and she gave Viviana the same sultry wink he'd seen her give Tony. "You should get that dress."

AJ couldn't read minds, but he could read body language. Viviana's parted lips begged to be kissed. Her erect nipples strained to be touched, and her hips swayed in a do-me circle. Viviana stared at the dressing room door after Angela pulled it closed.

He was supposed to be gay, not getting turned on watching two women flirt with each other. Tony would punch him right in the face. And Cassidy, well, better not to think about her right now since he was trying his damnedest not be turned on by hot women.

Can you two just make a date and get this fashion show over with?

"Do you like it?" Viviana asked his opinion on the dress.

It's hot would probably blow his cover as much as *it'll be great to wear to your husband's funeral*. How do you play the role of a gay fashion guru? He motioned for her to spin with a swirl of his hand.

"It looks fabulous," he said, using Angela's trick of emphasizing the wrong syllables and gave what he hoped was a convincingly flagrant head wiggle. He got a moment's reprieve when Angela came out to compete for the mirror.

"I like the possibilities of this one." Angela spun in a dress that tied behind her neck and was long in the back and higher in the front. "Do you have any restaurant recommendations for the few days we're here?"

As Viviana rattled off the names of restaurants, he marveled at how Angela dropped in information to hit Viviana's hot buttons. She had a natural gift, or the CIA was training actors. No wonder after she joined the FBI, they had sent her undercover despite her official linguist job description.

By the time they decided on dresses, the two had revealed as much information as believable for women involved with a mafioso and an arms-cartel head. No names had been exchanged. No probing questions were asked. No numbers exchanged or dinner dates made. He prayed it would be enough as he carried the bag out and opened the car door for Angela.

TWENTY-NINE

"Mr. Dance Fever is back. He's parked in the marina lot," Mack reported from his position hidden up on the hill overlooking the entire marina.

Playing cards at the compact dining table in the yacht's salon with Dev and Linc, AJ looked over at Angela. It didn't surprise him to see the smug look on her face as she sat on the sofa with Tony, whose eyes didn't deviate from the soccer game on the large flat-screen television.

One of Avila's security team—a man who wore his hair like the lead character from *Saturday Night Fever*—had visited the marina a few hours after Viviana returned home from her shopping trip. Casually checking out Viviana's new friend's story.

AJ would've preferred a speedier meetup, but, so far, Angela had predicted every move as if she'd scripted it. And now it was time for them to put on a show. Bait the hook to draw in the big fish.

"He's got binoculars out."

"Just binoculars? No audio equipment?" Tony, who was also miked in addition to an earpiece, asked Mack.

"No. I'll let you know if it changes."

Showtime.

For the last few minutes of the soccer game, AJ, Dev, and Linc played their employee roles, keeping a layer of distance despite the close quarters. When the game ended, it was Angela who took the lead. She finished her drink, then rose and took position in front of Tony, blocking the TV in a demand for attention—as if the slinky new dress wasn't already an attention-getter.

Tony slid both hands up the back of Angela's thighs, taking hold of her ass and pulling her to him. She sank to her knees on the sofa, straddling him, his face inches from her cleavage. "You can go." He waved one hand at them in a dismissive gesture.

Dev and Linc retreated to their shared room, and AJ ducked into his.

"What's your guy doing now, Bird Dog?" Lundgren's deep voice reminded him the chief was out there, even if he had allowed Tony and Angela to call the plays on this.

"Looks like he's enjoying Vincenti's PDA." Mack's teasing statement filled in the picture of what AJ envisioned was transpiring on the other side of the wall based on the noises coming through from Tony's mike.

"It's not exactly public when we're inside," Tony commented between kisses and murmurs.

In front of a bank of windows. AJ could see Angela having the confidence to perform despite an audience. It wouldn't surprise him if Tony had sublime exhibitionist tendencies beyond playing a character. At least they'd ruled out a threesome for arousing Avila's interest and member.

"I swear the guy's giving himself a hand job now," Mack said.

"Sounds like our work is done. Bird Dog, keep an eye on

him, not Vincenti. Everyone else can tune out and turn in," Lundgren ordered.

"Not sure Vincenti's work is done yet," Dominguez cracked.

"Earpiece off, Dominguez!"

AJ set his earpiece on the dresser. Not that he needed the earpiece. He stripped down to his boxers, then dug his earbuds out of the nightstand drawer and cued up his favorite playlist. The music should drown out the sounds, and he could ignore any banging against the wall.

THIRTY

"Viviana is leaving with Felix?" Angela's eyes lit up as she blew on her second cup of morning coffee. "That tells me we passed muster with last night's performance, and Felix is coming to check out Viviana's new friend." She trailed a finger down Tony's shoulder.

Avila's captain had started prepping his fishing boat a half hour ago, giving them a heads-up. In AJ's mind, Viviana coming along was a complication. "So, we don't follow his boat but try to get him on our boat? How?"

"We don't want him getting spooked and blowing this. We play hard to get." Angela sounded like some of the girls he'd gone to high school with.

"But—"

"She's right," Tony cut him off. "No way my character would invite a stranger on his boat. And forcing him on when he's got bodyguards is too dangerous." He nodded toward Angela. "Not to mention authorities being called in. Cops on his payroll."

"I'll work Viviana, and you do your macho standoff with

Felix. And you"—she targeted AJ—"hang back as the mute protector. This is not a one-act play."

They gave Linc and Dev a heads-up, then waited for Avila, his security guys, and Viviana. AJ wiped his sweaty palms on his pants when Mack alerted them the car had pulled into the marina's lot. Sitting on the back deck, he refrained from straining to see which dock their party picked.

Angela continued her yoga workout, dropping to her mat —and out of sight—seconds after Viviana spotted her and pointed her out to Avila. The group disappeared from his view as they neared the boat. Remaining still had never been harder.

"*Hola.*" Viviana's melodic greeting nearly pulled him to his feet, but a raised hand from Angela cautioned him to wait.

"Can I help you?" Dev called down from the helm and slapped on the hull.

AJ rose and peered around the cabin from the deck.

"I was looking for—" Viviana broke off and waved at him from the dock.

He gave a curt nod, then pulled back as if speaking to Angela. She came to the railing where Avila and Viviana were just feet away, flanked by two of their bodyguards. It would be so easy to draw his weapon and place two rounds in Avila's head. But he couldn't—no, he wouldn't—do it with Angela in the line of fire. He'd also promised Cassidy—with a damn pinkie swear.

Tony emerged from the cruiser's cabin to investigate, blocking Angela's path to disembark. The two exchanged words in Italian, with Tony playing it up with gruff movements and a killer stare while Angela answered with a breezy tone and patronizing gestures. When she strode down the gangway, Tony followed, putting him in arm's reach of Avila.

AJ moved closer, trying to overhear. Viviana's explanation about seeing Angela while on the way to their boat for a fishing jaunt came off too rushed and detailed to be authentic to his trained ears. Introductions were made, rather awkwardly since the women didn't know each other's names, and no one mentioned last names.

"Nice vessel," Avila commented, taking in the length of the gleaming white hull. "You sail from Italy?" He turned back, equally drawn between the boat, Tony's chest, exposed by his half-buttoned shirt, and Angela's curves in tight yoga clothing.

"Florida Keys. Taking it for a test run to determine if I want to buy it," Tony answered.

"Ah, so, it's not yours." Avila stepped away from the women and checked the name and home port painted on the stern. "You came all this way to see this vessel? You couldn't buy one in Europe?"

"I had business here that worked out for me to see the boat. The owner and I share a banker who knew his client was looking to sell—out of necessity—and that I was in the market to trade up. Made it worth the trip." He looked over to where Angela and Viviana stood close, talking in low voices.

AJ's eyes locked on the two bodyguards. Both had bulges at their hips from concealed weapons. Not total amateurs. The odds were still on his side, though. He kept his Glock in plain view.

Bits of Tony and Avila's conversation about fishing drifted up to him, but he refrained from moving closer to listen in.

Come on board. We'll take you on a fishing trip that I promise you will regret.

Only no one moved to board.

Avila swept his arm toward his boat before casting an envious eye at the *Fine Print*.

Seriously, dude. It's a nice vessel. You should check it out.
Instead, Avila moved away toward the women.

After Avila, Viviana, and their goons departed, Angela and the men gathered in the yacht's salon.

"How'd it go?" Dev asked.

"It went great," Tony answered.

"What do you mean 'great'? You didn't get them on the boat." AJ didn't care if his frustration showed.

"Patience, grasshopper. Avila wouldn't have gotten on if I'd offered, just like I wasn't going with him today. No. Too many ways for that to go wrong, and me not to come back. Now he has names and can check us out and decide to take me up on my invitation to go fishing tomorrow."

"If we get that far." Angela led with a confident smile. "Viviana was tossing down breadcrumbs, so I left a trail of New York-sized bagels. Told her we went to one of the restaurants she recommended last night. She said the other was her favorite. Hinted she'd be there."

"You'll go there tonight for a meetup?" That possibility offset AJ's disappointment that they weren't currently cruising out to sea.

"No. Too obvious, and the idea is to get them here, not us invited to their villa," she pointed out.

Damn. Should have realized that. No wonder that he sucked at the game-playing in relationships.

"I suggested they drop by for drinks tonight. And I may have dropped a hint about Felix checking out the boat."

"You're going to sell the boat out from under me, babe?" Tony acted wounded.

"Not like we could afford this one. Maybe after you get

your twenty years in and retire, we can start a charter-boat business. I think we'll have to start with something smaller."

Tony nodded as if giving it some thought, except the chances of him retiring when he hit the twenty-year mark seemed highly unlikely.

For now, AJ continued to count down the hours until he could pay back Avila for Hal's forced "retirement."

THIRTY-ONE

Here. Spotted me. Restaurant 2, AJ typed. Send. And delete —just in case. Leaning against the car, he bit into his tortilla. He ignored Avila's driver and soaked up the evening sun and breeze. He waited to see if Avila and his wife stayed in the restaurant or came out in search of Tony and Angela.

After five minutes, he finally decided the Avilas were not going to hunt down their new friends for dinner. This was in line with Tony's plan, though it left things too wide open for AJ to relax.

He strolled to the trash can, tossed in the wadded food wrapper and empty cup, and pretended to finally notice Avila's driver smoking a cigarette. He gave a slight head jerk in acknowledgment. Neither man moved to make small talk while their "employers" dined, leaving the hired muscle to eat the Mexican equivalent of fast food.

He wanted to tell Cassidy how close they were and assure her they were going to nab Avila—one way or another—but he couldn't. Not only because of operational security, but with the marshals confiscating her phone, he'd have to rely on secure channels once this was over.

It killed him, but he agreed they needed to keep playing it slowly to get Avila to let his guard down. So far, Avila had come to them. Still, when Tony and Angela headed to the car a half hour later, the last thing he wanted to do was drive away and leave Avila to enjoy his gourmet meal. Though the idea it could be his last gave AJ a jolt of excitement.

"How was dinner?" he asked.

"Great. Good food. Good company. Just the two of us." Angela slid into the back seat.

Tony joined her, and AJ closed the door. Yup, Avila's goon was keeping an eye on them.

"Home, James," Tony threw out with an aristocratic inflection.

He better not get too used to this. Reality was gonna crash down on him when they got back to Bragg.

"Did Felix and Viviana see you or just their driver?" Angela asked.

"Pretty sure Viviana did." She hadn't waved at him like earlier on the dock, but she'd certainly walked into the restaurant like a woman on a mission after glancing his way.

There was a fine line between playing hard to get and snubbing someone. Angela had finessed it perfectly, drawing Viviana in. Except Felix Avila was a wild card, and they couldn't risk losing him.

If it didn't happen tonight, they had a shot tomorrow—provided that Avila and his boat captain joined them for a fishing trip. Realistically, there were more factors out of their control in that scenario.

"What? No doggie bag?" Linc greeted them as they boarded the *Fine Print*.

"With him?" Angela jerked a thumb toward Tony. "Besides, Luca and Julia wouldn't take home leftovers." She touched her fingertips to her chest and spoke in a disdainful tone, though giving them one of her characteristic winks.

In the salon, she poured an ounce or two of port wine and raised the glass to her lips, taking a sip before turning the glass and leaving a second set of lipstick marks on the rim. She set it on the table beside the couch. While Tony stripped off his tie and rolled up his sleeves, she poured a splash of scotch into a crystal rocks glass and dropped in a few ice cubes. She placed the glass next to her wineglass.

AJ liked her optimism in setting the stage.

The phone rang, cutting the silent tension that came with waiting. All eyes were on Tony as he put the cell phone on speaker.

"They left the restaurant and turned toward the marina, not the villa," Juan filled them in.

Angela's smile grew like the Cheshire cat's. "Prepare to cast off, Captain Grant. Alert our real friends we hope to be setting sail."

Linc and Dev went above deck to make final preparations.

"I say we show off the boat's speed and get Avila as far out as possible. We'll do what we can to keep him from noticing how far." Tony eyed Angela, who nodded in silent agreement.

"Hanlon said they're pulling into the lot now," Linc called down. On the deck, he and Dev hauled in the gangway and began untying the lines securing the ship to the dock.

"You aren't leaving, are you?" Viviana's faintly panicked voice echoed into the vessel right on cue.

AJ trailed behind as Angela and Tony made for the deck. A lump of anticipation lodged in the back of his throat. Blood coursed through his body in an adrenaline-fueled race. If they could get Avila on board, this could be his last night as a free man and his first night of paying for his crimes.

"I thought it would be romantic to take a cruise to see the sun set over the city from the water." Angela leaned over the railing. Viviana, Avila, and the two bodyguards all appeared entranced by the dramatic sweep of Angela's arm toward the cityscape, or perhaps it was her generous display of cleavage. "You could join us, though you've probably seen it many times," Angela offered as if it didn't matter if they joined or not.

Tony gave a reluctant wave of his hand, and Dev set the gangway back in place.

AJ willed Avila to take the steps—commit himself. Instead, he stood with both feet planted like he was rooted to the wooden dock. Angela made the first move, walking down the short metal gangway to join them. Tony followed, stopping close to Avila, angling between the man and his bodyguards.

"I hoped to see you at Santé's for dinner," Viviana probed.

"We were headed there until he saw Las Islitas' Seafood. But if you don't have anything to get back for, you can join us now." Angela led Viviana on board, leaving the men in their wake.

Tony and Avila looked at one another as if hoping the other would object and stop the women. Neither did.

"I thought this was a private party, but if she doesn't get her way, there won't be *any* party." Tony chuckled gruffly, not waiting for Avila's response as he left his side.

Come on. Do it this time. When Avila followed, AJ silently cheered from his observation spot.

Tony pulled up short before stepping onto the gangway.

He looked from the first of Avila's bodyguards to the second. "I thought this would be at least a semiprivate excursion. We don't need them."

"You have three of your protection detail," Avila countered.

"Really? Three? The captain and cook came with the trial run of the ship." He pointed to AJ. "He's *her* protection. I can take care of myself," Tony bragged. "You need someone; you can bring one. My boat, my rules."

"It's not *your* boat yet, is it?"

"You wouldn't try to buy it out from under me?" Tony laughed.

"That wouldn't be the gentlemanly thing to do. I'll give you first shot, but if you pass, I might be interested."

Tony snorted. "Like either of us are gentlemen." He strode up the gangway.

Avila motioned to his driver, who backed off, turned, and cautiously headed back up the dock while the bigger goon sauntered up with a badass expression.

We'll see how badass you are in an hour.

Angela was already giving Viviana a peek at the staterooms while Avila took in the well-outfitted salon.

"Drink?" Tony picked up his glass.

Avila nodded. "Whatever you're having."

Tony's chin jutted up in an unspoken order to AJ. "I'm sure our generous host won't mind."

I read you loud and clear. AJ poured four fingers of scotch over ice. *Drink up.* He handed the glass to Avila. "For you. Ma'am?"

"Try the port. It's from my home village." Angela took a sip.

Viviana nodded, and AJ filled a clean goblet.

The engines rumbled to life, and the yacht slowly pulled away from the dock.

"How did you two meet?" Avila cut his eyes from Tony to Angela over the rim of his glass, taking a swig of scotch.

"I was working at an art gallery in Milan. Luca had business with one of my clients that brought us together," Angela answered easily.

"You a collector?" Avila continued to probe.

"I do some buying and selling."

"What kind of business did you say you're in?"

"I didn't say." Tony deflected.

"Let's go enjoy the view." Angela headed out to the rear deck as if bored by the men and business.

Dev brought the boat to a stop after a leisurely cruise, putting them about two miles from shore, which might as well be a million miles from international waters.

AJ widened his stance as the boat rocked in the light chop of the waves. Other than this bozo with a handgun—who they could easily take down—what was keeping them from dropping the ruse and making a run for open water? Avila got on the boat willingly. It wouldn't be kidnapping even if he requested they return to shore. Or would it?

This wasn't all that different than how they'd gotten Samir el-Shehri on a jet owned and operated by the United States Army instead of the private jet of a Saudi oil billionaire. Sometimes, with a big target, playing to their egos or needs worked better than guns and bullets.

He faked bored indifference as the two couples lingered over the railing, watching the sun sink behind the city. Not overly impressive, but the colorful sky served its purpose.

Tony kept a hand on Angela's lower back, just over her ass, and the contact at their hips should produce smoke or flames soon. Based on the tilt of Avila's head, he noticed the arousal building between the two as well.

Within minutes, the orange globe disappeared, and the colors faded to a deepening gray-blue.

Tony eased upright, making eye contact with Avila. "Light show's over. How about I show you what this lady can do." He tapped the rail.

"What kind of speed does she get?" Avila asked.

"We had her over forty knots in calm waters." Tony climbed the stairs to the bridge.

"How far are you planning on going?"

"As far as you want to see how she cruises." Tony's voice trailed off as they joined Dev on the bridge.

Seconds later, the engine noise and whipping wind kept AJ from eavesdropping on Angela and Viviana's conversation after they slipped into two deck chairs.

Ten more minutes at this speed, and they'd be in international waters. The adrenaline kicked up another notch, and he couldn't help but smile in the twilight, his gaze skimming the sea for the U.S. Navy ship waiting somewhere beyond the horizon.

Tony led Avila back down to the main deck. He made eye contact with Angela, conveying a telepathic message she apparently received because she gracefully rose, empty wineglass in hand. Viviana drained her glass and got to her feet.

Angela took Viviana by the arm, converging with their partners, as they entered the salon. Though AJ had no idea what she said to Avila when she released Viviana's arm to touch his, he could read the thought flashing across Avila's face.

Avila's bodyguard didn't wait for an invitation. He left his post on deck and followed the group inside.

Tony handed his glass to AJ. "Refill?" he asked Avila.

Avila downed a swig, then passed his glass to AJ.

"We can head back and hit the club or casino if you're a gambling man. Or …" Tony locked his focus on the women. "We keep cruising and have our own private party."

Even from several feet away, AJ could see Avila swallow while watching Angela brush a windswept lock of hair from Viviana's face.

"I'm in no hurry to get back."

Tony gave a short throaty chuckle. His smile sent shivers creeping up AJ's limbs. "We both seem to like living on the edge. Not afraid to take risks and get a rush."

Avila tore his gaze from the women to Tony, and his expression was like a teenage boy's who'd found his dad's stash of porn magazines.

"Tell the captain to cruise the coastline for a while. Then you're dismissed." Tony waved AJ off.

"We won't be needing you further." Avila also released his muscle, who hesitated but didn't verbally object. "Go."

AJ shot him a resigned we're do-as-we're-told look before exiting the salon. He closed the door behind Avila's guard, indicated for him to follow, then navigated to the flybridge.

"Boss wants you to cruise for a while," AJ relayed to Dev. Linc lounged beside Dev in the second seat.

Avila's guy edged close enough to study the GPS display on the helm.

Yeah, we're still inside the territorial-waters limit—for now, you prick.

"They're, uh, gonna be occupied for a while?" Dev asked.

"Probably a good while." AJ blocked Avila's guard from retreating.

Dev reached down and opened the door to the mini fridge. "Help yourself." He gave one of his innocent smiles and kept a hand on the wheel.

A smile finally broke on the guard's face, like a prisoner given reprieve. He dropped to one knee, bypassing the water bottles to snag a can of beer.

"Don't forget us," AJ told him.

He and Dev both drew their weapons when he reached in to grab more cans. He froze as the steel suppressor touched his temple.

"Don't make any sudden moves and keep your mouth shut, so I won't have to kill you and then your boss." Dev gave his best Dirty Harry impersonation.

"Naw, we don't want to kill him. Make him bleed a little is all. We'll let the sharks do the rest," Linc taunted.

"Sharks?" The thug's hands clenched around the beer cans, his skin paling in the light cast from the helm's displays.

"Ones other than your boss. You know how to swim? Oh, never mind. It wouldn't matter." AJ retrieved the semi-automatic pistol from the thug's waistband. "Sorry, no *cerveza* for you. Hands behind your back." He forced the man into a sitting position.

Linc gagged, then flex-cuffed the hands and feet of Avila's protector. Then he hauled him up to tuck him into the corner of the bridge.

Dev handed AJ his cell phone, the message window already opened.

Threat contained. Mission go, AJ typed and hit send. "Let me check on the situation down below."

He slipped outside to the narrow expanse of deck alongside the flybridge. After he lay on his belly, he set the movie function on the phone to record and lowered the phone down the side of the ship, turning it to pan the salon.

He played the short video clip of the white hull. "Dammit," he grumbled. He pressed his body against the railing to keep from tumbling into the churning water and extended his arm to its max reach and repeated his amateur filmmaking attempt. This time he was rewarded with a blurry, bouncing glimpse of the salon and its occupants. Clear enough for him to scramble to his feet and back to the flybridge.

"How long until we're in position?"

"Seven minutes," Dev calculated after checking their coordinates and speed.

That should be fast enough. Or would it be? How far would they go to see this through? "See if you can make it six," he said, thinking of Angela and how she might prefer having her clothes on when they were joined by a naval-assault team.

Linc checked Dev's phone. "They've launched," he confirmed as Dev increased the speed a notch, then another and another.

AJ picked up the night-vision binoculars and scanned the portside horizon. A sigh of relief escaped his lungs when he detected two zodiac boats racing over the waves toward them.

Linc used the phone's flashlight app to signal them. Dev gradually slowed and steered to his starboard, giving the zodiacs a covert approach to the rear of the craft.

The trio acted as if they were alone on the open sea. With a weapon aimed at his chest, Avila's once cocky bodyguard didn't so much as thump his bound feet against the hull. Apparently, the idea of being taken into custody had more appeal than an evening swim in shark-infested waters while bleeding from bullet wounds. He had a better chance of surviving on the outs with a powerful arms-cartel head.

Grappling hooks sailed over the rails, securing a zodiac to each side of the yacht. Despite AJ's instincts kicking into defensive mode, he remained as immobile as a statue. Seconds later, camouflaged bodies flowed up the ropes onto the deck.

Linc moved first to lay his weapon at his feet; Dev and AJ followed. All three fished out their federal credentials and held them in raised hands. A pair of SEALs assaulted the flybridge. Their M-4s swept over the men, before lowering the muzzles. Dev killed the engines, bringing the vessel to a rapid halt.

"What the hell is—" Tony's voice boomed, then broke off like a twig snapped in two.

Familiarity helped AJ catch the tinge of amusement in his buddy's indignant tone.

AJ stepped to the deck as Avila emerged. He attempted to duck inside upon seeing the armed men, but Angela apparently blocked his path because she rushed out, forcing Avila back on the deck, where he attempted to maintain his distance from Tony, who stood with hands raised.

Avila slunk into himself, his gaze fixed downward, but he couldn't disappear.

"Felix Avila, you're under arrest for—"

"Me? Wait!" Avila's mouth opened in stunned disbelief. He glowered at Tony. Hostility hardened his face when it hit him, and hatred fired arrows from his eyes.

Tony lowered his hands and leaned closer to Avila. "They always say we guys shouldn't think with our dicks. It'll get us in trouble." He stepped out of the line of fire, wearing a triumphant you're-a-total-shithead grin.

AJ's mouth curved into a vengeful smile when all the SEALs trained their weapons on Avila.

"You betrayed us?" Viviana rounded on Angela. Her arms raised with hands poised to attack.

At least four men moved to intervene. Angela blocked the strike first. In a blur, she pinned Viviana's arm behind her back, twisting it high enough to immobilize the enraged woman.

"You can go with him to face charges, or you can go home to your kids. Your decision. I hope you'll make a better choice than your past ones."

Just like that, Felix Avila ended up in the custody of U.S. forces. To AJ, it seemed too anticlimactic to be true.

Instead of relief or the satisfaction of a completed mission, a twinge of regret took hold that Avila's arrest went down without bloodshed. He'd made a promise, but what if Avila's arrest and conviction only doomed Cassidy to spending the rest of her life in WITSEC hiding from his reach?

Damn. She might never see her family again. It'd tear her up to cut ties to her sister and even her mother, despite her flaws. Even as crazy as his family made him, he didn't want to cut them from his life.

But Cassidy didn't have to be alone. There was nothing to connect her to him. The Marshals Service could place her near an Army base. He'd have to leave the team since it wouldn't be Fort Bragg—not with her having a past there, but he could transfer if that's what it came down to.

THIRTY-TWO

"That was awesome. Thanks for cooking." Marshal Suzanne Evans cleared her plate while Cassidy finished her breakfast.

"No problem. It gives me something to do."

"I get it.

"I can tell. This is no picnic for you, either." The marshal showed up at the nondescript, two-story safe house on her first day with two jigsaw puzzles, a sudoku book, knitting needles, a crochet hook, and yarn to help them both pass the time.

Back at Elmwood Manor, Cassidy had learned to crochet from the senior ladies while they congregated in the common room to watch *Wheel of Fortune* and *Jeopardy*. It'd taken her a little practice, but after four days, her hands moved by rote, looping soft yarn over the hook. She'd finished a baby blanket for Kristie Hanlon and started on a second.

She switched to the puzzles while Marshal Rodriguez binge-watched *Chicago P.D.* and *Chicago Med* during his evening shifts. The shows sparked comments between them on the unreality of many story lines from their perspectives in law enforcement and the medical field. Occasionally, she caught glimpses of familiar places, but she didn't miss the city like she once had. She didn't see Champ adjusting to the traffic and crowds of a city, either.

He was recovering well, though she still caved to his big eyes and slipped him half a strip of her bacon. She didn't have Hal anymore, but she had Champ. He'd saved her and helped fill the Hal-sized hole in her heart.

The two had also brought AJ into her life. But any future with him was still so up in the air due to Avila.

Avila's business was guns, and that kept AJ and his team in her prayers. What if he or someone on his team got shot—or worse? She'd asked AJ about the bullet wound on his left thigh. Just like Hal would have done, AJ shrugged it off without giving her any details.

She loaded the dishwasher when Suzanne surged to her feet, drawing her weapon. "Stay back. Get down. A car stopped in front of the house."

Cassidy dropped to the floor, next to Champ, her heart pounding in her ears.

Suzanne moved to the window and peered out, then lowered her arm and holstered her gun. "It's just DeLong."

Cassidy released a breath and lowered her face to Champ's. "It's okay, boy."

The dog nuzzled her cheek as if to say he wasn't worried. What was Flint doing here, though?

Suzanne opened the front door, and Flint strode in, beaming uncharacteristically as Cassidy got to her feet.

"I admit, I didn't think they could do it." Admiration laced Flint's usually monotone voice. "But your buddies came through."

"What?" Could he mean what she thought? Scarcely breathing, she waited for Flint to continue. Her stomach tightened, and hope spread wings in her chest, but she feared it taking flight too soon and crashing back to earth.

"Last night, Felix Avila was picked up on a U.S.-flagged vessel in international waters. At this moment, the U.S. Navy is transporting him to Miami, Florida."

"Finally!" Suzanne broke into a smile.

The news knocked Cassidy off-balance. She slumped into the chair, drawing in a series of deep breaths. Her fingers threaded through Champ's fur. "Is everyone all right?" she asked as the fog of shock cleared.

"From what I heard, neither side even fired a shot. He'll be arraigned no later than tomorrow."

"Will he be held, or will he be released on bail?" The idea of him walking out of a courtroom, pissed and free to orchestrate more anarchy, kept her from celebrating yet.

"Even without his passport, he'd be considered a flight risk. Though, I'm not a legal expert," Flint clarified, "so it could depend on the judge."

"If the judge sets bail, it's gonna be a shitload of money. With his reputation, it's gonna be difficult to find a bail bondsman who's able and willing to put up that amount of cash." Suzanne tried to assure her.

Cassidy suspected Avila had access to a few million and could skip the bail-bondsman step. She strained to see some glimmer of light to guide her out of this abyss. "What does this mean for me?"

"The Chicago DA has been sitting on the Flores case waiting for this—for Avila to be in custody. He'll put Flores on the expedited docket. Flores could be in a courtroom in a couple of weeks. Though more likely in a month."

"Weeks?" The light she'd hoped for flicked on, chasing away the darkness enveloping her life the past two years.

"Yes, weeks. Which is why we don't see a need to set up

a new identity and relocate you. We're certainly not going to drop protection, but we need you to stick it out here or in another safe house until we get you through the trial."

When she first went into protective custody, she thought she'd return to her old life in a matter of months. But District Attorney Clary had withheld the crucial fact that they'd offered Flores a deal, and he wouldn't see the inside of a courtroom until they had Avila. So, sacrifice a few more weeks to get her life back? Hell, yes!

She nodded gratefully, her mind shifting to AJ and his team. It'd be expecting too much that they would be her protection during that time, but at least she could talk to AJ. After the trial was over, she could go to Fort Bragg to see him and thank the team. Then? At least now she could decide. Be herself instead of living a lie.

THIRTY-THREE

AJ TRIED to focus on the NBA game on TV instead of staring at his phone, willing it to ring. He checked the time on his phone—again. Eight-eighteen. No missed calls.

From what he'd experienced with Cassidy, she ran early, not late. *What if ...?* No. There was no need to go worst-case scenario. There could be plenty of reasons, starting with the marshals needing to run the call through secure channels.

He hadn't wanted to be distracted when the call came, but instead of sitting on the couch waiting uselessly, he should find something to do. In his bedroom, he scooped up his dirty laundry. He'd just poured detergent in the machine when his phone rang. Pulling the phone from his pocket, his hands fumbled, and he nearly dropped it into the filling tub.

"Jesus," he breathed in relief. "Hello."

"Mr. Rozanski?" A male voice greeted him, not Cassidy's sweet drawl.

"Yes." He let the incorrect salutation slide.

"This is Marshal Rodriguez. Before I put the call through to Ms. O'Shea, I need to be sure you reviewed the security protocols forwarded to you."

"I have." He returned to the couch.

"At no time can you discuss Ms. O'Shea's current location, or anything related to her whereabouts."

"I understand. I'm familiar with operational security."

"The call will be monitored for Ms. O'Shea's protection."

He didn't know if that meant over the line or if some marshal would be standing over Cassidy. He didn't care.

"Ms. O'Shea is now on the line."

"AJ?"

"Hey."

"Sorry, I'm late. Thanks to you guys, I had a lot to talk about with my mom and sister."

"It's okay. It's great to hear your voice."

"It's good to hear yours, too, and know you're all right. I was told everyone's okay. That no shots were even fired."

"That's true." Other than Viviana getting her arm wrenched behind her back, not a hair on anyone's head had been harmed.

"I already respected you guys and your skills, but wow. Less than two weeks and you managed to do what all those other government agencies couldn't for how many years? And without anyone getting hurt. That's impressive."

The esteem she voiced brought a smile to his face. "It was a group effort. Angela deserves a lot of the credit. It was her insight and ability to read and play the characters that made it work."

"I'll need to thank her when I see her—*and you*—again." Cassidy's tone dropped to a sultry timbre.

The implied promise warmed the blood racing to AJ's groin. "That'd be good. So, what's next?"

"They've set a court date for Flores. A little over two weeks from now." The hesitation in her voice told him not to mark the calendar yet. "I've already talked to the prosecutors to go over my statement and what kinds of questions the defense will likely throw at me."

"They able to tell you how long the trial may take?"

"They expect me to be on the stand for a few hours to go over the few minutes I was with him. Then three days to a week for the trial. I can't go anywhere until the jury comes back." A trace of doubt tainted her confidence.

"What are your plans after that?" He usually took orders, didn't ask questions, but he needed answers to see where she saw things going without him sounding needy.

"First, go see my mom and my sister and her family."

The longing in her voice reminded him that she hadn't seen them in two years. They deserved priority. He dug out dirt from under his short fingernails and didn't press her.

"After that, a trip to Fayetteville is in order."

"I'd like that."

"In addition to seeing you, I just learned, after talking with Mom, that Hal named me as executor of his estate. Only his attorney has had a little trouble finding me, so they finally found her."

"Go figure."

"I wasn't expecting that. I'll see if there's anything I need to do before I start applying for jobs."

"I'm sure the hospitals in Fayetteville could use someone with your experience." He laid out an invitation. He didn't want to pressure her after she'd given up so much already.

"They have a level-three trauma center there. UNC, Duke, and WakeMed all have level-one centers."

She'd apparently checked, sending a clear message about where she saw things going, even if she referenced jobs that would be an hour and a half away. They had time to see where things went and work from there.

"How's Champ doing?" he asked.

"Good. He's about ninety percent recovered. My other hero, right, boy?" Her tone shifted as she spoke to the dog. "Say hi to AJ."

Champ gave a short, low bark in response.

A man cleared his throat in the background, reminding them both of his presence. Not that AJ'd been contemplating phone sex. Well, not seriously. They talked for a half an hour before the marshal said their time was up. Not long enough, but in a few weeks, they could have real conversations whenever they wanted. Go on a date. Spend time together without marshals or half the Bad Karma team under the same roof.

Not giving in to the temptation to draw Avila and his goons into a showdown finally felt like the right decision. Soon, he'd be able to look Cassidy in the eye and have no fear he'd broken his word or lost her respect. He'd kept his pinkie promise.

THIRTY-FOUR

THE SUN WAS out as Cassidy tossed the tennis ball in the safe house's backyard. She enjoyed the cool fall temperatures, the color of the leaves, and the way they crunched under her feet.

With Marshal Evans on her detail, Cassidy had a female to talk to, keeping her from going totally stir-crazy. When Suzanne had asked to bring her own dog along, the women had further bonded over her labradoodle, Indy, who hit it off with Champ.

Indy trotted to Suzanne, dropping the ball at her feet. She threw it, and the dogs raced after the ball as it disappeared in a layer of leaves. As they bounded back, Indy kept going past the women. They turned and saw Flint Delong as he rounded the side of the house.

The sullen set of Flint's mouth stole the joy of the day. Cassidy had seen expressions similar to his too many times—every time a doctor had to tell family members a patient had died. Her core locked like gears grinding to a halt.

"Who's dead?"

"How did you—"

"Tell me!" Fear knifed through her. Did Avila have the reach, even from prison, to get to her family? Who? Her mother? Sherri? Sherri's kids?

"Daniel Kraus was found dead in his cell this morning."

"Oh, wow," Suzanne muttered.

Kraus? Kraus was dead? Relief coursed through Cassidy. She couldn't dredge up a crumb of remorse that that man was dead. Someone did the world a favor.

"Which means they're pushing back Flores's trial," Flint went on.

"What? Why? We were ready to go to court."

"That's when Kraus was going to testify against Avila."

"They've got to have Kraus's interviews or written testimony by now, though," Cassidy protested.

"The case against Avila isn't strong enough without Kraus on the stand. They need Flores' testimony." Flint was unyielding.

"Why can't they try Flores and then, I don't know, reduce his sentence if he testifies against Avila?" She grasped for anything to keep from being pulled into a black hole of hopelessness.

"They won't take the chance Flores gets off," Suzanne spoke up.

"How could he? He confessed to killing people. Don't the police have evidence for the murder in Chicago?"

"Nothing that will stand up on its own. There's no telling what his attorney, who, no doubt, Avila is paying for, would pull to get Flores off. Try to argue the confession isn't valid because you'd given him drugs. Or even though an excited utterance is admissible, it was made to a priest with a reasonable expectation of privacy." Suzanne made logical arguments rather than empty promises.

"Why the hell am I doing this if it's for nothing?" Defeat weighted Cassidy's limbs.

"I'm not saying that he will get off," Suzanne attempted to assure her. "Lamont Clary is a brilliant prosecutor, but there's always a chance."

"If Flores is convicted, Avila's people could get to him in prison, too," Flint pointed out. "Look, they have Avila in custody now. They can move forward."

"How long until his trial? A month? A year?" A decade? If they would give her a firm timetable, it might resurrect hope.

Instead, Flint shook his head in a helpless gesture. "That is totally out of my control."

"Do you have any guarantees Flores will even testify against Avila?" The air grew heavy in the silence that met Cassidy's question.

"He knows he's likely to go to prison if he doesn't." Suzanne offered, but it didn't instill Cassidy with any confidence.

"In the meantime, I'm even more of a threat to Avila than before he was in custody. There's already an open contract on me and Kraus killed my stepfather. He had pictures of my family. What about them?"

"We can put them in protective custody. I'm sure Clary will sign off on it," Flint said.

"No." Cassidy couldn't stop shaking her head. "No. I've given up everything—my family, my job, my friends—because you hope some thug will get on the stand with enough credible testimony to convict a major foreign-arms dealer. I can't ask my family to give up their lives just because I heard Flores confess. Tell him to say a thousand Hail Marys or whatever to give him absolution, but I'm done."

"You don't mean that. If you don't testify, Flores goes free," Flint said.

"He hasn't sinned against me and I'm not providing more temptation." Kraus killed Hal Boswell, and he was dead. She'd let God deal with Flores and Avila if the DA and Federal Prosecutor couldn't.

"You'll be out of protective custody and we can't protect you." Suzanne joined forces with Flint.

"I can protect myself."

The plan that began as a crazy, desperate last resort in a dark closet hadn't stayed locked in there. Before AJ and his team caught Avila, she'd grappled with that idea to form a plan from start to finish. She could walk away. Prove she wasn't a threat to Avila. Show him there was no reason to go after her family. And, if he didn't believe it, they could follow her all the damn way to Africa and kill her there. At least she could do something meaningful, and save lives, in the meantime.

"I understand you're upset, but don't make a rash decision," Flint said.

She'd passed upset. Rushed right past it to the resignation that her future, if she had one, sucked.

"Give the Feds a chance to get Flores to talk," he pleaded.

"You tell the prosecutor that he has two days to get Flores to take a deal and talk. If he can't prove to me that Flores is going to tell them what they need to put Avila away and for you to give me a trial date, then I'm walking out of here."

"Two days? That's not enough time. Be reasonable."

"Reasonable? They've had two years." Two years she'd never get back. A stepfather—the one man who'd consistently been there for her—she'd never get back. She couldn't risk anyone else getting hurt because of her. "You want more time? Fine. Tell the DA he's got until noon on Friday. My bags will be packed, and I will walk out of here at twelve oh-one. I'm done being a pawn in the government's chess game with Avila. When it comes to my life, I. Am. Taking. Back. Control."

THIRTY-FIVE

AJ STUDIED the contents of his fridge, not finding much to tempt him. It was only eighteen hundred hours, but he really didn't want to go out. He hadn't heard anything from the marshals regarding his call with Cassidy—maybe they assumed he knew the designated time didn't change, but he didn't want to take any chances on missing it and having to wait another two weeks.

While he debated between a bowl of microwave chili and a can of vegetable beef soup, the doorbell rang.

"I told you I wasn't going," he muttered. Juan could find someone else to be his wingman. Prepared to shut his buddy down, he opened the door to what sounded like a bark.

It wasn't Juan or a mirage or a joke. It was Cassidy. Beautiful, in the flesh, Cassidy, with Champ, who rushed forward.

AJ gave Champ a quick head pat, then his embrace swept Cassidy off her feet. He sensed a slight resistance as he held her to him and inhaled her scent and absorbed her warmth. He carried her inside and kicked the door closed. "I thought the trial was next week."

"That plan hit a wall when they found Kraus dead in his cell a few days ago."

His hold on her slipped away. Was she serious? Her somber tone wasn't the "ding-dong the assassin's dead" song he wanted to hear.

"Without Kraus to testify against Avila, it falls back to Flores having to turn on his boss. And he's only going to do that to save his own ass."

AJ led her to the couch, where she sank down like she'd just finished a twenty-mile march. He dropped next to her, trying to process this news. Champ sat between their legs and put his chin on AJ's thigh for more rubbing.

"Apparently, the Chicago DA is afraid that my testimony might not be enough to convict Flores."

Fuck. He figured what was coming.

"So, the federal prosecutor wants Avila's trial first. Who knows how the hell long that will take? They said at least a year. Two is more likely. Even if Avila does go to trial first, Flores may not testify. Kicker is that Flores doesn't want to incriminate himself, so he hasn't talked yet."

Give me and the Bad Karma team ten minutes with Flores, and we'll make him talk. This time, Cassidy didn't give him the I-know-what-you're-thinking look.

"If Flores's attorney gets his way and his case goes to court first, it's the *Deal or No Deal* dilemma. If he gets off, he doesn't have to testify or make a deal. And it sounds like he's willing to risk finding out the verdict in his case at the end of his trial."

Cassidy's entire body deflated with her sigh even as AJ' frustration reached epic levels.

"That gives Avila a chance to get another assassin to find me or go after my family. I can't take the risk when the DA hasn't persuaded Flores to talk yet." She stared at Champ instead of looking AJ in the eye. "I'm putting an end to the game now. I've waved the white flag, and I'm going someplace where I'll be safe and pray they leave my family alone. If that means Flores and Avila walk, so be it. It's not my war. They can get together and celebrate their victory in getting away with murder over drinks, but I can't be the reason more of the people I love end up dead."

"I hardly think Flores and Avila will be getting together for drinks—unless they plan to try and poison each other. The trust between them is shot."

"You guys put your lives on the line. I'm sorry you went after Avila for nothing."

"No. You did more than anyone else, and like you said, this isn't your war. It's not your fault the DA can't get Flores to cooperate. Now that they have Avila in custody, they can try to convict him on gun-running and money-laundering charges."

It was a distant second to locking him up for good, but he understood her decision. Not testifying meant she could leave protective custody. Not end up in WITSEC forever. It was what she wanted, except it didn't guarantee her safety. She had to know that and she'd come to him.

He'd contemplated leaving the team to be with her, but was there a way to keep her here with him now? "We'll come up with a way to keep you safe," he promised. Though he didn't have a plan, or even a clue yet, on how.

"I've already got that figured out. Once I get a passport, I'm going to Africa. Working with Doctors Without Borders, I can make a difference. Save lives instead of looking over my shoulder, trying to save mine every minute of every day."

"Af—Africa?" That took him back a step. If they were going to have a relationship, she'd have to endure his deployments; he could deal with this. "For how long?"

"Until Flores and Avila aren't a threat. Or until they're dead. So, indefinitely."

Dammit. He should have gone with his gut, taken out Avila. Then she could still have a life here. Get to see her family instead of running off to hide in Africa. "How will you know when that happens?"

"I won't." Her stern tone matched that of an adult catching a teen about to do something spectacularly stupid. "That's not why I'm here. AJ, you can't wait around. We both have to accept that this is how it has to be. I can't take Champ to Africa. I know you can't keep him with your deployments, but I need you to find him a home. With someone who'll appreciate his service." She ran a hand over the dog's head.

"What if I say no?" *Think. Think. Think.* He needed more time to come up with an alternative.

"Then I'll take him to Lundgren's or to Tony's or find Dev."

Shit. "All right. I'll do it—on one condition." He crossed his arms over his chest.

Cassidy cocked her head at him and released an exasperated sigh. "What condition?"

"Before you leave, I take you on a real date." That would give him time to come up with something versus her heading to Lundgren's now.

"It won't change anything." Pervasive sadness infused each syllable.

"Maybe not, but I promised you I would. I keep my promises. You owe me that," AJ pushed. "If this weren't our situation, what would be your ideal date?"

Cassidy thought for a moment, her eyes flitting around rather than making extended contact. "I would've loved to have gotten glammed up and gone to your unit ball."

The idea of her being his date for the annual ball packed

an emotional blow of loss through his chest. "That's a few months off."

"I wouldn't have anything to wear if it were tonight anyway."

"Plan B, then. Dinner and a movie? It's not exactly original, but I can take you someplace nice. You deserve better than canned soup or processed lunch meat. That's about all I have to work with."

"One date won't change anything," she said again, but by her tone, acquiescing.

Yes! A minor victory. And she had no idea the offensive maneuvers he'd resort to in order to improve his chances.

THIRTY-SIX

AJ's HEAD pounded from the headache brought on by working his ass off to show Cassidy a good time while his mind raced to think of a way to keep her from relocating to Africa. With Avila in jail, that limited his options. Keeping her locked up in his apartment rated about a seven point two percent chance of success.

Settling in at his apartment to watch the movie after dinner, his mind operated in mission-planning mode. It was hard to concentrate with Cassidy's hand on his thigh, and if he wasn't mistaken, it had inched higher.

She caught him staring at her profile. The heated look on her face told him watching the comedic sci-fi movie they'd picked out wasn't how she wanted to spend their last night together. He hadn't wanted to be the first to go there, even if it seemed better to use their time for better purposes.

Still, he let her make the first move. She shifted from her position beside him, then rotated to straddle his lap. Subtle had never been her MO. She draped her arms over his shoulders, and they stared into each other's eyes in silent, anticipatory foreplay.

His hands started at her thighs, ran up, and lingered on her firm, curvy ass, then he pulled her sweet-smelling body against his chest. She lowered her face, and their mouths met for a hot, open-mouthed tango of tongues that made him feel desperately wanted and desired. Kisses that made his body ache with need.

He slid his hands under the lightweight sweater to stroke silky skin. Her breasts pressed against him, only layers of fabric were in the way. She lifted her arms when he tugged her sweater up, and then he tossed it aside. She wore a sexy blue lace bra, which he peeled off to bare her dark nipples that begged to be licked and sucked and teased. Not that he'd make her beg.

She murmured in pleasure when his tongue swirled over the hard, raised tip. The moan as he lightly bit into her flesh and the way her hips thrust against him encouraged him to take his time. "You like?"

She cradled his head to her chest answer. He fondled her other breast with his thumb, then rubbed and pinched her nipple. Her fingers moved to grip his shirt, inching it up.

"Off," she requested, and he raised his arms and let her pull his shirt over his head.

Now seemed like a good time to take advantage of having free hands to grope for the button on her pants. After he unzipped them, the logistics of getting her pants off when her legs were on either side of his presented a challenge, but only for a moment.

With one arm, he hugged her waist and pushed up to standing while Cassidy clung to him. He debated carrying her to the bedroom, but her legs unwrapped from his waist and dropped to the floor. On their own accord, his thumbs hooked over the band of her low-slung jeans and eased them down her hips. He swallowed in anticipation as she lifted a leg free, then kicked the pants clear. God, she had great legs. The lacy panties matched the bra, but since that was off, the panties had to go, too.

She read his mind, or maybe his open-mouthed breathing, and skimmed them off. He hurriedly unbuckled his belt, but she pushed his hands aside. In a flashback to their first time at the mountain cabin, she unfastened his pants and pushed them down. If he'd gone commando, they'd be ready. Instead, his erection strained his boxers to an obscene angle. Smiling, Cassidy stretched the elastic band and slipped a hand inside to ease him upward and the cotton down.

Then she sank to her knees in front of him.

What the ...? No way.

With the fingers of one hand wrapped around him in an enticing hold, she used her other hand to work the boxers to his ankles. He had no objections to her holding him captive this way. Not exactly what he'd planned, but then again, he'd been winging it since she showed up.

She scooted forward on her knees. *Yes*. This was really happening. "You don't have to. We can go …"

Her mouth opened wide, taking him in in a highly satisfying way, and he sighed when her lips closed around his shaft. Her tongue circled the tip's ridge. He should resist. Make this about giving her something to remember. Or at least mutual gratification. Though it wasn't like he asked for or suggested this.

Her fingertips dug into his butt, and he gave up any idea of resistance. He was a guy, after all. And she was freaking amazing. Her lips, tongue, and teeth applied intoxicating pressure as she sucked on the head of his penis, then she took him deep to the back of her throat. Her mouth glided up and down. Her lips and tongue worked together to give him a blow job of epic satisfaction.

He cradled her head in both hands, silently praying she wouldn't pull away when he came in her hot, slick mouth. She held on, cupping his balls, adding to the orgasmic finale that left him unsteady on his feet.

"Thank you." He pulled her up. The satisfied glint in her eyes motivated him to give as good as he got. If she were so damned set on going to Africa, he'd give her something to remember.

She took a drink from the beer bottle on the end table while he spread a fleece blanket over the leather couch. He guided her to sit. Her eyes held a question, but as soon as he dropped to his knees and tugged her bottom to the edge, an understanding smile lit up her features. He started by kissing her mouth, her neck, then each breast.

He took his time before he leaned her back. Even then, he concentrated on foreplay as he kissed the inside of her thighs, nipping lightly. His hands roamed and caressed her body. Her needy moans became more insistent, and her hips lifted signaling it was time to complete this mission.

"Seriously, Champ?" Cassidy muttered groggily after being awakened by the dog's whine.

Beside her, AJ lay motionless, his breathing heavy and even as she slid out from under the covers. She followed Champ out of the bedroom to search for her clothes. She found her underwear and pulled on AJ's mossy-green, waffle-weave Henley to cover her while she let Champ out to do his business.

Outside, in the predawn darkness, Champ sniffed the shrubs and grass as if marking his spot were of critical consequence. Meanwhile, her mind taunted her to remember something important that hung just out of reach. Had she been dreaming when Champ woke her? Or had there been an idea or thought that came to her before she'd drifted off to sleep?

"Pick a spot, Champ." She wrapped her arms around her chest, trying to keep warm while doing the foot-to-foot switch with her bare feet to minimize contact with the cold concrete. Soon, she'd be in Africa dealing with the heat. Hot and dusty, with no air conditioning, and the stink of human bodies. No sitting around a pool, enjoying a cold, alcoholic beverage like she'd envisioned Avila and Flores would do if they were set free.

Though, what had AJ said? That they'd want to poison each other? Wouldn't that be nice. It sure would solve most of her problems. Usually, her MO was to be the peacekeeper. Back at Elmwood Manor, Nidia had made a good point about keeping a safe distance rather than being a target of both sides. Just let the opposing parties go at each other.

If Flores and Avila got together, they might resolve their differences—considering Flores hadn't talked. If only the fire between the two could be stoked before a meet-and-drink. Except the marshals had Flores tucked away. Avila was in jail or a holding cell, and the only one getting access to him would be his attorney.

Like the sun breaking over the horizon, an idea dawned on her. She couldn't get to Avila, but what about his attorney? Could she get to him? Convince him to relay to Avila that she wasn't a threat? To leave her family alone? Even throw the spotlight off her and in a different direction?

Champ padded up and nudged her leg as if to say, *"it's cold. Let's go inside."*

He plopped down on his dog bed, but with Cassidy's mind racing, sleep was no longer an option for her.

She snatched up AJ's cell phone from the counter. Within

minutes, her internet search rewarded her with an article about Avila's arrest and arraignment. It even provided her with the name of his attorney in Miami.

Could she speak to him and then get herself hidden away until her passport arrived? She climbed upstairs to the bedroom, debating whether to wake AJ to run her idea past him.

Staring at him in bed, she wanted to crawl in next to him. Only she couldn't stay. Not when she'd come here to give them closure. She'd learned from all the men who disappeared from her mom's, and effectively, her life over the years that it was easier, and healthier, to move on than cling to the false hope that one day the person you loved would return and things would be different and better.

Hal taught her that with the way he'd been the one to tell her he'd filed for divorce from Tiffany. AJ might be able to help, or he might try to stop her, but she couldn't leave him with false hope.

She gathered her clothes and dressed silently. After scrounging in drawers for paper, she settled for the back of an envelope and scribbled a short note.

The lump in her throat didn't budge when she swallowed. She kissed her fingertips and pressed them to her signature.

Tears ran down her cheeks as she knelt next to Champ and stroked the sleepy dog's soft coat. She pressed a kiss to his head.

"Thank you. You've saved my life, and I'm sorry I can't take you with me, boy." She did her best to stifle the sobs that made it hard to catch her breath. Champ licked away the tears on her cheek. "I love you, too." She sniffled, her heart breaking more than she could bear. But she had one last shot, and she had to take it.

AJ STRETCHED and reached to turn off the alarm. His strained muscles groaned in protest. Though accustomed to waking alone, he immediately realized that shouldn't be the case this morning. Where was Cassidy?

The space beside him held residual warmth, and he sniffed the air for the aroma of coffee or breakfast cooking.

Pulling on a pair of gym shorts, he listened for sounds of her puttering in the kitchen.

Nothing.

Champ raised alert eyes as AJ emerged from the bedroom. "Where's Cassidy, boy?" The dog laid his head back down.

It took less than thirty seconds to check the small apartment. His heart rate accelerated despite his mind willing his body to stay calm. He looked out the front door at the parking spot where Cassidy's car was *not*. "Dammit." He couldn't believe she'd left without a goodbye—but at the same time, it screamed two hundred percent Ms. Independent O'Shea. Hadn't she learned anything?

He didn't even have a number to call her should he come up with a plan that allowed her to stay—which he hadn't. And he knew better than to expect the marshals to help him out and tell him where they were keeping her sequestered until her passport came in.

"How could you let her go?" He directed his aggravation at the helpless dog. Shit. He should have taken out Avila. One bullet. It would have been a life-changer. Or ender. Only he'd given Cassidy his word. A promise he wished he'd broken. As much as he wanted to, he couldn't change the past.

"Arghh!" A smidgeon of common sense kept him from punching the wall.

Champ ambled over to the counter and yipped. "You already need to be fed?" he grumbled and bent to get the food bowl and fill it.

Next to the coffee maker, he spotted the feminine script on an envelope, pulling a heavy sigh from his lungs. He set down the bowl and picked up the note.

AJ,

Thank you for everything. I so wish things could be different. Take care of yourself, and I'll do the same.

Love,

Cassidy

Love. She'd written, *Love, Cassidy*, though neither had said the word. Like idiots, they both probably thought it best not to take it to that level in their current situation. Now that lack of communication might be the second biggest regret of his life.

THIRTY-SEVEN

ONCE THE MORNING mission briefing ended, Linc and Dev picked back up with their telling of the Carolina Panthers game they'd gone to yesterday. AJ followed them as they exited the conference room, except the line of men stacked up when Angela Hoffman blocked the doorway. Her raised hand forced them back into the room.

"Hey. What's up, babe?" Tony's voice held an inviting tone.

"I got some news on Felix Avila."

News, not intel. AJ's head cocked as he took in her victorious smile.

"Felix Avila is dead."

Dead? It didn't get any better than that. "You'd better not be joking."

"I'd never kid about this."

"He get shanked in jail? That would be karma," Mack remarked.

"No. Judge granted bail."

"Bail? I thought—" Tony started.

"With Cassidy not testifying against Flores," Angela interrupted, "they had to drop most of the charges."

He'd told the team about Cassidy's visit. They understood her decision to leave protective custody and the country. They'd done what they could, but even the Bad Karma team had no sway with the legal system.

"What happened?" Lundgren asked.

"Someone got a big surprise in the long-term remote parking lot at Miami International yesterday morning. Found a body in the back of an SUV. He'd been shot in the stomach at close range."

Ouch. Brows furrowed on several of his teammate's faces as they waited for Angela to continue.

"Avila?" Tony asked.

"No. But police matched the stiff's prints to a Mexican national with ties to Avila."

AJ's upper body leaned forward. *Tell me how Avila died.*

"Once authorities made the connection, they pinged Avila's ankle bracelet—condition of his bail. He was at his house, but not moving. They found two bodyguards and Avila. All dead."

"Any leads?" Tony asked.

"Besides a few rivals?" Walt Shuler chuckled. "Maybe his wife ordered a hit?"

"No arrests yet. Authorities are pulling footage. I'm sure Avila had a security system with video surveillance at his place in Miami," Angela said.

Who cared who killed the piece of crap? Now Cassidy could testify against Flores, put his ass in jail, and be safe. No more delays. No more protective custody. She could stay here. They could be together. "Chief, do you have the contact info for the marshal handling Cassidy?"

Lundgren shook his head. "The colonel should. Though I'm sure that the marshals are looped in."

"I'll check on getting that for you. I like her." Angela winked at AJ, sending his hopes soaring another notch.

In the two weeks since she'd left, the ache of losing her grew each day. Now, in the space of five minutes, his world had taken a one-eighty. Something solid had gone his way. It was almost too good to be true.

ANGELA BURST into the shooting house a split second before the team began a hostage-scenario run-through with live fire.

"Whoa! Hold up. Hold up!" Lundgren ordered. "You can't—"

"This couldn't wait." She ignored the chief's scowl. "I have news. Not good news."

"Don't tell us Avila is still alive," Mack said.

"No, he is dead. But so is the priest Flores confessed to at the hospital in front of Cassidy."

"What? How?" Chill bumps broke out on AJ's body.

"Shot to death in a confessional in Jacksonville, Florida."

"*Madre de Dios*," Juan muttered.

"He'd transferred to a new parish, but probably wasn't hard to find."

"It's got to be related," Lundgren said.

"Yeah. Flores," Angela said with certainty.

"I thought he was in protective custody?" Mack protested.

"Without Cassidy to testify, they had no case. He was released after Cassidy left the program. They got a positive ID on him from video footage at the airport parking lot."

"She *already* left? I thought ... Shit." AJ wanted to believe she'd stay in protective custody until she left for

Africa, but he hadn't asked. He'd been so fixated on what he wanted that he'd failed to communicate. "Did you or the marshals get in touch with her?

"They've tried to reach her, but she either ditched or turned off the cell she had."

"Her mother or sister—" He grasped for an alternate.

"Already ahead of you. Cassidy went to see her mom and sister right after she left the program. She's been checking in with them, probably a burner phone, but she hasn't told them where she is. I've already told them if they hear from Cassidy to have her contact me, you, any of us, or the Marshals Service. And I got the email address she's been using and sent her a message."

"Good." That gave them a plan, and AJ hope.

"Cassidy contacted her mother yesterday. She's safe right now, but if Flores decides she's a loose end ... we need to find her ASAP because the timeline of what went down in Miami is not matching up with what the authorities first speculated."

Angela's tone was equivalent to tossing a grenade at AJ's feet.

"What do you mean?" the chief asked.

Angela's fingers brushed over the screen of the tablet in her hand. "This is footage from the long-term lot where they found the first victim, Jaime Guzman."

His teammates jockeyed for a view of the small screen. The angle sucked, and the footage was grainy and dark, but AJ could make out two men getting out of a dark sedan.

"This is Flores." Angela tapped on the man getting out of an SUV. "This is Guzman getting the duffle bag out of the sedan. He opens it, probably to show Flores cash. But watch what happens."

From what they could see, Guzman took his time

putting the bag in the back of Flores's SUV. When he turned, Flores shoved the man. In a blur, Flores drew a handgun, Guzman doubled over, dropping what had to be a pistol.

Flores had his weapon pointed at Guzman's partner before the man could react. The man raised his hands and stepped back. Flores shoved Guzman, landing him awkwardly in the back of the SUV.

Keeping his own gun pointed at the man's chest, Flores tucked Guzman's weapon in the waistband of his pants, then scanned the lot. AJ imagined the conversation between the two.

Avila sent you to kill me?

No, we brought you money. Please don't shoot me.

Give me your gun.

He might be right on that since the younger man slowly moved his left hand across his body, gingerly pulling a pistol from under his shirt. But the idiot tried to get the drop on Flores. He ended up writhing on the ground, clutching his thigh.

Flores confiscated the man's weapon. He tugged the bag and a suitcase out of the back of the SUV before cramming Guzman's legs inside.

A car pulled into the lot several rows over, the lights sweeping their way. Flores hauled up the man on the ground and forced him into the passenger seat of the sedan. He loaded the suitcase and bag into the back seat and drove away.

"The time stamp on this is ten thirty-two p.m." Angela paused the video. "Security footage at Avila's shows this car pulling in around eleven. Which means he didn't kill Avila and then head to the airport."

"Please tell me he went back, missed his plane, and the

cops found him. Or, hell, that he made his flight or even a cruise and left the country." AJ practically begged.

Angela shook her head. "Not that they've established yet."

"He could have a fake ID or driven to Mexico. Did he leave Avila's place in that same car?" Tony asked.

"I'm not sure on that."

"My money's on him ditching whatever vehicle he has and boosting one," Lundgren speculated.

"Which is exactly what he had already done once," Angela added. "The SUV Flores arrived in was stolen in Jacksonville two days ago."

"Where he killed the priest. Flores is going to hell." Tony shook his head.

"Why go after the priest who didn't talk?" Frustration leeched into Juan's voice.

"He's wrapping up loose ends. Show Avila there's no threat hanging over him." Mack said.

"Except Avila decides not to risk it," Lundgren said. "Sends his men to eliminate Flores. Want to bet that bag was not filled with big bills."

"He'd switched the plates with a the same make and model beige Hyundai in Miami. That's why authorities didn't immediately connect Flores to the priests murder sooner."

"Cassidy? Would Flores still see her as a threat?" AJ wanted someone to assure him this was over for her.

"We need to find her," Lundgren said instead.

"We know she's not with her family and wouldn't put them in danger," Angela said.

AJ grasped for ideas. "What about what we taught her? To double back to someplace safe."

"Dad was in the mountains last weekend. She's not there," Dev said

"That leaves Hal's place or his cabin. No one would be using either location," Lundgren said. "She might be thinking Kraus only found the cabin due to Champ's tracker and he's not with her, so she might think it's safe."

"She doesn't have any place else to go where she wouldn't worry about putting other people in danger." That AJ knew of.

"I can ask the authorities to check out Hal's house and cabin," Angela said.

"I need to go. Having strangers, even in uniform, show up, might spook her." AJ needed to lay eyes on her. To convince her that she didn't have to leave the country, he would keep her safe—whatever it took.

"We'll knock off for the day," Lundgren commanded. "Dominguez, you and Grant go by Hal's house. AJ and I'll go to the cabin."

"I'm in, too," Tony stated.

"This is a little overkill to convince her to come in." AJ tried to downplay the concern gnawing through his gut.

"No such thing as overkill when you're dealing with someone like Flores. I'd rather err on the side of safety." Lundgren tucked his sidearm into its holster.

"You sure you don't need us?" Mack asked, standing with the rest of the team.

"Go home. We'll update you later." Lundgren waved them off.

"Thanks, babe. I'll see you later." Tony gave Angela a kiss on the cheek.

"Be careful." Holding on to his arm, she stared him down.

He nodded crisply, then ushered her out of the shooting house, ahead of the rest of the men.

AJ took the back seat in Lundgren's SUV, feeling like he

was on the roller coaster from hell. He'd gone from the high of thinking Cassidy wouldn't have to leave the country or go back into WITSEC, to the rush of anticipating the chance to tell her he loved her. Now things had flipped upside down, and he prayed they could find her and keep her alive.

THIRTY-EIGHT

Cassidy drank in the view of the lake through the trees as she neared the cabin. This peaceful view of fall colors would be another thing she'd miss when she left for Africa. In addition to her family. And Champ. And, damn, she missed AJ so much it hurt.

They'd had a rocky start, but there was something undeniable about their connection. She should have fought it, considering her circumstances. But once AJ's team caught Avila, she'd had hope of this nightmare ending, and she let her guard down. Way down. Let her heart lead over her head. Just like always.

She should have known better.

Avila's reach extended to jail or wherever they had Kraus, shooting down her hope of him testifying. If moving to Africa didn't assure Avila that she wasn't a threat, nothing would. But maybe it would be far enough to protect her family.

Half the reason she'd wanted to see Avila's attorney was to deliver the message that his client needed to leave her family alone. Along with the promise that if he didn't, her friends wouldn't give Avila an outing on a yacht and then turn him over to the authorities next time.

But an hour after leaving AJ's, hell-bent on going to Miami, she realized confronting Avila's attorney face-to-face was an epically bad idea. He represented Avila, and that said a lot about his morals and ethics. What would stop him from having security detain her or follow her?

Instead, she'd resorted to a safe and hopefully effective phone call, where she'd taken the opportunity to drive home the message that *she* wasn't a threat to Avila. She was not testifying against Flores. Flores was the one who could testify against Avila. *Flores. Flores. Flores. He's who you want. Keep me the hell out of it.*

She'd almost gone back to AJ's that day. Except leaving Champ broke her heart. She couldn't do that again. She'd accomplished what she went for—kind of. Her plan to tell AJ goodbye and give him closure so he could move on had *not* gone as planned. Making love to him had been a spontaneous decision after he'd gone all romantic, insisting on a real date.

She knew from Hal's explanation to her mother about time-of-service commitments that AJ couldn't just give notice and leave the Army. It showed her how much he cared that he even considered giving up his spot on the team and the job he loved. Maybe he even loved her. But she couldn't ask him to give up his family and the job he loved.

She regretted giving up Champ so soon as she could have used his company and the peace of mind he provided. But she'd stayed strong and overrode each temptation to call AJ or go back to them.

Her rash decision to attend Hal's funeral had been exactly what Kraus wanted. Thanks to a flat tire, she dodged that bullet, and Champ saved her from a second. Playing it smart and safe was her motto now. She'd cut her hair and colored it blond. She wore glasses on her daily walks, and, like now, she watched to make sure no one followed.

Her luck just had to hold on a little longer. Any day now, her mom would say her passport had arrived. She'd give Tiffany the address to the shipping place, and off she'd go into the wilds of Africa.

She'd have a purpose. People to talk to. Freedom. It'd be an adventure. A life. Yeah. But a life without AJ.

She scanned the other cabins around Hal's before parking. The only signs of life came from the dots of light across the lake where people occupied the few homes.

She carried the first load of groceries in and set them on the counter, along with her purse. As she lugged the package of bottled water to the cabin, a man emerged from between the other cabins. She froze. Where had he come from?

The man, dressed casually in jeans, loafers, and a brown jacket, didn't mesh with her vision of a hunter or fisherman.

He smiled at her.

Her brain shot a warning signal through her nervous system. It wasn't a smile—more like a harbinger of death.

Flores! She recognized him despite the new goatee and shaved head.

The case of water slipped from her grasp and fell to the dirt. Several bottles exploded from the plastic wrapping, and she bolted around them for the cabin. The man limped forward a step, reaching into his jacket.

A bullet hit the cabin's log exterior as she charged up the steps. She slammed the door closed and locked it. That wouldn't keep Flores out for long.

The safe room!

She turned and swiped up her purse, then raced to the bedroom, skidding to a stop at the metal door.

She wrestled the bar out of the brackets. Thank God,

Tony hadn't made it a permanent fixture that Flores could use to lock her in. With adrenaline flooding her body, she shoved open the heavy metal door and shut it behind her. She dropped the bar onto the floor and slid the interior bolt into place with a satisfying clang.

The dragging footsteps on the front porch made her sink to the floor, bumping against the ottoman she'd shoved back in to keep out of the way in the cramped cabin.

Her heart pounded so hard her whole body shook as she fumbled in her purse for her phone. She dialed 9-1-1 and waited for a voice to come on the line.

Another gunshot made her jump. Panic stole her breath. She shrank back against the metal lining the closet walls as wood splintered, and the front door banged open.

She checked the phone's screen. No connection. "No!" The word escaped as a wail. The service was sketchy out here, but she just needed one bar. Fifteen seconds of connectivity. *Please.*

Redialing, she held the phone over her head, praying for reception. *Come on. Come on.*

Nothing.

The metal walls had to be blocking the already weak signal. Dammit.

In the darkness of the closet, she listened to him moving through the small cabin. Profanities streamed from his mouth when he encountered the metal plate in place of the closet door. He pounded on it, making the metal reverberate.

She wrapped her arms around her legs, unable to ward off the chill from his throaty growl and string of cursing. How had he found her? Somewhere, there'd been a flaw in her plan. Or seven. She'd expected Flores would go free eventually, but why couldn't he accept that her not testifying was a victory and leave her the hell alone? His being here and the gunshot were hardly indications of his coming to say thanks for not sending his ass to prison for the rest of his life.

"Come out, and I'll make it quick and relatively painless," Flores taunted her.

She didn't believe a word from the son of bitch's mouth. "You don't have to do this," she yelled back. "I'm not testifying. What more do you want?"

"You should have kept your mouth shut, you little bitch. WITSEC would be better than prison, but you went and destroyed my reputation and put a target on my back."

Did he mean because Avila had put a hit on his life, too, or had her phone call succeeded in reminding Avila who the real threat was?

"You can't stay in there forever. I can wait you out. I have food. Water. A bathroom."

The sneering tune of Flores's words made Cassidy wish his injuries had proved fatal. Silence reigned while the truth of his statement seeped into her core.

Her body jerked when something heavy slammed against the door. It was Flores, based on the repetitive drop of *chinga*—the Spanish equivalent of the f-bomb. *Serves you right, asshole.* A bullet struck the door, and she jumped a foot off the floor.

What were the chances someone heard the gunfire and called the police? Considering this was a haven for hunters, not likely.

Hal would have killed Flores if he'd known the depths of evil in this man's soul—or lack of one. Why had she made AJ promise not to kill Avila? If he had, this wouldn't be happening. She wanted to protect his honor, but now, he'd blame himself when someone eventually found her body.

Flores rapped on the wood walls on both sides of the door, his growl resounding outside the safe room.

She drew in several breaths and tried to focus. Clanking sounds came from the kitchen. What the hell was he doing? Already eating the food that she'd brought? He would have to sleep sometime. She didn't have to keep watch. She could sleep and wait for a chance to make a break for it. This. Was. Not. Over. She wasn't giving in.

The ottoman. What had Juan put in there? She flipped open the top, feeling inside the cube in the dark. Yes! The items Juan had put inside were still there. Was there a weapon of any sort? Flicking on the flashlight, she took inventory: a lightweight blanket and a bottle of water. No food. No knife. But it'd help her get through a day.

Knocking on the outside walls of the cabin made her jump again. If Flores were outside, trying to find a way in, this could be her chance. Open the door long enough to make a call. Get to her car. Grab a knife from the kitchen.

Precious seconds passed as she debated her chances. If Flores saw her through the bedroom window, that could be the end.

A bullet cracked through the side of the cabin. A second shot impacted the metal plate lining the back of the closet. what sounded like This guy was not giving up. What if he found a way under the cabin and shot through the floor?

She had to take her chances. She dug out her keys before sliding back the bolt, then opened the door enough to edge out. Ducking under the window, she dashed through the living room and through the kicked-in front door. On the second porch step, she froze, staring at both flat tires on the driver's side.

She was screwed.

Or could she make a run for it in the daylight? With his bum leg, she could outrun him. Hide in the woods.

Before stepping to the ground, Flores rounded the corner of the cabin.

Cassidy nearly fell, scrambling up the steps. A bullet whizzed past, alarmingly close to her head. Several shots rang out as she made it through the doorway.

In the kitchen, she yanked open the drawer next to the sink and snatched Hal's wicked-sharp filet knife.

Should she try to stab him when she had the element of surprise? Her mind switched from pure survival mode to justifiable murder. The Nightingale pledge didn't apply anymore.

With Flores clomping up the porch steps, she grabbed the closest bag of groceries and raced back to the safe room, praying she didn't regret her decision.

Flores dragged into the room. Furniture scraped against the wooden floor. Was he trying to block the door? That would suck. But she'd inch her way under the bed if she had to. She was not giving up. Hal had taught her too much.

"There's no back door, *chica*," Flores sang in a taunting manner, grunting as he pushed furniture. "This is your last chance. I don't have time to mess with you, bitch. I was supposed to prove to Avila there was no reason to worry. Finding the priest was easy. But you—"

Cassidy gasped. Priest? The priest who'd given him the last rites? The man who refused to divulge Flores's dying confession?

What had Flores done?

She knew. Knew because his soul was darker than the inside of this closet.

"I figured you'd be harder to find. After two years in protective custody, I knew the first thing you'd do is go see family. Only you had enough of a head start that you were already gone."

Oh God. Had he done something to her mom? To Sherri or her family? She went worst-case-scenario crazy before grasping to the fact she'd texted her mother yesterday.

Breathe. Don't do anything stupid.

"You haven't made any of this easy, so you're lucky I'm offering to make it quick." He pressed on the door, then grunted as if satisfied. "Your mother was easy to find, though. And ridiculously easy to get close enough to clone her phone."

Clone the phone? What did that mean? That he'd found a way to listen to their conversations? She'd been so careful. Yet here he was.

"Gotta give you credit. Using untraceable prepaid calling cards was smart. You didn't give anything away in your calls, either."

Numbness spread through her body as she helplessly listened to Flores continue.

"Your mom and sister weren't as careful. A little piece of the puzzle there." Furniture slammed against a wall. "Had to get your birth certificate here. You know Genealogy dot com doesn't list your father?"

That still cut through her like a scalpel. As much as Hal taught her to be independent, you still needed others—family. It's why being in protective custody was so hard. Why she let in AJ so quickly.

"Your mom is an attractive lady. Guess that's how she managed to land four husbands." His voice trailed off, then he shuffled back into the room. "Took a lot of digging, but Hal Boswell, hubby number three. I thought it was a long shot. But here you are. Gotta love the internet putting property records online. If only I'd managed to find you earlier."

He gave a gruff, hollow laugh. "Avila might have sent me back to Mexico. That was his mistake. Double-crossed me after I kept my mouth shut. You're my last loose end. And I'm done offering you an easy out."

A soothing whoosh made every hair on her body stand up.

"*Hasta la vista*, bitch."

She didn't hear anything else from Flores, just the soft crackling and popping before the smoke seeped in through the narrow crack at the base of the door.

THIRTY-NINE

THE MECHANICAL RINGTONE broke the heavy silence in the chief's SUV. It startled AJ and jerked Tony's attention from his phone.

"Go for Lundgren."

"Chief, Cassidy's not at Hal's." Dev's voice came over the vehicle's speakers. "We talked to the neighbor—"

"Who pulled his weapon on us," Juan interrupted.

"No sign *she's* been there."

AJ caught the inflection in Dev's voice. Tony's head angled toward Lundgren.

"Go on," Lundgren ordered.

"Something set off the neighbor's dog early this morning. He saw someone skulking around Hal's, but by the time he got out, the guy—and he's certain it was a guy and not Cassidy—took off."

"What kind of car?" Lundgren's deep voice dropped even lower in timbre.

"You're not gonna like it. The car was parked a few houses down, so the neighbor we talked to didn't get the make or plate. Said a dark sedan with what looked like Florida plates."

Flores. No one said the name aloud; however, the SUV accelerated under Lundgren's already heavy foot.

"You want us to hang out? See if the guy comes back?" Dev asked.

"Think that's a waste of time. We'll keep you updated."

"We're headed out then."

Lundgren clicked off.

AJ's throat constricted. He looked for landmarks to estimate how much longer. Flores had at least half a day head start. *Please, don't let Flores have found out about the cabin.* It wouldn't be easy to find out Hal owned another property in another county, but it was certainly possible.

Lundgren turned off the highway, not slowing on the rural road. AJ slid back and willed his body to relax. Conserve energy. Think positively.

Lundgren drew in a sharp breath. "You see that?"

"What?" AJ shifted into high-alert mode again.

"Yeah. How far are we from the cabin?" Tony reached for his phone.

AJ's heart thumped up into his throat. "Uh, couple of miles. Five to seven minutes. Why?" *Shit.* "What did you see?"

"Fire," Tony spoke calmly into the phone, not to AJ. "What's the address?"

Fire! "I don't know. It's, uh, Beaver Dam Creek Road. North off Hoover." He leaned forward to get a better view out the windshield.

He only got a view of trees. Then he saw it. Churning, aggressive black smoke. Not white smoke rising from a chimney or burning leaves. AJ dropped his head and swallowed the vomit that had worked its way up from the pit of his stomach. There was no way to pinpoint where the fire was from this distance. Yet, his limbs trembled with an all-consuming certainty while Tony spoke to the 9-1-1 operator and requested fire and medic be dispatched.

How long would it take for them to get out here? What if they were too late? *Please, Lord, don't let us be too late. Let us be wrong. Let it be something other than Hal's cabin.*

The SUV raced over the patched-up asphalt. Lundgren took the turn onto the dirt road at high speed. The SUV slid before gaining traction and narrowly avoided a massive tree trunk.

AJ caught another glimpse of the smoke—just as angry. Just as black. It rolled in billows. He unbuckled his seat belt and managed to drag his bag over the back seat and dug inside for his T-shirt and uniform top. He cut the T-shirt down the middle and into strips.

"Looks like her car," Tony exclaimed. And beyond it, orange flames danced along the roofline of the cabin.

"Someone is out front—and it's *not* Cassidy." Lundgren drew out the words as they closed the distance.

"Our firebug's armed." Tony clicked off his weapon's safety.

"We got Flores. AJ, find Cassidy," Lundgren ordered. He braked between the tango and cabin, though AJ would've preferred his boss run over the guy.

Dust swirled into the air. Before they came to a complete stop, AJ threw open his door. On the other side of the vehicle, Tony's door flew open.

"Whoa, guys. It's okay. I've already called nine—"

The satisfying crunch of flesh and bone shut off his words. AJ charged up the front porch steps without looking back.

The cabin's front door hung open at an odd angle. Smoke

poured out from the master bedroom and rolled along the ceiling. There was no sign of Cassidy in the main room or adjoining kitchen area.

In the master bedroom, the wooden dresser blocked the window. The drawers were pulled out, their contents burning. He scanned the floor, dreading the sight of a body. Even with the thick smoke, he could make out the bare wood.

With heat singeing his face and hands, he wrapped the T-shirt strips around his hands, then tried the bathroom door. Locked. The second bedroom was locked, too. He kicked open the bathroom door—empty. Smoke choked him. Coughing, he spun and kicked open the bedroom door.

"Cassidy!" No answer. No sign of her.

Like the main bedroom, the dresser and bed had been pushed in front of the window and set ablaze. Smoke escaped out the shattered window.

With his lungs straining for oxygen, he dropped to his hands and knees. Where—? It hit him before the question fully formed.

Fuck. He'd hoped she locked herself in the other rooms, but the bastard had locked her out to close off those escape routes. She'd fled to the safe room they'd created, except it wasn't designed to be fireproof.

He dropped lower, his nose scraping the floor as he crawled on his forearms and knees to the closet. Using his wrapped hand, he pushed.

It didn't budge.

He pounded on the door. "Cassidy!" He gave into a fit of coughing, sucked in hot air. Sweat poured off his body from the heat. He pushed again with no results. What if she'd succumbed to the heat, smoke, or carbon monoxide? Had they created a coffin? Was she dead? If he stayed in here much longer, he wouldn't make it out alive.

Already, he struggled to think clearly. "Cassidy! It's AJ. Unbolt the door!" He got the words out before coughs wracked his body.

Along with the roar and crackles and pops came the grate of metal on metal.

Don't let that be my imagination.

The door budged when he pushed again—a few inches. Thank God. Adrenaline rushed to his oxygen-starved muscles and cooled him a few degrees.

"Get back!" He dropped to the floor, flipped, and spun on his ass, taking in a lungful of smoke. He pressed both feet against the door. Heat from the metal penetrated the soles of his sneakers as the door swung inward.

Smoke stung his eyes, but the blurry image of Cassidy curled up, away from the door, summoned up the moisture he needed to clear his vision.

She held a blanket over her mouth and nose. She squinted past him with an alarmed, dazed expression.

"Come on!" He motioned for her to move. Her head bobbed, and the blanket dropped to her lap. She coughed as smoke swirled into the closet and surrounded her. A chunk of burning wood crashed to the floor by his elbow. He shoved it aside, burning his hand.

He wasn't going to lose her now. No way. He drew in a deep, smoke-filled breath, then pushed to his feet. Keeping his head low, he reached for her. Their hands came together as if in slow motion. He pulled, propelling her upward.

"It is you."

Cassidy's weak words penetrated the din that assaulted his ears while he hefted her over his shoulder. As he turned with her, a large figure loomed in the doorway.

"This way." The chief grabbed AJ's sleeve, guiding him

through the thick smoke. Seconds later, they stumbled into the twilight and fresh air.

AJ collapsed to his knees, then hands. Cassidy slipped off his shoulder to the ground.

Lundgren dropped to his knee beside her, checking her for injuries.

"Flores …" She coughed and sputtered for air.

"We got him. You're safe." The chief spoke in soothing tones.

When she managed to stop coughing, her gaze locked on AJ. She smiled and reached for him. He lifted the heel of his throbbing right hand to take hold of hers, then awkwardly pressed a kiss to her cheek before plopping down on his belly.

Tony and Flores were nowhere in sight, though if Tony were digging a hole in the woods for Flores's body, AJ would say the eulogy and dance on the grave.

Cassidy sat in the back of the ambulance, an oxygen mask over her nose and mouth.

"You should let us take you to the hospital to check you both out," the medic said to her this time.

She pulled the mask away. "Run the IV. I'll be fine. Trust me, I make a terrible patient."

"She's a nurse," AJ said in response to the medic's quizzical expression. "ER."

"Trauma," Cassidy corrected.

"So, you know it all? Put your mask back on then. Both of you." The medic's authoritative tone made AJ smirk, but they complied.

The medic inserted an 18-gauge needle in her hand to start an IV.

The lights from the firetruck lit up the firefighters who sprayed what remained of the cabin. Smoke and steam tainted the air.

Ray and Tony talked with the sheriff's deputies, whose prisoner sat in the back seat of the patrol car. Probably the only thing that kept her from kicking Flores so hard in the nuts that he'd be incapacitated for at least a few hours.

The medic examined AJ's burned hands, then inserted the IV into his arm. "Stay here," the medic said, then ambled over to Ray, likely to plead his case for taking them to the hospital.

She pulled the mask away to ask, "How'd you know Flores was coming after me and where I was?"

"We found out Avila was dead. Angela was trying to find you for me, so I could stop you from leaving the country." He took a hit of oxygen. "Marshals said you'd already left. Then we got intel it was Flores, and the priest had been killed. We guessed." He put on the mask when the frowning medic pointed at his mouth.

Thank God, they'd guessed right and made it here. She shivered, despite the blankets wrapped around her. She could still be in there. Dead. How close had she been? She remembered the heat. Suffocating heat. So hot, her skin felt on fire. Then, AJ's voice.

She'd thought she was hallucinating, but she had to risk Flores shooting her. Death by fire. Death by bullet through the heart.

Instead, she survived. Because AJ and his friends had risked their lives—again—to save her.

Had she set it in motion? Lobbed the grenade that started the war? It sounded like it, from what Flores had said and AJ confirmed. She'd expected it to go the other way. But as long as she stayed out of the battle and remained alive, she'd count it as a victory. Especially since Avila wouldn't be around to pay out on the contract on her. With Flores in custody, she might actually wake up from this nightmare.

"I have something important to ask you," AJ said when the medic turned his gaze away.

"Okay." She had no idea what was coming.

"Will you stick around and be my date for the unit ball?"

A delighted chuckle erupted, and she broke into a smile that banished the dark cloud that had loomed over her for so long. "I'd get to dance with you in your dress uniform?"

He gave a bashful head waggle. "Yeah."

"Hell, yes, I'll be your date. On one condition," she added.

"What's that?" He stopped mid move to her.

"Help me get Champ back."

"Done." He held out his pinkie.

She laughed and hooked hers with his.

He tugged her closer. "I love you. And no one is going to hurt you again." He sealed his promise with a kiss.

EPILOGUE

Cassidy held up the black sweater, then tossed it to the reject pile on the bed. Too depressing. This wasn't a funeral.

"You ready to go?" AJ stuck his head around the doorframe, then took another step to fill the bedroom doorway, Champ at his side.

"Almost."

"You're stalling. Pick something. It's not like he's going to care." His lips curled at the discarded pile of clothing.

Instead of his usual jeans and T-shirt or Henley, AJ wore a plaid flannel button-down tucked into a pair of khakis. He wore his Sunday loafers, and rather than his Saturday scruff, his strong jawline was clean-shaven.

She sighed and pulled on an emerald V-neck sweater. Ready was not the word she'd use—she would never be ready—but with AJ's support, she could do this. And she needed the closure to move on.

Champ bounded to AJ's car as she locked the front door of Hal's house. No, she had to start thinking of it as *her* home, even if a part of him would always dwell there. With AJ's help, she was transforming it from an outdated man cave to a bright and welcoming place. A home where she'd have the kind of stable family life she'd had when she first lived here.

AJ opened the passenger door and motioned Champ into the back seat. He waited for her to get situated before he closed the door and came around. Neither said much on the drive, talking more to Champ than each other. Her arms tingled with nervous anticipation, and her mouth went dry when AJ turned into the cemetery. He parked at the end of an even row of white headstones.

In the distance, she picked out the mausoleum she'd used as cover when changing for Hal's funeral. Today, there were no groups of mourners gathered for a service, only a middle-aged couple with a white-haired woman a few rows over. On the slight rise near the back of the cemetery, where unbroken expanses of grass laid, a backhoe dug a grave, piling soil in a heap.

Champ didn't notice the somber atmosphere. He nudged the back of her seat as soon as AJ opened the door, then wriggled out, sniffing the air. AJ's hand enveloped hers, warding off the cold. It gave her strength as he led her past tombstones marked with the names, ranks, branch of service, and wars the deceased fought in.

A cross was cut into the snow-white stone above Hal's name. Under his name were the dates of his birth and death. It listed Iraq and Afghanistan, but she knew there were other places he served. It said: *Bronze Star*, though she found two in a drawer in his wardrobe. The word that caught her eye, and made them moist, and caused the lump in her throat, was the word mentor.

Small American flags rose out of the soil on either side of the headstone, and a shot glass with the Army star, half full with amber liquid, sat on top. Two brass shell casings rested between the shot glass and two flat stones, one with black writing. The Yoda action figure that rounded out the collection made her smile.

AJ acknowledged it with a shoulder shrug. "You need privacy?"

So she wouldn't look crazy talking to a headstone? She shook her head, wondering how to start. Over the years, she'd seen enough people pass away to believe in a physical body and separate spirit. Hal's body was in the ground; it wouldn't hear her. Would his spirit?

She closed her eyes, conjuring his face as if she were speaking to him and not a slab of stone.

"I brought Champ," she started. "I'm taking care of him. And he's taking care of me. He saved my life. He misses you. We all do. I'm sorry ..." Her composure broke.

"You don't have to—"

"Yes, I do *need* to say it," she cut AJ off. "I know I can't change the past, but it's my fault you're dead. Even if I'd known who we were up against, you would have told me the same thing. To testify. But you could have been prepared and might still be alive. I know you'd forgive me, and my counselor says I need to forgive myself. I'm working on that. Some days are harder than others." *Like today.* She took a deep, cleansing breath.

"You made an impact, and your legacy will be carried on by the men you trained. Men like AJ. Honorable men. You know, for someone who'd become pretty cynical about love, you were a damn good matchmaker. I see why you wanted me to meet him." Tears blurred her vision as she smiled at AJ. "Why you knew we'd be good together. Because he's like you."

AJ handed her a tissue. She wiped away tears, and Champ gave her leg a nudge.

"And I'll do everything I can to make you proud. I'm staying in Fayetteville. I'm working at Womack Army Hospital, helping soldiers. And I'm taking psychology courses at the college so I can help soldiers with PTSD." After her ordeal, she had a first-hand understanding of its effects. The coping techniques her psychologist taught her had inspired her. That and AJ's insistence that she stay in Fayetteville instead of heading off to Africa.

"I wouldn't be doing any of this if it weren't for you. You may be gone, but you're still teaching me. Like, while it's good to be independent that doesn't mean I have to do everything by myself. I can accept help."

"She's still working on that, especially in the kitchen," AJ threw in.

"Hey, now." She rocked against his shoulder. "It's a learning process. It doesn't happen overnight."

"I'm still learning, too," AJ admitted. "The whole 'getting my family to respect what I do' thing. I'm realizing you can't always change the way people think, but you should have heard Cassidy give them her American-hero speech, telling them we save lives."

"Including mine." She wanted his family to like her, but she wasn't kissing up if it meant putting down Hal or AJ's service. The visit started rocky, but the rest of the long weekend had gone better than she expected.

"They came around a little, and I'm cutting them some slack. Myself, too. Figured it was more important to keep the respect I'd already earned." He wrapped his arm around Cassidy and hugged her to his side. "I'll take good care of her."

She reached into her pocket and pulled out the baggie with two dog treats. She laid one on top of the headstone.

"That one's from you, not for you," she informed a suddenly interested Champ, then gave him the other.

She stuffed the baggie back in her pocket and fished out the cigar case and cutter. AJ took them from her hands when she fumbled with what to do. He snipped the end, then clamped the cigar between his lips. He held the lighter's flame to the tip, then drew air in, and the tip glowed red.

Champ and sniffed the fragrant aroma that scented the air. His head cocked questioningly at AJ before looking around for Hal.

AJ blew out smoke, then handed Cassidy the cigar. She took it from him, taking her time to bring it to her lips. Even the slight breath she inhaled made her cough and sputter. AJ took it back, grinning at her. He took another draw on the stogie, then laid it atop the headstone with the other remembrances.

"This time, I won't guilt you about smoking them." She ran her fingers over the letters carved into the stone. "Thank you for everything. I love you."

Holding hands, she and AJ walked away with Champ a few steps ahead of them. The dog paused near the end of the row. He looked back at Hal's grave so long, she and AJ both stared back. "What is it, boy?"

Champ angled his head as if to get a better view. Was it the familiar scent of the cigar, wafting up like incense as a memorial to the man who'd touched their lives, that held the dog's attention? Or did he sense Hal's spirit? Champ gave a happy yip before trotting toward the car. Whichever it was, she knew Hal would approve of her decisions—how to deal with Flores and Avila, to help wounded warriors, to continue her education, but most of all, he'd approve of her with AJ.

Dear Reader,

Thank you for choosing *In the Wrong Sights*. I hope you enjoyed AJ and Cassidy's story. If you have not read the other books in the Bad Karma Special Ops Series, you can start with *Desperate Choices*, the prequel novella to the series. Then read *Deadly Aim* and *A Shot Worth Taking*. You can also get my novelette, *Undercover Angel*, which is Tony and Angela's backstory free by subscribing to my newsletter via my website.

I love all the guys on my Bad Karma team and hope to give them all their own happily-ever-afters—someday. However, I'm switching gears up at this time. I have dozens of ideas in my head (it's kind of a scary place) and I'm starting on a romantic comedy next.

Faking It With the Bachelor will feature a former Army soldier hero looking for his shot at love on a reality TV show. Read on for an early sample (AKA subject to change) and tune in to my newsletter or social media to get updates of what's coming and when.

Happy reading.

Tracy

FAKING IT WITH THE BACHELOR EXCERPT

CASTING

Tears were Nate Crenshaw's Kryptonite. Always had been and probably always would be.

He shook his head before turning off the TV and leaning back against his couch, exhaling long and loud. He'd thought he could do it, but it'd only taken fast-forwarding through a few episodes of *Say Yes to the Rose* to change his mind.

Some of the guys had shed a tear or two on Sienna's season. But from what he'd just seen, with a guy as the lead, *every* woman cried. The mascara running, my-heart-is-breaking, life-is-cruel, sobbing kind of tears.

It wasn't the kind of program he and his Army buds watched. More like made fun of the few times he'd seen a commercial promoting it. But, thanks to his sisters nominating him, he'd ended up cast on the matchmaking show even though he'd never seen a single episode for the reality show and had no idea what to expect—other than his buddies giving him grief prior to going on.

Being the next lead had been a nice fantasy for a few

hours but, nope, he was not going to be the one to cause that kind of waterworks. For the first time, he was in control on his life, his future, and he didn't need that kind of stress in it.

With only a second of hesitation, he hit the call back function on the voicemail screen.

"Nate. How are you doing, buddy?" Chase Parker greeted him like a trusted old friend. Which he was—kind of.

"Good, thanks. I, ah, got your message."

"I was hoping you'd answer, so I could tell you directly, but you haven't been picking up."

"I thought it was solicitation or political calls since you didn't leave a message the other times. You are persistent. I about blocked the number."

"Glad you didn't. So, what do you think? Are you ready to be our next featured bachelor on *Say Yes to the Rose*?"

"I have to say I was tempted, but I'm going to pass."

"Pass? Are you seeing someone already?" Chase sounded happy at that possibility, but Nate knew better.

"No. I think I'd do better just doing things the normal way. Give internet dating a try to find someone local."

"I understand but think about the odds this time. You'll have twenty-five women—all there for you."

Not exactly. A few would have other reasons for being there, but he let Chase continue.

"Fabulous dates. All paid for by the network."

"I know, but … I thought Chet was a lock for next season." They hadn't announced the next bachelor on the finale, but as the third to last man standing on Sienna's season, and with the way Chet talked, Nate thought it was a done deal. It's not like he'd ever expressed interest in doing it.

"The finale showed it was clear how much the fans love

you. They. Want. You. We want to keep them happy. What'll it take for you to say yes? I'm authorized to sweeten the pot."

"What, give me thirty women to pick from?"

"If that's what you want, consider it done."

"No," Nate laughed. More women to cry?

"How does two hundred thousand to be the lead sound?

"Seriously?" He sat forward trying to process what he'd just heard.

"Like I said. The fans love you."

Two hundred thousand dollars?

"Think it over. Talk to your family," Chase encouraged him. "Just don't say no yet."

For a few months "work" he'd have enough cash to cover two years of a living salary, secure a line of credit for his construction business's start-up, and pay salaries. Damn, it was tempting.

Was it too good to be true? Nothing had ever been handed to him in his life. Ever. But for two hundred thousand dollars he might be willing endure a lot of tears.

"I'll think on it." It's almost like Chase knew there was a Crenshaw family dinner tonight.

"Call me as soon as you make a decision." Chase's voice held a tinge of victory.

CHAPTER ONE

PRE-PRODUCTION

If CJ were a gambler, she'd be broke. Nevertheless, she opened her desk drawer and took out her purse and pulled out a ten-dollar bill for the obligatory betting pool. In her four years and eight seasons working on *Say Yes to The Rose,* she hadn't managed to pick the "winner." Her picks might make it to the top three, but that was the best she'd done.

Staring at the composite of twenty-five airbrushed beauties, she tapped her finger on one face, then another, wavering over a third. She only got to pick one.

Who should she doom to not get the final rose? She had to go with her gut.

"My money's on Donna." She handed the bill to Megan. Goodbye to two cups of Starbucks.

"The teacher? Has any teacher ever made it to the end?" Megan asked.

"Maybe it'll be a first." CJ shrugged. It's not like she anticipated a "happily ever after" outcome. There'd been a few couples that actually stuck—mostly in the early seasons.

Donna looked sweet. Had a real job—now. But she could easily be banking on becoming a reality TV star. Or she could be the bat-shit crazy contestant. Or the crier. Or one of the other half dozen drama types. CJ didn't have any insider information on the women like those who worked in casting.

Donna's simple, innocent beauty matched up with what CJ pictured at Nate's side. If this was finally the season that she picked the winner, she'd win a little cash. Not that a few hundred dollars would cover half a month's rent in LA. But a promotion to scriptwriter next season would give her a nice bump in pay. *If* there was a twenty-third season.

Her sigh resonated in her cubicle as Megan moved on. Please let ratings go up with no catastrophes this season, she pleaded silently to any powers that be.

She'd be back at square one if the show folded. Just one season of writing would be enough credits to join the Screen Writers Guild. With that magic accreditation, she'd be taken seriously, and the doors that had slammed in her face the past five years in Los Angeles would at least open a crack. Since she landed a job on the show, she'd paid her dues, clawed her way up, and it was time she got her big break writing the scripts for the "reality" show.

Her role might be limited, but she'd damned well do her part when it came to reviving the success of the show within the parameters she controlled. She'd come up with some fresh ideas for the dates. Not the controversial, cringeworthy kind of dates that cost the show many of its rabid fan base and her predecessor his job.

"Who'd you pick?" CJ's assistant, Yvonne, leaned against the entrance to CJ's cubicle. With her long dark-blonde hair and slender figure, Yvonne could be one of the contestants. She even wore a dreamy, lovestruck smile as she hugged her binder to her chest as if it were a romance novel.

Ha. As if. More like "happily *never* after."

"Donna, the elementary school teacher. You?"

"Imani. This is so exciting!"

"I know." CJ faked enthusiasm. Yvonne's excitement needed to last long enough for CJ to train her. Then the producers wouldn't have an excuse to leave her in the production-assistant role, planning the fabulous dates any longer. It was easy for the bachelor looking for love to come off as the "king of romance" when someone else planned the dates. And, of course, the show footed the bill for the extravagant adventures.

CJ checked the clock on her tablet. Showtime. "Let's see what Nate has to say, so we can begin planning." She led Yvonne to a private conference room. While Yvonne situated her chair nearly on top of CJ's, she pulled up Nate Crenshaw's contact information. While the line rang, she propped up the tablet.

Four rings. Five, six, and no Nate—even though he'd promised he'd be available. This was not like him.

It was another ring before Nate appeared on the screen. "Sorry. A buddy called from Afghanistan to rib me about being on the show." He gave an uneasy smile. One far short of the genuine, money-maker smile that won over the hearts of viewers last season.

"No problem," CJ assured him. "This is my assistant, Yvonne. She'll be learning the ropes and helping set up the dates this season, so I wanted her to sit in with us today."

"Hi!" Yvonne waved. "I still can't believe Sienna didn't pick you, but I'm so glad you are our next bachelor."

"Uh, thanks," Nate said but wouldn't hold eye contact over the screen.

"Yup. From the minute you stepped out of the limo in

your dress uniform, I was totally Team Nate." Yvonne fanned herself.

"That was my sisters' idea. They figured my wearing the uniform would make me stand out."

"It definitely did, and in a better way than coming in a costume," CJ said. Nate stood in the background, observing. made a power statement by simply standing there as though he was on a mission to defeat his twenty-four opponents. His quiet confidence had been part of why fans quickly rooted for him.

CJ picked him in the last betting pool. He'd made it to the final four men and "Meet the Family" date before Sienna let him go.

"Are you going to wear your uniform opening night?" Yvonne asked.

"I hadn't thought about it yet. I'd probably go with a suit since now I'm officially out of the Army."

"That'll still make them swoon. That and when you take your shirt off."

Oh, brother. Yvonne needed to stop rambling. Now. CJ refrained from elbowing her.

"Chet was the workout fiend with eight-pack abs. It's not too late to replace me if he's free." Nate didn't laugh when he said it.

Chet wanted the role—bad. But viewers loved Nate. Was it possible Nate still wasn't active in the Twitterverse to know about Chet's meltdown? The guy had managed to alienate the producers *and* a good portion of the show's fans after not being chosen. Now, something felt off with Nate. Not good. CJ needed to get this back on track. "No. *You're* our guy."

"Team Nate all the way," Yvonne sang out.

"Ah, thanks. My sister Kathy thought it'd be Chet while

Melanie was convinced they'd want me. What do you think, CJ? Were you Team Chet or Team Nate?"

"You're definitely the one I want to see get a 'happily ever after.'" Which was why CJ had been Team Chet originally. From what she'd seen—albeit after edits—Nate really did want to find love. A wife. To start a family. He deserved those things. He also stood a helluva a lot better shot at finding them off screen.

***

I hope you enjoyed this excerpt. This project is a different vibe and tone than the *Bad Karma* series, and I'd love to hear if this is something you'd click to grab a copy. Let me know at tracybrodybooks@yahoo.com. ☺

Also by Tracy Brody
Available Now!

DESPERATE CHOICES

DEADLY AIM

FREE Newsletter Subscriber Exclusive

A SHOT WORTH TAKING

UNDERCOVER ANGEL

ACKNOWLEDGMENTS

I want to thank all the people who've read my *Bad Karma* series. It's been exciting to have readers fall in love with my characters and stories. While I had all the full-length books written prior to 2018, I've been able to publish these three books, a novella, and a novelette in nine months—despite a pandemic—because of the support from my family, friends, and other writers.

Thanks to my Golden Heart Sisters who've shared their experiences, especially with indie publishing: Jeanne, Christy, Suzanne, Arlene, Marty, Barbara, and many more. Being a Golden Heart finalist with all the Dragonflies, Mermaids, Rebelles, Persisters, and Omegas has blessed me with many fabulous friends, and I wish you all much joy and success in writing.

Thanks to Dale Simpson for always responding to my questions, whether they relate to military tactics or mindset. To Kathryn Barnsley for those early edits and letting me make you cry over the military-funeral scene. Melanie, when I attended Robbie's funeral, I had no idea of the friendship that would later grow. Thank you for being my fun travel buddy and listening to my story ideas.

Jen Graybeal, thank you for donating the edit for a great cause. Angi Morgan, I so appreciate all your great ideas and suggestions. Your insights were invaluable. To my work wife and friend, JJ Kirkmon, as usual, you rocked the copy edits, and I look forward to the end of this pandemic and returning to our meetup times!

Thank you to our Armed Forces and their families for serving and sacrificing. You're my inspiration and heroes.

Lastly, much thanks and love to my family for their support and patience, allowing me to do what I love.

ABOUT THE AUTHOR

Tracy Brody has written a series of single-title romances featuring the Bad Karma Special Ops team whose love lives are as dangerous as their missions. A SHOT WORTH TAKING and IN THE WRONG SIGHTS won the Golden Heart® for romantic suspense in 2015 and 2016. DEADLY AIM was a four-time finalist in the Golden Heart.

She has a background in banking, retired to become a domestic engineer, and aims to supplement her husband's retirement using her overactive imagination. Tracy began writing spec movie and TV scripts, however, when two friends gave her the same feedback on a script, saying that they'd love to see it as a book, she didn't need to be hit over the head with a literal 2" x 4" to get the message. She joined RWA® and developed her craft and is still working on using commas correctly

Tracy and her husband live in North Carolina. She's the proud mother of a daughter and son and now a mother-in-law. She invokes her sense of humor while volunteering at the USO. You may spot her dancing in the grocery story aisles or talking to herself as she plots books and scenes while walking in her neighborhood, the park, or at the beach on retreats with friends.

You can connect with me on:
https://www.tracybrody.com/
https://twitter.com/TracyBrodyBooks
https://www.facebook.com/tracybrodyauthor
https://www.instagram.com/tracybrodybooks/
https://www.bookbub.com/authors/tracy-brody

Printed in Great Britain
by Amazon